LIGHT
of the MOON

LUANNE RICE

LIGHT
of the MOON

Bantam Books

LIGHT OF THE MOON
A Bantam Book / February 2008

Published by Bantam Dell
A Division of Random House, Inc.
New York, New York

This is a work of fiction. Names, characters, places, and incidents
either are the product of the author's imagination or are used fictitiously.
Any resemblance to actual persons, living or dead, events,
or locales is entirely coincidental.

Book design by Virginia Norey

Bantam Books is a registered trademark of Random House, Inc.,
and the colophon is a trademark of Random House, Inc.

ISBN: 978-0-553-80511-6

Printed in the United States of America

To Karen Covert
with love

LIGHT
of the MOON

PROLOGUE

*She ran out the kitchen door into the darkness and fog, hear-*ing her own footsteps pounding in her ears. She slipped, caught herself, kept running. Her shoulder seared—she could still feel her mother's strong hand, shoving her away, shoving her down. She tugged at the barn door; it was so heavy, and the handle was too high. When she got it open, she smelled the horses and heard them rustling in their stalls. They sensed disaster—they knew her mother was leaving, knew she had to try to stop her.

Her heart was racing. She'd heard the voices whispering. They woke her up and she'd thought it was a dream, but then she'd looked out the window and seen the bags, known in the pit of her stomach that something bad was happening. She was down the stairs in seconds and flew to her mother in the doorway, grabbing her hand.

But he was waiting in the yard, his big ugly face and bristly moustache telling her mother to hurry, they had to go. And her mother had locked furious eyes with her—as if she was angry her child loved her so much, as if she felt rage because her daughter didn't want her to go—and she'd pushed her away, sent her stumbling back into the wall.

Sari had cried out for her father, but there was no time. Her mother was running across the yard, climbing into the car. Sari had flown outside, known she had to catch up, realized Mystère was the only way.

The big white horse tossed her head. No time for a saddle or bridle; just a scramble up the rough boards, a jump onto her back. Small hands tangled in the mane. Her mother's favorite horse, so much bigger than her own pony.

Sari clucked her tongue, making Mystère move. Out of the barn, into the blackness. Fog swirled off the marsh; it was night, pitch dark, and rain was starting to fall. She rode blindly, by instinct, toward the road, her ears straining for the sound of the car.

All she could hear were hoofbeats and the pounding of the rain. It soaked her clothes through to her skin, made her hair fall into her eyes. Her shoulder burned, and the raindrops felt like needles, and she wanted her mother to pull her off the horse and dry her with a towel and say she was so sorry for hurting her. She wanted to feel the rough towel and her mother's soft hands, and she wanted it right now.

"Mama!" she called.

She kicked Mystère once, then again, to make her move. Riding was as easy as walking—she'd grown up doing it. But now it was night, and she'd been sound asleep, and the fury in her mother's face and the thrust of her hand had shocked her into numbness. She thought she heard her mother whispering to the man, but it was just wind whispering through the reeds. Mist rising from the creeks and lagoon made it impossible to see. She knew they had reached the main road only because the horse's hoofbeats suddenly sounded sharp instead of soft.

The only sounds: hoofbeats and rain and the rustling marsh grass.

And then, up ahead: glowing monster eyes.

Red, burning through the fog, staring straight at her. But instead of being afraid, she felt her heart leap. She wasn't too late. She was awake, this wasn't a dream, she wasn't too late.

She kicked the horse, and felt her take off as if she knew, as if Mystère knew even more than she did. She'd never gone so fast—a pure gallop, hoofbeats clanging in her ears, the storm wind rising and shrieking, or was that her own voice? The rain came down hard, stinging her eyes and blurring her vision.

The red eyes winked, blinked—brake lights being tapped. Her skin drenched, hair dripping, mouth wide open and filling with tears so fast she might choke, might not be able to get the words out. Getting closer, she saw the car beginning to pull away.

She saw the beautiful face—turned half-around, looking over the back of the car seat, out the back window, arm reached out as if to touch her. She kicked Mystère faster, faster.

"Mama!" she heard herself wail, letting go of Mystère's flowing mane as she leaned forward, reaching out to her mother with all her might.

But the car pulled away, faster than any horse could gallop, its lights receding. Fog and rain and night filled the distance between them, swallowing the car and making it invisible, and she was crying so hard she didn't hear the other car coming, didn't hear the wheels splashing up water. And then she was flying through the air as the big white horse suddenly dodged sideways on the glittering wet pavement.

But she had no wings, this wasn't a dream, and the whispering voices had been real, and the bags had been real, and the violent shove had been real, and the red eyes had belonged to a monster that had come to destroy her family. She catapulted over the horse's head and opened her mouth to scream, but it never came out.

The scream went in instead of out, and it was caught inside, the scream was trapped inside, and she hit the ground and broke into pieces, and she saw those glowing red eyes, and then the world turned to gray.

Five Years Later

ONE

Air France 321, scheduled to leave Boston's Logan Airport at 7:50 that night, was full. Susannah Connolly sat in seat 22A; she had her tray table stowed, seat in the upright position, and carry-on bag tucked under the seat in front of her. She'd slipped her passport into her jacket pocket, and at this very moment, she was missing a surprise party—hers.

Her seat belt was tightly buckled. She had the window seat, and two strangers—a couple, whispering comfortably to each other—had the middle and aisle. She had a novel, a magazine, and a guidebook to read. She hoped the party guests were enjoying champagne and birthday cake. She couldn't think of many things she felt less equipped to do than pretend to be having fun at her own surprise party.

Every seat on the plane was taken. The captain's voice crackled over the loudspeaker, telling them they were third in line for takeoff. His French accent was soft, alluring, and sexy, but she barely noticed.

Staring out the window, she felt the plane begin to move, its wheels bumping slowly along the accessway. Susannah traveled a lot. Her passport had been stamped so often, the customs officials had to search for a clean page. Work had taken her away from home a hundred times in the last few years. But this was different—brand new territory: this was a journey for herself, to connect with her mother.

Her mother . . . Although she had died six months earlier, it still didn't seem real.

Susannah was a cultural anthropologist, on the fast track in a competitive field. She taught at Connecticut College, but this was a sabbatical year. Her specialty was cave paintings—specifically those with a spiritual bent—with a concentration on horse illustrations. Cave dwellers had looked to the sun, the sea, the great bear, the forest deer, the blue whale, the wild horse. They'd created saints before the birth of the church, and she'd always been impressed and moved by the inspiration they'd found in the world around them.

Susannah had traveled the world to crawl, wriggle, dive, and spelunk into the planet's deepest, most hidden crevasses—dark, usually slimy, frequently precarious holes, where other humans had gone before, to leave messages, stories, splashes of hope, despair, and beauty.

She had crawled deeper into caves than anyone else would dare to go. She'd lie on her stomach, inching forward as the rock walls closed in on her, fighting claustrophobia, knowing that if only she made it a few feet farther, she'd be rewarded with the sight of something no one had seen in thousands of years.

Ian had seemed to understand. He'd often traveled with her, but rarely entered the caves; he'd wait outside, review the data she sent back via the miracle of fiber optics. He'd had a phobia of being trapped, and no matter how hard he'd fought it, he couldn't overcome the fear—but it hadn't mattered; his analysis of the images had been without peer.

Susannah had met him when they were both grad students at Yale. They'd started out studying together; they took the same classes, had the same professors. The work was hard, so they encouraged each other. Susannah would get lost in her research, the love of her subject matter, and Ian would remind her to apply for grants, submit her work to journals.

Once they were studying in his room, and Susannah fell asleep on his bed. It was December, just before break, and an icy draft was coming through the old windows. She woke up to find him curled beside her, and she pressed against him for warmth. They lay there for a long time, and then he began to kiss her.

His arms were around her. She felt so cold and tired, and she knew she should stop him. But he stroked her hair, and whispered that he'd been feeling this way for so long. Susannah let him hold her, shivering in the cold. Her father had died not long before, and she'd buried herself in work, and she felt starved for closeness.

Susannah remembered that moment so well—the instant they'd gone from good friends and work partners to something confusing. They studied so well together, balanced each other out. She delved deeply into the raw subject matter, and he organized the material. They worked separately on their own dissertations, but coauthored several papers published in journals. Ian never missed a chance to publish. . . .

Ian gave her jade earrings for Christmas, red roses for Valentine's Day. Susannah had felt herself becoming part of a couple—almost by accident. She had so much in common with Ian. He was always there. Curious about her work, involved in her research, interested in her discoveries, sympathetic when they found her mother had lymphoma.

But was this love? He began talking about what they'd do after leaving Yale. There seemed to be an assumption that they'd be making decisions together. And since he had his mind set on Stanford, Susannah felt herself being pulled to the West Coast. She'd resisted at the time—told Ian she wanted to accept a position at Connecticut College.

He hadn't understood, but he also hadn't given up. Although they'd made their academic homes on opposite coasts, Ian kept trying to convince her they should be together. Years went by; they both advanced, working together on projects when they could. He kept up his campaign, telling her they already knew each other so well; they were passionate about the same field; and he'd spoken with the publisher of an academic press, who thought the idea of a couple visiting sites together could make a wonderful series of books.

Susannah's mother had tried not to laugh when she told her.

"Oh, darling," Susannah's mother said. "How romantic . . . he's courting you with a book deal!"

"Mom," Susannah had warned.

Margaret Connolly chuckled. She was thin and pale, her skin yellowed from the disease and treatment. But her eyes were as bright and blue as ever.

"Sweetheart, tell me your hopes and dreams . . ."

"About what, Mom?"

"About everything."

They were sitting in the oncologist's office on Temple Street, waiting for Margaret Connolly to be seen. Her lymphoma had come back. It had been in remission for years, but now it had returned and spread. Susannah sat by her side, waiting to hear the results of the latest radiation treatments. At that moment, she wanted never to leave Connecticut again. She wanted to be with her mother every second she had left.

"My hopes and dreams? To plant a garden, to walk on the beach, to ride again . . . on a beautiful white horse . . ."

"Those are mine, too," her mother whispered.

"We'll do them together," Susannah said.

"Okay," her mother said, smiling. "Maybe we'll finally take that trip together . . ."

"The Camargue!" Susannah exclaimed. "To see Sarah! Could we? Do you really think . . ."

Her mother just looked over, her gaze full of love and sadness.

"No," Susannah said, answering her own question. "No, we'll stay home instead. We'll garden, and walk on the beach . . ."

Her mother shook her head. "No, Susannah . . . that's not how it will be."

"What do you mean?"

"I mean that you're not going to stay home and wait. . . . I want you to take that trip."

"Mom. Not without you."

"Yes, sweetheart. And others, too. Your work takes you where you need to be, and that's how I want it."

"Not now, though," Susannah said. "I should cancel everything. Lascaux, Istanbul . . ."

"Listen to me. You're the best daughter anyone's ever had. I know you'd do anything you could to make me well. You'd find a cure for cancer if you could, and I know that. But that's not your work . . ."

"Work doesn't matter now," Susannah whispered.

"Yes," her mother said, nodding. "It does. Life's work matters so much. It's the distillation of who you are, what you believe. You care about the past, because you love everything and everyone, and you want to learn all there is to know."

"You taught me to be that way."

"I tried," her mother said. "Your father and I both did. And we're so proud of who you've become. So don't hold back now, Susannah. . . . Go see Sarah."

"Maybe Ian and I should—"

"Not Ian," her mother said, her voice surprisingly sharp.

Susannah looked deeply into her mother's blue eyes.

"You think Ian is as passionate about anthropology as you

are," her mother said. "But he's not. He's ambitious, darling. There's a difference."

If Susannah hadn't already known that, her mother's words might not have rung so true. The more Ian pushed, the more Susannah pulled back. And then early last fall, on a trip to Lascaux, he'd unexpectedly arrived and surprised her with a question. Susannah sat back in her seat, eyes closed, remembering it now.

He'd planned so well; he'd known how excited she'd be after exploring a new chamber, seeing cave paintings she'd never seen before. And he knew, too, how worried she was about her mother. Susannah had continued her work, her travels, because her mother insisted. But her entire spirit was pulled home, every minute. She felt ripped in half.

Susannah walked out of the cave, and Ian caught her in his arms. She was sweaty, covered with dirt, but he didn't seem to care. He held her, listening to her describe the delicate drawings, the subtle colors. She'd seen images of a mother and children, close by the fire, and tears streamed down her cheeks as she thought of her own mother.

"Those drawings," he said, "are our future."

"Our what?"

"You'll document them, I'll get everything ready for the publisher. We're a team, Susannah. You don't want to come to Stanford—fine. We'll go somewhere else, but we'll do it together. It just makes so much sense. . . ."

"Ian . . ." She wanted to ask him: *Weren't you listening to me?* But she held the words inside. He just kept talking, making his plans, and she stood there, rocked by the beautiful, ancient paintings of a mother and her family.

"What's wrong?" he asked, finally noticing her tears.

"I'm just thinking of my mother," she said.

He stood there, silent for a moment. She suddenly felt overwhelmed. She wanted him to hold her tight, understand the grief she felt—knowing her mother's illness was advancing, and there was nothing they could do.

"You're so sad," he said.

"I am," she'd whispered. Something about the cave, the earth, the almost eternal quality of the paintings, had made the idea of losing her mother all the more vivid.

"Susannah, maybe if you rethought your priorities . . . made other choices . . ."

"What are you talking about?"

"Taking time for the people you love. Relationships," Ian said, "take work. Even now, with your mother dying, it was your choice to come here . . ."

"God, stop!"

"I want us to be together," he said. "Really together. Working, traveling . . ."

She stared, in shock.

"Will you marry me, Susannah?"

"Oh, Ian . . ." She felt her eyes flood again. He knew by her non-answer what her true answer was. They stared at each other for a long moment. Susannah's face was streaked with dirt and tears. Ian looked immaculate, as always.

"You're making the wrong choice," he said, and it sounded like a warning. "But then, I've watched you do that for years."

Sitting on the plane, Susannah thought of Ian. He was for the most part gone from her life now—she'd told him she needed a break, and although he'd made some recent overtures, they hadn't seen each other since then. But his words haunted her.

After fighting the cancer so hard for so long, her mother had died. Susannah had been in Istanbul. She'd rushed back from the Pavan Caves, but she'd been too late. And now in April, half a year later, it was Susannah's birthday, the first without her mother, and she'd known it was finally time to take that trip. . . .

"Flight attendants, prepare for takeoff," the pilot said in French.

The cabin lights dimmed. The big jet began to lumber down the runway. Slow, faster, gathering speed. The engines droned and roared. Susannah's seat shook slightly. The plane rose.

When she'd lost her mother, she'd lost her cheering section. She could hear her mother's voice; after returning home from Lascaux, Susannah had told her what he'd said, and her mother had replied, eyes flashing, "Ian doesn't know us, sweetheart. How could he even try to make you feel guilty? You don't, do you?"

"He said it was my choice . . . to go to France, instead of staying with you."

"What does he know? Besides, he's not your true love."

"What if he is?" Susannah had asked.

Her mother had smiled, taken her hand. "If he was, you'd know it by now."

"I hope you're right."

"You'll feel it—with someone else, when the time is right," her mother had said. "It will have nothing to do with your head, so stop thinking about it. You'll feel it in your heart."

As the plane gained altitude, nose pointing into the sky, Susannah's back pressed into the seat. She stared out the window, gazing down through the darkness at the beautiful yellow lights painting New England, highways straight and roads winding, neighborhoods hugging the coastline, the great black expanse of the North Atlantic stretching out beneath them in never-ending waves as the plane flew on and left the eastern seaboard of the United States—and her surprise party back in Black Hall—far behind.

With her mother gone, Connecticut seemed cold and empty. Susannah had missed the chance to say goodbye. But there was another place, where Susannah knew she could find her mother's spirit. . . . They had always talked of going there together, but then it was too late. Before her death, Margaret Connolly had made her only child promise to make the trip herself. Until now, that promise had never been kept.

Flying east, Susannah thought of her mother, and slept.

Hours later, after landing in Paris and connecting to Arles, Susannah drove out of the rental car lot, both hands on the wheel. Black parasol pines and olive trees, leaves pale green and silvery, lined the sides of the road.

Arles was a canvas by van Gogh: wild colors everywhere. Terracotta terraces, ochre and sepia walls, houses the color of sunflowers, the shadowed black arches of the Arènes. It was a celebratory city, light exploding from the river's surface and reflecting in bright shimmers on ancient Roman walls, markets alive with produce and flowers so beautiful they might have been painted by Vincent himself. Susannah bought a fresh almond croissant from the *boulangerie;* passing a market stall selling brightly colored silks and other fabrics, she stopped. On a whim, she bought herself a birthday present: a red hair ribbon.

Tying the ribbon around her hair, she left the city behind, pulled onward by sea. She was going to the Camargue, the starkly beautiful area of southern France where the water and the land seemed to merge in an endless expanse of silver. Helen Oakes—the head of the anthropology department, and Susannah's boss and mentor—had offered Susannah an apartment in Arles, but she'd declined and rented a place sight unseen off the Internet.

Helen had tried to insist—Susannah had promised to do a small amount of work while she was over here, to review documents at a particular library that Helen had been unable to visit herself. She'd said the apartment loan was the least she could do, but Susannah had thanked her and remained firm. She needed to be on her own.

Right now she held on to the promise she'd made her mother: to visit Sarah.

Susannah's family history included a miracle performed by a slave girl. Her parents, unable to conceive after ten years of marriage, had taken a vacation to the Camargue. While there, they had stumbled upon an ancient church in a seaside town. Inside they'd found a statue of a not-quite-official saint imbued with healing, holy powers. Susannah's mother had knelt by the statue, unbelieving but with the sort of desperation known to attract miracles.

The town itself was full of grace, named for three Marys: legend had it that in A.D. 45, a group of Christians was forced onto a small boat without sails and set adrift in the Sea of Galilee. They included Mary Magdalene; Mary Salome, mother of the apostles John and James; Mary Jacoby, sister of the Virgin; Saint Martha; Lazarus; and an Egyptian slave girl named Sarah. Swept along through storms and hundreds of miles, their small boat at last washed ashore on the coast of the Camargue.

While pilgrims from all over came to beg the Marys for help and healing, Susannah's mother had been drawn to the statue of Sarah, the slave girl. Carved of black wood, her face was humble and sweet, her head and shoulders were draped with ribbons and tinsel, and her bare feet were surrounded by handwritten prayers and dozens of glowing votive candles—offerings left by her own devoted followers. Susannah's mother had fallen to her knees, touched by the thought of this young girl, so far from her home.

Margaret Connolly believed their daughter had been conceived that very night. Growing up, Susannah had heard the story of Sarah, almost too mystical and dangerous for a young girl to comprehend. She had loved it, especially along with the stories about the white horses.

The famous white horses of the Camargue had also been part of Susannah's family fairy tale, a mixture of story, truth, and enchanted, sacred places. Her mother had never forgotten the sight of those pure white horses running free on the endless salt grass plain, and she'd woven them into Susannah's bedtime stories. Susannah had begged for riding lessons, and her parents had obliged. Her father had taken her to the stable every Saturday morning.

Sometimes, crawling into the deepest, darkest caves, she'd calmed herself by imagining the white horses, so wild and free, unfettered and unrestrained, galloping over the marsh. When she was wedged into damp, stony chasms, or pressed by her schedule, her constant travel, her classes, the thought of those horses, and the exhilaration she herself felt in the saddle, freed her mind. They'd saved her from panicking, helped her get through the worst places.

Now Susannah was going to the Camargue to see the white horses. She wanted to hear their hoofbeats—feel them pounding the marsh beneath her feet as she stood in their midst. Her own riding, at home, at the Connecticut College stable behind the Arboretum, had ceased as she'd gotten so absorbed with work and travel. Her body and spirit felt pent up, and deep down she believed that those white horses running by the sea could somehow release them. And she had promised her mother.

Her mother had so often steered her in wonderful directions. Even her position at the college . . . after she'd graduated from Wheaton, gotten her master's and then her doctorate at Yale, she had piles of letters ready to go out to anthropology departments all over the country. With Ian pressuring her to apply to departments on the West Coast, her mother had gently suggested Connecticut College, just a few miles away from their home in Black Hall. Susannah had sent a resumé to Professor Helen Oakes, and she'd never once regretted it.

In Arles, bright sun had streamed down from a sparkling sky, beckoning her south. But as the road wound into the marshland, silver haze first filmed and then obliterated the sun. She rolled down the car windows, letting the cool, damp air touch her skin. She knew that the Camargue was 220,000 acres of wild marsh, pastures, and dunes.

The light was mysterious, the endless marshland flat and hypnotic. No matter which way she looked, she saw only salt grass blowing in waves. Her car was alone on the road in this primeval landscape. A strong wind was kicking up from the sea, rippling the marsh. The sun faded a little more; the haze turned to fog, swirling and thickening as she drove south.

The wind was filled with energy. It didn't feel like a storm; it just made her want to jump on a horse and ride for miles, beyond the horizon. Her eyes were peeled for the white horses; she felt they were near. She pulled the car over to the side of the road. A guidebook was open on the seat beside her; copies of pages she'd printed from the Internet lay beneath.

Stepping out of the car, Susannah breathed the salt air. Stretching her limbs, she felt as if she'd been trapped in a box. The car, the plane, her office, her mother's hospital room, the caves, her life. Every muscle ached.

Her eyes watered in the sharp wind. Facing toward the sea, she opened her arms and felt the wind against her body. Glancing down, she saw hoofprints and felt prickles on the back of her neck: the horses were nearby.

Looking around, she realized she might be lost. There were no signs, and everything was unfamiliar. Perhaps this was a dream. Or maybe she had conjured it all out of a near-forgotten bedtime story. The wind was charged, and in that moment she felt magic.

About to return to the car, she heard distant pounding and felt the ground start to shake. Instead of fear she felt pure exhilaration: they were coming. She knew it, and started running through the fog toward the sound.

First the ground was dry and solid and then it was damp. The tall green grass brushed her ankles and calves, and her sneakers squished in clammy mud. Graceful bone-white egrets flapped their wings and took slow, ungainly flight to escape her, bright blurs in the thick fog. A horse whinnied in the near distance, and Susannah took a deep breath and listened.

The animals were coming hard and fast. She felt their energy before she saw them. Waiting for streaks of white, instead she saw black. Dark shapes charging toward her: blue-black hides, murderous curved horns, flashing red eyes, flaring nostrils. Thudding past her, they wheeled back in rage, and suddenly Susannah was surrounded, not by gentle white horses, but by twenty wild black bulls.

She wanted to drop to her knees, cover her eyes, but she was frozen in a moment surreal, ridiculous, and terrifying. The bulls were exquisite, pure power, beautiful animals. But they wanted to kill her. They had furious eyes; Susannah had invaded their territory. One bull was larger than the others, and he stood in the forefront. He sputtered and pawed the ground. And he was staring at her, straight at her head, right at the red ribbon she'd bought at the marketplace in Arles.

It was the ribbon! The red was infuriating him; she'd seen enough movies to know that. If she dropped the ribbon on the ground and backed away, he'd let her alone. She felt the entire herd inching toward her. Reaching up slowly, she started to take it off. Took hold of one end, untied the bow . . . and the red ribbon unspooled and the strong wind took it, made it stand straight out in her fingers like a red flag, and the large bull let out a deep, guttural sound and began to paw the ground harder.

And then Susannah heard the horse's whinny again, and out of the fog, out of nowhere, saw the white horse coming fast and heard a voice saying sharply, *"Donnez-moi votre main!"*

Give me your hand . . .

She reached out blindly, felt rough fingers close around her wrist, pull her onto the broad white back of the galloping horse. It happened so fast, before she could even think, and she was electrified. Suddenly she was flying across the marsh, her arms around a stranger, a French cowboy. She felt her heart beating against his backbone, and she heard the bulls charging from behind, swore she could feel their hot breath on the back of her neck.

The rider galloped them away, through the marsh, onto a sandy trail. Her sensations were intense and alive. She smelled the man's sweat and the horse's scent, and she felt the rock-hardness of his back against her chest, and the beautiful white horse beneath her. But as the adrenaline stopped rushing, and she had the chance to replay it, she felt a rush of fear and shock at what had almost just happened.

"I'm sorry," she said into his windblown hair.

"You nearly got killed," he said.

"I know."

The horse had been racing along, but now it slowed down. Susannah's arms remained locked around the man, though. Even when the horse stopped, she couldn't let go. She was trembling, and the emotions dammed up by sudden terror flooded out.

He turned half-around, looked at her over his shoulder, through a lock of gray-brown hair falling across the brightest blue eyes she'd ever seen. His skin was weather-beaten, darkly tanned.

"What were you doing back there?" he asked. His accent was American, not French.

"I was looking for white horses, and instead I found wild bulls."

"They inhabit the same places."

"I didn't realize."

"People think the Camargue is so romantic," he said. "All white horses."

"I'm not romantic," she said. "I'm academic."

He flashed such a quick, wonderful smile, for a moment she saw starbursts around his eyes, smile lines around his mouth, white teeth. He reached around, pried her fingers open, took the red ribbon she still held from her hand.

"I shouldn't have worn red," she said.

"Bulls are colorblind," he said.

"Was it the movement that angered them? The fact it was waving?"

"Smart. You *are* an academic," he said, laughing.

Then he stuck the ribbon into the pocket of his shirt, gave his horse a quick kick, and started riding back the way they'd come. Susannah tensed up, thinking they were going to encounter the herd again. He must have felt the fear in her body.

"Don't worry," he said. "They're gone now."

"How do you know?"

"I just do."

The horse carried them through the fog, straight to her car. Susannah felt confused, turned around. Jet lag had taken hold, as well as the aftermath of nearly being gored. The marsh was flat and endless. She had no idea where she was, and when the horse stopped again, the rider had to gently pry her arms from around his waist. Swinging her leg over, she let herself drop to the ground.

She stared up into his blue eyes. "Thank you," she said.

"I'm glad I was there," he said. "You're a good rider."

"Thanks. I surprised myself. It's been a while since I was on a horse."

"Well, that was some jump up."

Susannah smiled. "Maybe I should join the circus."

His eyes flickered. The easy friendliness and humor were still there, but he stared out over the marsh, and she felt him wanting to ride away.

She blinked, turning in a slow circle, trying to get her bearings. Her legs wobbled, and she realized she was feeling the effects of fear and the short, intense ride. The man glanced down again. Edging closer, she reached up and petted the horse's white neck and velvety muzzle, tangled her fingers in the white mane, long and glorious.

"You saved my life, right?" she asked the horse.

"Probably," the man answered for the animal.

"Then I need to know his name."

"Her name," he said, "is Mystère." He gazed at her without expression in his sky-blue eyes. He stared for a long time.

"What?" she asked.

But he just shook his head, gesturing at her car. "Go on, get in," he said. "I want to make sure you have a safe getaway."

"Which way . . ." she started to say, but he just gestured left, down the road in the direction her car was already pointing.

"Six miles, straight to the sea," he said. "Stes.-Maries-de-la-Mer."

"How do you know that's where I want to go?"

He just smiled. "I'm a mind reader."

She smiled back. She walked over to her car, opened the door, climbed in. He stayed right where he was while she turned the ignition key and started the car up. Mystère's long white tail swished back and forth.

"Remember," he said, "no waving ribbons in the marsh."

"I remember," she said. "But oh, I wish . . ."

"What do you wish?"

She swallowed, gazing up at the man on the white horse. He looked tall and lean and brown, maybe forty-five, three or so years older than she was. He wore jeans and a blue cotton shirt. For the first time she noticed that there was no saddle; not only had she just executed a pretty amazing circus trick, she'd done it bareback.

"That my parents could have seen that," she said quietly. "The way you held out your hand, and I grabbed it and jumped on."

"Your parents?"

"My father used to take me to riding lessons. And my mother told me about the white horses here."

"She should have told you about the bulls, too. There's a lot of danger if you're not careful . . ."

"Then I'll be careful," she said steadily, suddenly afraid—not of the bulls, but of the cold fog enveloping the endless marsh and the town where she was heading. She feared it seeping its way into her mood. She'd come here to feel better, and stave off the dark pain of her mother's death, and her own guilt. She gazed into the man's blue eyes. She didn't want to drive away.

He hesitated, as if he understood—or as if he didn't want to leave either.

But then he made a clucking sound with his tongue, gave Mystère a little kick, and rode off into the fog. Susannah watched him disappear. Alone again, she felt a quick bolt of fear. But she chased it away. The marsh was wide and lovely, and the bulls lived here with the horses, and she had just been rescued by a blue-eyed cowboy. Quite an introduction to the Camargue. She wished she'd remembered to ask him for her red ribbon back.

She felt oddly empty, as if she'd just awakened from a dream. She realized she hadn't even asked his name. Trying to hold on to scraps—the sounds and sights and feelings of something unbelievable, otherworldly—she turned south, toward the town. She knew it was inhabited by the Rom—Romanies, known to some as Gypsies. Her mother had told her they had adopted Sarah as their honorary saint. Every year at the end of May, they held the *Pèlerinage des Gitans:* the Gypsies' Pilgrimage. Families would flock from all over, to beg Sarah for miracles and thank her for ones already granted.

In that moment, Susannah recalled the strange look in Helen Oakes's eyes when Susannah had agreed to go to Stes.-Maries-de-la-Mer, and the conversation that had followed. And now, although Helen had written a letter of introduction for Susannah to present at the library in Arles, and had written out a list of topics and questions, this was Susannah's journey and no one else's.

She put the car into gear, and drove toward the sea.

One hand on the wheel, the other holding the printout, Susannah drove slowly into the town, through streets lined with white houses, down to the harbor. She glimpsed the fortified Romanesque church, with its simple, pure lines, its battlements and a bell tower. She felt an instant pull toward it, but jet lag was getting the better of her. Glancing at the paper in her hand, she drove along the wharf and looked for Rue Magdalene.

A flamenco guitarist leaned against a tall stone wall, singing in a language that sounded unfamiliar. Clotheslines stretched between houses, and bright laundry and seaweed-flecked fishing nets flapped in the wind. The afternoon sun had burned a hole in the fog, and diamond patches of light sparkled on the choppy surface of the harbor, where colorful fishing boats strained at their moorings. Susannah saw Rue Magdalene, and turned right.

Number 14 stood a half block off the water, on a narrow cobbled side street. Susannah parked at the curb, pulled her bags from the back seat, and walked toward the house. It was two stories, pale pink, the color of the inside of a cockle shell; there were white shutters at the windows, and a front porch with a round table and furled white market umbrella. Like all its neighbors, the house had a red-tiled roof.

Before Susannah could climb the steps, the door opened. A woman came forward, smiling. She was darkly tanned, petite, but very strong looking—toned shoulders and bare arms under a sleeveless purple dress. She had a dragon tattoo on one bicep and one of the Virgin Mary on the other. Hoop earrings showed through tumbles of curly black hair.

"You must be Susannah Connolly," she said in thickly accented English.

"Yes," Susannah said.

"I'm Topaz Avila," the woman said, taking one of Susannah's bags. "Let me show you around the house, and then I'll be on my way. Did you have a good trip?"

"It was . . ." Susannah began. She'd been about to say "eventful," and rush into a story about the horses and bulls and the man in the marsh. But instead she just said, "It was fine."

Topaz gazed at her, as if waiting for her to say more. But when Susannah didn't continue, she smiled and led her into the house.

She showed her the kitchen and bathroom, the living room and bedroom; told her how to prime the well if the water ran out; pointed out a list of contact numbers, including her own, hanging by the phone in the kitchen. She opened the back door and gestured to the *pièce de résistance*: a small swimming pool.

"You see there's a parasol—umbrella—for sunny days. But do not put it up now, or it will blow itself out. The wind, you see."

"Yes," Susannah said. "Is there a storm coming?"

Topaz laughed. "A storm? Oh, no. This is normal for this time of year."

"The wind blows like this all the time?"

"It's the mistral," Topaz said.

Mistral. The word seemed so exotic and beautiful. Susannah felt herself grin, and Topaz returned the smile, wide and wonderful. Susannah's knees were just about buckling with exhaustion, so she just accepted the keys from Topaz, thanked her for her trouble, and saw her out. Then she walked upstairs to the bedroom, dropped her bags on the floor, stumbled over to the bed, and fell into a deep sleep.

TWO

Sari Dempsey stood in the back room of her house, sorting laundry. Everything she touched burned her skin. Her father's socks singed her fingers; her own cotton shirts seared them, too. She'd caught a fever long ago, and she couldn't be cured. That's because the malady was in her soul, not her body.

The injuries to her body had been quite terrible, at the time—a broken arm, a shattered pelvis, a hairline fracture to her skull. A bad concussion that gave her piercing headaches, that impaired her vision—bleached the world of color and, for the weeks immediately following her accident, made her see double. The double vision had abated, but the colors never came back. Sari had been colorblind ever since that night five years ago.

Ever since that night . . .

If anyone ever wrote a song about her, painted a picture of

her, wrote her biography, the title would have to be *Ever Since That Night*. Nothing had been right since then. The world had turned gray, her dreams had gone dark, and all she could think of was her mother's face in a desperate knot, her mother's strong arms taut and rough as she'd pushed Sari away, running out the kitchen door to be with the man she loved—a man Sari hated.

Of course she'd hate any man her mother loved who wasn't her father. Her father was the best, even though she didn't always let him know she felt that way. Ever Since That Night, she and her father had lived in the same house, but they were a little bit like ghosts. They didn't talk much. They hardly ever laughed. And Sari often caught him watching her with such terrible sorrow, as if he blamed himself for letting Sari's mother run away. Or for not stopping Sari from climbing up onto her horse, riding after the car, and all that happened after that.

For the way she was now.

Sari didn't mind work. Now that Rosalie had left, housework kept her busy and prevented her from thinking. She liked doing chores; she knew that other girls did them with their mothers. Her mother had never really been the housework type, even before she'd left. But Sari enjoyed it, keeping her home nice for her and her father. Sometimes she imagined her mother would come back, and see how beautiful it was, and want to stay.

Her father gave her an allowance for helping with the housework, and she saved it in a jar she kept in her closet. Sometimes she imagined paying for an operation, so she could see colors again—even though the doctors had told her father there was nothing organically wrong.

That meant she was crazy. The fact she saw the world in black and white, like an old movie, was all in her head. She had stayed in the hospital for weeks after the accident. They'd kept her in traction, allowing her pelvis and arm to heal. They'd given her painkillers that kept her in a fog. They'd sent in neurologists who'd given her test after test to figure out why she'd stopped seeing colors. After that the parade of shrinks began.

Shrinks in the hospital, shrinks in Arles and Paris, even a special-expert shrink and neurologists in Providence, Rhode Island, and New York City, on a summer trip to see her grandparents. No one could really figure it out, because the truth was too simple: her mother had taken all the colors away when she left.

Missing someone so much was complicated. Especially because it had been her mother's choice to go. Sometimes Sari's shoulder still burned, from where her mother had shoved her. Slapped her. Grabbing her mother's hand, holding on to her, Sari had gotten hit. Her mother had never done that before; she'd been so despairing, so desperate to get away from Sari and her father, she'd turned violent.

Sari curved inward as she remembered. She missed her mother, but she didn't think she loved her anymore. That hurt more than anything: five years after that night, she'd stopped loving her mother. Well, sort of. Even now, her eyes filled up with tears to think about it.

Rosalie, her mother's best friend, had been their housekeeper after that. But Sari had upset her a few weeks ago by talking about her mother, triggering Rosalie's fierce loyalty to her friend. She'd driven Rosalie away, too. Now it was just Sari and her father.

So Sari folded the clothes. She saved up her allowance for a dream so secret she could never say it out loud. Her dreams were of nature and poetry and horses and staying with the people you love forever, of colors coming back, and of something too treacherous to say. Sometimes she thought Laurent—her next-door neighbor and oldest friend—might guess. No one knew her better than Laurent. . . .

The laundry smelled like wet horses. It always did. Her father spent so much time riding, tending to the herds, his clothes were basically permeated with equine odor. It reminded Sari of happy times, before she'd stopped riding. Times riding with her parents, and with Laurent. But sometimes those memories were so happy, they made her weep.

Even though she hadn't been on a horse in five years, since she was eight—she hadn't approached Mystère in all that time—she liked the fact her father just kept riding. He treated the horses with enough love for both of them. There was comfort in the constancy. He woke up before dawn every day, hauled himself out of bed to feed the herds, rode into the marsh, took tourists on rides through the Parc.

The tourists came here to see the white horses. Sari didn't blame them: the horses were magical. Most of the tourists liked the horses because they looked pretty, not because of their rare and ancient bloodlines, dating back to the Solutre horses of the Lascaux cave paintings, many miles away.

The people flew here from New York and Florida and London and Berlin and wherever else tourists came from, to stand on the boardwalks and click pictures of the bulls and flamingos and wild white ponies. They'd pay handsomely to take trail rides in a pack, led by Sari's father and Laurent's father, Claude. Sometimes they'd ride at night, when the marsh was painted silver with moonlight. And when they'd had enough of horses, they'd all go down to Stes.-Maries and take pictures of the Romanies.

Sari patted trail dust and mud off her father's jeans, checked to make sure his pockets were empty, and threw them into the washing machine. Then she did the same to his shirt. He was usually pretty good about taking things out of his pockets, but he'd missed something here—she reached into his shirt pocket, pulled out a ribbon.

The sight of it made her stomach hurt.

It was long, fine, made of satin: a Gypsy ribbon. Sari stared at it, her heart skipped a few beats—and she felt her eyes fill with tears. What was he doing? Sari's mother had worn ribbons like this—individually, tied in her hair, and in the hundreds, all colors, streaming from her costume. Sari pictured her mother's favorite robe, as brilliant and vivid as the stained glass windows at church in Arles, flowing with fine purple, saffron, rose, red, emerald ribbons. They'd looked like rainbows, trailing off behind her as she'd ridden into the arena. . . . Sari could no longer see colors, but she could remember them.

Had her father been talking to her mother's people? But that was impossible—to them, he didn't exist. He was as dead to them as Sari's mother was. Had he fallen in love with another Rom woman? Or maybe, or maybe, or maybe he'd seen *her.*

Sari's heart skipped and began to pound: could her mother have come back? She must have! And the only reason her father hadn't told her was because she didn't want to see Sari.

She finished throwing the laundry into the washer, measured out soap, and turned on the machine. She heard the sound of rushing water, scalding hot, washing away all the horse smells, and all the Gypsy touch.

Walking through the house, she went to stand by the kitchen window. It was after six; her father should be home soon. She'd finished school early today, and the rest of her class had taken a trip to the museum in Nîmes. Laurent tried to convince her to go, but she'd told him she had to go home to do chores. Gazing out at the front yard, the pastures and long fences and marsh stretching into green nothing, she tried to stay calm.

Two black cats circled around and around her ankles. Their names were Oscar and Bruno, and Sari bent down to pick them up now. She held one in each arm, eyes closed while they licked and nuzzled her face, purring like tiny race cars. Someone had left them on her doorstep almost five years ago, in a covered basket, the lid on tight so they couldn't escape.

It was just a few months after her mother had left, right after Sari had come home from the hospital. At first she had imagined that her mother had come back, left the cats on the doorstep as a gift or coded promise. Was she trying to tell Sari she was coming back? Was she saying that if Sari took care of the kittens well, proved that she could love and respect two tiny living things, she'd return? Maybe she'd been trying to teach Sari a lesson: how hard it was to take care of things.

Sari knew how hard it had been for her mother to take care of a baby. She'd been a great beauty, a riding genius, a circus princess, born to ride white horses, her black hair flowing like her own mane. She had defied everyone to marry the American, the man everyone in Stes.-Maries-de-la-Mer saw as nothing better than a robber: he'd stolen the most beautiful, talented, high-strung Romany for himself.

Her mother's people—all of them except Rosalie—despised her father, and they'd cut her off for marrying him and having Sari. That must have killed her—how could it not? Moving out of town, to live in the middle of the Parc, with a man who knew nothing of her traditions, nothing of her life. He had tried to turn her into a housewife. Someone who went to market, cooked, mucked out stalls, had a baby.

Sari stood at the kitchen counter. She kissed Bruno and Oscar, let them down to walk across the sink and try to drink from the faucet. She stared at their black fur, and still believed her mother had been trying to tell her something, leaving the kittens for her to take care of. Glancing down at her hands, she saw her mother's skin.

Tan, burnished with Romany blood, nothing like her father's. He was from America, and Americans were all from somewhere else. His family had roots in Ireland, England, and Canada. From what Sari had been able to see—either on her visits to Rhode Island, or when her grandparents and uncles and aunts would come here—they had all been as different from her mother as day and night. Her mother's family, people without a territory, had settled years and years ago in Stes.-Maries. It was just down the road, but they wanted nothing to do with her.

Bruno stood on the windowsill, meowing. Sari wondered whether he still remembered those first days on the ranch, when she'd let the two kittens scoot outside and play. Everyone she knew had outdoor cats. Let them run free in the marsh, catching rats and birds, sunning themselves on the mudflats, chasing flies, playing in the hayloft, hiding in the stables.

But after just one week, Sari had been unable to stand it. Not knowing where they were, worrying that they might not come home. She moved slowly, because her pelvis was still healing, and she'd lost sleep, worrying about her two little kittens. She'd feared monsters in the swamp, the dreaded Tarasque of the Rhone, navigating the creeks behind her house, ready to kill her boys. So she had brought them indoors and kept them there. They were house cats now, and had been for five years.

All beings had a home, and that's where they were supposed to stay.

Her father was late for dinner. Sari was almost glad, because her feelings were wild and she didn't want him to see her this way; knowing her mother had come back and didn't want to see her was like losing her mother all over again. She balled the ribbon up in her hand, pressed it into her face, and began to sob.

Astride the white mare, Grey Dempsey had taken the last kilometer slowly, giving everyone a chance to take more pictures. The fog had finally lifted, and late-day caramel light spread over the marsh, painting everything gold. He led the riders into the paddock, and everyone dismounted, thanking him. He obliged people by taking photos of them with the white horses. Several asked where he was from in the States, and how he had ended up in the Camargue, and he'd told them the basic story, that he'd grown up around horses, had come to France and made his way down here to horse country, and never gone back.

Close enough.

Once he and Claude had gotten the horses rubbed down and most of them stabled, he'd paid Claude and said he'd see him tomorrow. Claude had walked home to Anne and Laurent, leaving Grey to head over to the main paddock, where he'd left Mystère for last.

She stood there, her withers almost pure gold in the setting sun. He reached into his pocket, pulled out a carrot, fed it to her while tangling his hand in her mane, petting the side of her neck.

"You're a good girl," he said. "You worked hard today. But it wasn't like yesterday, was it?"

She ate the carrot, then he led her across the yard toward the barn. He'd ridden her since early morning, and she'd been incredible. Ever since yesterday he'd been reliving that moment in the marsh, when he'd come upon that woman standing among the bulls. He'd reacted more than thought— kicking Mystère into a dead run, stretching out his hand, pulling the woman up behind him.

She'd asked if Mystère had saved her life, and he'd said yes, and it hadn't been a lie. The bulls were wild and aggressive, and he'd never once ridden that close to them when they'd been ready to charge. The woman, fine satin ribbon waving in her hand, had been thirty seconds from being gored to death.

"But she could ride, couldn't she?" he asked now. "Couldn't she jump up? Did you see that?"

It was as if she'd had wings on her feet. Their timing had been perfect; he'd leaned over, reached down, and she'd put up her hand just in time, in the split second it took to grab her. And somehow she'd had enough momentum—nothing like a running start, because she hadn't been moving, she'd been stock-still, her instincts had told her to do that—to spring straight up, swing her leg over, and hold on tight.

Wings on her feet; that's what it had to be.

Grey had known one other woman like that. She'd been able to ride like an angel, standing tall on her horse's back, robe flowing out behind her. She'd had wings, too. And she'd spread them and flown away.

Leading Mystère into the barn, Grey opened the door to her stall. His heart ached a little, looking into her eyes. Horses felt things strongly; in that way, they were like people. She'd been missing a woman's touch for years now. Maria and Grey had bought the horse on their daughter's fourth birthday— and Sari had given her the magical name.

Maria had ridden Mystère, trained her, started teaching Sari some easy tricks. Sari had taken to riding as if she'd been born for it. But all that had ended the night Maria left. Sari had stopped riding after her fall.

And no woman had ridden Mystère until yesterday.

Was it Grey's imagination, or was she looking more alert, holding her head higher? He had his own feelings about grief and loss here in the Parc Régional de Camargue; he and Sari hadn't been the only ones affected. But petting Mystère, giving her one last carrot, heading toward the house, he knew that nothing compared to what Sari still felt.

His stomach clenched even before he walked through the kitchen door. Just knowing he'd find his daughter in there, hiding out in her own home, seeing the world in shades of gray, made him ache with the sort of dull hurt and anger he'd long stopped trying to get rid of.

"Hey there," he said, stomping his boots, closing the door behind him. She stood at the stove, stirring something in a copper pot. *"Ça va?"*

She shrugged without turning around.

"You decided not to go to Nîmes?" he asked in English.

They spoke it here at home, and during summers in Rhode Island.

"Yes," she replied. "I didn't want to."

"I thought Laurent was trying to get you to change your mind."

"I've been to the museum enough times."

"You might have seen something new this time, something you missed before. A beautiful painting, or statue."

"Paintings look dull to me," she said quietly, and he felt stabbed through the heart. He saw the tension in her shoulders as she stirred whatever she was cooking. Seeing his daughter standing at the stove, knowing paintings, landscapes, the world looked dull to her, filled him with fresh despair.

"Sari. Let me call Rosalie again, and see if she'll come back. I don't want you doing all this—you should be out, having fun, going on these trips."

"She doesn't want to be here. I just remind her of who she'd rather see."

Grey stood in the middle of the kitchen. Sari had her back to him and gave no indication of turning around any time soon. The two cats had jumped down from the windowsills and were investigating his boots. He bent down to pet them without taking his eyes off his daughter.

"What's the matter, Sari?" he asked.

She didn't reply. Instead, she reached for the pepper mill and twisted it over the pot. She was often silent and distant, but right now he saw her shoulders shaking, and her hand trembling as she cracked the pepper.

"Sari?" he asked, as he stood up from the cats and took a step closer to the stove.

"When were you going to tell me?" she asked, her voice breaking.

The look in her eyes shocked him: beseeching, filled with despair. Tears ran down her face, and her chin wobbled, as if he'd broken her heart.

"Tell you what?"

"That you saw her!"

"Sari, saw who? What are you talking about?"

Dropping the spoon back into the copper pot, she reached into the pocket of her jeans and pulled out a red ribbon. He stared at it, remembering yesterday.

"I took it from a woman in the marsh," he said.

She shook her head, dark hair flying. "No," she wailed. "You didn't. I know she's back. She's somewhere nearby, isn't she? And she doesn't want to see me?"

"No, of course not! Your mother—"

"Where did you meet her? Was it accidental? Or did she call you, and you didn't want to tell me?"

"Sari," he said.

"What color is it?" she wept. "What color ribbon was she wearing, Papa?"

He was shaking, and wanted to grab her to him. Lead her into the living room, sit her down, talk sense into her. He struggled to make his voice gentle, the way he always had, in the weeks and months after Maria had first left. He'd felt like a hypnotist, a soothsayer, trying to talk his daughter—and himself—into becoming sane. But that had stopped working some time ago. Sari had stopped listening. And he had stopped believing the lies he'd been telling all along, that her mother would be back, that she'd never forget them, never forget *her.*

"Sweetheart . . ."

"What color, Papa?" she begged.

"It's a red ribbon."

"She was wearing it, right? She's back . . . Don't lie to me, Papa. Don't make something up. Tell me the truth."

"I just did."

"You got this from a woman in the marsh?" Sari asked with disbelief, waving the ribbon. "It's a Gypsy ribbon."

"I know," he said.

"Was she Rom?"

"No," Grey said, picturing the woman's light brown hair, freckled skin, violet eyes. "No, she wasn't."

"Then what was she doing—"

"Sari, I have no idea where she got it. Maybe she bought it at a souvenir stand. Maybe she picked it up off the street. How do I know?"

"Well, how did you wind up with it? Did she give it to you?"

"Not exactly."

"What does *that* mean?" she asked, her voice inching toward hysteria.

"Whoa," Grey said, as if he were gentling a wild horse. She was very sensitive about anything concerning women. The few dates he'd had were completely secret, behind Sari's back. She lived on the tightrope of wanting her mother to come home while claiming to never want to see her again. No other woman was allowed into the picture. His grieving, wounded daughter needed him all to herself.

He knew, on some level, he was doing her a disservice. Sari wanted to believe that Grey still loved Maria, that he would forgive her for leaving, and would always keep the door open for her. It wasn't supposed to matter that her mother was with someone else now, and had been since before the night she'd left. Grey had gotten advice, telling him to be straight with Sari. But right now there was nothing to tell.

"Tell me what's going on!" she wept.

"Sari, nothing is."

"Then how'd you get the ribbon?"

"I'll tell you, sweetheart," he said. "I was out on Mystère yesterday, and we came upon a woman, a stranger, about to get trampled by twenty bulls. We rescued her, and I took the ribbon from her. She was holding it, it was blowing in the wind, and it was provoking the bulls."

"You and Mystère rescued her?" Sari asked, her lower lip trembling.

"Yes."

"Were the bulls . . ."

"They were ready to charge."

"You could have been hurt!"

He narrowed his eyes. She was right, and he could read her mind: what would she do if something ever happened to him? "We were fine."

"What kind of lady would be dumb enough to get that close to the bulls?"

"Stop that, Sari. She didn't know."

"Did she ride Mystère?"

He put his hands up, stopping her before they went down this road. Sari wouldn't ride her, but for a long time, no one else was supposed to either—not even Grey. Now Sari seemed to gain comfort from seeing her father ride her mother's favorite horse, but certainly no strange woman would be welcome to. The tension was thick between them, lightning about to strike, when suddenly he saw it drain right out of her; she thrust the ribbon at him and crouched down to pet the cats, dropping the fight for now.

"I'm just glad you're okay," she whispered, more to the cats than to her father.

"I'm fine. Everyone's fine."

"You'd better get ready for dinner."

"It smells good."

"It's *daube de boeuf*."

"I'll go change," he said. He walked upstairs to his bedroom. Taking off his work clothes, he made a mental note to wash them himself later. Sari had talked him into letting her do the chores, but that was wrong. She needed to be a kid for as long as she could. He'd call Rosalie and beg her to come back, after Sari went to bed.

Just then he heard the screen door squeak open and softly close. He walked over to the window. It gave onto the backyard and barn and salt plain as far as the eye could see. They lived on the edge of a world of water, the sea-silvered marsh sliced into a puzzle of islands by hundreds of dark creeks. He liked this time of night, when the colors drained away, when his daughter could see what everyone else saw.

As he watched, Sari crossed the yard. Her limp was completely gone; she walked straight and tall, then stood alone, facing the barn. The top halves of the stall doors were open, and one white horse had heard her approach, and was standing at the door.

They looked at each other, girl and horse. This was as close as Sari ever let herself get to Mystère. She never touched her, never rode her. Grey stared down at his daughter, standing there in the yard. Then he turned away from the window.

He lifted the red ribbon from his nightstand, where he'd dropped it a minute ago. Gazed at it for a few minutes, remembered how it had looked waving in the woman's hand. She had jumped up like such a champ.

He wound the ribbon into a tight coil, placed it behind a book on the shelf beside his bed, and headed downstairs for dinner.

THREE

Susannah had intended to go to the church first thing in the morning after she arrived, but she'd been unable to move. She never experienced jet lag like this when she was working, but it had tugged her down, back into bed. The fog had turned to rain, and the wind blew harder. Lying still, covers pulled up, she listened to the rain on the roof.

So far from home, she felt months' worth of grief rising to the surface. The latest issue of the *Journal of Cultural Anthropology* had just come out, her name on the cover and her article on Paleolithic art in the caves of Corsica inside. Her work in Turkey had gained attention, too, and she'd received a grant to continue there. But Susannah couldn't focus on any of that.

Eyes closed, she felt rocked by sorrow, and for the first time in all the months since she'd lost her mother, she at last gave herself over to the overwhelming guilt that haunted her. Her mother had been sick with lymphoma for so long, Susannah had gotten used to her illness as a way of life. Margaret had remained relatively stable, but Susannah wouldn't have stayed so long in Istanbul if she'd known how quickly things would change, no matter what her mother said.

Imagined images of her mother's last days had become a familiar tape: lying in the hospital, getting weaker and sicker so fast, needing higher doses of morphine, while Susannah was so far away. Had she hoped Susannah would come back on her own? Had she tried to hold on for one last goodbye?

All of that talk about "life's work" . . .

Susannah could hear her mother's voice now. She knew what Margaret believed, that a person's work and spirit were completely entwined. By encouraging Susannah to continue traveling and making discoveries, Margaret was choosing life. She never would have wanted her daughter to sit at home, waiting for her to die.

Just before Susannah left for Istanbul, there had been signs that Margaret's condition was changing; she'd felt more tired than usual. A blood test had come back with an elevated white cell count. Susannah had wanted to cancel her trip. But her mother had insisted; she'd told Susannah she felt fine, that everything would be okay.

"You have to go, sweetheart. I've never been to Istanbul, but it's always sounded so beautiful. Imagine, you'll be right there on the Bosporus. . . . You'll be seeing it for me, too," she'd said.

Three days after Susannah had arrived in Istanbul, she'd gotten word that her mother was in the hospital. She'd called Shoreline General immediately; she remembered being in her hotel room overlooking the Bosporus as they spoke together. Her mother had asked her to describe the view from her window— the city skyline, minarets, blue water—and reassured her that she was fine.

But she'd known deep inside that it was bad; she should have trusted her instincts, not her mother's soothing words.

Susannah should have been at the hospital, dealing with the doctors, holding her mother's hand. But her mother had died there alone.

Lying in a strange bed, in a rented house, Susannah wept. She'd come here, to the Camargue, to feel closer to her mother—to find a way to forgive herself. Instead, she felt the mistral seeping into her soul and wondered whether she'd ever get over what she'd done.

We die alone, the saying went. But Susannah had never believed it. Not when you come from a close family, not when you are surrounded by love. Her mother had nursed her father after his heart attack; Susannah doubted she'd ever left him for more than a few hours. And she'd been right by his side when he died.

Her mother had deserved the same from the daughter she had raised with such overflowing love. Susannah should have been there for her, not just when she died, but so many other times. She'd told herself she was making her mother proud—her parents had always encouraged her, wanted her to succeed at the college, and in her field. Her life's work . . . Susannah had told herself she was leaving Margaret with excellent health care, that she'd cancel any trip, cut it short and head right home—if things changed.

But there hadn't been time. By the time Susannah had gotten the final call, her mother was already in a coma. She'd died with no one holding her hand, while Susannah was in the air, flying home from Istanbul.

The rain beat in rhythm with her heart. The weather held its own despair. She curled into a ball under the covers, shivering and wondering why she had come.

But one day later, the sun was shining. Susannah climbed out of bed—determined to fight yesterday's darkness, the overwhelming loneliness that had swept over her in the foreign place, so distant from her home. She had traveled so often on business. The field of cultural anthropology was rich and deep, and her studies and work had taken her all over the world. She'd had moments of difficulty along the way, but she'd always stayed strong and positive, keeping the focus on her work and reveling in the exotic surroundings.

She plugged in her laptop, connected to the local phone line, and checked her email. There were birthday messages from Heather, Amy, and other friends. Reading Heather's email, Susannah smiled. *How did you do it? Slip out of town JUST in the nick of time?!?! Serves me right—I know I'd always promised* never *to do that, to throw you a surprise party. Helen got you off the hook in the classiest way possible. We'd invited her, and instead of coming, she sent a case of champagne with a note that she'd sent you to France on top-secret Connecticut College business. I can't quite imagine what that is, but it doesn't matter. Without going into details, you're lucky you didn't come—there was a mystery guest you'd probably just as soon have avoided. Just have a fantastic time, and don't worry about a thing.*

A mystery guest. Susannah wasn't sorry to have missed him. Seeing Ian was the last thing she needed right now. Even after their rift, he never gave up. She sent back a reply to Heather, as well as one to Amy. Then she wrote to Helen, thanking her for sending the champagne, and for keeping her secret—Susannah had found out about the party and the "mystery guest" and bought the champagne herself.

Helen had been kind enough to have the champagne delivered; she'd understood that Susannah just wasn't up to a surprise party this year. Susannah closed her email to the professor by confirming she'd contacted the library in Arles before she left, made arrangements to research in the rare book room later in the week, reminding Helen to fax the library director her credentials; Susannah had a duplicate set, just in case.

Her credentials. They fit on five 8½ × 11 pieces of paper, her whole professional life boiled down into a curriculum vitae of degrees, awards, publications, grants. Wheaton. Yale. She'd started working at Connecticut College that following summer, after completing her doctorate.

She'd loved reading about world cultures, and had wanted to be an anthropologist for as long as she could remember. Her mother had been a middle-school English teacher. When Susannah was young, she would beg to help correct papers. Once Margaret had said yes, but only if Susannah read the book she'd assigned her class.

It was *Horses in the Cave: The Paintings of Lascaux,* by Anna McNeil. Susannah had gotten lost in the story about Paleolithic hunters in southwest France, the incredible, vivid paintings they had done in the caves of Lascaux. She'd been moved by the author's understanding of the people who had lived back then, and of depictions—in the color plates—of beautiful horses, some of them shot with arrows.

Susannah's mother had told her to turn to the back of the book, look at the list of source material. There, cited for quotes in chapter three, was Professor Helen Oakes of nearby Connecticut College. Susannah must have filed that information deeply away.

At Yale, she often researched in the Beinecke Library, one of the most exquisite buildings in the world, with translucent marble walls through which drifted soft, gray, diffused light. It was a cozy and romantic sanctuary, and it was there that she'd begun delving into cultures that revered horses—inspired by her early reading, and by the fact she'd always loved the animals so much.

Again, there in the library, she encountered the name of Helen Oakes; the professor had written a book called *Women, Beasts, and the Myth of True Love.* Susannah had admired the playfulness of the title and the scholarship of the work, and she'd cited the text in her own dissertation, on the cave paintings of Lascaux.

"Susannah, I'm so proud of you," her mother had said after she finished at Yale, toasting her doctorate. They were having dinner at the Renwick Inn, their favorite restaurant, right on the riverbank in Black Hall, a spot they'd always chosen for special family occasions. "Your father would be over the moon."

"I wish he were here," Susannah had said.

"I know, honey," her mother had said. "So do I. But you have him with you always; you know that."

And she did. In symbols and memories, and the big silver watch of his she always wore, and in the strength and knowledge he'd passed on to her during his lifetime—her connection with her father would last forever.

"So, now what?" her mother had asked at that special dinner. They'd been determined to make it festive, regardless of the fact they missed him so much. "What is the next step on your amazing journey?"

"You mean, where am I going to get a job?" Susannah had laughed.

"Exactly."

"Well, I'm applying to Michigan, and I've sent letters to the departments at Harvard and Stanford. Ian's really pushing for me to apply there."

"Ian wants you where he can keep an eye on you," her mother said.

"Mom, he's not that bad . . ."

"Susannah, he lets you scramble around the caves while he sits outside, not getting dirty, taking notes on your discoveries—and sharing the credit! When I spoke to him at graduation, he made me feel as if *you* were lucky to have worked with him. It makes my blood boil."

"That's just teamwork, Mom," Susannah had said.

"Not my kind of team," her mother had said, stubbornly.

"He's envious of you . . . I watched him when you won the Fabbri Prize."

"Well, he probably should have won," Susannah said, remembering how he'd sulked. "His grades . . ."

Her mother stopped her, placing her hand over Susannah's on the table. "Don't you ever let me hear you say that again. You worked so hard for that prize. Honey, don't ever let anyone demean you—and don't you do it to yourself. You and Ian share a love of the caves . . . but you love the beauty and mystery. He loves the way your research will advance him."

"Thanks, Mom," she'd said.

"I get it," her mother said. "Time to change the subject." They sat still for a few minutes, quietly gazing out through the bright green leaves of maple and birch trees, across the long green lawn toward the golden river.

"What about," her mother asked finally, as if she'd been holding the idea inside all evening, "Connecticut College?"

"I hadn't really thought about it," Susannah said. And immediately she'd wondered why not. Its department had such an excellent reputation, partly because of its star professor.

"I read an article in the *Day,* not long ago, about an anthropologist there. Professor Helen Oakes," her mother said.

"Mom," Susannah had laughed. "Don't you remember? Her name was listed in that book you gave me to read years and years ago. The one that got me started! *Horses in the Cave: The Paintings of Lascaux,* by Anna McNeil."

"Hmm," her mother had said thoughtfully. "I do seem to remember that."

"Sure, I'll apply to Connecticut College. It's so close to home—that would be a plus."

"Well, so is Yale," her mother said. "I'm not suggesting this to keep you nearby. You know that, don't you? I want you to spread your wings. . . . Even Stanford, if that's what you want."

"Of course, Mom," Susannah had teased. "You'd much

rather have me working in California, all the way across the country."

"If that's what made you happy, I absolutely would," her mother had said resolutely.

And Susannah had believed her, too. Her parents had never tried to hold her back—they'd done the opposite, encouraged her to travel, explore, and do her best, wherever that took her. But nonetheless, she'd applied for a job just ten miles from home, been accepted by Professor Helen Oakes herself, and—in spite of Ian's disappointment and derision— never once doubted herself.

She'd continued working with him through the years; because of their shared interests, they often wound up writing about the same sites. But as time went on, and he kept pressing for more, she'd been very glad they lived on opposite sides of the country.

Now, glancing around the kitchen of her rented house in Stes.-Maries, she knew she was right to have traveled back to France. The sense of her parents was everywhere. Yet the place seemed entirely new and mysterious at the same time. Her adventure in the marsh attested to that.

Checking the schedule of town events hanging by the kitchen phone, she saw that today was market day in Stes.-Maries-de-la-Mer, and she decided to check it out.

Susannah stopped first at a café at the foot of her street. She ordered a croissant and café au lait, and enjoyed them on the terrace, overlooking the harbor. Her thighs and shoulders ached from her wild horseback ride, and her wrist was chafed, from where the man had grabbed her. She rubbed her wrist now, looking around.

The horizon was low and limitless, and everything was scoured by light from above and reflected off the river and bay. Although the land- and seascape reminded her of Connecticut, it was also vastly different. Without trees to diffuse the sun, the light was scalding here, vivid and intense.

Wearing a sunhat and dark glasses, carrying the wicker market basket from her kitchen, Susannah headed through town to the Place des Gitanes. There were stands for charcuterie, *poulet, poisson, fromage, boulangerie,* and fresh Provence vegetables. She moved slowly through the *marché,* stopping to savor every stand, filling her basket with beautiful food, wrapped by each individual vendor in crisp white paper.

The street was bustling, as if everyone in the region had come out to enjoy the sun and do their week's shopping. One woman was selling embroidered blouses—bright flowers and symbols stitched on fine muslin—and they hung from the stall's awning, moving in the quiet breeze. Susannah bought one. Then she stopped at a stand to buy postcards to send home to Heather, Amy, and Helen.

"*Bonjour!* Mademoiselle Connolly!"

Turning, Susannah saw her landlady coming toward her—Topaz Avila, dressed today in a flowing emerald silk skirt and one of the embroidered peasant blouses. Topaz carried a string bag, a baguette wedged in among white paper packages.

"Mademoiselle Avila," she said.

"*S'il vous plaît*—call me Topaz."

"And call me Susannah."

The two women fell into step with each other as they walked along. Susannah glanced up at the old church. Once again she had planned to go inside this morning, but with the sun shining so brightly she just wanted to stay out in the streets and soak it up. Topaz caught her glance, and nodded.

"Have you been yet?"

"No, although it's one of the reasons I came here."

"That's true for many people. We have many pilgrims."

Susannah nodded, thinking of her own family story. "I can imagine."

"Do you know about the legend?"

"Some," Susannah said elusively. Although she had grown up hearing it from her mother, and despite the fact her boss had a particular academic interest in some of the details, Susannah really wanted to know the perspective of a person who lived here.

"Would you like to walk awhile? I'll tell you about it."

"That would be wonderful," Susannah said.

As the two women strolled along, Topaz told the story of the ship, drifting all the way from Galilee in the year 45, of how the three Marys, Martha, Lazarus, and Sarah made landfall right here in this ancient town, here on the edge of the marshland.

"Lazarus . . ." Susannah said.

"Yes," Topaz said. "Brought back from the dead by his best friend, Christ. But the company in this boat was so *exceptionnel*, he barely stood out. There were also Jesus's aunts—both named Mary—and Saint Martha, and, of course, Mary Magdalene. While Lazarus went on to Marseille, to found a church there, the Marys stayed. They were grateful for having landed safely, and they built a chapel right here."

"That one?" Susannah asked, gazing up at the mysterious towered structure.

"Yes, indeed."

Susannah studied the imposing Romanesque architecture. Her mind raced with thoughts regarding its historical importance, but her heart was touched by the idea that Mary Magdalene had walked this very ground, and founded this church out of pure gratitude.

"Is it a true story?" she asked softly, wanting to draw Topaz out, knowing that not all the scholarship in the world could hold a candle to a true believer.

"Of course!" Topaz said, as if there could never be any doubt.

"But how do you know?"

"The bones," Topaz said, launching into a story that Susannah already knew well. "Two female skeletons were found in the chapel crypt, beneath the Altar of Juno, during the fifteenth century. It's been determined that the women had been very old when they died; we are sure they were Mary Salome and Mary Jacoby. You see, Sarah had stayed here in this town with them, even after all the others had left."

"Sarah, the young servant girl," Susannah said, thinking of her mother's stories.

"Yes," Topaz said. "She cared for them into their old age. They were relatives of Mary Magdalene as well as Jesus Christ. Sarah stayed with them until the end."

Topaz's words pierced Susannah's heart. *Stayed with them until the end* . . .

Topaz must have seen the expression in Susannah's eyes; her own filled with compassion. "Would you like to see Sarah's statue? It's in the church . . . you really must, to understand what she means to people."

Wordlessly, Susannah nodded. She walked with Topaz across the street, up the stone walk bleached nearly white by age and the sun. Her blood was racing so fast, she could barely breathe. Was it because her parents had come here so long ago, that she was walking in their footsteps? Was it because Sarah—who had blessed Susannah's mother so many years ago—had done something Susannah herself had not—or could not—do for her mother at the end? When Topaz held open the heavy church door, Susannah stood out in the sunlight, unable to move.

"Come in," Topaz said, then smiled. "Sarah is waiting."

The sun had blinded her, and she couldn't see in the darkness in the back of the church. Topaz led her down the aisle, Susannah walking as slowly as possible. Candles burned everywhere. Her eyes became accustomed to the dim light—the church had very few windows, and those few were tiny.

"It was here, in 1449, that the former church nave was destroyed," Topaz said in a low whisper. "Right here, at L'Oreiller des Saintes . . . the skeletons were found."

Susannah bowed her head, feeling the ghosts of her beloved dead.

"There," Topaz said, pointing to the left. "Unbelievers say that in ancient times, that was a pagan altar where bulls were sacrificed in worship to Mithra." Seeing Susannah shiver, Topaz went on quickly. "But in any case, that was long ago, before the ship landed, before the Marys came. Here, past the Christian altar, is our Sarah. *Sara-la-Kali . . .*"

Gazing at the beautiful statue, ebony wood dressed in gold leaf, the statue draped with layers of real clothes, the young girl's face so kind and loving, Susannah felt her eyes fill with tears. People had left behind crutches, canes, braces, even old bandages, evidence of every sort of hurt. They had surrounded Sarah's statue with candles, and they were burning now, so that the statue's black wood seemed to gleam from within.

Susannah knelt. She knew that her mother had been *right here.* Her parents, lovers of nature, had discovered the Camargue in their search for birds and wild horses. That they had arrived in this church at the very end of the windswept plain, perched right on the edge of the Gulf of Lions, seemed a miracle in itself. As if sensing that Susannah needed privacy, Topaz backed away.

There was something so sweet and comforting about Sarah, Susannah could instantly see why her mother had loved her. She was reminiscent of the Black Madonnas studied by colleagues of Susannah and Helen, yet not a Madonna at all. She was a young slave girl, humble for having lived an entire life of service. Yet something in her eyes—even in this statue carved centuries ago—spoke of life, curiosity, a desire to embrace everything and everyone.

And people loved her: that was obvious. She wore real clothes; her visitors dressed her in skirts, blouses, jackets, scarves. Over what appeared to Susannah to be a lovingly ragtag wardrobe was a tattered gold brocade coat with recent darns on the sleeves and pockets.

Susannah reached out, touched the cloth.

"Hello, Sarah," she whispered. "My mother loved you. You brought me to her. She asked me to come . . ."

Susannah listened. Voices carried from other parts of the church, and she swore she heard familiar whispers. She thought of the stories she'd been told as a child, and whispered her thanks to Sarah, for what she had done for her parents, for herself. She whispered the name Topaz had said earlier: *Sara-la-Kali*. And she felt her mother's presence.

After a few minutes, Susannah wiped her eyes and stood. She paused by the crypt where statues of Mary Jacoby and Mary Salome stood. As she moved away, she felt the pull of the ebony statue behind her, and she was unsure of whether it was Sarah's own power, or knowing that her parents had been here before her—or the sense that her mother was with her now. But she continued toward the door, where Topaz waited.

The dark-haired woman smiled brilliantly.

"Now that you've met her, what do you think?"

"She's wonderful. More beautiful even than I'd expected. Who dresses her that way?" Susannah asked as they walked out the door into the bright sunshine.

"The faithful," Topaz said. "We take turns. Sarah is the patron saint of the Romany people. So much so, it used to be forbidden for anyone else to enter the church. Only the Rom had that right."

"I'm glad that changed," Susannah said. "If it hadn't, I might not be here."

"What do you mean?" Topaz asked.

Susannah took a deep breath. She felt shaken by what had happened inside the church, and she wanted to preserve the feeling of her mother's presence. Talking about it helped her hold on. "My parents came here a long time ago . . . they'd been married for many years, with no children. They visited this church on a vacation to France—it was almost by accident. They'd actually wanted to see the white horses of the Camargue, and something made them follow the road a little farther . . . down here to Stes.-Maries. My mother walked into the church, and she knelt by Sarah. My mother always said . . ."

"That Sarah blessed them with you."

"Yes," Susannah said.

"They were right," Topaz said. "Although of course it was no accident that they wound up here. It never is. Stes.-Maries calls those who need to come. Your parents were drawn to Sarah by divine inspiration." She smiled as widely as before, tilting her head. A group of Gypsy women walked past, skirts flowing; they waved at Topaz, and she back at them. Everything felt so exotic. "I shall tell . . ." Topaz began, trailing off.

"What?" Susannah asked.

Topaz hesitated, seeming to consider whether to continue. Her gaze seemed to seek out the women who'd walked past, disappearing around the back of the church. "Nothing," Topaz said. "I have friends that will be interested in your story. That is all. Now I must go. I own several houses other than the one you are renting, and they must be cleaned and readied for the next tenants."

"Well, thank you for showing me the church," Susannah said. "And Sarah. My mother and I always meant to come here together."

"You would have found her yourself," Topaz said. She flashed a smile, but it instantly disappeared. Susannah felt Topaz gazing over her shoulder toward the street, watched the woman's eyes narrow and harden.

When Susannah turned to see what had changed Topaz's mood, she saw her friend from the marsh climbing out of an old Citroën. He was tall and rangy, with that streak of silver in his brown hair, and blue eyes so bright it seemed he must never look into the sun, and the sight of him hit her like a lightning bolt. A decal of a white horse was stuck to the back window of his car; Susannah wondered how he had managed to get a sticker that looked exactly like Mystère.

"What's that man's name?" she asked Topaz.

But when she turned back to her landlady, she saw Topaz hurrying away, toward the other women, the brilliant green silk of her skirt whisking around the corner of the stone church. Susannah watched her go, then gazed back toward the man she had last seen on a white horse in the fog-shrouded marsh. She remembered her body pressed into his, riding for their lives through the mist. She smiled, waved, and ran down the steps to meet him.

Grey had come to town looking for Rosalie—never an easy proposition—and instead found the woman of the red ribbon. Here she came, beaming and looking so happy to see him that it made his heart flip. He felt the same way, and started to grin. The sunlight was white, bouncing off the sea and the stone of the church, and it made him squint and shade his eyes with his hand, and he couldn't stop smiling.

"Hello," he said, stopping beside her.

"It's you," she said. "I thought it was."

"Yep, it's me. How are you doing, since our wild ride?"

She laughed, a really wonderful, startling trill, as if the question had taken her by surprise, and just seeing her made him want to ride off with her again. He felt a physical rush that nearly knocked him over, and that put him on guard.

"It *was* a wild ride, wasn't it? Well, my legs ache, and my wrist feels like one big rope burn, but otherwise I'm fine. I'm glad the weather has cleared up. That fog was a little spooky."

"It must have been," he said, feeling spooked by a whole lot more than the fog.

"I have a question about the bulls," she said. "I just heard about how they used to be sacrificed right here, back in pagan times—is it true?"

"Supposedly," he said, gazing into her eyes. She'd been be-hind him on the horse, and he hadn't realized how clear, and darkly beautiful, and intelligent her eyes were. "But not all the legends around here should be believed . . ."

"But some should," she said softly.

He shrugged and said nothing.

"Those bulls," she went on, shaking her head. "They're magnificent. It's awful to think of them being sacrificed."

"I know," he said. "Even to this day."

"Bullfights?" she asked.

He nodded. "They're common here. Most ranchers don't allow the bulls to be killed—but there are some."

"I'll avoid those ranchers," she said. "And I'll watch out for bulls in the Parc."

"Just pay attention and leave them alone. If you give them plenty of distance, and don't wave ribbons at them, they won't bother you. I'd be more worried about quicksand."

"Quicksand?" she asked.

He nodded. "It's everywhere in the Parc. It's more like sea mud, really, left behind when the tide goes out. We lose horses to it." He peered into her dark violet eyes. He wanted so much to offer to show her around; they were standing so close he could smell her hair. He remembered the feel of her—it wasn't something he'd soon forget. She seemed to be exerting a pull he hadn't encountered since Maria. It felt dangerous, so he kept his tone steady, took a half step back. "Wouldn't want to lose you. Stay on the boardwalks, and you'll be fine."

"Thanks for the warning," she said, looking down. He saw the color rising in her cheeks; he'd made her blush. Was he being too alarmist, scaring her all over again? Or was it something else? Was she feeling on edge, too? He saw sadness just behind her eyes, and wondered what had happened to cause it.

"It's not all bad in the Parc," he said. "I didn't mean that."

"I know. As a matter of fact, I was thinking about taking a trail ride," she said, looking up again, emotion even closer to the surface. He watched her wage some kind of private battle with herself. A smile emerged. "On one of those white horses I came here to see."

The bright sun beat down, paradoxically making her eyes darken. He thought of how beautifully she had made that leap, how expertly she had ridden. He imagined leading her into parts of the Parc no one else would go, where the horses could gallop through silver plains of sea grass. He'd show her himself how to avoid the quicksand. But then he thought of Sari, of the way that ribbon had set off a panic, and he knew he had to shut this down. Sari needed all his attention.

"Well, there are plenty of ranches," he said.

"I need to find a good one," she said. "One that has a nice rancher who doesn't kill the bulls."

He nodded, and it took everything to hold himself back from offering.

"I was wondering," she said. "Since this is the second time we've met, do you think we could actually introduce ourselves?"

"Sure," he said, smiling. There couldn't be any harm in that, could there?

"I'm Susannah Connolly," she said.

"Grey Dempsey," he said, shaking her hand.

"You're American?"

He nodded. "Born and raised there," he said. "But I moved here a long time ago."

"You're an expatriate?" she asked.

He chuckled. The way she said the word, with mystery and allure, reminded him of how he'd felt when he'd first come to France in his twenties. "Yes, you can say that," he said. "I wanted to be Hemingway."

"Really? Because of the bulls?" she asked.

"I was a journalist," he said.

Something shifted in her gaze. She'd been categorizing him in a certain way—horses, bulls, the great outdoors. But suddenly her perception changed; he felt her curiosity building, and that was true for him as well. He'd felt her hand, just now, shaking it, and earlier, in the marsh; it was a little rough, surprising him. Her eyes were deep and sensitive, but also challenging; she was in charge of her own life. For some reason he'd had the feeling she worked with books.

"I'd better get going," he said.

"Oh," she said, sounding disappointed. "Okay."

"Take care," he said. "Enjoy your time here."

"Thank you. I will."

With a last look into those eyes, he turned to walk away. Sari came first, and she needed everything he had, his traumatized, colorblind child. He'd trained himself to keep from getting involved with women, but this time it hurt like hell.

Rosalie Daquin lived in the caravans on the outskirts of town, but she spent most of her days in and around the church; he needed to see her in person, to convince her to come back to work. He'd only taken a few steps when he heard Susannah call his name.

"Grey Dempsey!" she said.

He glanced back.

"That was your byline?" she asked.

"Yep," he said. "It was."

"Well, you might be a journalist, but you sure know how to ride a white horse."

"So do you, Susannah Connolly," he said.

They waved at each other once more, and then he followed the path behind the church, where he'd seen Topaz running, pretending she hadn't seen him, no doubt on her way to warn Rosalie he was coming. He tried again to put Susannah and her midnight eyes out of his mind, but he couldn't do it.

She was right there, and he knew he was in uncharted territory.

FOUR

Susannah felt exhilarated. She'd loved seeing Grey again, and she felt a little shocked by how happy it had made her. She stopped at the newsstand and picked up a local guide, listing fifteen places offering trail rides within a short drive of Stes.-Maries. The third one was called *Manade du Dempsey:* Dempsey's herd. The owner's name was listed right there: Grey Dempsey.

Her high spirits evaporated at the sight of his name. Why hadn't he told her that he owned and operated a horse ranch?

Her feelings were hurt. She had to admit it. Why had he so deliberately steered her to go somewhere else? Her recklessness in the marsh must have really appalled him—a stranger just barreling in.

She knew how that felt. When she was in the field, maneuvering into a cave, she moved very carefully, and felt intensely territorial about "her caves." One wrong move could damage everything, and she had little patience for amateurs.

Back at her little house, she put all the things she'd gotten at the market away and made herself a lunch of fresh yogurt and dark ripe figs, drizzled with lavender honey. It tasted delicious, and she found herself wondering whether Grey shopped at the market, whether he cooked for himself, whether he had someone to share meals with. She liked thinking of him as a journalist, and wondered how that and his ranch were connected. Did he still write? Or did all his effort go into caring for horses, taking visitors on rides through the Camargue?

Sitting at the kitchen table, she told herself to stop it. He'd pushed her away—that was that. She should know; she'd done the same thing to Ian. Lately when Ian wanted to attend conferences on the East Coast, and suggested they meet up or go together, Susannah would make excuses. He'd finally gotten the message, but it had taken a while.

Reaching for her notebook, she began to record her observations about the church, Sarah, and everything Topaz had told her, retreating into the comfortable habits of her profession. Anthropology was the study of humanity. Susannah's interest lay in the way human beings related to each other and their environments at various periods of history. But at the moment, all she could think of was Grey Dempsey.

Putting down her pen, she looked around the room. This was ridiculous; she hadn't come here for this; she'd traveled to the Camargue to keep a promise and see Sarah, experience a new culture.

And she wasn't just observing Gypsy culture—she was living in it. It felt exotic, thrilling, and completely unfamiliar. Throughout Topaz's house were icons and symbols: talismans to chase the evil eye? Susannah stood, walked over to a feather hanging by the door. She knew that it was meant to repel wickedness and danger; beside it was an icon of the almost-saint Sarah.

Sara-la-Kali.

Susannah felt intrigued by the Rom, the way they'd carried their customs and beliefs into the present, woven them into everyday life, made their saint a part of their families.

Lost in thought, Susannah was startled when the phone rang. Who knew she was here? She hadn't given the house number to anyone—she didn't even know what it was. Reaching for the wall phone, she answered.

"Hello?"

"Susannah, it's Topaz."

"Oh, hi," Susannah said. "You ran off so quickly earlier, I didn't get to thank you properly for showing me the church. And Sarah."

"It was my pleasure. Listen, do you remember that I mentioned to you about some friends I have, who would be interested in the story of how Sarah blessed your family?"

"Yes, I do."

"Well, we are getting together tonight. We would love for you to join us, tell us about what happened. Would you come?"

Susannah paused. She thought of her mother, knew how much this would mean to her.

"Yes. I'd like that very much," she heard herself say. "Thank you."

"I'll pick you up at seven," Topaz said.

"You don't have to," Susannah said. "If you just give me the address, I can—"

"It's rather a long way out of town," Topaz said. "I'll be happy to drive you."

"Thank you, then. I have a question," Susannah said. "You called Sarah 'Sara-la-Kali.' I know that Sarah is from Kali's lineage, but is it commonly known? Do you think of her that way?"

"We'll explain that to you tonight," Topaz said, her voice rich and gentle, as if the very question had warmed her. *"À tout à l'heure!"*

"À tout à l'heure," Susannah said.

After she hung up the phone, she sat very still. Her eyes fell upon the page she'd been writing. It was filled with her first impressions of encountering Sarah: the dark church, the blazing votive candles, the feeling of peace that had come over her. Sarah was everywhere. It was almost as if by writing about her, Susannah had summoned Topaz's call.

As Susannah sat at the table, continuing her precise note-taking, she concentrated on her observations at the *église*. But every so often her pen wavered and she thought of those blue eyes, and knew it was futile: she had the rancher on her mind, and he wasn't going away.

Turning on her laptop, she logged on and went straight to Google. Typing in "Grey Dempsey," she found mention of the Manade du Dempsey—travel articles, or blogs by people who'd visited, glowing reviews of Grey's horses, ranch, and trail rides. It wasn't until Susannah had scrolled through four pages that she found what she'd been looking for: references to articles written by Grey Dempsey.

The most recent dateline was fourteen years old. He had written for the *International Herald Tribune,* as well as *Paris Match.* Looking further, she found reference to pieces he had published in *Harper's, The New Yorker,* and *The Atlantic Monthly.* She couldn't find any entire articles—only citations of them in other work.

But she could see from all the mentions that his subject matter had been very specific. He had written about the Rom.

Gypsies from Prague to Madrid, and especially in France. She could tell from one story that he had been based in Paris, and had come to the South of France to witness their devotion to what he referred to as "the slave saint." Sarah.

And that was the last reference she found.

How had he gone from journalist/observer of the Romany people to living right here, among them? Perhaps his desire to be Hemingway had gone deeper than he'd admitted, and the outdoors and the bulls and the horses had worked their magic on him, convinced him to put down roots in this enchanted place.

Somehow Susannah thought there was more to it than that. But since it didn't really matter anyway, she shut down the computer and pulled out the list of ranches again. She had a map of the countryside; it seemed like a good time to go exploring. She'd give the Manade du Dempsey wide berth and leave him alone—that was obviously what he wanted.

It hurt her. Susannah never felt this way. She'd always been happy to go on her way, absorbed in her work and all the discoveries the world had to offer. Now she was stunned, overwhelmed with feelings she'd never had before, and for a man who was just a stranger.

As much as she didn't want to admit it, Sari's heart jumped when she saw her father pull up with Rosalie. She was sitting at the kitchen counter, Bruno and Oscar at her feet. She'd just finished her schoolwork and had started in on dinner preparations. She'd decided to fix a gratin, and began slicing *courgettes* and tiny potatoes, grating Gruyère cheese.

Rosalie was a great cook, and she'd always put something secret in her gratins. Sari had been wracking her brain for what that ingredient might be—and here Rosalie came, through the door. The cats scattered for hiding places as they always did when non–family members entered the house.

"*Bonjour*, Sari," Rosalie said, preceding Sari's father into the kitchen.

"*Bonjour*," Sari replied, sheepishly and quite shyly, considering she'd known Rosalie since birth.

"You didn't think you'd see me again, did you?" Rosalie asked in English.

"*Pas vraiment*," Sari answered in French, just to be contrary.

"Not really?" Rosalie asked, eyebrows raised.

"Sari's sorry for what she said," her father said now. He was standing behind Rosalie, out of her sight. Only Sari could see the desperation in his eyes. Sari knew they needed help around the house; she wanted to do the right thing.

Rosalie stood very still. She gazed steadily, patiently, at Sari. Her dark hair was long and wavy, her eyes huge black pools. Sari's mother had had the same coloring. Sari shivered.

Her father watched her. Sari felt that buzzing feeling she sometimes got when she was afraid she'd disappoint him. She wanted to make everything right, make Rosalie want to stay; all she had to do was apologize.

"What are you making?" Rosalie asked, drifting toward the counter.

"A gratin," Sari asked. She wanted to ask Rosalie about her special touch, but she didn't dare. Her heart was aching too much, and her arm throbbed; it hardly ever hurt anymore, only when something really made her think about her mother, about that night. Seeing Rosalie was almost like looking into the eyes of her mother.

"We have things to talk about," Rosalie said, arms folded across her chest.

"I know," Sari whispered. But the rest of her thoughts, words that might make things right, were stuck in her throat.

"It hasn't been working out," Rosalie said.

"We want it to," Sari's father said. "We know you've gone out of your way to help us, and we'd like to ask you to come back. Right, Sari?"

But Sari couldn't speak, or even nod. The kitchen was silent, all except for the wall clock ticking. Outside, a rooster crowed. From the barn, someone whinnied. There had been an afternoon trail ride today, and Claude had taken the horses out, leaving just a few behind. His son, Sari's best friend, Laurent, was in the stable now, cleaning up. Sari heard the scrape of his pitchfork on the stable floor.

"You know how I feel about Maria, don't you?" Rosalie asked. "You know how hard it was for me to hear you talk about your mother the way you did?"

"I do know," Sari said quietly. "I'm very sorry."

"For what?"

Rosalie was going to make her spell it out. Sari felt heat rise in her face, making her head ache the way it had in the months after her accident.

"For what I said about my mother," Sari said.

"Were you wrong?"

"I was wrong to hurt your feelings."

"Sari," her father began.

"That's not the same thing," Rosalie said softly, her voice shaking. "Your mother is my best friend, and I love her. I know you've been through a lot, Sari. But saying you hate her was wrong. Do you understand that?"

Sari stared down at the floor. It was made of thick tiles, chalky and dotted with animal tracks from where they'd been left to dry in the sun. There were mice tracks with whispery tail marks dragging between the tiny claw prints, and chicken tracks, and even human baby footprints. Sari's own . . . The tiles were terracotta, and Sari knew—from a five-year-old memory—that they were pink. But right now they just looked dull, the shade of mud, without any color.

"Sweetheart, say it," her father pleaded.

Sari thought back to the moment Rosalie and her father wanted her to apologize for. It had happened late last month, one of March's warmest days. The horses had had spring fever, and so had Sari.

The night before, she'd dreamed of her mother, how on one of the first warm spring days of the year she would always take Sari into Stes.-Maries to walk on the promenade, balance on the narrow white rail, pretend it was a tightrope. Sari would walk, and her mother would hold her hand. That's how Sari had learned balance, holding her mother's hand.

That memory had been so vivid. Rosalie had been standing in the yard, washing dishcloths in a tub of fresh soap suds. She'd turned, to hang the cloths to dry on a clothesline, just the way Sari's mother had used to do, and Sari had gone crazy.

Sari had upset the tub of water, soap bubbles bursting and flying into the breeze, drifting into the beautiful marsh, delicate little things breaking on every spike of tall grass. Sari had watched the bubbles, remembering how they used to look like little rainbows, and she'd started to weep.

"What's wrong?" Rosalie had asked.

"The bubbles," Sari had cried. "They're clear and empty."

"Yes . . ." Rosalie had said, not understanding.

"They used to be so pretty," Sari had sobbed. "When my mother was here, they were like rainbows. They *shimmered*."

"Sari . . ."

"It's so ugly now," Sari had wept. "The whole world . . . it's just so ugly . . ."

"Sari, that's not true."

"You don't know what it's like," Sari said. "No blue sky, no green grass! I'm forgetting what it used to be like. Every day I forget another color. Today I can barely even remember the color of her cheeks—they used to be so rosy! I can't remember what that color looks like!"

Rosalie had looked shocked, as if she had no idea Sari had been storing up so much pain, and that made something explode inside.

Sari grabbed her hand. "She's never coming back, is she? She's gone forever. She's with that stupid man, and they have their horrible circus in the desert, and you don't care. You don't care my mother doesn't want me! I cracked my head open, and all the colors drained out with my blood! I can't see colors, and it's all because of her! How can you be her best friend—a person like that?" Sari had cried to Rosalie.

Rosalie had pulled back. Sari's mother had left over five years ago. Perhaps Rosalie thought she should be all better by now. Maybe she didn't know how awful it was, to go to bed at night and know her mother wasn't coming in to say good-night ever again. Or how it felt to know her mother had slapped her away, pushed her down and driven away while Mystère bolted and Sari lay in pieces on the road. Didn't Rosalie care that Sari had never been put together right? Her bones worked now, and the pain in her head was mostly gone, but the world was gray, and the bubbles were clear, and Sari would never see another rainbow.

"Sari, you know your mother will always love you. She went away for a reason, too deep for you to understand. Grown-up reasons; yes, she rides in a circus, and yes, it's in the desert. But that's not why she left. One day you'll be old enough to know why she did what she did."

"What she *did*? I'm here, and so is Papa. What she did was leave us! She's the most selfish person in the world, a terrible person. I hate her. I swear on my life that I hate her and hope she never comes back. She's not welcome here ever again. Do you hear me?"

"I hear you," Rosalie had said, backing away from Sari.

And just looking in her eyes, Sari could see that she'd wrecked something. Rosalie had been with them since Maria had left, but in that instant, it was over. And Sari broke again, knowing that Rosalie's reasons for working for them in the first place had had more to do with loyalty to her friend than with love and care for Sari and her father.

Now, her heart scratching at her throat, Sari tried to swallow and speak. She knew what she had to say. But she couldn't. The crazy thing was, she hadn't completely meant what she said: sometimes she hated her mother and sometimes she loved her. Sometimes she dreamed of flying to Las Vegas and finding her, and sometimes she never wanted to see her again.

"Sari?" Rosalie asked.

"I was wrong to tell you," Sari whispered, scalding tears

starting to flow. "Because I know she's your friend. But I can't explain the way I feel; you want me to feel only one way about her, and I don't. She shouldn't have left. Sometimes I still hate her for it."

"Sari, don't say that. Someday you'll understand."

Sari shook her head hard. "I don't *want* to understand."

Looking up finally, Sari saw her father's face fall. She saw Rosalie's expression harden. Sari's chest ached, because she was holding in a sob. She knew that the adults were trying to work things out—being around her father had never been easy for Rosalie. Rosalie was Rom, like Sari's mother, and they held her father responsible for getting Maria to marry outside the circle. The only reason Rosalie had worked here at all—and why she had come back now—had been out of sheer devotion to Maria.

Rosalie looked helpless; Sari wanted her to leave. And Rosalie did. She turned, walked back out through the door, across the yard, and climbed into the Citroën, waiting for Sari's father to drive her home.

Standing alone with him in the kitchen, Sari waited for her punishment. Her father didn't yell, but he knew how to admonish.

He'd give her a lecture. He'd tell her she'd spoiled everything, and now they were back to cooking and cleaning all on their own. No one in Stes.-Maries would work for them—because he was such a pariah in the community. Only Rosalie had ever crossed the boundary and come here.

But he didn't say a word. To Sari's shock, he walked over and hugged her so hard, it almost hurt. His arms locked around her with urgency, as if his hug could fill the world with color. His embrace felt red, yellow, blue, green, pink, violet. She felt him shaking; she wanted to say something, but she knew if she spoke she'd start to sob and never stop. Maybe he felt the same way, because he let go and walked out of the kitchen. He climbed into the car, started it up, and turned it around in the yard.

Sari watched them drive away. Rosalie stared sadly out the car window, and waved. Sari waved back. Then the car disappeared down the long road that led back to town.

Walking out into the yard, Sari stood right in the place where she'd spilled the soapy water. The ground was dry, but she swore she saw a mark, a big dark blotch permanently etched in the dirt, where most of the water had splashed. Gazing down at it, she thought she imagined a shimmer of iridescence: the ghost of one of those bubbles that had set her off.

She turned to face the barn. Her heart was pounding. She needed comfort; she needed Mystère. Even though she couldn't ride anymore—would never get up on her horse again—she needed to know she was right here.

And Mystère knew, too. Like Rosalie and all her sisters, like Sari's mother and all Rom women, Mystère had a touch of second sight as well. The wind was blowing in the other direction, so she couldn't smell Sari's scent. But nonetheless, as if Sari had called her name, Mystère came out of her stall. Sari heard her heavy footfalls on the sawdust floor, clomping out to the paddock.

They stared into each other's eyes, girl and horse. The hot tears that had been building up broke free. She didn't sob though, and the feeling stayed locked in her chest. Gazing at Mystère, Sari was rooted to the spot in the dirt. She reached out her hand, half wishing she could just walk over and pet her horse. But she knew she couldn't. She knew that if her fingers touched the white fur or soft gray muzzle, if she buried her face in that flowing mane, the rock in her chest would crack, and she would die.

She would die of grief. So she just stayed where she was, on the wet spot that would never dry, and stared at her beautiful horse.

FIVE

There were white sails in the harbor, and the water sparkled, and the sea meadow rippled endlessly. Susannah drove out of town, into the marsh plain of the Rhône estuary, leaving the sea behind. The road twisted around *étangs*, saltwater lagoons filled with hundreds of pale pink flamingos, and over narrow creeks lined with herons and egrets. The scenery was magical and vast, and from the safety of her car she could enjoy glimpses of black bulls grazing on the salt grass.

The ranches seemed to be clustered in the northwest. She crossed a graceful bridge curving over a canal, and began her search. Most of the farmhouses were white with woven straw roofs, and nearly every one bore a sign saying *Promenade Équestre*. Horseback rides.

She continued on, getting lost in her search. Just the thought of riding made her feel happy. She remembered all the times her father had taken her to her lessons, how they'd driven together through the Connecticut countryside, to the beautiful stable on the Farmington River. They hadn't had much money; her mother had been a teacher, and her father had had a lamp store on the main street of a dying industrial town. But they'd seen how much Susannah had loved horses, so they'd set money aside so she could ride.

She was lost in thoughts of her parents when she reached the crest of a narrow bridge. She stopped at the top, gazing out at the hypnotic sea of grass. Hearing a car approach, she quickly pulled over—and as the car passed, she saw that the driver was Grey Dempsey. He had a beautiful dark-haired woman beside him, and they were heading toward town.

He met Susannah's eyes as they passed. She nodded, shocked to see him—hadn't she just left him in town, two hours earlier? In any case, he was with a woman. That made everything clearer.

She drove a zigzag north and then west. Suddenly, on the left, she saw the sign: *Manade du Dempsey*. The ranch looked like many of the others she had just passed: white house, thatched roof, large barn and paddock, trails leading into the marsh. Pausing by the side of the road, she gazed at the setting. She intended to just drive on, but then she saw the white horse.

Mystère stood in the paddock, in the shade of the salt-silvered barn. Although shadowed, her white coat gleamed like a beacon, pulling Susannah off the road. Just as she started driving in, she saw the young girl. She'd been standing as still as a post, right in Susannah's path—and with Susannah's attention on the horse, she hadn't seen her. Susannah stopped dead. They locked eyes, and Susannah had the quick impression of someone about twelve or thirteen, with long brown hair, dark green eyes, and tawny skin. One look at her, and Susannah knew the girl was part Romany.

But even though the young girl's eyes were such a different color than Grey's blue ones, the bright life in them left no question—this was his daughter. The child stared at Susannah for another second, then turned and bolted into the farmhouse.

Feeling like an intruder, Susannah nearly turned around. But she'd stopped to see Mystère, so she drove into the dusty parking area and parked beside a group of other cars. Did they all belong to Grey, or was there a trail ride in progress? And if so, with him on his way to Stes.-Maries, who was leading it?

The questions melted away as she walked across the yard toward the white horse. Leaning on the paddock fence, she reached out her hand. Mystère came right over, nuzzled her arm, right in the crook of her elbow. Susannah leaned against her strong neck, resting her head on the horse.

"Excusez-moi, madame? Est-ce que je peux vous aider?"

Turning to look, Susannah saw a teenaged boy standing there. He was tall and lean, with sensitive eyes and a sulky mouth; he wore a dusty black shirt and blue jeans, worn cowboy boots, and work gloves.

"I was just stopping to see the horse . . ." she said in French.

"Américaine?" he asked, catching her accent.

"Yes," she said.

"A lot of Americans come to our ranch," he said in English. "Because Monsieur Dempsey is from there—from Rhode Island. I'm sorry, but the afternoon ride has already left. In fact, they should be back at any moment. Perhaps you can pick out a horse you like, and come back tomorrow. We will give you first choice."

"Oh," she said. "I—I wasn't coming to ride. Not here. I just wanted to stop and see Mystère."

"You know Mystère?"

"Very well," Susannah said. "She saved my life."

"You're the lady from the marsh!" he said, his eyes growing wide, his mouth stretching in a huge smile. "The one who was nearly trampled!"

"Ah, my secret is out," she laughed. "I guess Grey must be spreading the word."

"Yes. He couldn't stop talking about you."

"Because I was such a prize idiot?"

"No," the boy said. "Because you can ride like someone in a dream. '*Comme un rêve.*'" Then he said, "'*Comme sur un nuage.*'"

"As if on a cloud?" she translated.

"That's what he said."

Susannah turned back to Mystère, gazing into her dark, knowing eyes. If Grey felt that way about her riding, why had he not suggested she come to his ranch? It confused her, and although she was happy to hear the praise, she felt as if perhaps she shouldn't have stopped here at all.

"Will you come with me?" the boy asked.

"Where?" Susannah asked, giving him a questioning look.

"Just for a moment. Over there, to the house . . ."

Susannah glanced at the farmhouse. She saw a checked curtain at the window move, and guessed it was the girl she'd seen in the yard before.

"Sure," she said. There'd been something about the girl—her age, or her posture, or the intensity of her gaze—that had reminded Susannah of herself as a young teenager. It was when her own passion for horses was at its peak, and she imagined how wonderful it must be for a girl that age to live on a ranch, with white horses to ride any time she felt like it.

The boy led her through the yard, up a stone sidewalk to the kitchen door. He knocked once, and then walked right in. As she followed him, Susannah wondered what his relationship to the family might be; he'd called Grey "Monsieur Dempsey." She stood just inside the doorway, looking around the room.

The kitchen was large, with windows overlooking the paddock. One black cat lay on the windowsill; another was curled up on the rush seat of a ladder-back chair. The floor was rustic sun-baked tiles, the walls were soft yellow, and all around the ceiling moldings was a hand-painted garland of laurel leaves and rose, lavender, and gold flowers. In the center of the kitchen, the scarred wooden countertop was covered with the ingredients for what looked like a gratin. Sliced potatoes and zucchini had been arranged in an oval copper pan.

"Sari," he said. "Come on, I know you're here. We just saw you looking out the window. Don't be rude."

"I'm not rude," came a soft voice. An instant later, the girl Susannah had seen outside stepped from behind a tall wooden armoire that was also painted in the style of the garland. She was small and slim, her eyes red from crying.

"This is the lady," Laurent said.

Sari didn't reply; she looked as if she wanted to run away.

"You know, didn't your father tell you? The one who went looking for ponies and found bulls instead."

"The lady who waved her ribbon?" Sari asked, turning a shy but somehow charged gaze on Susannah.

"Yep," Susannah said. "Pretty foolish, right?"

Sari just stared, as if frozen.

"Sari, she asked you a question . . ." Laurent said gently.

"Not foolish," Sari said. "But dangerous. Terrible things can happen in the marsh. The worst things of all . . ."

Susannah nodded. She heard the girl's voice shaking, saw emotion in her eyes. "What kinds of things?"

Laurent stepped closer to Sari, as if he was worried about her. The gesture seemed sweet and protective, and Susannah saw Sari look up at him.

"You're talking about the bulls, right?" Susannah asked.

"Yes, that's right," Laurent said, eyes locked with Sari's. "We grew up here, and we know to stay away from the areas where the bulls roam free. We tell the tourists the bulls are called 'black death,' just so they'll stay away from those places."

By the way Sari looked down, Susannah knew that Laurent was covering for her somehow—protecting her from something she'd been about to say? Susannah wasn't sure, but she knew from the way Laurent stood so close by that his feelings for Sari were strong.

"Why did you come back?" Sari asked after a moment.

"Me?" Susannah asked. "Well, I wanted to . . ."

"She's looking for a place that offers trail rides," Laurent said.

"That's right," Susannah said. "And when I saw Mystère—"

"You know her name?" Sari asked.

Susannah nodded. "Yes. Your father told me . . ."

Sari drew in a sharp breath. She looked around, and Susannah could feel her tension, sense her wanting to escape. Susannah knew she'd said something to upset her—was it the mention of Mystère, or her father?

"You know," Laurent said quietly, looking at Sari. "This could be such a good thing."

"What?" Sari asked.

"The best for everyone. Our visitor wants a trail ride, and she's already been on Mystère. Mystère needs to be ridden. You know that, don't you? Your father and my father both say—"

"Laurent!" Sari said.

"Sari, I think you should let her ride Mystère."

The girl lowered her eyes. Susannah saw her sway slightly, steady herself by touching the butcher-block island. Her beauty was sharp and dark, her deep golden skin sun-kissed and glowing. But as Susannah watched, the color drained out of it, and there were storms going on behind her eyes. She shut them.

"She's a great rider. Your father said so. Come on, Sari. Mystère needs contact, too, she needs to be ridden, and since this woman—Madame . . ."

"Susannah," she said. "Just call me Susannah." She watched

Sari stand there with her eyes closed, as if she could shut herself in and block Laurent's words out, watched the girl growing paler by the moment, and she felt a tremor go through her body. "Thank you, Laurent, but I think Mystère is a one-girl horse."

"Pardon?" Laurent asked.

"I don't know." Susannah shook her head. "There was just something about Mystère that made me realize she's completely devoted to just one person. Horses are very loyal. What am I telling you for? You know horses better than I do. In fact, until the other day, I hadn't ridden in a very long time. Years, in fact."

Sari had opened her eyes. She didn't speak, but she was listening.

"Our horses are trained for many people to ride them," Laurent said quietly. "My father has been working for Monsieur Dempsey since before I was born. He has always made sure the horses were ready for any rider. All the horses—yes, Sari, you know this: even Mystère—"

"That might be true," Susannah said, interrupting, her eyes on Sari. "When necessary, even the most special, particular, horse can be ridden by strangers. But every horse has her own person. And I have the feeling that Mystère's person is standing right here."

"Me," Sari whispered.

Susannah nodded. "Yes. That's how it seems to me."

"That's right," Sari said.

"I could tell."

"Nobody else rides her. Except my father."

"I understand," Susannah said.

"He has to," Laurent said darkly. "Someone has to exercise her; horses need to be ridden."

Susannah opened her mouth to speak, but Sari tore from the room. She heard the girl's feet pounding upstairs. Laurent gave her an apologetic look, then went running after Sari.

And Susannah was left standing alone in another family's kitchen.

Laurent had seen this happen before. No two events were ever exactly the same. But certain elements always added up for a big explosion. He walked down the hallway, pausing outside Sari's bedroom door. How many times had he been up here? Hundreds, at least. When he and Sari were little, they'd gone in and out of each others' houses, equally welcome in both.

But lately it had started feeling different. They were growing up, and although he loved her as much as ever, he'd started feeling as if they both had their own private places. He couldn't just barge through the door the way he had when they were little; but he wanted to see what was on the other side even more.

"Sari," he said, knocking.

"Go away," she wept.

"Open up."

"I don't want to talk to you."

"You're acting terrible."

"I don't care."

"Not to me," he said. "To the woman downstairs. She's a visitor, and you're being awful."

After a minute, the door opened a crack. He pushed it, saw her standing just inside. Her face was wet, but she'd stopped crying now, and he saw despair in her gaze, and all he wanted to do was make it right, make her sadness go away.

"I'm not terrible," she said, her voice husky and choked. "How can you say that to me? Do you really think I don't care about Mystère?"

"I'm sorry," he said, wanting to touch her, wipe her tears. He held himself back. "For pushing you about Mystère."

"Don't you think I worry about her?" she asked.

"I know you do. I see you standing in the yard looking at her."

"You should do your homework instead," she whispered.

"Someone has to watch you," he said, trying to joke.

But she wouldn't smile. She just stood there shaking, as if she might break apart. He stepped closer, trying to keep his mind straight. If he focused on Mystère, maybe he could get through to her; maybe he could help.

"I know you care about Mystère. But listen, letting her loose in the paddock is just 'exercise.' She needs . . ." He couldn't make himself say "love," but that's what he'd heard his father say.

"Is that lady still here?" Sari asked.

"Of course," he said. "She looked very worried, the way you went flying up the stairs. She's probably afraid she upset you."

"I wish she would go," Sari whispered.

"Oh, Sari. People are nice, you know? Didn't you hear her say that she understands no one rides Mystère but you?"

Sari looked at him with red, swollen eyes. She turned back toward the window in her bedroom, then walked over to look out at the ring. Laurent stood beside her; he saw her staring at the paddock, at Mystère standing by the fence. He felt the air crackling between them. It came from inside Sari—she was filled with thunder and lightning. But he knew it also came from him, from the electricity she made him feel.

"She *is* still here," Sari asked, staring at the car parked right outside.

"Well, she wants to make sure you're okay, I guess."

"Tell her I am, please?"

"Why don't you come down with me?" Laurent asked. "So she can see for herself."

Sari hesitated, then nodded.

And that surprised Laurent—it honestly did. He hadn't expected her to agree to go downstairs again. On another day, he might have taken her hand. Just as a friend, the brother he'd always been to her, showing her support for doing the right thing. But today he kept his distance, following her down the hall. He smelled her shampoo, and thinking about her taking a shower, washing her hair, made his chest tighten.

They walked down the stairs. Sure enough, Susannah was right where they'd left her, standing in the middle of the kitchen with a concerned look in her eyes.

"Is everything okay?" she asked.

"Fine," Sari said.

"I'm sorry if I upset you," Susannah said. "I didn't mean to . . ."

"You didn't," Sari said, her voice clipped. "It's just . . . you're right about my horse. No one but my father rides her right now. I . . . I had an injury, so I can't."

"Well," Susannah said, "I hope you recover soon."

Laurent was careful not to look at Sari. It wasn't that she had lied exactly; it was more that she'd given the barest hint of the true story.

"Thank you," Sari said stoically.

"Well," Susannah said. "I've gotten to see Mystère again, and I'd like to thank you, Sari—and now I should be on my way."

"Will you come back tomorrow for a trail ride?" Laurent asked. "I can hurry home from school, and help lead it. I'll make sure you get a good horse, almost as good as Mystère."

Laurent noticed the tension in Sari's jaw. He was back on thin ice with her, but he didn't care. He liked this woman, and he liked the fact Sari was talking to her.

"No," Susannah said. "I'm afraid I won't be able to." She shook Laurent's hand, said she was happy to have met him. She glanced at Sari. As she did, her gaze fell again on the counter, and all the ingredients there. "That gratin looks delicious," she said.

"Sari's a good cook," Laurent said.

"I can see that. When I went to the market in Stes.-Maries today, all the vegetables looked so good. Seeing them coming together, I'm inspired to cook one for myself tonight."

"Don't forget to add a little sage," Sari said.

"Sage? What a great idea. I'd never have thought of that," Susannah said. "I always add a tiny bit of cinnamon and nutmeg when I make gratin."

"The secret ingredients!" Sari burst out, shocking Laurent with the excitement in her voice.

Susannah smiled. "It's the way my mother taught me. There's something about the spices that works well with the cheese and cream. Sharpens them up, or something. Well, enjoy your dinner."

"You too," Sari said.

Susannah turned to go. Laurent saw her glance up at the flower garland painted on the plaster wall. He wondered what she was thinking about it. It looked so pretty. He felt like telling her those flowers were as full of poison as belladonna. Sari's mother had painted them.

Laurent knew he should follow Susannah into the yard, but he didn't. He stayed inside the kitchen with Sari. He watched Susannah walk past the paddock toward her car. Mystère stood at the fence, hazy sun glinting in her dark eyes.

The wind had kicked up again, tossing Mystère's mane and tail. Susannah paused as if she wanted to give her one last pat before she left. Laurent knew she sensed Sari watching, so she just smiled at the horse and continued to her car.

Sari followed the car with her eyes. Backing up, turning around, driving out. Laurent's stomach tensed, as if he and Sari were one and the same. Did she relive her mother's departure every time? Is that why she was frowning, brows knit, eyes flashing? Laurent knew she wouldn't relax until after the car had disappeared.

"She's gone now," he said, when it had.

"I know," Sari said. Outside, a veil of high clouds had slid in, painting a penumbra around the sun.

After a minute, she turned to the counter. She stared at the food she'd been preparing as if she'd never seen it before. Then she went to the spice cupboard and took out two small jars: nutmeg and cinnamon.

Laurent watched her season the gratin. He stared at her for a few seconds, waiting for her to say something. But she seemed lost in thought, all words locked inside, so he just walked out the kitchen door and over to the paddock to visit her horse before the rain started to fall.

SIX

Grey drove home, trying to keep his focus on the road. Rosalie had simmered the whole way back to Stes.-Maries. He'd looked over, seen her eyes welling with angry tears.

"I'm in an impossible position," she said, just as they pulled into town. "I care about Sari, yes, but Maria's my oldest and best friend. That's why I agreed to work at the Manade in the first place."

"And we appreciate it," Grey said.

"You say that," she said, shaking her head. "But you don't. I remind you of Maria—that's the real problem."

"Maria's in the past," Grey replied.

Rosalie shook her head, as if she didn't believe him. "You just want to convince yourself of that. She's in your life every minute of every day; I see the way you look at me, with such anger, and I know you're thinking of her."

"All I care about is Sari," he said harshly, wishing she'd get it. For a time, he'd thought about Maria—about confronting her in Las Vegas, forcing her to see Sari and face what she'd done to their daughter. "I need help with the house, and I don't want Sari doing it. She has schoolwork, and I want her to have time for fun. I'm worried that the more pressure she feels, the harder it will be for her to get better." He paused, giving her a hard look. "Not everything is about Maria, Rosalie."

"You blame her for everything. She made a mistake . . ."

"By marrying me, okay," he said. "But not by having Sari."

"She hates that Sari suffered."

"Suffers," Grey said through clenched teeth.

Rosalie had started to retort, but seemed to think better of it and sat deep in silent thought, until Grey stopped the car. Hand on the door handle, she gave him one last look, then shook her head and got out. She wasn't coming back to work—that was clear. He saw her friends watching from the church steps. They didn't acknowledge him in any way as he turned the car around, nor he them.

Now, approaching the kitchen door, he steeled himself. Sari would be angry and upset about what had happened with Rosalie, and he half expected to see the gratin she'd been making in the garbage. He took a deep breath and pulled the door open.

She was huddled on the window seat, shoulders hunched, arms wrapped around her knees. Staring out at the paddock, she didn't even turn around to greet him. He walked right over and stood next to her, stroking her hair.

"Rosalie hates me," Sari said. "Doesn't she?"

"Of course not."

"But she quit."

"Let that be her problem, Sari. She misses your mother. It's hard for her to be around here."

"Other people miss her, too," Sari said. "Not just Rosalie."

"I know," Grey said, still cradling her head in his hand.

She tilted her neck, looked up at him. "But you don't, do you, Papa?" she asked.

"She left a long time ago, Sari. I've gotten used to it."

"So have I," Sari said. But Grey knew that was a lie.

He dropped his hand then, turned toward the stove. If she'd ditched the gratin, he'd have to make something else for them. But there it was—golden brown and bubbling—cooling on top of the stove.

"This looks great," he said.

"Yeah," she said. "It came out well."

He washed his hands, and silently they set the table. He felt her unwinding, warming up a little. Sari put out a pitcher of water, and he filled their glasses. To his surprise, she lifted her glass and reached up to clink with his.

"Here's to . . . Mystère," she said.

Grey nodded, taken aback by the toast. "I'll drink to that," he said as they clinked glasses.

Sari served them both helpings of the gratin, and he felt her watching him eat. She had learned to cook when she was very young. Her mother had always avoided the kitchen, preferring to be in the barn, or at a different ranch, with other riders training for the circus ring. But Grey liked to cook, and he'd taught Sari the best he could. She'd also picked things up on trips to Rhode Island, visiting his parents, from Anne, Laurent's mother, and from Rosalie.

"This is delicious," he said.

"There's a reason," she said.

"Because you made it?" he asked, smiling.

"No." She put down her fork. Suddenly the warmth in her eyes disappeared, and they were back in the deep freeze. "Someone told me the secret ingredient."

"Really? Who?"

"The lady with the ribbon."

Grey kept eating. He didn't believe her. She was testing him. Over the years, he'd discovered the danger of talking about any woman to his daughter, so he never did it. He was the father of a sweet, troubled girl who'd been abandoned by her mother, and he had learned to tread very lightly, to protect her carefully, and to not take the bait when she dangled it in front of him.

"It's true, Papa," she said.

"Sari, stop. Eat your dinner, okay?"

"She stood right here, in our kitchen."

Grey refilled his water glass, drank it down. A cool breeze blew through the open window. He smelled the marsh and the sea, and he heard the cries of distant shorebirds, and he thought of the horses in the barn. He couldn't meet his daughter's eyes.

"Can't you taste the secret ingredient?" she prodded.

"Something does taste extra good," he said, taking another bite.

"It's a combination of cinnamon and nutmeg!" she said. "Rosalie left without telling me, but that's okay, it really is. Because now I know. Because the lady with the ribbon told me."

Grey slammed his hand down, and his fork clattered onto his plate. She was pushing him, and he felt his frustration boiling oven. There were no women in his life. No matter how much he'd have liked to invite Susannah back to the ranch, it wasn't going to happen. Now she was blaming him for it anyway. He looked up, saw Sari's eyes shining with tears.

"Why are you so mad?" she asked.

He spoke carefully. "Because I don't want you saying that about 'the lady with the ribbon.' I didn't bring her here, Sari. I don't even know her—it was an accidental meeting, just like I told you. She went her way, and I went mine. I know you don't like—"

"She might have gone her own way, but she found her way back here," Sari shot out.

"What do you mean?"

"I looked out the window, and there was this person lean-ing over the paddock fence. Just looking at Mystère."

Grey felt a jolt—she *had* been here. He wasn't sure why that image did the trick—but suddenly he pictured Susannah Connolly standing by the ring, greeting the horse who had rescued her. He could see it completely, and he knew Sari was telling him the truth.

"When was she here?"

"So now you believe me?" she asked.

"Yes," he said, taking a deep breath. She sounded both bit-ter and hurt. He saw her eyes cloud over and knew she was about to cry. "And now you believe me, too, right? I told you she was a stranger," he said.

"Yes. You didn't get the ribbon from my mother. I believe you now. Why should I have ever thought my mother would come back? What kind of idiotic idea would that be?"

"Sari . . ."

"You asked when the woman was here," Sari said. "It was while you were driving Rosalie home. She was standing right here in the kitchen, and you know what she said? That Mys-tère is a one-girl horse."

"She's right," Grey said.

"Most people don't get that," she said. "They think Mystère needs to be ridden more than she needs to be ridden by me. Even Laurent thinks that!"

"Mystère's doing fine," Grey said. "I make sure she gets enough exercise. You don't have to worry."

"Laurent says Susannah rides *comme un rêve*."

"Like a dream," Grey said, bowing his head as he ate, glad his daughter couldn't see the color rising in his cheeks and know that those had been his own words. *And like a cloud . . .*

"Is that true, Papa?" Sari said.

"Something like that."

"As good as my mother?"

"No one rides like your mother," Grey said.

They stared at each other across the table and their half-eaten dinners. Outside, one of the horses whinnied; Claude or Laurent must have gone into the barn. Grey thought of how Maria used to do that, visit the horses every evening. Was Sari remembering that, too?

"Exercise isn't the same as love," Sari said.

"What do you mean?"

"Mystère," she said. "Laurent says Mystère needs love."

"You love her, honey."

"But I don't ride her," Sari whispered.

Grey nodded. He'd never tried to push her. But there'd been so many times when he saw his daughter feeling the pain of missing her mother, and knew that she was also missing her horse. That night when Maria left had robbed Sari of more than just her mother.

"I could, maybe," Sari said now.

"Could what?"

"Ride again."

Grey couldn't believe his ears. Had she really said that? It was the first time in over five years that she'd even suggested riding. The doctors had told him she would heal; first her bones would knit together, then the physical pain would go away, then she'd want to live life again. And one day she'd wake up and she'd see colors.

As he watched, Sari carried her plate over to the sink and gazed out the window. He followed with his own plate and saw what she was looking at: Laurent leading one of the new ponies into the ring.

"Do you want to go out now?" Grey asked. "It's not too late, and I could get Mystère saddled up and . . ."

"Not tonight," Sari whispered.

"Okay," he said, not wanting to push.

"That lady wants to ride," Sari said softly, after a couple of minutes. The water was running, nearly drowning out her voice. "She was looking for a ranch, and Laurent asked if she wanted to come back here, but she said no."

Grey thought of their meeting on the street in Stes.-Maries, and how he hadn't told Susannah about his ranch. She'd probably thought that strange—he knew he would have. And he assumed that she'd picked up on Sari's antagonism, and not wanted anything to do with them.

"She'll find a good place," Grey said. "She said she hasn't ridden a lot lately. She probably wants to take her time finding the right horse."

"The right horse is Mystère," Sari whispered.

"She's *your* horse," Grey said.

"If that woman rides like a dream, time doesn't matter," Sari said, looking up at him with blank eyes, like a sleep-walker. "In dreams, time is nothing at all. That's how it will be for me and Mystère, too. I ride her in my sleep—I always have. I could do it right now if I wanted."

"Dreams aren't life," he said. "Sari, let me take you out, okay? We'll go easy at first, and . . ."

Sari's eyes were suddenly blazing, full of tears.

"Why did she go?" Sari whispered hotly.

Grey looked at her. They'd been over this so often in the past. Recently, he'd tried to stay away from the subject of Maria, not wanting to upset her. But something was making it all bubble back up now. "Your mother?" he asked. "I told you, sweetheart. It had nothing to do with you." He reached out to take his daughter's hand, but she turned away, her shoulders shaking with silent sobs.

"That's almost worse," she managed to say. "It's almost worse, that something so big had nothing to do with me."

"Sari . . ."

"She pushed me away from her," Sari wept, burying her face in her hands. "Right here, in the kitchen. That was worse than falling off Mystère. That was the worst of all."

"Sari," he said.

She walked out of the room. He heard her heading upstairs, listened for her door to slam. He just stood at the kitchen window, watching Laurent in the ring with the white pony. He saw the boy gaze upward and knew that Sari's light had just gone on.

Grey stared out at the paddock, thinking of Susannah Connolly standing there. Thinking of her behind him on Mystère, pressed tight against his back, her hips jammed into his, the feel of her arms locked around his waist.

The two black cats circled his feet, waiting to be fed. But he couldn't quite move. He closed his eyes, listening to the hoofbeats in the ring outside, wondering where Susannah was, what she was doing, why she had really come to the ranch.

Topaz picked Susannah up right on time, and drove through the town, past the fortified church, and into the darkening countryside. Night birds and crickets called through the open windows as Topaz sped along roads so narrow, reeds and rushes brushed the car as it passed.

Purple clouds raced across stars and moon, and Susannah felt as if a storm was coming. Topaz had seemed distracted, silent, since she'd picked up Susannah, but now she shot her a quick look.

"Is the breeze too much? I could put up the windows."

"I like it," Susannah said. It matched her mood. She'd felt all stirred up after visiting the Dempsey Ranch. That child, Sari, was so lovely and seemed so lost. And who was that woman Susannah had seen with Grey?

Susannah closed her eyes, trying to stop thinking of Grey Dempsey, struggling to understand her feelings about him. They were so unprecedented, such a bolt from the blue. Obviously he had a family. But even knowing that, she was so curious about him, so drawn to him. After years of building her career, worrying about her sick mother, keeping Ian at arm's length, she felt knocked out by the intensity of her attraction to him.

She glanced over at Topaz. She was tempted to ask about the Dempseys, but she'd seen how Topaz had reacted to the sight of Grey earlier, outside the church. She opened her mouth to speak, but Topaz turned and spoke first.

"I am sorry for being so quiet," she said. "I have things on my mind."

"Would you rather postpone this?" Susannah said. "I'll be here for nearly two more weeks. We can do it another time."

"No," Topaz said, flashing her wonderful smile. "It is when life is challenging that I need nights like this most."

"Nights like this?"

"With the Circle," Topaz said.

She drove in silence for another few kilometers, then turned into a driveway marked with a sign that said *Mas SLK*.

"What does that mean?" Susannah asked.

"*Mas* means farmhouse," Topaz said.

"And SLK?"

Again, the wide smile. "Sara-la-Kali," Topaz said.

Topaz drove along a rutted road, into a field behind a small white house. Big boxy shapes, silhouetted by the cloud-filmed moon, were set in a wide circle around the land's perimeter. As they drove closer, Susannah thought they were cottages, many with lights glowing in their windows. But when Topaz parked the car beside one, and Susannah climbed out, she saw that the cottage had wheels.

"*Ma roulotte,*" Topaz said, gesturing with welcome.

Susannah stood looking around. The caravans were brightly painted—that was obvious, even in the shifting light. Topaz's was a warm shade of pumpkin, decorated with a painted garland of flowers over the door and windows. The flowers were bright red, cool lavender, and gold, entwined with ropes of silver-green laurel. Now, turning around, Susannah looked at the other caravans—painted in shades of brick red, dark purple, saffron yellow, and sage green. All were painted with flower garlands. Susannah thought of the Dempseys' kitchen, and felt prickles on the back of her neck.

"They're so beautiful," Susannah said.

"The flowers are familiar to you, yes?" Topaz asked.

Susannah nodded. "I just saw some, very similar, today . . . how did you know?"

"Rosalie saw you driving toward the Manade du Dempsey. And you asked me about him earlier, no?"

Him; realizing she meant Grey, sent a jolt down Susannah's spine. Feeling Topaz's eyes on her now, Susannah felt a rush of apprehension and didn't respond. Suddenly she wondered why she'd been brought here.

"Don't be afraid," Topaz said, putting her hand on Susannah's arm. "You, of all people, should have no fear."

Susannah wanted to tell her she wasn't afraid. She took risks in her work all the time and reveled in exotic cultures. Visiting a gypsy camp was nothing compared with crawling into a skinny crack in the rock. But her emotions were raw and unfamiliar, and right at the surface, and that was scaring her. She wished she had driven her own car, so she could leave right now. Topaz's hand closed gently around Susannah's wrist, and her gaze was calm and steady.

"Please," she said. "Everyone is so eager to meet you."

"Who painted the garlands in their kitchen?" Susannah asked. She needed to know, needed to hear that Grey was married so she could stop feeling this way.

"The Circle will tell you," Topaz said. "And they're inside right now. Please, come let me introduce you."

And Susannah swallowed her fear, allowing herself to be led up the steep, narrow stairs to the doorway of Topaz's caravan. The door opened, and Susannah stepped inside. She saw candles burning everywhere, and had the fleeting impression of

Sarah's crypt—this had exactly the same feeling of candlelit devotion in a small, enclosed space.

Only instead of the lone statue of Sarah, the dark almost-saint, Topaz's caravan was filled with women. Every spot was filled—the small table and three straight-back chairs, the loveseat, the floor. Only one chair was vacant—a large comfortable-looking armchair, all the way in the back.

"Everyone," Topaz said in a thrilling voice, "this is Susannah Connolly. The person I told you about."

One by one, the women stood. Topaz conducted Susannah through the cramped, narrow interior. Susannah looked into each face, and saw that they were women of all ages, from teenaged to very old. And as Susannah went to shake each woman's hand, she was met instead with a kiss. One, clearly the oldest, had tears in her eyes.

Susannah felt overwhelmed by all the love and emotion in the room. With Topaz's arm around her shoulders, she was led to the back of the caravan, pressed down to sit in the empty armchair, the seat of honor.

"But why?" she asked. "I don't understand."

"Because your mother was blessed by Sarah," Topaz explained. "And that is why you are here."

"Here, in Stes.-Maries?" Susannah asked.

"Here on this earth," the oldest woman said. "Sarah performed a miracle, so that your mother became pregnant with you. And so you could be born."

"That's what she always said," Susannah whispered.

"To a woman who longs for a child, who prays to have a baby and can't," the old woman said, "there's no greater pain. None in the world."

"She told me she prayed all the time," Susannah said. "Every month. But never . . ."

"Until she visited Sarah," another woman said.

"And she didn't even know about Sarah," Susannah said quietly. "I mean no disrespect by this—and my mother certainly wouldn't either. But in America, in the Catholic Church, Sarah is not known. Or not talked about . . ."

"She belongs to us," a young woman said proudly. "She's *our* saint. She's of and for the Rom."

"That's right, *petite chérie*." Topaz laughed. "But Susannah is proof that Sarah looks beyond."

"I never believed such a thing," the young woman said. She had a short, spiky haircut, the tips tinged with gold.

"That is why I wanted Susannah to visit the Circle," Topaz said.

"For proof?" someone else asked.

"Yes," Topaz said. "So you could meet her, and hear her story."

SEVEN

"You . . ." Susannah said, *looking around the candlelit room* at all the faces turned in her direction. "All of you . . . are the 'Circle'?"

"We are," Topaz said. "The Sarah Circle. Let me introduce everyone."

Going around the room, Topaz pointed out Anaïs, Naguine, Isabel, Zuna, Eugénie, Jeanne-Marie, Zin-Zin, Florine, Ana, Étoile, and Rosalie. Susannah nodded to each woman, locking eyes with Rosalie. She had been the one in the car with Grey, and the one who had reported Susannah's trip to the ranch to Topaz, and she regarded Susannah with suspicious eyes now.

"Pleased to meet you," Susannah said to the room.

"And to meet you," said Zin-Zin, the old woman, in heavily accented English.

"Tell me about the Sarah Circle," Susannah said quietly, looking at Topaz, but taking in the whole group.

"We're devoted to Sara-la-Kali," Topaz explained. Everyone took turns talking, while Susannah listened intently.

The women were part of a clan of Manouche Gypsies. Their group had branches all over northern Europe, mainly in France and Belgium. Romanies romanced the road, and were beset by a constant, everlasting yearning for whatever lay beyond the next hill, the next town, the next country.

Every woman in the room had grown up traveling, living in caravans, helping to support their families by basket weaving, bracelet making, singing, and guitar playing. The single constant in their lives had been the yearly pilgrimage here every summer, to this wild land of the Camargue, to pay respect to Sarah. Now they had settled in town year-round.

Zin-Zin told of early days, when the fields were filled with music, and the families would congregate around the caravans. Django Reinhardt, the legendary guitarist who'd influenced B.B. King, was part of the Manouche clan, and had come here to this very spot every May 24, during the *Pèlerinage des Gitans,* to pay homage to Sarah. The room fell absolutely silent, with love and reverence, listening to the old woman talk.

"Sara-la-Kali," she said. "Black Sarah. She was like us: a girl who traveled far and wide. Her skin was dark, her spirit was pure. She served the aunts of Jesus, she arranged for their safe passage over the sea, through storms, from Palestine. She was not accepted as a saint by the Catholic Church, but that didn't matter to us."

"The Manouche has roots in India, you see," Topaz said. "We originated there, wandered through Byzantium, gained the name 'Tziganes' for our work as animal traders and trainers, moved onto Egypt. 'Gypsy' is just a corruption of 'Egyptian,' but even that wasn't right. We were enslaved and persecuted; we were called the 'Gypsy Scourge.' Louis XIV made Gypsy men his slaves."

"And he had Gypsy women flogged and deported," Zuna said.

"Yet we always had Sarah to protect us," Rosalie said, her eyes glaring at Susannah, as if she could read her mind, saw her as an interloper. "Sara-la-Kali."

"Kali," Susannah said.

"What do *you* know of her?" Rosalie asked, the question a challenge.

"Leave it!" Topaz warned.

Rosalie said something fast and harsh in a language Susannah didn't understand. But it was clear that Rosalie mistrusted and disliked her. Susannah studied the beautiful woman, with her deep brown eyes and cascading black hair, and wondered what her relationship with Grey and Sari could be.

"I just want to know," Rosalie said sharply, "what she thinks she knows about Kali."

"Don't grill her, she's our guest," Topaz said. But Susannah wanted to answer.

"I'm an anthropologist," she said.

"You're here to study us?" Rosalie asked, looking around. "Like someone else we know, eh?"

The room buzzed quietly, and Susannah thought of what she had read regarding Grey Dempsey's background as a journalist.

"I'm not here to study you," she said quietly.

"Not at all?" Rosalie challenged. "That's not why you've come?"

Susannah shook her head, trying to be as truthful as possible without saying too much. "I have work to do, it's true. The first rainy day, I'll be going to the library in Arles to do some research for a colleague . . ."

"On us?"

"Not specifically," Susannah said. "But I can't help making observations. My colleague, Helen Oakes, has taken many trips to India. One of her most important papers was on the feminine power of Sakti, and the Kali Age, on the mother-goddess and fertility cults. My understanding is that 'Sara-la-Kali' relates to that Kali. Does it also refer to your clan's origins in India?"

"Yes!" Topaz said, smiling and gleaming, as if with pride for a prize student. She gave Rosalie a quick, hard glance, then looked back at Susannah. "Kali, the essence of divine feminine spirit, of mother-love and feminine energy."

"*Sakti*," Susannah said. "Sanskrit for feminine energy."

Topaz nodded. "That is what Sarah means to us. She has the spirit of Kali, our connection to the divine, and to our ancient Eastern roots. For us, Sarah represents the primal, the source, the Great Mother."

"We all need her," Zuna said.

"Especially those of us who have lost our mothers," Zin-Zin said with what seemed to be secret, deeply held sorrow. "No matter how old one is, one never stops needing her mother."

The words brought tears to Susannah's eyes. She suddenly sensed her mother's spirit in the room, as strongly as she had felt it at the church earlier that day, and her chest filled with the most penetrating ache she'd ever felt. "I miss mine," she said, glancing at Rosalie. "More than I ever thought was possible. More than anything else, that's what brought me here."

"Not research," Topaz said to Rosalie, as if punctuating the point.

Zin-Zin reached over and took her hand. Susannah closed her eyes, remembered the last months of her mother's life, the times she'd sat with her, so close, just like this. Why hadn't she done it more? Why hadn't she thrown her work aside and paid attention to what was important?

"What happened to your mother?" Zin-Zin asked.

"She died of cancer," Susannah said. "Lymphoma."

"Were you with her?"

Susannah's throat caught. "Some of the time, yes," she said.

"I tried to be. Her illness lasted a long time. I . . . have to travel for my job. Grants are so hard to come by, and sometimes I'd have to keep to a schedule set by my benefactors. I'd be on-site, but I'd be thinking of my mother. . . ."

"You were torn," Topaz said.

Susannah hesitated. She'd never opened up about this before, but something about these women made the words pour out. "Completely. I love my work, and she was so proud of what I did. I'd feel I was doing it for her, as well as for myself. But I'd also be feeling such guilt, knowing she was sick at home, wanting to be with her."

"Her illness progressed?" Zin-Zin asked.

"Yes. But it didn't happen fast—we kept having hope. She would go into remission. But it always came back. At the end, it overtook her." She bowed her head, feeling all the tears and guilt and emotion come welling up. "It ran all through her body, all at once. She always handled everything with such grace, even at the end. She tried to protect me from knowing how bad it was, so I'd go to Istanbul and do my work."

"What happened?"

Susannah listened to the wind and rain outside, trying to hold herself together. "I was in Turkey, on-site. I saw such beautiful paintings . . . the most incredible of my career. I took pictures, knowing she'd love to see them. And then I got the call . . ." Remembering, she started to weep. "Her nurse said my mother wouldn't let her phone me until then. She had started to get worse, and from then on it was so fast. I called her doctor, and he told me he was putting her in hospice, and on morphine, and . . . I got on a plane, and she died while I was in the air."

Susannah cried, and she heard some of the other women crying with her.

Zin-Zin's grip on Susannah's hand tightened. "Don't blame yourself. She wouldn't want you to."

"But I do blame myself," she wept. "How can I not? I wasn't there. . . ."

"She didn't want you there," Zin-Zin whispered.

Susannah raised her eyes. "What?"

"It was her decision to have the nurses not call you. This was her journey—her own death. Perhaps she *waited* for you to travel so far away before she let herself start on it."

"What do you mean?"

Zin-Zin was old and wise, and as Susannah gazed into her eyes, she knew that she had seen many deaths. "When a mother loves her child as much as yours loved you, she might find it impossible to let go, to leave you, if you were sitting right there. She had to wait for you to go away before she could die." She paused. "You're such a smart woman—why have you not realized that?

"Listen to your own heart," she went on. "You know I'm right, don't you? I can see it in your eyes. . . ."

Susannah nodded slowly. What Zin-Zin said made such perfect sense. Susannah and her mother had been so close. It would have been impossible for them to say goodbye, for her mother to have let go.

"She's with you now," Zin-Zin said. "Right here."

Susannah looked around, just like a child who really hoped to see her mother standing right there. But all she saw were the kind, concerned faces of the Romany women.

"She brought you here," Florine said. "You know that, don't you?"

Susannah looked up, startled. She remembered her mother's words: *Visit Sarah.*

"She told me to come," Susannah said.

"To Stes.-Maries?" Naguine asked.

"To see Sarah," Topaz said gently. "Your mother knew that you needed her."

"We're blessed to have you," Ana said. "You, whose life has been such a miracle."

"It has?" Susannah asked, looking around the faces. Sometimes she felt so guarded and alone. She spent her days delving into faded wall paintings and dusty books, researching people and cultures long dead. She'd gotten tangled up in the old habit of Ian. Just because he was there, he'd kept her from looking for anything like real love.

Suddenly she heard the name *Grey*—and she swore it was her mother who'd said it. She shivered, shaking her head with disbelief. Looking around the room, she saw candlelight flickering in mirrors and the window glass, burnishing the faces around her.

"You feel something, don't you?" Topaz asked.

Susannah nodded. Her skin tingled, as if she'd just been brushed by a ghost—which, she was positive, she had.

Zin-Zin began to talk again. She told stories of Sarah and her works, and what she meant to the women of the Circle. They were the caretakers of Sarah's crypt. And they were the watchers over all the miracles she had performed.

"Topaz has brought us several like you," Zin-Zin said. "Occasionally people, women, whose lives have been touched by Sarah, have rented her house in town. But mostly they're Romany. Or with at least a connection to the clan. Some had a grandmother who was Rom, or an aunt, or a cousin. Most had grown up as devoted to Sarah as we ourselves are. They come here, crippled or ill, and when they depart town, they leave their crutches behind."

"They don't need them anymore," Susannah said, picturing Sarah's crypt, lined with offerings, its ceiling blackened with centuries' worth of soot from votive candles.

"But you," Zin-Zin continued, "you are not Rom. You're not from our lineage."

"That's what makes you so special to us right now," Topaz said. "The thing that sets you apart. Sarah has performed a miracle in your life, yet you're not a Gypsy. That is very unusual. It's why I had to introduce you to the Circle."

"Thank you," Susannah said. "I'm so glad to have met you all . . ." She trailed off, hesitating.

"What is it?" Topaz asked. "Do you have questions for us?"

"Several," Susannah said, laughing. "Do you all live here, at the Mas SLK?"

"Yes," Florine said. "These are our *roulottes* . . . many of them were driven down, over a number of years, from Flache os Courbos."

"The Pond of the Ravens," Topaz translated. "In Belgium."

"Is it just women?"

"Just women in the Circle," Ana said. "But many of us have husbands and sons. We have families, of course—family is more important to us than anything in the world."

The women murmured their assent, smiling and nodding. Susannah felt a sharp twinge; that was true for her, too. It always had been. Yet once again, looking at Zin-Zin, she saw deep pain. The old woman closed her eyes, as if feeling private anguish. Susannah tried to catch her eye, but Zin-Zin wouldn't look up. Surrounded by these women, united by their connection to Sarah, and their devotion to her and Kali, she was struck by the fact that they also had husbands and children. How had she let herself miss out on that?

"Do you have children of your own?" Zin-Zin asked softly, suddenly raising her eyes.

The question stopped Susannah short, wondering how the old woman had read her mind. "No," she replied.

"You will," the woman said. She squeezed Susannah's hand again, then grinned, her tan and weathered face beautiful in spite of, or perhaps because of, her many wrinkles. "I feel certain of it."

Topaz had set water to boil, and when the whistle blew, she and some of the others began to pass out teacups. She'd brewed green tea that tasted of honey and lavender, and Susannah sipped it, letting it warm her hands and insides. The mistral blew, rattling the windows, shaking the caravan from side to side.

"Your caravans are very beautiful," she said after a long moment.

"Thank you," some of the women replied.

"Topaz said the Circle paints the garlands," she said. "You're all artists?"

"Creativity runs in Romany people," Zin-Zin said. "Music, poetry, painting, riding horses . . . it all comes from the same source."

"You like the garlands?" Rosalie asked sharply.

"Very much," Susannah said.

"Did you like Maria's? The one in her kitchen?"

"Stop it," Topaz warned.

"Maria's?" some of the others asked, sounding shocked.

"She was at Maria's house today!" Rosalie said. "I saw her driving there!"

"Who is Maria?" Susannah asked.

Zin-Zin dropped Susannah's hand, and a cool silence fell over the Circle. Susannah felt all eyes on her, and it took all her strength to not look away. She gazed from one face to the next, waiting for someone to answer.

"She was one of us," Florine said.

"*Is* one of us," Rosalie corrected.

Zuna let out a laugh, said something in the language Susannah couldn't understand, and Rosalie reacted as if she'd been slapped. Topaz, shrugging, said in French, "She's right. You're the only one of us who's gone to the Manade du Dempsey since Maria left. So you of all people should suspend judgment and criticism of our guest."

"It was only for the child," Rosalie said. "But that's over now."

Were they speaking of Sari? What did she mean—*that's over now*? Susannah thought of Grey; was Rosalie involved with him or not?

Just then Zin-Zin clapped her hands. *"Écoutez!"* she said sharply. "We must not fight. Not in front of an outsider." But then, turning slowly to face Susannah, she asked, in the same heavily accented English as before, "Why *were* you at the Manade?"

"The white horses," Susannah said.

"She wants to take a ride through the Parc, of course!"

"Bien sûr!"

Was it her imagination, or did the tension in the room diffuse, fly away? There was much laughing and nodding, and she heard Florine say that with their focus on Sarah, they forgot that people had other reasons for visiting the Camargue: the white horses, the black bulls, and pink clouds of flamingos—*les fleurs qui volent*, "the flowers who fly"—winging across the endless sea plain.

"There are other ranches with white horses," Rosalie said.

"True, but none are better than the Manade du Dempsey," Zin-Zin said. "Grey has the best horses in the region, and no one knows the park better. Except my father, of course, and he has been dead for fifty years."

"She asked about Maria," Rosalie said. "Perhaps we should tell her."

"Enough for tonight!" Topaz said, standing up with a quick glance at Florine that made her start to collect teacups. "I must get Susannah back home before the mistral blows trees down across the road."

Susannah stood. In spite of the hostility she felt coming from Rosalie, she realized that she didn't want to leave. She felt so snug in Topaz's caravan, surrounded by the Sarah Circle. She wanted to hear about Maria, and about Grey and Sari.

"Thank you so much," she said, gazing at each person. "I have had a wonderful time."

"We are so glad Topaz brought you," Zin-Zin said, clutching Susannah's hands. The old woman's eyes gleamed, tears pooling. "You have honored us by coming."

"I'll never forget you," Susannah said, gazing into her eyes, kissing her cheek. Topaz led Susannah through the caravan, exchanging hugs and kisses with all the other women. Only Rosalie held back, arms folded across her chest, just watching from the back of the *roulotte*.

Susannah walked out into the strong wind and driving rain, heard the door close quietly behind her. Topaz drove her out of the *mas*, and Susannah took one last look back at the caravan.

The curtains had been pulled, and the glow of candlelight was no longer visible. She closed her eyes, almost wondering whether she had imagined everything. But there was Topaz sitting beside her, fiercely concentrating on the tempest-washed roadway, and there was the small medallion of Sarah hanging from the rearview mirror.

Susannah wanted to ask about Maria, but didn't dare distract Topaz from driving. The storm raged outside the car, and Susannah imagined it was fifty percent Topaz's skill and fifty percent Sarah's grace keeping them safe on the road.

EIGHT

It was late; Sari didn't know what time, but the dream had awakened her again. A jumble of horses, and car lights, and her own scream. Had the sound actually come out of her mouth? She lay still, listening, as if she could hear it echo.

Sometimes she woke her father when she cried out in her sleep. But tonight there were no sounds coming from down the hall. No, instead, she heard them outside her window, a voice talking down below.

Heading over to the window, she peered into the darkness. The storm that had blown up earlier had broken and someone stood in the horse ring. She squinted, trying to see. It was Laurent, trying to climb onto the back of a colt, one of the new, wild ones, talking quietly, giving the yearling—or maybe himself—a pep talk.

Sari went downstairs—she moved stiffly, her bones aching, as if the dream had reminded them of how broken they'd been. She opened the kitchen door, careful not to let the cats out, and hurried barefoot into the yard. Laurent was so intent doing what he was doing, he didn't even see her.

He held the colt by a short line attached to a leather halter. Then he jumped up onto the fence, holding tight to the line, and stepped onto the colt's bare back. One careful foot, then the other . . . The colt didn't even have to rear up—he just gave a good shake, and Laurent fell off into the soft dirt.

Sari laughed.

"What's so funny?" Laurent asked, standing up and brushing himself off.

"What were you trying to do, kill yourself?"

"That would make you laugh?" he asked.

She shook her head; it would be the worst thing she could imagine. But after the bad dream she'd just had, and the upsetting events of the day, it just felt so good to laugh with her friend.

"No," she said. "It would make me cry."

He took a step closer to her. She felt his warm breath on her forehead. She wrapped her arms around herself. Her thin cotton nightgown rippled in the breeze. He was so close; squeezing her eyes tightly shut, she imagined her arms were his, that he was holding her. The thought scared and excited her so much, she stepped back and fell over flat.

"C'mere," he said, giving her his hand. "I fall off the horse, and you trip over your own feet."

"I guess I won't be joining the circus any time soon," she said, letting him help her up. "And you shouldn't either. What were you trying to do—ride standing up?"

"Yeah," he said, and suddenly they were standing close again.

Sari stared past him, at the colt in the ring. He was excited, being out so late at night in such changeable weather. The wind seemed to be coming from all directions. She shivered, and felt Laurent drape something around her shoulders—his sweater.

"I wanted to see what it was like," he said.

"Riding standing up?"

He nodded.

"What's so great about riding standing up?"

"You should know—you could do it."

"I haven't even ridden sitting down in a long, long time."

"You have circus blood in you," he said.

"Shhh."

"You do."

"Don't say that."

"It's true," he said. He paused, and she worried he was about to start talking about her mother. But to her relief, he didn't. "That woman who came here? Susannah Connolly?"

"What about her?" Sari asked. Hearing her name made her feel funny, and she wasn't sure why. There'd been something so nice about her, about the way she'd offered that suggestion about the spices, and about the way she'd said that Mystère was a one-girl horse.

"Your father said she rides like a dream, but that's nothing compared to . . ." Laurent trailed off.

Sari looked up into his deep eyes, saw the way he was watching her. She felt herself blush.

"Nothing compared to you," Laurent finished.

"But I don't ride anymore," Sari said.

"You're going to start," he said. "I can feel it. You want to. You're better now; your body is healed, and you're dying to ride."

"Yes," she whispered. "But I'm still afraid."

"That's okay," he said, tugging his sweater more tightly around her, keeping her shoulders warm. "You won't be forever. You'll start riding again, and once you do, I won't be able to keep up with you."

"But you're the best rider I know!" she said. "Our age, that is."

"I don't have what you have," he whispered, his eyes burning.

"Don't say it," she said, wanting to block her ears.

"Gypsy blood," he said. "You'll ride the way your mother rode. And you'll leave me here in the ring . . ."

"Laurent," she said, "I'm not like her. Don't say that!"

"I didn't say you were like her. I said you'll ride . . ."

"Shhhh," she said, putting her hand over his mouth. But he just pushed her hand away.

"Once you start, I want to make sure I'm as good as you, so we can ride together. But since you have it in you already, I have to work twice as hard."

"That's why you're out here in the middle of the night? Trying to break your neck?" she asked, touching his chest. "What would I do if you crashed down and got trampled? If I woke up in the morning and found you in a lump, with hoof-prints all over your sad body? Do you think I'd be able to eat my breakfast, go to school, live my life?"

"Without even a thought," he said, grinning.

"You're an idiot," she said, and she couldn't even smile. What was wrong with him? Didn't he know what could happen to people who fooled around on horseback? She pulled his sweater from around her neck, handed it to him.

"Sari!"

"Go to sleep, Laurent. We have school in the morning."

"You want to ride, I know it," he said. "Let me get Mystère. . . ."

"No," she said, facing him. "No."

He stared at her, and she knew he saw her trembling. This time it wasn't from the chilly air. She stood still, shaking, and he reached for her. But she wouldn't let him touch her. She felt confused, her emotions wild.

"Come with me," he said, finally taking her hand. She wanted to pull back, but even more, she wanted to follow him. He led her toward the barn. Digging her heels in, she couldn't step over the threshold. "It's okay. You know who we're going to see."

"Mystère," Sari whispered, and all at once she let him pull her inside.

She never came in here anymore. Having spent just about every possible minute in this barn the first years of her life, she felt the electric memory of her last time in here: the night her mother had left. A huge shiver ran down her spine, and she felt dizzy.

But Laurent held her by the hand, and he led her over to Mystère's stall. The lights were low, and the air was cold. Mystère knew immediately that Sari was there; the horse still remembered her smell, knew her voice. Mystère turned around in the big box stall and walked over to the door, tail swishing once—as if in greeting or admonishment: *What took you so long?*

With Laurent holding her hand, Sari reached toward her horse. She held her hand out, palm up, and felt Mystère's velvety muzzle brush her fingers, and the feeling of it made her weak in the knees, made her eyes flood with tears. She hadn't touched her beloved horse once since her mother had left.

"Je t'aime," she whispered, staring into her horse's huge dark eyes, feeling as if the last five years had just disappeared. She wanted to throw her arms around the strong neck, pull herself up onto the wide back. But instead she just stood there, staring into her horse's eyes, feeling tears on her cheeks.

"She's missed you," Laurent said.

"I know," Sari whispered, thinking about what he had said before about the difference between love and exercise, knowing that he'd been right, that nothing could be truer. Being let loose in the ring, allowed to run around, wasn't the same as this: girl and horse together, looking into each other's hurt eyes.

"You know what I think?"

"What?" she asked.

"That if you ride again, something amazing will happen."

"But I *can't*."

"You have to," he said, the words rushing out. "It will help you."

"Help me what?"

"See colors again."

"Laurent," she gasped, closing her eyes tight. She knew that he knew about her problems, but they never talked about it. Having him say it out loud made her feel so embarrassed—but also, in the strangest way—so good. To know he cared . . .

"What will make you able to ride again?" he whispered.

"I'm not sure," she whispered, feeling Mystère's warm breath on her hand, wishing she had Laurent's sweater around her shoulders again. She was icy cold, but not from the weather; from the inside out, as if her heart were a chunk of ice.

"Maybe someone could take you," he said. "So you don't have to ride alone."

"Stop," she said.

"And maybe that could happen soon," he said.

"Shhhh," she whispered, not really thinking, not wanting to do anything or be anywhere but right here, standing with her horse and Laurent, just being together. She closed her eyes so she wouldn't have to see the world in black and white. With her eyes shut, feeling the warmth of Laurent and Mystère, everything was perfect. Everything was fine. . . .

Laurent had an idea of who should take Sari riding. The next morning, the storm had renewed itself, and it was raging again, wind blowing the rain sideways. His body ached from the fall he'd taken, and pulling on his jeans, he saw that he had a big bruise on his hip. But he thought of the injuries Sari had suffered, knew that this was nothing. He ate breakfast fast, getting outside before Sari did. He caught up with Grey, standing in the barn's feed room.

"Bonjour," Laurent said.

"Ça va?" Grey asked, hauling down a new bale of hay. Lau-

rent went over to help him, shouldering the heavy bale out of the loft, down to the floor. "Thank you," Grey said. He looked a little surprised to see Laurent in the barn so early.

"At this hour I'm used to seeing you running out to make the school bus, with no time to stop and see the horses," Grey said.

"I didn't come to see them. I came to see you."

Again, Grey looked surprised. He was used to viewing Laurent as the little kid next door. He'd grown up playing with Sari, and if he had anything serious to talk about—well, that's what his father was for. But Grey nodded, beckoned Laurent into the stable office, gestured at the chair across the wide desk.

"What is it, Laurent?"

Maybe Grey thought he'd come to ask about more work, or a raise, or permission to ride Django, the big stallion—he had an all-business look in his eyes. So Laurent cleared his throat, feeling nervous, and said, "It's Sari."

"What about her?" Grey said in a way that let Laurent know he had his total attention—he sat up straighter, looked sharper. He always looked troubled—Laurent knew Sari gave him a lot to worry about. And right now all that concern was focused across the desk, at Laurent.

"She needs to ride."

"Well, I'd like her to," Grey said. "When she's ready. But she hasn't been . . ."

"She's ready," Laurent said. "I know her . . . better than anyone except you." He watched for Grey's reaction to that, then continued. "She stands out in the yard, looking at the horses. At night I look up and see her in her window, staring toward Mystère. And last night . . ."

"What happened last night?"

"She came into the barn."

"She did?" Grey asked, staring at him, taking that in. "By herself?"

"With me. This is the closest she's let herself come, ever since the accident," Laurent said.

"I know. Well, I'm glad to hear she went in. That's a big step."

"We have to help her ride," Laurent said, the words pouring out. "That night, Sari's heart was broken, and if we could help her in the right way, if we could make everything right for her, help her go back to the way she was before she fell, before her mother left . . ."

"Laurent—" Grey began, clearly disturbed by Laurent's direction.

"No, listen—I know I'm right! We have to help her!"

"Of course I want to help her," Grey said. "More than anything, you know that."

"She lives in the dark," Laurent said, his voice thick. "In a colorless world. I think of all the things Sari can't see, all the beautiful colors, and I try to think of ways that she could see them again."

"The doctor said that one day her ability to see colors will come back," Grey said. "It could come back gradually, or all at once." But he sounded like he was repeating long-ago words in which he'd lost hope.

Laurent already knew what the doctors had said, kept saying. He'd grown up with Sari. He'd heard his parents talking about her condition. He knew there were different kinds of colorblindness, and that hers was one of the most unusual: not only was her ability to see red and green impaired, but all colors.

"I want it to happen now," Laurent said to her father. "I want her to see colors now, and I think it will happen if she rides."

"Laurent . . ."

"I know there's a way to help her. She needs someone . . ." He trailed off, thinking of how he wished that could be him. He wished Sari would let him help her ride again; nothing mattered to him more. But somehow he knew she needed more than he could give her right now, and as he watched Grey look more intent, he knew he had to say it.

"Go ahead," Grey said. His tone had been steady and almost patronizing, as if he thought Laurent was just a kid, stupid and naive. He'd been just going along with Laurent, but suddenly he seemed to be really listening. "Tell me what you're thinking."

"You know she needs her mother," Laurent said.

Grey stared at him, hard and cold. For a minute, Laurent thought he was going to stand up and walk out of the office. But he stayed at his desk, his hands holding on to the edge. "Yes, I know," Grey said steadily. "But that's not going to happen."

Laurent nodded. "I think a woman could help her," he said.

"Like who?" Grey asked. "Sari doesn't want any women around here, doesn't want anyone to take her mother's place. Not even Rosalie."

"Not Rosalie," Laurent said. "Susannah Connolly. The woman from the marsh, with the red ribbon . . ."

"I know who you mean," Grey said. His eyes brightened so sharply, Laurent wondered what was going on. But quickly the clouds came back. "But she's not going to ride here. For one thing, she's only visiting the area for a short time. For another, Sari wants nothing to do with her."

"I think you're wrong," Laurent said quietly, picturing the expression in Sari's eyes, standing by Mystère. She wanted to ride so badly—her longing was completely obvious. And it had been unlocked somehow by Susannah's arrival here at the ranch. That couldn't be a coincidence.

"Sari would never go for it."

"But what if she did?" Laurent pressed. "What if she did, and we let the chance pass by?"

Just then the phone rang; the Dempseys had one line that went to both the house and the barn. Grey answered while

Laurent thought furiously about how he could convince him to try the plan.

When Grey hung up, the brightness was back in his eyes—along with a look of puzzlement, as if he wasn't quite sure what was going on. "Did you talk to anyone else about this?" he asked Laurent, sounding almost accusatory.

"About Sari riding? No—who would I talk to?"

Grey just stared at him; he had to know he was telling the truth. Just then the bus's horn sounded, and Laurent heard Sari's voice calling him. He grabbed his book satchel and headed for the door. "I hope you'll ask Susannah," he began.

"I'll think about it," Grey said. Frowning, he looked from Laurent back to the telephone, leaving Laurent to wonder who had called, and what was said. Then the boy pulled up his collar, ducked his head, and ran through the driving rain to the bus waiting in the road.

When Susannah woke up, she saw that rain was coming down hard. She had thought she might meander through the region, looking for another ranch that offered trail rides, but the mistral was too intense. Today would be the day she went to Arles.

Inspired by the night before, by the energy of the storm, the warmth of the caravan, and the women's stories, she felt more at peace than she had in months. Somehow last night had given her mother back to her.

Climbing out of bed, she looked out the window as she dressed, confirming that today would be a terrible day to ride. She thought of Grey, wondering what he did on days like this. She supposed ranchers had to work outside no matter what the weather was.

The drive to Arles took her right through the wildest part of the Parc, not far from where she'd encountered the bulls. The rain came sideways, blowing hard. When she passed the spot where she'd parked on that first day, gotten in trouble in the marsh, she noticed a car idling on the side of the road.

It looked like the one she had seen Grey driving—an old green Citroën. The sight of it made her heart bump; she looked over as she went past, trying to see inside the car, but the windows were slick with rain and fogged with steam. Glancing into her rearview mirror, she saw the car pull onto the road behind her.

Had she just conjured him up? Driving past this spot was completely visceral: her skin remembered the terror of the bulls, the excitement of leaping onto the horse behind Grey, of holding on to him. She needed all her concentration to drive, and lost track of the car. But when she rounded a bend, just past the wide lagoon, she saw a green blur in the rearview mirror. It might have been the mistral bending the reeds, or perhaps it was the green Citroën, on an errand all its own.

Susannah started to feel nervous. She'd already had one close call here in the Parc. There were no other cars on the road. She told herself she was being paranoid—why would Grey be following her, and how would he even know she'd be passing through? She hadn't decided, for sure, to go to the library in Arles until this morning, when she'd seen the weather.

But the heavy rain soon became a deluge, and she drove carefully along, both hands on the wheel, straight into Arles without another glance back at the road behind her. She couldn't believe how different this small city looked in the mistral from her first visit just a few days earlier; all the vibrant color had drained away, leaving gray and sepia stone. She found it even more romantic: mysterious, ancient, and haunted by ghosts.

She passed the obelisk at the Place de la République, and following the printed directions she held in one hand, drove through Old Town, into a maze of cobbled streets. Tall ochre houses lined the byways, their shutters painted in muted tones of sage, lavender, mint, and marsh rose, and Susannah couldn't help reflecting that they reminded her of the garlands on the caravans, and in Grey and Sari's kitchen.

Just past the Église St. Honorat, she parked the car, grabbed her briefcase, and ran for the alley between the medieval church and the building next door. Tucked at the very back of the narrow passage, she found a pillared enclosure with a small brass oval on the wall heralding *Bibliothèque du Cheval Blanc:* the White Horse Library.

She rang the bell, and was asked to give the password. Remembering Helen's note, she said the word *"Jardin"* into the speaker box. A buzzer sounded, then a series of quick, hard clicks as the locks were opened, and Susannah entered, shaking the water off her raincoat, wiping her shoes on the mat inside. A security guard—young, muscular, and armed—stood at the door. He searched Susannah brusquely, then sent her to another guard seated at a desk in the foyer. Susannah handed him her credentials—a letter of introduction from the professor.

The man examined the letter. *"Très bien,"* he said. Seeing that Susannah hoped to do research in the Lamartine Room, he directed her down a corridor. As she thanked him and left the desk, she heard the buzzer sound again and saw him lift the phone to ask for the password.

Susannah knew that this house had once been the rectory of the Romanesque church next door. It was now a privately funded library, containing so many rare books, manuscripts, and works of art that it required very intense security, especially since the theft by armed men, five years ago, of several priceless documents, including letters written by Saint Martha.

As Susannah approached the Lamartine Room, she noticed the heavy wooden doors, the barrel-vaulted ceilings, the solid Romanesque columns. Yet in striking contrast, the columns' capitals were decorated with bursts of lilies on one side and horses on the other, carved in high relief, an unusually decorative touch. It was a striking departure from the building's otherwise austere symmetry.

Entering through the heavy doors, Susannah settled down at a long mahogany table halfway down the room. She gave a call slip to the librarian on duty. Waiting for her request to be delivered, she noticed an unsmiling guard, machine gun held across his chest, at the entrance to the reference department. Looking up at the ceiling, Susannah saw the furrow left by a bullet five years earlier.

The robbery had been audacious. Susannah had heard all about it from Helen, who had been in Arles at the time. The thieves had entered, guns drawn, and tied up all the librarians and researchers. They'd known exactly what they were looking for: letters written by Saint Martha describing the Tarasque—the dragon that had lived in the Rhône River, attacking farmers and destroying bridges.

Saint Martha had tamed the beast with hymns and prayers.

Helen's field of interest had always been strong women. She'd studied groups influenced by powerful female figures, and one of her great passions was the study of Provence. Previously she had concentrated on Tarascon—the town on the Rhône closest to where the dragon lived.

But this trip, Susannah had promised to return to Connecticut College with material relating to the sea voyage from Galilee—for Saint Martha had been one of the group set adrift, including Lazarus and the three Marys and Sarah, who had landed in Stes.-Maries.

The librarian delivered the book to Susannah's table. Titled *Le Livre du Grand Voyage*, it was so ancient—jewel encrusted and bound by leather, with a raised cross just below the title—Susannah was required to wear special gloves so her skin oils wouldn't damage the parchment. The light overhead was dim and diffused: the parchment was so old and fragile, stronger light could harm the fibers.

Susannah made careful notes, sketching the book's cover—ruby eyes embedded in the green dragon's face, the heavy gold cross beneath the title. Gently turning the pages, she felt the thrill of touching a volume that had been created by a saint.

Time slid away. As Susannah delved into the book, she lost track of the hours and minutes—even of the century. She was swept into a timeless story of a woman voyaging from her native land, landing in the Camargue, encountering a legendary monster along the way, taming it with love—just like Beauty and the Beast.

Susannah's mentor had told her to pay special attention to page 321. The professor had examined this book before—but back then her focus had been the Tarascon locale, not that of Stes.-Maries, located farther south in Provence. Now, reading the page, Susannah made notes on Saint Martha's gratitude to Sarah, the young slave girl. When she'd finished recording her impressions, she went back and transcribed the page, word by word.

As she wrote, Susannah thought of how deeply Sarah had affected everyone she met. She remembered last night, the emotion she'd seen in the faces of all the Circle; the fact that there was an entire clan of Manouche women who had moved to Stes.-Maries, just to be closer to Sarah; and especially the profound gratitude of her own mother.

She'd been so lost in her research, she barely heard the heavy doors open and close. But when a slight shadow fell across the page, she flinched and looked into the dim light. She saw the outline of big shoulders and a lean torso.

"Hi," she said, shocked and happy to see Grey. She smiled, but saw the seriousness in his eyes. "What are you doing here?" she asked.

"Hi, Susannah . . . I was hoping to talk to you."

"Talk to me?" Again, she wanted to smile, but his expression didn't invite friendliness. Hands stuck into his pockets, he stood back from the table, staring down at her. "How did you find me? How did you even get in?"

"I've researched stories here," he said. "I'm in touch with the director, and he gave me the password."

"Were you researching a story in the marsh?" she asked.

"You saw me, did you?"

"Parked right in the same spot where I first met you? How could I possibly miss you?"

"I'm sorry. But I have to—"

The security guard stepped forward, standing right beside Susannah. She glanced up at him, noticed the alarm in his eyes and the way he had his finger on the trigger of his gun. Her heart skipped so hard it hurt.

"There are strict rules about the examination of *Le Livre*," he said sternly to Grey as the librarian came forward, as if to provide backup. "I must ask you to step away."

Grey stared at Susannah. He seemed determined, intense, and suddenly she felt annoyed—what was he thinking, interrupting her research? He had had ample opportunity to approach her. She didn't know what he was trying to tell her, or why he had come, but she knew that she had to take care of this right now, and fast. He was undermining her credibility with the library staff. No one messed with her work.

She pushed her chair back, and in that instant the librarian removed the priceless book from the table. Susannah watched as she whisked it behind the counter, behind the smoked-glass enclosure where the rarest books were stored. Her blood was racing, and suddenly she felt full of fury. She peeled the white gloves off, stashed her notes in her briefcase, gestured that she would like to speak with Grey out in the hall.

They stepped outside, the heavy wooden door swinging shut behind them.

"What do you think you're doing?" she asked, her voice rising, echoing down the vaulted corridor.

"I'm sorry to interrupt your research. I really am."

"Then why are you here? What do you want?"

"It's important."

"So is my work! My colleague made special arrangements for me to look at that book. Do you know how much back-and-forth it took? She had to fax my credentials—*and* hers! They only allow it out of the vault once or twice a year!"

"I didn't realize you were here to view *Le Livre du Grand Voyage*. If I'd known, I'd have waited for you to come out. But you've been in here for a few hours already, and I started thinking maybe you'd left through the catacombs or something."

"How *could* you know what I was here to see? Or anything about me?" she asked, her temper rising further. "How could you possibly?"

"Look," he said. "I need to talk to you, and I had to do it out of town—away from Stes.-Maries."

"Away from—" she began. "Did you really follow me here?"

"Yes," he said.

"How did you know I was coming, when I didn't even know myself?"

"I . . . was told what you do . . . that you'd be visiting the library."

She stared at him. Whom had she told? Helen had contacted the director of the library and given Susannah's name, saying that she would visit sometime during the month. And last night Susannah had mentioned to the Circle that she was doing research and planned, generally, to visit a library in Arles. But she hadn't been specific about a time—had she?

"Who told you?" she asked.

"It doesn't matter. The point is, I couldn't talk to you in town."

"But no one even knows me there! I'm only visiting. What difference—"

"They know *me*," he said quietly, and they both fell silent.

Susannah thought of Rosalie, the hostility she had shown last night, the allusions to Maria. She gazed at his eyes, bright blue, intent on her and whatever he wanted to talk to her about. His broad shoulders filled his dark green oilskin, and she could see tremendous tension just pouring off, and his eyes were full of worry, and suddenly all her anger melted away and she knew.

"Is this about Sari?" she asked.

He nodded. "Yes, it is. I know you met my daughter at the ranch, when you stopped by yesterday."

Susannah hesitated. "I saw Mystère, and stopped. Why didn't you tell me you had a ranch?" she asked.

"For the same reason I didn't want to talk to you in Stes.-Maries. Because my daughter is very vulnerable, and I walk a fine line with her. And because the town is small, and people see everything that goes on."

"What would it matter if you talked to me?"

She watched him wage a private battle of some sort. His forehead was creased with worry, yet he was gazing at her with something veering between tenderness and concern, and it made her bones feel liquid. "It's not that I wouldn't want that," he said finally. "It's just that you've walked into a very complicated situation."

"I haven't really," she said softly. "I barely know you."

"That may be so," he said, "but I'm persona non grata to a lot of people in Stes.-Maries. They might misinterpret."

"Misinterpret what?"

"What I want from you."

"From me?"

"I want you to help my daughter."

"Sari . . ."

He nodded, then bowed his head as if he couldn't believe he was about to ask. A security guard walked by, and they exchanged nods. Grey had said he had done research here, but standing in the hallway now, he looked only like an outdoorsman. Tan, rangy, dressed in a slicker, jeans, and boots, looking as if he wanted to jump on a white horse and ride away as far and as fast as he could go.

"I would like you to . . ." He trailed off.

"Like me to what?"

"Take her riding," he said finally.

"But I'm just a tourist," she said. "I haven't ridden in such a long time."

"I know. That's what I said . . ."

"This isn't your idea? Then whose is it?"

"Laurent's. Her friend—he . . ."

"I know who you mean," she said, remembering the tall boy standing so protectively by Sari. Susannah pictured the young girl, the sadness in her supernaturally dark-green eyes, the way she'd closed those eyes as if to withdraw from the world. Susannah's heart had gone out to her.

"She has you," Susannah said quietly. "And she has Mystère . . . that's her horse, right?"

"Yes. But she hasn't ridden her in five years."

"How old is she now?"

"Thirteen."

"What happened?"

Grey hesitated. She saw him weighing his options. He didn't want to tell her at all, but he knew that he had to explain, or she might not agree to do it.

"She had a terrible fall," he said slowly. "She was eight. The mistral was blowing, and it was . . . well, very late at night. She rode off the ranch, into the marsh. It was so dark, and she took Mystère onto the main road. They . . . well, never mind. Mystère got spooked and reared up, and Sari fell."

"Was she all right?"

"Not at first," Grey said. He gazed at Susannah for a long moment, blinking slowly, holding himself together. "No, she wasn't all right at all." Susannah waited for him to go on, but it seemed he couldn't.

"Is she better now?" Susannah asked softly.

"Yes," Grey said. "But not completely." He hesitated, then told her: "The night she fell, she went colorblind."

"Oh, Grey!"

"It's lasted all this time. We've had every test possible; she's been to neurologists and psychiatrists here and in Paris, New England, New York. There's no physical reason for it. The doctors say she'll 'outgrow' it."

"How awful for her," Susannah whispered. And how awful for Grey: she looked into his face and finally understood why there was so much pain in his blue eyes.

"I just want life to be good for her," he said. "Right, and happy, and good . . . She used to love riding so much. You can't imagine how much she loved her horse. Yesterday was the first time in five years that she's set foot inside the barn."

"That's good," Susannah said.

"It was right after you'd been there—just a few hours later."

"But just a coincidence, right?" Susannah asked, both shocked and honored that he would think there was a link.

"I'm not completely sure. She doesn't trust people easily. Especially . . . not women. She doesn't like me talking to anyone, spending time with them. I'm all she's got. She tends to be . . . well, possessive. She's needed me all to herself, and I've understood that."

"Then why would you want her to ride with me?"

He stood there watching her, a hundred unspoken reasons in his eyes. "It was Laurent's idea," he said.

"He cares about her."

"Very much."

"But why me?"

"Laurent thinks it would be good if she could go riding with a woman. The more I think about it, the more that makes sense. And she—well, she really appreciated your kindness the other day." He spoke as calmly as he could, but Susannah could see the tension and worry behind his eyes.

"It was easy to be kind to her," Susannah said.

"Thank you."

"I'll ride with her," Susannah said.

"You will?"

"As soon as the rain stops—assuming it does before I have to leave, to go back home to the States," she said. "I'll come to the ranch on the first dry day."

"She gets home from school at three-thirty," Grey said.

"I'll be there," Susannah said. "I can't promise it will work—she might want nothing to do with me."

"That's possible," he admitted. "I hope that doesn't happen . . . and if it does, I hope you won't feel hurt."

"I'll try not to," she said.

Grey nodded. He said he'd let Laurent know she'd be coming, then jammed his hands into the pockets of his oilskin. He turned to walk away; as he did, his arm brushed Susannah's shoulder. He stood still, and the contact lasted a few seconds longer than it had to.

Susannah watched him go, still feeling the pressure of his arm. She heard the echo of his footsteps down the long hall. The security guard stood to greet him again, and the two men stood talking for a moment: vestiges of his former life as a journalist? She wondered what kind of research he had done here, and how a man studying the Gypsies had wound up living on a ranch in the midst of them.

Then she turned away, to go back to Saint Martha, the woman who had entered the world of a dragon. As she let the heavy wooden doors close behind her, she thought about the beauty of jeweled books and garlanded kitchens, about the deeper truth that lay behind pretty things, and what life was like for the young girl with the burning green eyes who couldn't see colors.

NINE

It rained for days, but the atmosphere had changed, and Susannah didn't think it had much to do with barometric pressure. She made brief, solitary expeditions into the town for supplies and sat in her house writing up notes on the research she'd done at the library, and working on other articles. She couldn't concentrate. Her shoulder tingled, the spot where Grey had brushed her. Sitting at her table, she could have sworn he was standing right there, just behind her.

The telephone rang, making her jump. She picked up the receiver, but no one was there. She hung on, listening to the dial tone. Thinking of Grey so hard, she was sure it had been him. Maybe he wanted to tell her he'd changed his mind, that she shouldn't come to the ranch. Or maybe he wanted her to come sooner. . . .

When the phone rang again, she answered quickly.

"Hello?"

"Susannah . . ."

The voice made her go silent.

"It's Ian. How are you?" he asked.

"I'm fine," she said.

"You're a hard woman to track down," he said.

"I know," she said. "I had to get away . . ."

Now he was silent. She could hear the hurt pouring through the line. Their lives had been connected for so long. . . .

"Get away . . . from what?" he asked after a few moments.

"It's been rough since Mom died," she said. "I wanted to spend some time thinking about her. . . . I miss her, Ian."

"I know," he said. "Of course you do. You were close."

"That's why I came here," she said. "We'd always talked about visiting Stes.-Maries together. But somehow it never happened."

He didn't speak for a moment. She heard him breathing, felt his anger.

"I wonder why," he said after a moment, "it never happened."

"You didn't have to say that to me," she said quietly. "I say it often enough to myself."

"Susannah, what's happened to us?" he asked. "You used to tell me everything, call me all the time. You'd never take a trip like this without talking it over with me."

"I've never taken a trip like this before, ever," she said. "Everything feels new."

"You got on a plane," he said. "You flew to France. You missed a hell of a party. From what Helen told me, you're doing research. How new is any of that?" He paused, as if hearing the bitterness in his own voice. "Look, I'm sorry. But I don't understand. Why are you shutting me out?"

"Ian . . ."

"Are you going to Cosquer? Is that what you're studying?"

"Please, Ian. Stop."

He paused, catching his breath. "Look. My timing was

off—it couldn't have been worse, proposing to you when you were going through so much with Margaret, when she was getting so sick. But don't hold that against me, Susannah."

"I don't hold it against you," she said.

"Then what? We have so much in common; you know how right we are for each other. No one will ever support you and your work the way I do."

"You've been . . ." she said, but stopped, hearing the past tense. He heard it, too.

"You want to tell me it's over," he said.

"Ian," she began.

"It's not, Susannah," he said. "I don't believe it, and I won't let it happen. Tell me where you're staying, and I'll fly over. I need to see you."

"No," she said. "I don't want that."

"Listen to me. You don't know what you want—you're too upset, you feel so guilty."

"I'm saying goodbye now, Ian," she said softly.

She hung up the phone and went to the window. Shaking, she stared out at the rain. The street glistened, black and gray. Raindrops bounced off the pavement. She thought of how long Ian had been part of her life, and how distant she felt from him now. Looking up at the clouds, she wondered when they would lift. She hoped it would be soon.

The phone rang again. She turned and stared. It had rung once earlier, and no one was there. She'd thought it might have been Grey, but now she knew it was Ian. So she stood where she was, feeling that spot on her shoulder where Grey had touched her, and deciding she'd said all to Ian she had to say.

Grey sat in his office in the barn, feeling like a teenager. He held the phone, listening to Susannah's number ring and ring. He'd called once, and she'd answered. Chickening out, he'd hung up. Then he'd tried again, and it was busy. Now no one was home.

What did he have to say to her anyway? His excuse for calling was to check in, make sure she was still coming to ride when the weather cleared. But the truth was, he just wanted to hear her voice. He just wanted to know she was there.

This was strange; it wasn't Grey. He was usually all business—running the ranch, taking care of Sari. He wasn't used to feeling like a kid.

Claude walked into the office, holding a saddlery catalogue. He stood across the desk, watching as Grey had to pretend he was on hold.

"Important business?" Claude asked.

"Yes," Grey said.

"Ah," Claude said. He stood there patiently, tapping the rolled-up catalogue with one leathery hand, his sweater stretched tight across his generous gut. Grey watched as Claude's gaze traveled over the desk. It came to rest on the notepad, just before Grey had the chance to cover it with his hand.

Susannah, he'd written. And not just once: *Susannah, Susannah.*

Grey watched as his stable foreman smiled. Claude lifted his eyes to meet his, and Grey felt himself redden.

"She's coming here to ride," Grey said.

"Ah," Claude said again, the smile getting bigger. "I was right, then: important business . . ."

"Laurent knows all about it," Grey said.

"Very good," Claude said. He gave the catalogue one last tap, then dropped it on Grey's desk. He left the office, leaving Grey to listen to the rain on the roof and the phone ringing endlessly in Susannah's rented house, just a few miles down the road.

*   *   *

Days passed, a blur of rain and fog. Laurent had said to expect a surprise on the first sunny day, and even though she wouldn't admit it to him, Sari found herself waiting for the sky to clear. She noticed that her father was being more quiet than usual—sitting in his chair at night, staring into space, as if he had serious matters on his mind. But when she asked him what was wrong, he just smiled and said, "Nothing at all. Everything's really good, Sari."

Okay . . . If he said so.

The rain was torrential. Sari tried to concentrate on her schoolwork, but lately she'd felt herself slipping. Especially when it came to writing assignments; sometimes she felt she lived in a different world than anyone else. How could she describe a scene if she couldn't really see it?

Laurent was with her when she got her paper back in history class. The teacher had asked them to write about Madame de Sévigné. They'd read her letters to Louis XIV, describing Paris, the Court of Versailles, and especially, her time spent in the South of France with her daughter.

The passages about the palace, the costumes, the dresses, the gardens, the sea, were all so vivid. But reading about lush blue satin, about butter-yellow silk, about bright red roses, about brilliant gold crowns, about the sparkling azure sea, meant nothing to Sari; they were just words, as hard as she tried to remember how colors like that looked. So she'd written an essay so drab and unenthusiastic, her teacher had given her a barely passing grade.

"That's not like you," Laurent had said.

"The teacher thinks it is," she'd said.

"Why didn't you try harder?"

"Because I don't care," she'd whispered.

"You have to care, Sari," Laurent had said. "Don't give up."

She remembered that now, staring out at the rain. She'd come to like inclement days, when the weather turned the marsh gray. When Laurent told her something good would happen as soon as the sun came out, she'd told him she hoped it never would. He'd seemed shocked at first, but then he understood. That's why she felt so lucky to have him as a friend: he was in her corner.

Finally, the mistral stopped blowing, the clouds blew away, and right after Sari got home from school, Susannah Connolly drove into the parking area. Sari stood in the pantry, watching out the small window.

Laurent walked out of the barn, greeted Susannah. As Sari watched, Susannah took a small bag from the car, holding it under her arm as she spoke to Laurent. Sari wrapped her arms around herself, wondering what they were saying.

A minute later, he came walking toward the house. She met him at the kitchen door.

"You know that surprise I mentioned?" he asked. "Well, put your riding boots on."

Sari grabbed his hand, stared into his eyes. "What are you talking about?"

"I know you want to ride," he said. "Wanting to is the biggest part of it. Just come outside. I'm going to saddle up Mystère."

"No," Sari said.

"Sari, please . . ."

"You should know I'd never ride with a stranger," she said. "I can't, Laurent."

He stared at her as if he knew she could do it. The cats jumped down from sunny spots on the window ledges, and circled around Laurent's feet, but he ignored them.

"I think you can," he said quietly.

She shook her head.

"Then we'll have to tell her," he said, looking crestfallen.

Sari felt a twinge of doubt—she hated upsetting Laurent, and knew that he wanted the best for her. She felt like asking him to tell the woman himself, but pulled herself up straight and followed him outside.

When Sari stepped out into the yard, Susannah came to meet her. She was dressed for riding herself: dark jeans, low boots, and a denim jacket. Her face was glowing, as if the idea of riding made her so happy she couldn't hide it. Sari tried to fight her nervousness and smile back, but she found it just a little too hard.

"Hi, Sari," Susannah said.

"*Bonjour,* Susannah," Sari said shyly.

"Thank you for coming," Laurent said.

"I can't think of anything I'd rather do than ride with you," Susannah said, smiling at Sari. The words were so gentle, and Sari had the feeling she really meant them.

"It's very kind of you," Sari said, feeling stiff. "But I won't be able to ride today."

"No?" Susannah said. "Oh, I'm sorry."

"Of course, *you* can still ride," Laurent said to Susannah. "I'll go saddle up a horse for you. I'll go with you, if you'd like."

"Thank you," Susannah said. Laurent turned and walked away, leaving Sari alone with Susannah.

"I—" Sari stammered, feeling awkward, knowing she should explain a little. "I used to be a good rider, but it has been a long time."

"I'd say the same thing about myself," Susannah said.

"But," Sari said, "my father said you ride very well. *Comme un rêve.*"

Susannah laughed. She shook her head. "Hardly like a dream! I managed out of pure necessity. You remember about the bulls, right?"

Sari nodded, trying to smile. But it seemed her mouth wouldn't oblige. Her face was frozen. Her thoughts kept darting backward and forward: to the last time she'd been on a horse, that terrible night.

"I brought you something," Susannah said, handing Sari the package she had been holding.

Sari accepted it with surprise. She looked up at Susannah, who was watching her with a patient smile. Sari opened the bag, saw the wrapped present. The paper was a pale shade, tied with a satin ribbon.

"This is for me?" she asked. "Even though I'm not going to ride?"

"Yes," Susannah said.

Sari held the package. She couldn't remember the last time she'd gotten a present just because. Her father always remembered her birthday, and there was Noël, but this . . . just for nothing . . . no special reason . . . a day like all the others on the calendar. "Why?" she asked.

"Because I wanted to," Susannah said, as if that was all the explanation that was needed.

Hands trembling, Sari untied the ribbon. She slid her finger under the paper's fold, undid the tape, tugged it open. The paper fell away, and Sari pulled out a dragon—a child's plush toy. She held it, staring down at the dragon's glittering eyes, the line of spiny scales down its curved back.

"I got it for you in Arles," Susannah said. "After your father came to ask me to ride with you."

"This was his idea?" Sari asked.

"Actually, he told me it was Laurent's."

Sari held the toy, lifted it to her face, brushed the soft fur against her cheek. She closed her eyes. The feeling carried her back a long way. She shut her eyes tighter; going inward had always been such a good way to hide. Right now she was hiding from how much she loved being given a present for no reason whatsoever, and how touched she was, that Laurent was looking after her.

"What color . . ." she heard herself whisper.

"The dragon is bright green; his eyes are red."

Sari kept her eyes closed shut.

"Your father told me about your fall," Susannah said softly. "I know what it's like to have something happen that keeps you from doing things you used to love. I've felt that way lately. And when I was at the library in Arles, doing research on Saint Martha and the Tarasque, I thought of both of us."

"You and me?" Sari asked, barely able to talk.

Susannah nodded. "Yes."

"But why?"

"Well, you know the story of Saint Martha . . . how she traveled so far, in that small boat, across the stormy sea . . . with her wonderful friends . . . how they survived all that, and landed in Stes.-Maries . . ."

"The town was named for her friends," Sari said. "The three Marys . . ."

Susannah nodded. "Yes. And from there, Martha went up the Rhône, and she settled in a town that was tormented by a dragon. A ferocious creature who destroyed boats, and attacked townspeople, and lived under bridges, keeping everyone afraid."

Sari stood still, thinking of all the stories she'd heard about the Tarasque. When she was young, her mother had told her about the beast. And once, on a trip to Tarascon, her father had shown her the riverbanks where the dragon had prowled, the curved stone bridge under which it had made its lair.

"It lived in seaweed," she said to Susannah now. "A nest of horrible, slimy weed. And it killed birds, just plucked them out of the air to eat. And it frightened children, and tried to catch them and eat them, too. Everyone in the town was terrorized. The dragon had fangs and red eyes, and it never, never slept. It just *hunted*."

Susannah nodded. "Yes," she said. "It was tormented, poor thing."

"Poor thing? *It?*" Sari asked, shocked to think of the Tarasque as an object of pity. Fear, yes. Terror . . .

"Saint Martha knew that it suffered terribly," Susannah said. "That's why it had to be so fierce and dangerous. So she went down to the river . . . not to slay it, but to make friends with it."

Sari stared at her. She heard horses' hooves clopping through the stable. A trickle of fear ran down her back.

"She calmed the dragon," Susannah said. "With hymns and prayers."

"Instead of killing it," Sari whispered, holding the dragon toy tighter.

"Yes," Susannah said.

"But I'm not scared of a dragon," Sari said, her voice not much more than a croak. Her senses were alive, alert right now. She smelled horse hair and saddle leather. Her nerves were screaming. She looked at Susannah standing so close and she remembered her mother wrestling her in the kitchen, shoving her away. That was the worst part, but she couldn't say it out loud, so she said something else instead. Her eyes brimmed with tears. "I'm afraid of my horse."

Susannah nodded. She held out her hand, and without even thinking, Sari put out hers, as tears rolled down her cheeks.

"You don't have to slay it, or chase it away, or pretend it doesn't exist," Susannah said. "As long as you know it's there, and you can help it find a way to leave, when it's ready."

"Like Saint Martha and the Tarasque?" Sari asked.

"Yes, like that," Susannah said.

Sari stared out over the marsh. She wondered why Susannah was being so nice to her—she was the girl who drove everyone away. When would Susannah discover that she was worse than a dragon? She pictured her mother speeding off, the car's taillights flashing, flashing, as it carried her away, bright as a dragon's red eyes, the last color she ever saw. And she thought of what Rosalie had told her, one time when Sari had been so badly behaved Rosalie couldn't take it anymore: that Zin-Zin said her mother must be cursed to have brought such pain on everyone, and Sari must be cursed, too.

The horses were right there. Laurent held them by their

bridles; he hadn't brought Mystère because Sari had said she wasn't riding. Her father's stallion stood in the paddock, his black eyes gleaming. She remembered him riding after her that night, finding her in the road, shouting into the fog. Maybe there really was a curse: what else could explain all the terrible things that had happened to her family?

Sari felt her father standing beside her right now. She couldn't look at him. If she did, she would start to sob and never stop.

"You decided not to ride?" her father asked now. "That's okay, sweetheart."

"Papa," she said, looking up at him. She was still holding Susannah's hand and the dragon toy. She handed the dragon to her father. "Will you keep this for me?"

"What do you mean, Sari?"

"I want to ride," she said.

"You don't have to . . ."

"She wants to," Laurent said, running into the barn—she knew he was going to saddle up Mystère.

"I'll be coming with you and Susannah," her father said, his eyes gleaming.

Sari shook her head. She couldn't explain this to him, but she had to go alone with Susannah. She couldn't have anyone there from that night. Only Mystère—because she knew that Mystère was damaged, too. That night had injured Sari's horse's spirit almost as much as it had hers.

"Are you sure?" Sari's father asked.

"I think she's sure," Susannah said softly, answering for her.

"You know to stay on the main trail?" he asked, locking eyes with Susannah. Sari watched a look pass between them that seemed too mysterious for her to begin to figure out. She was too busy trying to get her own heart under control.

"It's marked?" Susannah asked.

"Yes," he said. "You'll see blue diamonds nailed to fence

posts. Just keep them to your right. They lead in a big circle through the refuge, and will get you right back here in about forty minutes."

"What about the bulls?"

Sari's father shook his head. "The bulls are far away—you won't go anywhere near them if you keep the diamonds on your right."

"The horses know the way," Laurent said. And then, quietly, "So does Sari, from before."

"I don't want to go first," Sari said.

"You don't have to," Susannah said.

And then, Sari knew she was ready. She let go of Susannah's hand, walked over to Mystère, leaned her head against the strong white head. Forehead-to-forelock, she kissed her horse's face. Then she took the reins from Laurent. He gave her a long look, and she tried to smile, but her mouth was too dry.

She had grown a lot since she'd last ridden. She reached up to grasp Mystère's saddle, put her foot in the stirrup, and let Laurent give her a leg up. The distance from ground to horse was so much less than the last time, but it felt a thousand times as far. Her blood was racing so fast, she felt lightheaded enough to topple off.

But then Susannah mounted Arabella, and she was sitting right there beside Sari on Mystère. Sari took a second to notice how calm Susannah looked, how happy. Then she glanced down at her father and Laurent. Laurent looked happy, too. Sari wondered what her father must be thinking.

"Papa, I'm riding again," she said.

"So you are," he said, the smile on his face everywhere but in his eyes. The old tragedy was there in his eyes—it had never gone away, not ever since that night—but at least his mouth was smiling.

"Are you ready?" Susannah asked.

"I think so," Sari replied.

"Then let's go for a ride," Susannah said.

And very slowly the horses began to walk, single file with Susannah and Arabella ahead, into the endless, salt-silvered cradle of sea grass that Sari knew—from an ever-so-distant memory—was soft green.

"How are you, Sari?" Susannah called back.

"I'm fine," the girl said.

The horses walked along, and Susannah heard the rhythm of their footfalls—soft in the pliant marsh ground—and the sound of tall reeds brushing their legs, and her own steady breathing. The saddle took some getting used to. She was used to riding English, but this traditional Camargue saddle was more Western. When the trail widened, she pulled up and waited for Sari to catch up, and then they rode side by side.

"Mystère looks happy," Susannah said, smiling.

"She likes having me ride her," Sari said, smiling back and—for the first time since Susannah and she had first met—her smile looking relaxed and genuine.

"As I said the other day, she's a one-girl horse."

"That's why . . ." Sari began, trailing off. Susannah didn't push her, but after a moment Sari finished her thought: "I think that's why I wanted to ride with you."

"Because I knew that about Mystère?"

Sari nodded. "Not everyone would."

"It just seemed so clear," Susannah said.

They rode along. Susannah felt Sari watching her hands.

"What is it?" she asked.

"In the Camargue, we ride with the reins in one hand," Sari said.

"I learned to ride English," Susannah said, transferring both reins into her right hand and feeling like a cowgirl in a movie. "I'm not used to this . . ."

"You're doing well," Sari reassured her.

After a few minutes, Sari gave Mystère a little kick, and she began to trot. Susannah smiled and followed. They crossed a rustic wooden bridge, flushing an entire flock of flamingos. The birds flew up in a pink cloud, but the horses seemed unperturbed. So did Sari. A blue diamond appeared up ahead, nailed to a tilting pole, and Sari kept it to her right, breaking into a canter as she guided Mystère along the well-trod path.

Susannah and Sari cantered for about half a mile, then slowed to walk again. When Susannah looked over, she saw Sari grinning. It was how Susannah felt herself: joyous to be riding. She petted her horse, feeling deep love for the animal. She'd always felt bonded with the horses she'd ridden, in touch with the mysterious communication that had nothing to do with domination and everything to do with connection.

"My father's right. You're a good rider," Sari said.

"Thank you—so are you."

"When did you start?"

"So long ago, I can barely remember! Let's see . . ." Susannah thought back. "I was in Miss Heckler's class, and that was fourth grade. So I guess I was ten."

"That's a funny way to remember. What did your school have to do with it?"

"Nothing, really. It's just that I remember my father picking me up at school to take me to my lessons. I couldn't wait for the school day to end! I loved riding so much, I wore my riding habit all the time. Jodhpurs, boots, black velvet hat. Even to school on days when I didn't have riding lessons."

"That's so funny," Sari said.

"I dreamed horses."

At that, Sari didn't reply. Susannah glanced over, saw her gazing down at Mystère's mane with a troubled look in her eyes. Her face was a knot, just as it had been the first day Susannah met her in the kitchen. Suddenly, with that, Susannah watched the fear return to Sari's body. Her spine tensed up.

"Sari, did I say something wrong?"

"I have bad dreams," she said. "About horses."

"You're not dreaming now," Susannah said quietly, seeing the panic in Sari's face. "You're wide awake, and you're doing wonderfully."

"I'm afraid," Sari said, shutting her eyes in the way Susannah had begun to recognize as the girl's first defense against whatever was frightening her. Sari collapsed over Mystère's neck, encircling it with her arms, burying her face in the white mane.

"Remember Saint Martha," Susannah said. "The way she sang to the dragon . . . letting it know she was right there."

Sari didn't reply, but stayed hunched over as her horse walked along. Susannah watched, feeling her own panic rise, wondering what she should do. But as Laurent had said, Mystère knew the way. The beautiful white horse just stepped along, steady and calm, carrying Sari homeward.

"What would she sing?" Sari asked after a few moments, her mouth buried and her words muffled with tears. "To make the dragon not be so terrible?"

"I'm not sure," Susannah said. "What do you think?"

Sari began to sing then, her voice high and wavering. Susannah didn't recognize the song, but it sounded ineffably sweet and tender, like a lullaby one might sing a little girl beset by bad dreams. She drew up close by Sari, so she could listen better.

The strange thing was, as Sari's voice grew stronger and she felt better enough to sit up, start to guide Mystère again, turning down the last stretch toward the ranch—just visible at the end of the trail—Susannah's heart felt heavier. She felt a huge tug inside, and she knew she didn't want this moment to end.

Not just the ride, not just being on a white horse, not just spending time with Sari: but the whole thing. The blue sky and the smell of the sea and the fact that she could see Grey waiting for them up ahead.

He had walked to the end of the road, and was watching for them. She saw his hand shoot up, giving them an exuberant wave. And they waved back—both Susannah and Sari. Then he stuck his hands in his pockets, rocking back on the heels of his well-worn boots, grinning as he watched them approach.

Susannah wondered how he did it. How had he gone from being a journalist haunting the Bibliothèque du Cheval Blanc to running a ranch? How had he switched from a life of paper and books to a life outdoors, with a beautiful daughter? How did people go from research and documents and deeply embedded sorrow to fully living their own lives? Susannah felt happier than she had in months, and she realized—for the first time since her mother had died—she didn't feel guilty.

"Papa!" Sari called. "I did it!"

"I see that, sweetheart," he called back.

He glanced up at Susannah, gave her a questioning glance—had it really gone well? She nodded that yes, it had. She saw that he was still holding the little toy dragon she'd bought for Sari.

And she also saw something else: a tiny bit of hope in his eyes.

It reminded her of standing in a dark forest on a cloudy night. Looking up, through the tangle of branches and fringe of pine, and through layers and layers of scudding clouds, there might be a moon. You more knew it than saw it, but suddenly the wind would blow, and the branches would toss, and a scrap of cloud would clear, and there the moon would be.

That's what Susannah saw in Grey's eyes as he walked alongside her horse, across the main road, into the paddock of the Manade du Dempsey. Laurent was waiting, too, and he dashed over to Mystère, to reach up and help Sari jump down.

"Can you see everything?" Laurent asked in a rush. "Sari, could you see the colors out there?"

"No," she whispered.

Susannah saw Laurent's face crash. He'd wanted everything all at once. He'd hoped Sari's first ride would make her all better. Susannah looked into Grey's eyes, and saw him gazing back.

"She did okay?" he asked.

"She did a lot better than okay," she said.

Grey didn't reach up. And Susannah didn't climb down. They just stayed there, frozen. Susannah couldn't stop gazing into his eyes, searching, searching for that glint of hope. Because if she saw it again in his eyes, she might be able to believe it was reflecting something in her own.

TEN

The next morning was another brilliant, clear spring day.
Many people showed up for the early trail ride, but Grey let
Claude take them out, while he stayed at the stable. There
were things to do, no doubt about it. A stall door that needed
repair, from where one of the new, wild horses had kicked it
in. And some roof tiles that needed to be replaced after blowing off in the storm.

But the truth was, he stayed because he knew she was coming back. She hadn't said a word, and he hadn't asked her,
but he knew. He'd seen it in her eyes. The way she'd stared at
him, returning from the ride with Sari, sitting up there on
Arabella, gazing at him with those big violet eyes of hers.
She'd been telling him, in everything but words, that she
would be back.

So there he was, at the last stall in the stable, tool belt
strapped on and one nail in his hand and another in his

mouth, and the hammer swinging, and Tempest, the young and recalcitrant wild white horse bucking in the next stall and neighing like crazy, when she walked in.

"Hi," Susannah said.

"Hey," he said, grinning.

"You don't look surprised to see me," she said, smiling back.

He laughed. Tempest was really making a racket, going more than a little nuts. Susannah's gaze was calm, gentle, almost amused. He watched her take a step toward the stall, stare in at the colt.

"What's wrong?" she asked, holding out her hand.

Grey knew she was speaking to the horse, not him, but he answered anyway. "That's Tempest. Until last month, he was living wild on the plain. He's a yearling; some of his herd had a hard winter, and he was showing signs of wear. So Claude and I brought him in."

"He hates it," Susannah said.

"Yes," Grey admitted. "He did this."

Susannah looked at the wrecked stall—shattered door, splintered wood. Then she turned back to Tempest, regarded him with warm eyes.

"What is it?" she asked quietly. "Do you miss your herd?"

"Let's put him in the corral," Grey said, partly because he wanted her to talk to him instead of the angry white horse. Gesturing for Susannah to stand back, he opened the stall door, caught Tempest by the halter, and led him out the open stable door. Tempest tried to yank away, with a force that nearly pulled Grey's arm out of the socket.

Once they got outside, Susannah swung the paddock gate open, and Grey let go. The young horse ran in circles, bucking with furious energy. Grey and Susannah stood there, watching. He saw her frown, felt her sensing the horse's emotions. Her compassion was palpable. He stepped closer to her, just to feel it, like waves, pouring off her.

"Do you know a lot about horses?" he asked.

"Only that I've always loved them," she said.

"So have I," he said. "I grew up in the country, and rode almost as soon as I could walk. We had a farm across the street from Narragansett Bay, and once a year there'd be a big horse show on our land. My father was known all through the state for the horses he raised."

"That's how you wound up running a ranch here?"

"Sort of," Grey said after a pause.

She let that go. "What would your father say about Tempest?"

"That he's scared out of his mind. My father taught me that horses and people think completely differently. People have hunter mentality. We go after what we want, and don't stop until we get it. Horses think like prey, like the hunted . . ."

"Because they *were* hunted," Susannah said, watching Tempest. "The earliest cave drawings—Lascaux—right here in France, show horses with arrows piercing their sides."

He nodded. She was an anthropologist, a student of such things, but he knew she was speaking from a deeper part of herself right now—the part that loved horses.

"Horses are intrinsically wild. And they want to be free," Grey said. "Not 'owned.' As kind as a rancher might be, he's still his horses' jailer. That's what Tempest is feeling about me right now."

Susannah nodded. She watched the young horse run and buck for a few more moments, then turned to Grey. "You're a kind rancher," she said.

"Thank you." He stared down at her. "I wasn't sure you thought that—not after I followed you to Arles."

"I didn't mind that," she said. She touched his hand very lightly, sending shivers up his arm.

He had to face something: ever since he'd first met Susannah, he'd been unable to stop thinking of her. He'd made those crazy calls, and he'd had dreams about her. There was something about her that seemed as free as the white horses, and in his dreams she was pressed up against his back, as she'd been that day, her arms locked around his waist. All he wanted to do right now was turn, and kiss her, and never stop.

"Grey," she said, staring up at him as if she could read his mind. Her eyes were beautiful, her mouth just slightly open.

"I have to tell you something," he said.

"What?"

"I didn't just follow you to Arles. I called your house, too."

"What do you mean? When?"

He hesitated, embarrassed. "The other day—during the rain. You answered, and . . ."

"That was you?"

He nodded. "Then I called back, and it was . . ." He stopped himself. "Why, who did you think it was?"

Now it was her turn to look embarrassed, but she smiled through it. "Never mind," she said. "I got another call, but it doesn't really matter. You know what? I had the feeling it was you . . ."

He laughed. "Maybe we're connected. Because you know what? I knew you were going to come today."

"How did you know?"

He shrugged. "The way you looked, just before you drove away, after you and Sari came back from your ride. I felt it. . . . You stared at me, as if you wanted to say something."

"I wanted to ask you more about Sari," she said.

"She loved the ride," he said, but his heart fell a little; he was glad she was interested in Sari, but he hoped she'd been thinking about other things, too. "She hasn't talked about it much, but that's her way. She keeps things locked inside."

"I'm glad she has Laurent as a friend."

"So am I," Grey said. He waited a moment, then said, "Was there something else you wanted to say?"

She laughed lightly. "Oh, just all of it," she said.

"All of what?" he asked, stepping closer.

"I don't know," she said, looking across the salt meadow. Then, "Okay. This will sound strange, I know. But ever since I met you . . . I've felt as if I stepped out of time."

"Out of time?"

She nodded. "This place . . . it's so magical. And the way you rode out of the fog on a white horse . . ."

"I do that a lot," he said.

She laughed. "But not like that," she said.

"No," he agreed. "Never before like that . . ."

She nodded, smiling, as if she was glad to hear it.

"Would you like to take a ride?" he asked now, suddenly at a loss for words, knowing he had to move.

"I would," she said.

He saddled up Arabella for her, and took Django out of his stall, and led both horses into the yard. Giving Susannah a leg up, he held her hand for a moment and felt the connection come through his body.

He climbed up on the big stallion, and led Susannah out of the yard on the scarcely used trail that meandered down past the big lagoon. The tide came in here, flooding the plain, but he knew it was hours before that would happen, so they cantered along the silvery mud, into tall grass.

"What's your horse's name?" she asked.

"Django."

She paused for a moment, staring at him. "I heard that name just recently," she said.

He nodded, wondering who'd been talking to her.

Across the plain, they could see the long line of riders behind Claude, heading back toward the ranch. Grey steered Susannah away from them, taking the south trail, skirting the lagoon, feeling sun blast off the surface of the sparkling water. White egrets stood in the shallows, spearing silver fish with sharp bills.

Another mile. They rode flat out, just feeling the horses pounding across the soft marshland, the breeze freshening as they neared the sea, the sun warming their faces. And then they cleared the last stretch of green reeds, and he heard Susannah's intake of breath and turned to see the pleasure in her eyes as they rode out onto the beach that ran along the sparkling Gulf of Lions.

The Mediterranean Sea spread all the way to Africa, as bold and azure as the sky above. A wide pebbly beach stretched endlessly in both directions. Climbing down off Django, Grey held Arabella's bridle while Susannah swung her leg over and dismounted with a jump onto the sand. The beach was covered with black scallop shells, small delicate fans in shades ranging from silver to dark pewter to ebony, and he saw her bend down to examine them.

"You're good," he said when she stood. "You ride like a Camarguaise."

"Sari taught me to hold the reins in one hand."

"The first time I saw you ride," Grey said, "there were no reins."

"No saddle, either," she said.

He was standing right next to her. His heart was pounding from the last half mile, when the horses had really run it out. Or maybe it was her closeness, and the way her head was tilted back, and the electricity that just kept getting stronger, and the sense he had that the reality of being so near to her was merging with his dream.

He took her in his arms now, and pulled her close, and kissed her. Her lips tasted like sunlight, and her mouth was hot and cool at the same time, and he heard himself say her name right in the middle of the kiss.

He held her hand, and pulled her down—or maybe it was the other way around, because suddenly they were easing each other onto the sand. He was on fire with the way she brushed his hair back from his face, and touched his skin with such sureness, and the way her arms were around him now, as tight as the first time.

When they stopped, they just held each other, hardly able to breathe, gazing into each other's eyes. If Grey couldn't hear the horses right there, and if the sea breeze weren't blowing gently but steadily, washing over their skin, sharpening all of his senses, he might think this was another dream. He held her, afraid if he let go she'd disappear.

"How did that happen?" she whispered.

"I wanted it to," he said.

"So did I, I think," she said.

"You're not sure?"

"I told myself I was going to the ranch just to talk to you," she said. "When Sari wasn't there. And I knew you couldn't come to town . . ."

"Because everyone knows me there."

"Is that really so bad?"

"The surest way to ruin your good name in Stes.-Maries is to be seen talking to me."

"You have a bad reputation?"

"Yeah," he said, smoothing the coppery-brown hair back from her forehead, kissing it. "The worst."

She was sweating from their sunlit ride through the hot marsh, and the sheer physicality of it all made him need to kiss her again and again. His heart was wrecked by the whole thing, and he truly thought there was a possibility he'd never get out of it alive.

"What did you do to deserve your bad reputation?" she asked when they finally broke apart, laughing.

"I don't want to tell you," he said.

"Because you think I'll disapprove?"

"Something like that." Holding her hand, he looked into her eyes. Her hand was small, fine-boned, but it felt rough, and that excited him. "Your hands don't feel as if you spend all your time at your desk."

"I don't," she said. "I'm a cave person."

"Excuse me?" he laughed.

"Half the year I'm on my hands and knees, crawling down rock tunnels into caves, to study Paleolithic art."

"Cave paintings?"

"Mainly," she said. "Rock art of all sorts. Paintings, carvings . . ."

"Like the horses you mentioned—at Lascaux?"

"Horses are dominant," she said, nodding. "But there are many images . . . bison, ibex, reindeer, mammoths. And not just Lascaux. This part of the world has many sites. The Dordogne, Languedoc, Roussillon, Quercy."

"Wow," he said, gazing at her with admiration. "That's your work. You're not just an anthropologist—you're an explorer."

She laughed. "I don't usually think of it that way, but getting into the Cosquer Cave—near Marseilles—took some doing. The entrance to the site is below our present-day sea level, so I had to learn to dive. Took lessons, went on practice dives . . ."

"Was it worth it?"

She nodded. "Yes, certainly . . . it's spectacular. The dive went down forty meters, to a small opening under the sea, then sloped back up into a tremendous chamber filled with prehistoric paintings and hand stencils; the artists traced their own hands on the rock walls. It's so moving and powerful . . . archaeologists call them 'finger tracings'—the artists used flints to etch their handprints in the soft limestone walls."

"Their way of saying 'I was here,' " Grey said.

Susannah looked at him with bright eyes. "That's it, exactly. They wanted to make their mark; all around the cave are traces of charcoal—they burned fires to illuminate the space. It's incredible."

As she spoke, he traced her hand with his fingers. "I wish I could see it," he said.

"Do you dive?" she asked.

"Yes. I grew up in Rhode Island, diving on the wreck of an old U-boat. I got certified when I was eighteen."

"Then I'll take you to Cosquer," she laughed.

"You promise?"

"Absolutely!"

"Deal," he said, knowing they were just talking. Her time here was so short, and he knew he couldn't leave the ranch just as the season was getting busy. Sari was on high alert, anyway. "Do you work with the same team all the time?" he asked. He saw her shut down; it happened all at once, like a door closing.

"I used to," she said.

He knew she was talking about a man. Did he have to do with that other call, the one she said didn't matter? He stared at her. The thought of Sari, and of someone else in her life, had brought him back to reality.

"Okay, then," she said, closing the subject. "Tell me this: why did you name your horse Django?"

He paused, holding her hand. "He's named for Django Reinhardt, who was a great guitarist. Some say the best ever. I like guitar music . . ." He trailed off, knowing it was his turn to change the subject.

"Django Reinhardt used to come to Stes.-Maries," she said. "You obviously know that . . ."

"Yes," he said.

"To the caravan circle, up the road behind the church."

So she'd been there; so she knew. He lowered his eyes, pushed himself up so he was sitting. How soon before it was all over, and what did it matter, considering it hadn't really even started yet? What was there to start? He thought of Sari, thought of everything, closed his eyes and wondered about this other guy in her life. Of course there would be someone. . . .

"Who's Maria?" she asked softly.

"Sari's mother," he said.

"And your . . ."

"My wife, yes."

"You're still married?"

He laughed harshly. "The marriage was annulled," he said. He didn't feel like telling her the truth, that the marriage had never been legal in the first place. Sari might find out, if he started talking about it. "How did you hear about Maria? From the same place you heard about Django?"

"Yes," she said. "The Sarah Circle."

"Oh, yes," he said, and he heard the bitterness in his own voice. "Them."

"You came to France to be Hemingway," she said. "And be a journalist. You wrote about Gypsies."

"They told you that?"

She shook her head. "No," she said. "That's what Google is for."

He looked over the sweep of blue sea, both touched and troubled that she'd looked him up. It had been a long time since he'd researched anything; what was available to find out about his life? If she typed in enough details, would the whole story show up on her computer screen?

"What did you find out?" he asked slowly.

"Not very much. Just that you wrote some pieces on the Romany people. Is that how you wound up coming to Stes.-Maries?"

"Yes," he said. He thought back; it seemed a million years ago. "I was living in Paris. I used to drink at a place on Ile St. Louis where a bunch of writers hung out. One of them was a gypsiologist. He told us all about the Gypsy Lore Society, if you can believe that. There are some arcane fields of study, but none more than that. It's a closed, secret world. Meeting him, I got hooked."

"So you decided to write about it?"

Grey nodded. "I came down here with him. We stayed at a ranch—just a few miles from the one I own now. There was a woman there, gave trail rides, and trained horses herself, un-

der the tutelage of one of the Gypsies' greatest horse trainers.
She was a spectacular rider, rode in a circus act . . ."

"Maria?" Susannah asked.

"Yes. Maria Loisy," he said. He thought back to those first
days. It was hard to believe sometimes, when he realized that
his entire life had changed direction so completely, based on
one chance meeting at the Brasserie de l'Ile St. Louis.

"What happened?" Susannah asked.

Grey looked into her eyes. How could he explain this to her,
the way he'd felt so intoxicated by a place, and way of life,
and someone who could balance on the back of a galloping
white horse as though she were part of it. "Well," he said, "I
fell in love with her."

"Oh," she said.

Fell in love. The words sounded like what it was, so why
weren't people more afraid? Grey's father had once explained
to him the difference between falling in love with someone
and loving them. The old horseman had given his son the talk
one day while they rode together toward Middlebridge, and
he'd done it without looking him in the eye once.

"Falling in love," his father had said. "It's like taking a
horse over a brush fence—you get air, rise up, take the jump.
And you might land okay, or you might go flying. You want to
make sure you're on solid ground. That's what loving someone is like: you land safely. You have ground under your feet."

Grey had listened to his father, but what had he wanted to
land safely for? He'd been young and wild, with Hemingway
as his idol, and he'd come down to the South of France to
write about Gypsies, and fallen in love with the most exciting
one of all.

"And are you still?" Susannah asked, bringing him back to
earth. He couldn't believe how he was starting to feel about
her, in such a short time. It was different from Maria, but
happening just as fast, and it shocked him.

"Still?"

"In love with her?"

"No," Grey said. "I haven't been for a long time."

"But she's Sari's mother."

"She left five years ago," Grey said. "And we haven't seen her since. But she really left long before that. We fell in love fast, and Sari came, and reality set in. After Sari was born, we never turned to each other again. Not once. When the baby was big enough, she began spending most of her time at that ranch I told you about, with her horse trainer and friends. Our marriage was never accepted by them—or by any of her people—I'm the devil to them."

"It wasn't your fault!"

"Some of the older people blamed Maria as much as they did me. Supposedly, one put a curse on her, and all of her children."

"Oh, God—Sari?"

Grey shook his head impatiently. "Don't worry—I don't believe in it. Rosalie put the idea in her head one time, and I swear I nearly lost it. It's just Old World stupidity. But Maria took it to heart; she probably believes it to this day."

"Do they know where she is?"

"Of course," Grey said. "They know, I know. And so does Sari. Maria is with a circus in Nevada. She's the star—something she always wanted."

"But her daughter . . ."

Grey didn't respond. He wanted to stop talking about Maria. The waves broke gently on the shore, lulling him into a feeling of calm. His heart felt cracked open, talking to a woman who cared. He never let himself get this far. But Susannah really was different and so was all that was happening. It had to be. Grey looked at her now, touched her cheek.

"I'd started to think Sari would never ride again," he said, looking into Susannah's violet eyes.

"I'm glad she did," Susannah said. "And that I was there to see it."

"*See* it? You made it possible . . ."

"She's so good. And she obviously loves Mystère very much."

"She does. But she was badly traumatized . . . still is."

"How did she fall, Grey?" Susannah asked.

Grey paused. "She was chasing her mother. It was the night Maria left . . ."

"Oh my God!" Susannah said, closing her eyes. Grey could tell the picture was vivid in her mind, could see her imagining what it must have been like for his eight-year-old daughter.

"She fell off Mystère and just shattered," Grey said. "Completely. The physical breaks were only part of it."

Just then a group of riders from another ranch galloped out of the marsh and began riding along the beach. Grey felt them watching him and Susannah, so he gave her his hand, helped her up. He bent down and picked up a few scallop shells. Most were black, but he found two bright orange-apricot ones as well, and slipped them into his pocket.

They climbed back onto their horses and started riding home. Grey hated to leave the quiet beach. He wanted to keep talking with her, wanted to tell her everything, the whole story, but even more he wanted just to be with her.

Making their way back through the tall reeds, he felt reality returning. As they neared the stable, he heard voices: the morning trail ride had returned, and the afternoon ride would begin shortly. He pulled back on his reins, stopping Django. Susannah glanced over her shoulder, and Arabella circled around.

As if she knew what he wanted—or wanted the same thing herself—Susannah guided Arabella to stand side by side with Django. Grey leaned across the space between the horses, wrapped his arm around Susannah, and kissed her. It was rough and hurried, compared with their time on the beach, her lips salty from the sea breeze, and her hand clutching his as if she felt the same urgency he did.

"Once we get back to the barn, there'll be people around," he said.

"I know," she said.

"I want to see you again," he said. "How long are you here for?"

"I fly home on Sunday," she said.

The words hit him with a thud; it was Thursday now. His mind raced; how could he see her every minute? Sari would be home from school soon, and tomorrow he had a vet coming from Nîmes; Saturday belonged to Sari—he knew she'd have it all planned.

"Sunday is too soon," he said.

"I know," she said.

"Look . . ." he said. "Put it off for a few days, okay? You can do that, can't you?"

"I'm not sure; I paid full fare, so it might be possible to change my ticket. . . ."

"A tour group booked a night ride for Sunday. I do that sometimes, when the moon is full, or close to it. I'd love for you to come."

"What about Sari?" Susannah asked. "Won't she mind?"

"I'm not sure," he said hoarsely, touching her face. "She and I spend Saturday together; it's always been 'our' day. I wish I could see you then, too . . . and tomorrow. But I want you to take that ride. Will you? And if you stay a few extra days, I'll figure out a way to see you after that, as well. . . ." He reached into his pocket, pulled out the scallop shells he had picked up on the beach. He handed them to Susannah.

"For me?" she asked.

"While you're thinking about staying, I want you to remember today," he said.

"Do you think I could ever forget it?" she whispered.

And he shook his head, because he knew he never could forget it either, and they turned their horses toward home, and galloped back to the stable.

ELEVEN

Susannah returned to her house after leaving the ranch, stripped off her riding clothes, got into her blue bathing suit and dived into the pool. The sun was bright, beating down on her skin, and the sensuality of it filled her with almost more longing than she could bear.

She swam more laps than she could count, just to burn off the desire that seemed to be overtaking her. Her heart pumped from the exertion, and the turquoise water split into silver sparkles as she stroked up and down the pool's length, thinking of Grey the whole time.

He had spoken of falling in love. The image of falling filled Susannah's mind as the water held her steady. The danger of teetering, losing balance, plunging into the unknown: that's how she felt right now. She'd held herself back all these years; what she'd had with Ian hadn't even come close.

Grey had asked about her "team." She'd found herself

wanting to tell him about Ian. She worked so hard, all the time, and involving herself with Ian, mixing up their professional connection with something more, had kept her from being available to anything real. Even after his proposal, when she'd backed away, there had been no definite end between them. His call, as unwelcome as it had been, had at least helped her feel more clear about the fact that things were really over. If they had ever existed at all. What she felt for Grey was so different.

As she climbed out of the pool to dry herself off, she felt the towel—rough on her skin—and thought of him, and wanted him so badly she had to sit down. How had she let herself stay this alone for this long? She lay back on the terrace, letting the sun bake down, and feeling heat rise through her body from the hot blue stone beneath. She thought of how safely she had lived, how wrapped up in the cocoon of the college and the library. And she thought of Grey kissing her on the beach, and felt the world tilt beneath her.

But how could she live up to the relationship he'd had already, with Maria? When he had sat there, telling her about how fast they'd fallen in love, Susannah had had to stare down at the pebbles on the beach, just to keep herself steady, because she'd felt as if that's just what was happening to her: she was falling in love with Grey.

She took a shower in the open air, letting the warm water wash over her body, wondering how she could wait to see him again. She knew that he had ranch business tomorrow, and that Saturday belonged to Sari. It touched her, to think of him being so devoted to his daughter. . . . But she didn't know how she would make it till their next meeting. Sun streamed through the slats of the tall enclosure. She smoothed her skin with lavender wash, poured from a tall silver bottle, and knew she was already a much different woman than the one who had left Connecticut. She had to get back—she had obligations—but she had already decided to stay at least another day or two.

As she dried off and dressed, she knew that she owed a large debt to her mother, for telling her to visit Sarah. But also to Helen Oakes. The thought of coming to Stes.-Maries-de-la-Mer had been in Susannah's mind for a long time, but she'd felt so stalled after her mother's death.

Then, three days before her birthday, Susannah had been sitting at her desk. Surrounded by piles of books, papers, site maps, and photographs of findings from the Istanbul dig, she'd been lost. She heard the thump, thump of Helen's cane, just in time to look up into her mentor's patrician, austere face.

"Hello, Helen," she said.

"Susannah, may I interrupt you for a moment?" Helen asked.

"Of course," Susannah said, clearing a pile of papers from the chair beside her desk.

Helen Oakes was tall and reed thin, with white hair pulled back in an elegant French twist. She wore a hunter-green challis dress and sensible brown shoes. Her only piece of jewelry—which she always wore—was a thick gold chain from which dangled a heavy gold locket adorned by a mysterious raised cross on one side and a deeply scored monogram on the other. Heavy wool stockings hid the brace on her left leg.

"What can I do for you?" Susannah asked.

Helen had a glint in her eyes. "Well, it's rather delicate. I lay wide awake last night trying to decide what to do. I've been invited to a surprise party."

"Oh dear," Susannah said, smiling. They'd worked with each other long enough to know that neither one of them liked surprise parties.

"Yours," Helen said.

"Oh no," Susannah said, having a vision of herself walking into the party: widening her eyes, letting out a whoop of delight, pretending to be thrilled and totally surprised—she thought it over; no, that wasn't going to happen. Her eyes filled with tears.

"You've had a very hard year," Helen said.

Susannah nodded. She had a lump in her throat, and couldn't speak. She pictured all her loving, well-meaning friends planning the one thing she wouldn't be able to stand: forced gaiety was beyond her realm right now.

"When my mother died," Helen said, "I found myself quite incapacitated. I went on a lengthy retreat."

"You did?" Susannah managed to ask.

"Yes," Helen said. "To a Buddhist monastery in northern India. The serenity I found was unparalleled. I sat in meditation for hours each day, within sight of the snow-capped Himalayas. All the feelings that had been pressed down, swirling inside, were allowed to come to the surface. And I was able to let them out."

"How did you manage that?" Susannah asked. She thought of herself sitting cross-legged on the floor of a monastery. If she did, she was quite sure that she would start crying and never stop.

"It was simply necessary," Helen said. "As I sense it is for you. We're alike, you know."

"We are," Susannah said, grateful to have such a wonderful friend and mentor.

"You are mourning your mother, my dear," Helen said, leaning closer. "But also a sense of yourself that has been lost."

"Lost?"

"Yes. You've been chasing around the world for years now. Your scholarship has been superb, but the rest of it—" She gave a thumbs-down. "Believe me, I know. In excelling at work, you sacrificed a bit of yourself. I did the same thing. I'm not saying that we've made a mistake—only that in choosing this path, we've let some of life pass us by."

"I wasn't there for my mother," Susannah said. "That's what you're saying?"

"Not at all. You made your mother so happy, doing what you love to do. I'm talking about other areas of your life. Ian Stewart, to be precise."

"What about him?"

"Susannah . . . what are you doing with him?"

"He and I are taking a break."

Helen paused, staring at her. "Are you sure he knows that?"

"You sound like my mother," Susannah said, smiling sadly.

"Well, your mother was a very wise woman. Now, does Ian knew how you feel? Or, rather, how you don't feel?"

"I'm not sure he wants to know," Susannah said. "It doesn't seem to be sinking in. He has a talent for ignoring what he doesn't like. As you know, I've been trying to 'bond' with a group of anthropologists from Cambridge. Ian wasn't invited on my last trip with them—he just showed up."

"Well, prepare yourself," Helen said. "He's planning to 'show up' somewhere else."

"What are you talking about?"

"I made the most ridiculous mistake; I told him about your surprise party, and I believe he's insinuated himself into it. He contacted your friend Heather and asked to be invited," Helen said. "She told me when she called to invite me."

"Oh God," Susannah said. "I thought he was in Marseilles, giving a lecture about the Cosquer Cave right around now. Besides, he and I aren't together anymore."

"Well, as I said, I think maybe you need to let him know." Helen gazed at her. "He won't let go easily."

"No . . ." Susannah said. She'd already started to realize that Ian was holding on to her for all sorts of reasons.

"What are you going to do about the party?"

"I can't go, I just can't," Susannah said.

"Go to Stes.-Maries," Helen said gently.

"But my mother . . ." Susannah said. "That was going to be *our* trip."

"Let it be your trip," Helen said. "You and Margaret . . . She'll be with you every step of the way."

"Oh, Helen . . ."

"I'm not being selfless," Helen said. "I need something, and it happens to be in Arles."

"But . . ."

"There is a library there. The Bibliothèque du Cheval Blanc. It contains a magnificent work attributed to Saint Martha. There's a source of great feminine power in Stes.-Maries. I would like you to immerse yourself in that town, and make notes on what you discover."

"But my party."

"You can send them a case of champagne," Helen said. "And tell them that I've sent you to Europe on a top secret mission."

Susannah had almost laughed, but Helen suddenly looked completely serious. She gazed silently, the words "top secret" shimmering between them in a way that Susannah knew they were meant to be taken seriously.

"Are you available?"

Susannah thought of Ian. "Yes," she said. "Completely available."

Now, as she walked into the kitchen of her rented house, Susannah glanced down at the notes she had taken in Arles. The library, where Grey had found her . . . And she looked at the notes she'd made after visiting Sarah's crypt, and after attending the Sarah Circle. She wondered what Helen would think if she knew that instead of finding serenity and meditation here, Susannah was falling wildly in love.

And she had a plan; there were things she had to do, a promise she wanted to keep. She picked up the phone, called the airline, and changed her reservation. Her next calls were much more local.

*   *   *

That day after school, Laurent was working in the barn, and Sari joined him there. He had to put new hay down in the stalls, and she was helping him break apart the bales. It was heavy, dirty work. She never minded work—had her own chores to do around the house and farm—but this was the first time in five years, since they were little, that she'd come so close to the horses.

Almost everything had changed with that one ride. Seeing Sari coming through the marsh on Mystère, next to Susannah on Arabella, had filled Laurent with happiness . . . and pride. He had known what she needed, and he'd helped it to happen. Looking over at her now, seeing her face streaked with dirt as she threw another pitchforkful of hay into the stall, his only frustration was that she still couldn't see colors.

A few nights ago she'd caught him trying to ride one of the wild horses, and he'd told her a little of the truth—he wanted to improve his riding so he could keep up with her. But she had no idea how he felt about her. Tonight, for example; he wanted to ask her to study with him. They had the same homework, and lately he'd been concerned that her grades were falling. She could come over, and they could sit on the sofa, instead of working alone in their separate houses.

"What are you doing, leaning on your pitchfork?" she scolded. "Get to work!"

"Listen to you . . . first day back in the barn, and you start bossing me around."

"Someone has to."

"Your father's in his office—he signs my paycheck."

"Yes, well . . ."

She grinned and threw a handful of hay at him; he picked up a huge armful and dropped it on her head. She pretended to fight him off, then managed to sling her foot around his ankle and knock him down into the pile of hay. He grabbed her hand and pulled her in with him. One of the horses let out a whinny, and she laughed. It was so good to see her having fun, he hugged her. He nearly kissed her, but then their eyes met, and they pushed away.

"You're terrible," she said, "pulling me into the hay."

"Well, you knocked me down first," he said.

She was blushing, and he knew he was bright red. What was happening between them? They'd grown up practically brother and sister. Turning thirteen, the first thing that happened was that he'd started turning crazy every time Sari came near. This wasn't the first time he'd wanted to kiss her; it was just the closest they'd come.

The strangest thing was that he felt her wanting to do it, too. And he could see she felt as mixed about it as he did. Now she'd jumped up, run over to Mystère's stall. She reached for an apple from the bin, and worked off a section, holding it out toward the white mare.

Laurent walked over to stand next to her, just because if he didn't, he knew there would be weirdness between them. He'd already figured that out with other girls. But he didn't care about them; what he cared about was making sure there was no unfamiliar wall between him and Sari.

"She's so happy you're feeding her," he said, standing half behind Sari, looking down at the back of her head.

"I'm her person," Sari said.

"She always knew that, even when you stayed away."

"Of course she knew it," Sari said, turning to give Laurent the sternest, warmest, crazy-wildest look he'd ever seen. "Sometimes things are so obvious, you don't have to say it, don't have to be there, don't have to do anything at all . . ."

"Huh," Laurent said, paralyzed.

"And other times," she said, holding him still with her gaze, "you have to take drastic action."

He never saw it coming; she slid her foot behind his ankle again, and knocked him right back down. She stood there laughing, offering him a hand. He took it, and when she pulled him up, the words just came out.

"Come study with me tonight, okay? At my house?"

"That's awfully far," she teased.

Laurent felt ripples across his skin. It *was* awfully far—she had no idea what she was saying, or what he was feeling. If she had any idea that he'd long stopped thinking of her as a little sister, who knew what she'd do? So he just gave her a stupid grin, shook his head as if he thought she'd just said something ridiculous, and started forking hay into the stalls again.

"Well, how about this, too . . ." His throat was dry. Ever since he'd seen that bad grade on her history essay, he'd been thinking about how he could help. And now, Susannah had called, asked him to help *her*. He felt like part of a conspiracy—because as much as he liked her, and wanted to help, he was thrilled, because the end result meant more time with Sari. "How about studying with me at the library tomorrow?"

"Why? We can study here, can't we?"

"Yes, but it might be fun to be in town. I'll buy you some crêpes."

Sari paused, giving him a funny smile. He tried to keep a straight face, giving nothing away.

"Crêpes *sucre*?" she asked.

"Any kind you want."

"Okay, then. I'll go with you."

Laurent smiled. He glanced over at the office door. Her father was standing there, looking happy with the world. Laurent wondered whether Susannah had called him yet.

"Is there a group coming to ride tonight?" Laurent asked.

"No," Grey said. "That's scheduled for the full moon. Sunday night."

"Okay," Laurent said.

"I'm going to Laurent's to study tonight, Papa," Sari said, continuing to work. "Is that okay?"

"That's completely fine," Grey said. "Um, Sari, I wanted to talk to you about tomorrow . . ."

"Oh!" she said. "Laurent and I are going to the library after school. Is that okay, too?"

"Yes, Sari. That's great."

And Laurent could tell, by the way Grey was smiling, that it really was, that nothing could have made him happier than to know that his daughter would be busy and off on her own tomorrow evening.

Even though Susannah had told him she would change her departure to Tuesday, Grey felt time ticking away. After so many solitary years, trying to rebuild a world just for himself and Sari, he felt inseparable from a woman who would be flying across an ocean. Every minute that went by, he found himself feeling more impatient for the time to pass so he could see her. She'd called him at the barn, asked him if he could be free all the next day.

"The vet's coming, but I'll get Claude to cover for me here," he said. "Why?"

"Well, I'd need you all day," she said. "We couldn't make it there and back and do everything we'd have to do in time for Sari's school bus . . ."

"What are you talking about?" he laughed.

"I'm making good on my promise," she said.

"What promise?" he asked.

"You said you wanted to see the Cosquer Cave."

"You're kidding!"

"Get your swim trunks ready," she said. "We're going underwater."

"You don't mess around," he said.

"I hope you know the way to Marseille. Will it be a problem to pick me up early? Like . . . dawn? Will Sari worry?"

He laughed. "It's a ranch—I'm always out early. There's

one thing. I'm always here when she gets home from school. But she and Laurent are going to the library tomorrow . . ."

"I thought that might work out," she'd said, laughing. "At least, I hope it does. See you at sunrise!"

Now, sitting in his office, Grey stared out into the barn. Obviously Laurent was in on it—Susannah must have called him. He and Sari were working in the stalls, laughing and fooling around. Grey watched for a few minutes, trying to remember when he'd been that young.

Grey might not be a kid anymore, but right now he felt like one. This was unexplored territory for him. Susannah was different from anyone he'd ever known. He wanted to read everything she'd ever written, see the world and the places she explored, learn all there was to know about her.

Tomorrow at dawn, he'd be with her.

Susannah was taking Grey to the sea cave. That's all she could think about. There were several more calls she had to make, to secure permits, and access, and to make sure there would be dive equipment available. But she had always been efficient, expert at making things happen, cutting through red tape. She had a BlackBerry filled with contact information, and within an hour, the plans were set.

All she had to do was wait for today to pass so tomorrow could come.

Taking her market basket for later, she headed to the church. Making her way through the dark nave, she passed several women she recognized from the caravan: Zuna, Florine, Ana, and Étoile. They had changed Sarah's clothes—removed the gold brocade coat and replaced it with a shimmering pink cloak—and arranged fresh candles all around the statue. Topaz was down the aisle, polishing the stone floor.

Waiting for the women to leave, Susannah walked into Sarah's chapel. She paused before the beautiful dark statue.

Looking into Sarah's eyes, she thought of her mother, felt her right there beside her.

Zin-Zin had said she would have children. Would she really? She had just turned forty-two years old. By the time her mother had knelt here, she was only thirty-four, had been married for nine years, and had desired children for all of that time. Susannah had spent all her life studying and working, getting ahead in her field. Right now she felt overwhelmed with yearning, and it was all the more powerful because she'd never felt anything like it before.

Her eyes fell upon the base of Sarah's statue; people had left smooth stones, pieces of jewelry, handwritten notes, and scallop shells at her feet. Susannah thought of the seven shells that Grey had given her on the beach. Reaching into her pocket, she pulled them out. Five were black, but two were shades of peach. Choosing one of the palest ones, she added it to the pile of gifts for Sarah.

On her way out of the crypt, beyond the candles' light, she waved at Topaz, polishing the stone floor. Topaz waved back, and then rose to follow Susannah outside, into the sunlight.

"Good to see you," Topaz said, when they stood outside the church. "I notice you left Sarah an offering."

"A scallop shell," Susannah said.

"That is very powerful," Topaz said. "*Coquille Saint Jacques* . . . it's the symbol of pilgrims en route to the shrine of Saint James de Compostela, in northern Spain. They pass through here, and it's said the *coquilles* on our beach are black, in honor of Sarah. She will be most pleased that you left one for her."

Susannah peered at her, shielding her eyes from the sun. "Would you like to have a coffee with me? There's something I'd like to ask you about."

"Of course."

Linking arms with Susannah, Topaz began to walk her down the street. They strolled through the market, past stalls bright and vivid with fragrant flowers and ripe fruit, with squawking chickens in cages and large brown eggs piled in woven baskets, with racks of cotton dresses blowing gently in the breeze. Susannah spotted other women from the Sarah Circle: Anaïs, Naguine, Isabel, and Rosalie. They stood together talking, whispering as they saw Topaz walk by with Susannah.

Topaz waved lightly, ignoring several pointed stares, leading Susannah onto the terrace of the *café tabac*. They squeezed past a tall revolving rack of postcards, into one of the tables right in front. A faded red awning shaded them from the sun, and they both ordered double espresso from the elderly waiter. Sitting on a stone wall across the way, a young man played flamenco guitar.

"How have you enjoyed your time since we saw each other last?" Topaz asked.

"It's been wonderful," Susannah said, unable to hide a huge smile.

"We enjoyed having you join us at the caravan," Topaz said.

"I really appreciate your introducing me to the Sarah Circle," Susannah said, watching through the market stalls for Rosalie and the others.

Topaz laughed. "Not everyone is sure what to make of you. A few attitudes have shifted a bit. . . . It wasn't very long ago that we Romanies claimed Sarah all for our own. There's a certain distrust of 'outsiders.' Especially those for whom Sarah has performed miracles."

"But you seem so welcoming," Susannah said.

"I am," Topaz said. "Because I'm not one hundred percent Gypsy. My great-grandfather, on my father's side, was Spanish. It's where I get my name, Avila. He was making the pilgrimage in reverse—*from* St. Jacques—when he passed through here and met my great-grandmother. There was quite a scandal. It's taken generations for my family to really be accepted."

"Why is it so bad for a Gypsy to marry a non-Gypsy?"

Topaz laughed. "That's a good question. Have you got the next six months to listen? Because that's how long it would take for me to tell you everything I've ever heard about it. Mainly, it is because we have such a rich tradition and lineage, and because we've suffered such persecution. We're proud, and our elders want to be sure our traditions continue."

"The elders would be unhappy to see a Gypsy marry someone from outside?"

"Not just the elders, and unhappy is putting it rather mildly." Topaz turned to look Susannah in the eye. "Is this what you wanted to ask me about?"

"Yes. Maria," Susannah said.

"Ah," Topaz said. "You've found out about our Maria."

"You mentioned her the other night . . . and Rosalie . . ."

"Rosalie is very protective of Maria," Topaz said. "They were as close as sisters."

The waiter brought the two *cafés* on a small tray, and Topaz immediately added three sugar cubes to hers. Susannah sipped the strong coffee, waiting for her to go on.

"Love is miraculous, don't you agree?" Topaz asked.

"I do," Susannah said quietly.

"Well, for the Manouche—our clan—it is mysterious, magical, and always romantic. But there are certain expectations. We marry men we know, friends of the family, brothers of our girlfriends. But along came Grey Dempsey, with his notepad and tape recorder, his fancy job as a reporter, talking of Paris and America, and Maria was swept up . . ."

Susannah listened, shocked by how painful it was to hear about Grey with another woman.

"And Maria—she could take the breath from any man. She was an exquisite beauty, with supernaturally dark eyes, and the most knowing gaze . . . she could tiptoe on the back of a horse, and the horse wouldn't even know she was there. Every Gypsy man from here to Budapest wanted her."

"But she wanted Grey . . ."

Topaz nodded. "Sometimes I think it was because it was so forbidden. Maria was always ready to take a dare."

"Did you go to their wedding?"

Topaz laughed. "No—no one did. They eloped."

"Was her family very upset?"

"Not by that," Topaz said. "The Manouche allow what's called 'runaway marriage'—the couple disappears for a day or two on their own, but then returns to feasting and celebration. There was no wedding party for Maria and Grey. They went to a judge in Arles—never telling a soul. She moved to Paris with Grey, cut off ties with all of us."

"Paris? But I thought . . ."

"The ranch came later. He had assignments from American and French magazines, and he was based in Paris. She tried to love the city, but she was horribly homesick."

"For Stes.-Maries?"

"For horses. Maria's job had always been to look after horses at her trainer's farm. That's where she'd learned to ride the way she did—truly, like an angel. Balancing on the toes of one foot, arms outstretched, a ballerina on horseback. She performed in all our festivals, from the time she could walk."

"So Grey left Paris and moved down here . . ."

"He loved horses almost as much as Maria. And I think he would have done anything to make her happy."

"Were you close to her?"

"In some ways, very," Topaz said. "I was always hopeful for her and Grey. My great-grandparents, you see. My family is proof that love doesn't always happen according to plan. In fact, I think the best kind doesn't!"

"What happened between them?"

Topaz shrugged. "They were up against such opposition.

Our elders were outraged and hurt. Plus, there was Maria herself."

"What do you mean?"

"She was . . . very special. High-strung. More talented on horseback than one would believe humanly possible. Her parents died young; she was raised by Zin-Zin, who is as close to a Gypsy queen as we have. Maria was the apple of her eye! Zin-Zin was devoted to her; I think it made Maria feel so special, she always had to be the star. . . . In fact, sometimes I think that's why she married Grey. She knew such a marriage would make her stand out. It would make everyone talk. But it turned out to be wrong from the start."

"In what way?"

"A thousand ways. Maria thought she wanted love and nurturing, but she found that life with a husband was completely constricting to her. She needed complete freedom to pursue her art."

"Art?"

"Oh, yes," Topaz said. "What Maria does on horseback is nothing less than great art. Arabesques, leaps, grande jetés . . . She needed to ride free at any hour, and to travel wherever she wanted, to train and perform."

"Is that what she's doing now?" Susannah asked. "Grey mentioned a circus."

"Yes," Topaz said simply.

"But what about Sari? How could she leave her?"

"Maria . . . is not like other people."

Susannah thought of her own mother; she could not imagine her leaving Susannah, for any reason. Nor could Susannah envision herself ever leaving a child; she pictured Sari, the hurt she'd seen in her eyes, and shook her head. "No," Susannah agreed. "She must not be."

"It's easy to judge Maria," Topaz agreed. "But you don't know her. She's truly not of this world. She's like a butterfly."

"What do you mean?"

"Maria floats like air. She appears so delicate, almost fragile. But when she rides—she's filled with as much tensile strength as the horse itself. It's magnificent. She becomes one with the horse. If you believe that we are all here for a reason, then to see Maria you would believe God put her here to dance on horseback."

"And meanwhile, Sari suffers."

Topaz just shook her head. Then, looking Susannah straight in the eye, said, "You've gotten very attached, haven't you?"

Susannah hesitated, then nodded.

"To both of them," Topaz said. It was a statement, not a question, and it made the blood rise into Susannah's face.

"Yes," Susannah said.

Topaz nodded. A small smile touched her lips. Rosalie and the others were still watching from across the way. Susannah saw Topaz meet Rosalie's gaze; was there a hint of tension there?

"Did you manage to get to the library the other day?" Topaz asked.

"In Arles?" Susannah asked, surprised that Topaz would remember she'd mentioned it. "Yes, I did."

"And your research went well?"

"Yes. Topaz, I know I said I'm not here to study you, or any of the other women, but I have to confess, my colleague—a professor I work with—has a strong interest in Saint Martha. In particular, she asked me to study the connection with Sarah, and the women who are devoted . . ."

"Like the Sarah Circle."

"Well, yes."

Susannah glanced over, expecting to see anger on Topaz's face, but instead she saw a large, bright smile.

"That pleases me," Topaz said. "The more studies that are done, the more people will come to see Sarah. Who am I to stop the faithful? You, who've already known a miracle in your life, should know that."

Susannah laughed and nodded, sipping her coffee.

"So, tell me, Susannah: did Grey find you?"

"Excuse me?"

"At the library—in Arles?"

"Yes, but how did—" And then Susannah realized. "You told him! He said that someone had told him I was going to Arles. Was it you?"

Topaz strove to make her face blank. She stared up at the medieval church, at the blue sky behind the dark fortifications. But there was a sparkle in her eye that gave everything away: she was a Romany, but she'd been born and bred by people who believed more in love than tradition. She was the keeper of Sarah's chapel, and Sarah had already proven to be a guardian angel for Susannah and her family.

"It was you, wasn't it?" Susannah pressed.

"Perhaps I had a hand in it."

"But why?"

Topaz just shook her head, refusing to say more. Susannah paid for the espressos, and Topaz thanked her. She had to get back to the chapel, to finish cleaning before evening devotion. She hurried away and Susannah watched her disappear into the church. She was still feeling grateful and mystified, when she noticed Rosalie still staring from across the market street.

Susannah reached into her pocket; she still had six scallop shells, given to her by Grey, and her hand closed around them now. They jingled fragilely in her fingers, and reminded her that she wasn't alone.

It was a new feeling. She looked up in the sky, at the sun shining in the bright blue, and she knew she could hardly stand waiting for night to fall, and to pass, and for dawn to come, when she would see him again.

TWELVE

Dawn began as a pink shimmer in the east, blazing into a line of orange fire along the horizon, turning the sea from black to blue. Susannah had never felt so excited; at the same time, she'd never felt so calm. This morning, everything felt right with the world.

A little while later she heard tires crunching the white gravel in the driveway, and she slung her bag over her shoulder and ran outside. Grey sat in the green Citroën, grinning through the windshield. Her heart jumped just to see him. Climbing into the car, she hesitated for just a second. He didn't; he leaned over to kiss her hello.

"Good morning," she said.

"Good morning," he said, not letting go.

She leaned into his body, thinking that they could scrap the trip and just go back inside. But then he eased away, shifted into reverse to back out of her driveway and head out of town.

"Are you ready for this?" she asked.

"I am," he said. "Been looking forward to it so much, I couldn't sleep last night."

"Neither could I," she said.

They drove north to the N568, headed east onto the A55, and within an hour they were caught in Marseille commuter traffic. They skirted the bright, colorful port city, driving through dry white hills and pine-shaded olive orchards. Just beyond Cap Croisette, they angled into the Calanques— spectacular white limestone cliffs scored with fjords and sapphire bays. The massif stretched twenty kilometers along the coast road to Cassis.

"I live an hour away and hardly ever come here," Grey said, driving along the steep belvedere. "When we go to the city, it's almost always Arles or Paris. I've been to Marseille, but never driven east of the port. This is incredible."

"That's how I felt when I first came here," Susannah said, so happy she could be the one to show it to him. She explained about how the Calanques had formed at the end of the last ice age. The glacier retreated, scraping the earth's crust, leaving this spine of white mountains along the fault line. Tiny villages nestled down below, at the edge of the sea, home to fishing families.

"Where are the caves?" he asked.

"Right there," she said, pointing at Cap Morgiou. The next headland jutted boldly into the Mediterranean, the vertical drop dramatic and straight down to the sea. Following the signs on the steep switchback road, Grey turned onto a narrow one-car road that plummeted over and down the sea cliff. Several heart-stopping minutes and hairpin turns later, they'd reached the end of the road. Parking in an unpaved lot, they made the rest of the trek on foot.

They scrambled down steps carved into the rock face. Susannah reached for Grey's hand, wanting to make sure he didn't fall; she'd been here several times, and she knew how treacherous this path could be. Glancing into his eyes, she saw he had a wide smile on his face.

"What is it?" she asked.

"You," he said.

"What do you mean?"

"You're being protective; it's nice. No one ever does that for me."

She smiled back, and thought of how much she liked doing it. "Everyone needs protecting now and then," she said.

Grey just laughed, holding her hand tighter. They emerged in the tiny village at the foot of the precipice, but even on solid ground they kept holding hands. Houses painted blue, ochre, and coral lined the narrow street. They stopped in front of a dive shop: *Caratini Services Plongées.*

Inside, she greeted the owners, Felix and Jeanine Caratini. It was a wonderful reunion, involving much hugging and kissing and a steady stream of rapid French. Susannah introduced Grey; they asked him a few questions, and he told them about learning to dive off Narragansett, producing his logbook and medical certificate. They were fascinated to hear about his dives on the sunken U-boat; Susannah listened, touched by how humbly he established himself as an expert diver.

The building's plaster walls were lined with photographs of the many divers who'd come through the door. Smiling faces, everyone dressed in wet suits and wearing air tanks—all except one person. Ian. The picture showed him standing beside Susannah, his arm around her; she looked ready to dive, in black neoprene, while he was wearing a blue button-down shirt and chinos.

"Monsieur Stewart," Jeanine said to Susannah, following her gaze as Grey stepped away to examine the tanks. "He is here, in town."

"You saw him?" Susannah asked.

"He arrived yesterday. He came here hoping to see you."

"I just spoke to him . . . How would he know I'd come to Cap Morgiou?" she asked, frowning. "I didn't even know myself . . ."

Jeanine beamed, giving Susannah a quick hug. "Because how could you resist? Staying in the South of France, so close, and not diving the Grotte Cosquer?"

"As hard as that would be to do, my real reason for coming was to show Grey . . . I want him to see the cave."

Jeanine nodded, and Susannah saw happiness in her eyes. They'd known each other for several years, and Jeanine had seen the dynamic unfold between Susannah and Ian. Susannah had always thought what a good couple the Caratinis made— how independent they each were, yet how supportive, running this business together. She had envied them, and she knew Jeanine wished Susannah could have that kind of connection with someone.

"Where is he now?" Susannah asked.

Jeanine shrugged. "That I don't know. He took a room in one of the guesthouses near the lighthouse."

"He's waiting for me?"

"Yes, I believe so," Jeanine said.

"Who is waiting?" Grey asked, walking over to meet Susannah as Jeanine turned to help some other customers.

"Ian. An old colleague."

"Your old team?" Grey asked, grinning.

"Yes," she said. "He didn't dive, though."

"Is he on this wall?" Grey asked, peering at the gallery of divers.

Susannah pointed at the photo, and watched Grey lean forward to see more closely.

"You were with him?" Grey asked. "I mean, more than just colleagues?"

"We met in grad school," Susannah said slowly. "There was

so much to like about him . . . he's smart, and he loves our subject, and we worked well together. We tried . . . well, we made a stab at trying . . . for something more."

"But it didn't work out?" Grey asked.

"No," she said, shaking her head.

Grey grabbed her hand. "I'm glad it didn't work out," he said. "For whatever reason. I'd like to hear about it, if you want to tell me."

"Our breakup was a long time coming," she said slowly. "It wasn't any one thing. But once my mother got really sick . . . once I knew things were really changing—well, it made me look at everything differently."

"And you knew?"

She nodded. "I knew I couldn't be with him."

Grey took her hand, and pulled her against him. She stood there holding him, feeling a closeness she'd never felt with Ian.

Just then Felix came toward them with armloads of dive gear. Grey hugged her harder, and then they went into dressing rooms to change, came out dressed in wet suits, carrying masks, fins, and air tanks.

While Jeanine stayed at the counter to mind the shop, Felix led Susannah and Grey down the dock to his boat—*Le Chat Bleu*. Grey gave her a hand, and she stepped over the rail. The boat was captained by a friend of the Caratinis, Jean Olivier. Grey helped Jean cast off, then sat beside Susannah on the fiberglass seat as Jean started up the engine and headed into the bay.

Grey and Susannah linked fingers, feeling the sea breeze in their faces. The sun beat down, making the black wet suits feel so warm. Susannah leaned into Grey's strong body, thinking about how rough and ready and sweet and tender their brief time together had been. The horseback ride, this chance to dive. She'd never had anything like it with Ian, or with anyone. She felt so much support, connection, and trust.

As the boat left the inner harbor, it gained speed, bouncing across the azure waves. Grey's arm slid around Susannah's shoulder, and he held her tight. And she grabbed his free hand, and held him right back.

The water was so clear, and Grey's breath sounded loud in his ears, and he swore he could feel both their hearts beating—his and Susannah's—as they breathed into their regulators and swam side by side, slowly down toward the sea bottom.

The undersea world felt peaceful and private, as if it belonged only to him and Susannah. She glanced over at him, through their bubbles, making sure he was okay. It touched and amused him, and he gave her a thumbs-up. No one ever looked at him like that. He was always the one taking care of business, running the ranch, caring for the horses, looking after Sari.

Diving took him back to his youth. He had learned over twenty-five years ago, long before he'd met Maria. The years melted away; the realm of the Camargue was a distant memory. He didn't feel like a kid—he hadn't lost his wisdom and battle scars—but the everyday realities of his life seemed to be dissolving with every breath he took, every meter they descended.

Brightly colored fish swam by, some covered with spines, exotic and unknown—the clear water was itself a revelation to someone who had learned to dive in murky New England waters. As they got closer to the sea bottom, Susannah pointed out bright, spiky orange coral, enormous langoustes, red starfish, and a green eel.

She'd told him that Ian wouldn't dive with her, and Grey almost felt sorry for him. Who would choose to miss an experience like this? Not just the exhilaration of diving, but also the intensity of going this deep underwater—going anywhere—with Susannah.

Grey swam close by her, feeling the ripple of her leg against his. She was slim and muscular, and the wet suit clung to every inch of her body. He had to remind himself to breathe steadily; that's what deep dives were all about. But she was making it a challenge.

As she gestured to him that they'd come to the mouth of the cave, he held back briefly to hold on to the moment. Up in the boat, she'd given him some background. The cave was a relatively recent, incredible find: in 1991, a professional diver, Henri Cosquer, swam into one of a hundred caverns honeycombed along this stretch of the sea bottom. At one time, before the last ice age, these caves had been several miles inland. Cosquer became the first human being in thousands of years to enter and see what was inside.

And now, because of Susannah, Grey was getting that chance. She switched on her light, and he followed. Holding on to a previously set line, she began to swim into the dark opening, Grey a few feet back behind her, his eyes getting accustomed to the blackness.

It had been a long, long time since Grey had felt anything like this. As a journalist, he'd known the thrill of making discoveries. For so many years now, he'd buried himself in the routine of his work, living the life of a rancher, catering to the tourist trade. He hadn't flexed his reporter muscles in over a decade, and right now his senses were on high alert.

The cave was completely dark; their flashlight beams provided the only illumination. Large fish darted back and forth, prompting Grey to swim closer to Susannah, wanting to keep them away from her. But she gave him a calm look through her mask; the sight of her eyes reassured him, and he kept swimming.

After a few more minutes they began to rise. Their progress was slow, in stages, taking time to decompress. Grey loved those moments—hovering in the dark with Susannah, holding hands and waiting for their blood to stabilize so they could continue their ascent. He felt light-headed, but not from nitrogen narcosis. He was intoxicated being next to Susannah.

When they reached the surface, they broke out into a rock-walled chamber. Susannah swam over to a ledge where semipermanent staging lights had been set up by other research teams. She climbed out and flipped the switch, and the cave was filled with light.

Sliding back into the water, she swam over to Grey. They slipped off their masks. He stared around at the limestone walls rising and arching overhead, his heart hammering, his arm around her. She began pointing upward, and it took him a few moments to be able to focus on what she was seeing. But once he saw, he was awed.

"Paintings," he said. "They're everywhere."

"Yes," she said. "Over a hundred and fifty different animals are depicted."

She led him around, showing him images of horses, bulls, ibis, flamingos . . . the many species he lived beside every day, in the Parc Régional de Camargue. Then there were other, less familiar animals: mammoths, chamois, ibex, bear, even penguins. There were seals, auks, and jellyfish. The paintings were done in warm, beautiful earth tones. Some of the animals were marked with zigzags and squares. Others were pierced by spears.

The cavern was large, shaped approximately like a butterfly. She guided him through the different areas: the North Chamber, the Feline Chamber, the section nicknamed "the Beach." They swam under an arch, through a narrow passage, past the rock face anthropologists called "Chaos."

"Who did these?" he asked, gazing with amazement at the incredible images all around them.

"No one knows, exactly, but we think they were travelers," Susannah said. "We've found similar work in the Ardèche, as well as Valencia and Parpello, in Spain."

"The same artists?"

"That's my theory," she said. "I published a paper about it three years ago. We found evidence of charcoal—they built fires, and used flints. The animal paintings date back nearly nineteen thousand years. But see these?" She led him, swimming slowly, over to the large flooded shaft by the east wall, where he saw eerie images of human hands.

"You told me about these," he said, remembering when she'd first mentioned the cave.

"Hand stencils," she said. "These were done about twenty-seven thousand years ago. They're very distinctive—see how some of the fingers look incomplete?"

"Deformed, almost," he said, noticing the short, crooked digits.

"Maybe," she said. "Or perhaps the artists curled them under. It's very unusual, but I've seen the same patterns in Spain and the Ardèche . . . I found other hand stencils near Istanbul, but in those instances, the hands were more normal looking."

"What were the artists trying to communicate?" Grey asked, starting to think like a journalist for the first time in more years than he wanted to contemplate. His mind was racing, noticing how most of the hand tracings were black, with just a few done in red. Several had been scored with flints, others painted over with dots, bars, and the same zigzags he'd seen in the animal paintings.

"You already know," she said, smiling. "You told me, when we were sitting on the beach. You said they were telling us they were here."

"Making their mark?" Grey said, turning to face her.

She nodded. Their faces were inches apart. He felt her legs brushing against his, moving in rhythm, treading water. She laced her fingers with his, and he started to swim with her over to the cave wall. He scanned the surface, looking at all the hand stencils, the marks of so many who'd been there before them. Holding her hand against the rock, he gently traced her fingers with his, as he had done on the beach.

Leaning down, he kissed her. Her mouth tasted like salt, and her skin, pressing against his through two layers of neoprene, felt burning hot. He thought of their voices, still ringing in the air, and felt the reverberations in his body.

He was shaking, wanting to hold on to her forever. She pressed against him, pulling back, her eyes open wide.

At first he thought she felt shocked by the intensity of the kiss, maybe even upset. Her eyes drank him in, as if searching for an explanation. But then she cupped the back of his head in her hand, softly kissed him again, their eyes still open, as if they couldn't bear to let go or look away. They floated together, unanchored in the ancient space, as though they were suspended in time.

Finally, they broke apart. They had a long swim back, and then they'd have to decompress. They took a last look around the chamber, at the etched and painted animals and sea creatures, at the hand stencils, at the vaulted rock ceiling. Susannah extinguished the light, and Grey switched on the flashlights.

They kissed once more in the dim light, then plunged into the black water. Swimming through the underwater part of the cavern, Grey felt a blanket of darkness enclose them. They were under the sea, and that made him feel safe. No one could get to them here. No one from her college, no one from his ranch, not her one-time partner, not even, as much as he adored her, Sari. He and Susannah were moving through the underwater darkness together, and he didn't want to go up to the surface for air.

THIRTEEN

There is nothing quite like diving into a secret cave with a man with whom you're falling deeply in love. To leave the brightness of a sunny day, sift downward through the clear, clean water, and enter a new world. To swim together, holding his life in your hands, taking him into a narrow rock tunnel, deep into the earth, showing him things so few people have seen, art created in times before history.

Maybe that was the part that made it all so charged: the fact the paintings were so ancient. The hand stencils had lasted twenty-seven thousand years, in spite of the salt and damp and the fall and rise of the sea. To be swimming together, holding on to each other, bodies hot and soaking wet, legs entwined treading water, kissing under a canopy of art created millennia ago, was overwhelming.

It was primal, and intense, and beautiful, and reckless, and made them realize they were part of something huge and ever-lasting.

If only that could be true, Susannah thought. Twenty min-utes after Jean had driven them back, after they had changed into their clothes and finished up at the dive shop, she sat be-side Grey on the terrace of a small café overlooking the bay of Cap Morgiou. She tossed her hair, letting it dry in the late-af-ternoon sun; glancing over at him, she saw him peering across the cerulean water and wished that her time in France would never end, that it could last forever.

The waiter brought over a bottle of Côtes de Provence rosé, two glasses, and a small dish of niçoise olives. Grey asked if she liked shellfish, then ordered a *plateau de fruits de mer.* Lifting his glass, he looked over at her.

"To Henri Cosquer," he said. "If he hadn't discovered that cave, I never would have gotten to see it with you."

"Here's to you, Henri," Susannah said, laughing as they clinked glasses.

The Bandol tasted delicious and dry, magical in the sea air. It quenched Susannah's thirst, made her feel as if her holiday were just beginning. The olives looked glossy in the sun, shades of green, black, and lavender; they were too pretty to eat. Grey pulled out a pen, and started tracing her hand on the table's brown paper cover. Then she did the same to his.

The *plateau* came: oysters, mussels, some periwinkles, and sea urchins arranged on seaweed. Susannah had eaten at this café before, but the food had never tasted so wonderful. She watched Grey pick up a sea urchin, spines down in his palm, maneuver the brown stuff aside with a small spoon, and find the strips of coral inside. He fed them to her, and Susannah felt as if she were tasting the inside of the sea cave.

She caught his wrist midway through the second bite, and kissed it.

"What's that for?" he asked.

"Everything," she said.

"You're the one who gave me this day," he said. "Every single minute of it has been . . . I don't even have the words."

"It's been great," she said. "The best day I've ever had."

"I was thinking something along those lines," he said. "Do you think we can have another one just like it?"

She laughed. "Well, you're a dive expert. You know we can't dive two days in a row, and it's getting awfully close to the time I have to leave."

"Don't talk about that," he said.

"I won't," she said.

"We can't dive again, so we'll have to do something else. Something almost as wonderful."

"Like what?" she asked, thinking that an hour with him anywhere would be incredible.

"The moonlight ride," he said. "The night after tomorrow."

"At the ranch?" she asked.

He nodded. His eyes were bright, but she saw a familiar weariness settle over his face, as if even the mention of his ranch reminded him of his real life. She slipped her hand into his, to remind him that they didn't have to go home yet—that the afternoon wasn't over, they were still right here, on this sunlit terrace, surrounded by pots of beautiful flowers, the sea just beyond, the endless crystalline sky arching above.

"I'd love to," she said. "Nothing would make me happier."

He smiled. She thought of one thing: staying with him would make her happier. She wished they were on a real vacation, here in this little town, in a guesthouse overlooking the harbor. She laughed, wanting to tell him what she was thinking, when she saw his expression change.

"Here he comes," Grey said.

"Henri Cosquer?" she teased. "Or Felix or Jean?" Who else could it possibly be, who else would Grey know of here?

"I recognize him from his picture," Grey said.

Ian. Susannah knew even before she turned around. Her stomach tightened as his shadow fell across the table, and she looked up into the familiar brown eyes. He was dressed the way he always was: as if he were about to go into the class-room, not scramble around out in the field. Blue shirt, khakis, brown loafers.

"I heard you were going to be here," he said. No hello, no introducing himself to Grey.

"Well, here I am," she said. "Grey, this is Ian Stewart. Ian, Grey Dempsey."

The men shook hands. Ian gave Grey a long, suspicious look, and Grey managed to keep his face passive.

"You missed a hell of a party back in Connecticut," Ian said.

"You mentioned that," Susannah said.

"Well, at least you're here now," he said. Susannah stared at him. Was he not realizing that she was with Grey?

"Let's not do this now," she said.

"I'd like to talk to you in private," he said, gesturing at Grey.

"There's nothing to say," Susannah said, pushing her chair back and standing up to face him.

"You're running out again?" Ian asked sharply, grabbing her arm.

"Hey." Grey jumped up, pulling Ian's hand from Susannah's wrist.

"I'm not running out," Susannah said, wanting to calm everyone, easing Grey back down. "I just . . ."

"Yes, you are," Ian said. "That's what you do—run away."

"Ian . . ."

"From the people who care about you most. Me, all your friends waiting at your party."

"This is ridiculous," Susannah said. "Stop it, now."

She sat down again, glancing at Grey. Assured that she wanted to stay, he pulled his chair closer to hers, sitting beside her. Ian remained standing, staring down.

"You let your friends down," he said. "Running out on them."

"They don't think that about me," Susannah said. "I don't do that."

"No?" Ian said. "Just ask your mother."

Susannah gasped audibly; she felt her hands cover her mouth.

"Listen to me, Susannah," Ian said, reaching for her hand. "Why do you think I came here? I knew you'd be here. I know *you*. No one knows you better than I do. We go back a long way; I've sat at your mother's bedside, haven't I?"

Susannah's eyes filled with tears. It was true. Ian had met her mother, had spent hours at her house in Black Hall, had eaten meals with her, had shared stories of many trips, and projects, and papers. "That's what makes it so terrible," Susannah said. "You *did* know my mother. She was kind to you. But she wouldn't like what you just said to me."

"But you *weren't* there," Ian went on. "When she died. You're not there when it counts, Susannah. For your mother, for me . . ."

Grey pushed his chair back. It was cast iron, one of those pretty chairs that every sidewalk café in France seems to have, and the legs scraping on the concrete made a harsh sound. Susannah saw the fire in his blue eyes, and she put her hand out to stop him, but it was too late. Grey grabbed the front of Ian's shirt, pushed him across the sidewalk, right to the water's edge. There was a six-foot drop from the walkway to the harbor, and Grey stood there with Ian leaning out.

"Take it back," Grey said.

"What are you, twelve years old?" Ian asked, his voice sounding strangled. "Let go of me."

"Take it back," Grey said, perfectly calm. "Unless you want to go swimming."

"How perfect—she studies prehistoric art, and she's found herself a Neanderthal. I'll have you arrested," Ian said.

"He means it," Susannah said, grabbing Grey's arm. She remembered the trouble Ian had stirred up on sites, where he wanted local personnel off the job and his own people on. He knew how to manipulate situations, to involve the authorities. And she saw clearly, with no further room for denial, precisely how vindictive and small-spirited he was. "Please, Grey . . ."

Grey stared at him. Susannah could feel the energy, barely restrained, pouring off him. She stood there, knowing she should defuse the situation, make Grey stop, let Ian go. But Ian's words rang in her ears with others she had listened to for so long, and he looked so smug and superior, as if he believed Grey would never do it; she couldn't speak or act.

"Are you sorry for being rotten to Susannah?" Grey asked.

Ian managed to laugh. "What I said wasn't rotten. What she does, running off on the people who care about her, *that's—*"

Grey let go of Ian's shirt, and Ian fell into the harbor. Susannah looked down, watching Ian splash around. Grey gave her a long, serious look. "He was about to say you were rotten," Grey said.

"I know," Susannah replied, as people from the café came to stand along the seawall, watching Ian swim to the small curved beach by the boat launch.

"He shouldn't have said what he said about your mother."

"No, he shouldn't have," Susannah said.

Grey watched Ian stroke to shore. "Should we help him out?"

"I think he can take care of himself," Susannah said.

"Then should we leave?"

"Yes." Susannah nodded. "We should."

By the time they climbed back up to the parking area, the sun had started to set. It cast bright orange light across the white limestone cliffs, setting them afire. Susannah's heart was throbbing.

"Are you okay?" Grey asked, once they'd gotten into the car.

"I think so. Are you?"

He nodded. "What a jerk that guy was. He's a professor somewhere?"

"Stanford."

"That's hard to believe. A small-minded idiot like that. Are you sure you're all right?"

"I am, Grey," she said. She glanced over, saw him staring down the hill at the harbor, at the placid scene. She scanned the wharf, almost expecting to see police. But Ian wouldn't have called anyone, she realized; he'd be too embarrassed.

"I can't see you with him," Grey said quietly. "Not at all."

"I wasn't, really," she said.

"He was wrong about you," Grey said. "He's wrong, and he's a liar to say what he said."

"How do you know?"

"Because I know how much you care. I've seen it with Sari. I know you would have been the same with your mother . . ."

"I was," she said. Her voice broke, and her eyes filled with tears. She remembered what Zin-Zin had told her. "My mother had a journey to make, and I couldn't go with her."

Grey nodded, taking her hand. Susannah closed her eyes, wondering how she could have come so far—forgiving herself, and finding a way back to her mother—among people she had known for so brief a time.

"I feel as if you know me better than Ian ever did," she said.

He smiled, and his eyes bored into hers. "So do I," he said.

Susannah stared out the windshield as Grey drove carefully up the narrow mountain road. There were sheer drops off to the right, straight down to the sea. She trusted him completely, to get them up the hill safely. When he got to the top, he drove a few miles, then stopped at a turnoff overlooking the entire expanse of sea and sky.

They sat there in silence, but the car was full of electricity. Susannah's mind raced—with everything that had just happened, and the ticking clock that hung over them.

"There was a woman," he said after a few minutes. "She wasn't . . . we weren't serious at all, but we saw each other casually for a couple of months."

"After Maria, you mean?"

He nodded. "Yes. It was nice to have company, someone to have dinner with once in a while . . ."

"You don't have to tell me," Susannah said, shocked by how much she didn't want to hear about Grey and another woman.

"Sari couldn't deal with it," he said. "I tried it both ways—being honest and open with her about the fact I was going out to dinner, then lying straight out, telling her I was going to a farm auction near Nîmes. Didn't matter—she picked up on the truth, fell apart."

"Fell apart?"

Grey nodded. "Yeah. Big time. Nightmares, crying, stopped eating. It scared the hell out of me."

"Why is it so bad for her?"

"She's so insecure," he said. "It's out of control. I know that. But she lost her mother in such a terrible way . . ."

"And she's afraid she'll lose you, too."

Susannah reached for his hand, wanting to comfort him. She stared into his eyes, wondering if he felt the same despair she did, about their situation.

"I'm sitting here," he said, stroking her hand, "never wanting to let you go . . ."

"I feel that way, too," she said.

"It's crazy, I know that," he said. "You just got here. We just met. You're supposed to go back to the States . . . and I can't stand it."

She stared into his face as he reached over, brushed the hair back from her eyes.

"I swear," he said, "I think she's just starting to make real progress—a lot of it thanks to you. But if you had seen what it was like—I don't want to push her . . . don't know what I can do . . ."

"Grey, I know. But I'd be lying if I said I didn't wish there were some way," she said.

"We're going to drive home tonight," he said, "and I'll already be missing you. From the minute we start back, I'll know it's just a matter of time."

"I can't be apart from you," she whispered.

He grabbed her, pulled her toward him, kissed her hard. They were desperate to be together, not even an inch of space between them; he held her on his lap, stroking her hair, holding her tightly. A cool breeze blew through the open window, making them shiver. She pressed closer against him, kissing his lips. When they stopped, they looked into each other's eyes, as they had in the cave.

"Susannah," he said, as she eased herself away, back into her seat.

"I want this to last forever," she said, thinking of Sari. "But I know we should go back . . ."

He stared out over the sea. "I keep thinking, what if you just didn't leave? What if you did your work from here . . . what if you stayed?"

"For a few more days?" she asked.

"No," he said. "Just as you said: forever."

His words rang in the small car, just as their words had hung in the cavern, echoing above the water and against the ancient animal carvings and hand prints, stenciled into the rock walls.

There in the sea cave, Susannah had felt as if love could last forever, as if the feelings she had for Grey were as eternal as the limestone, the cavern, the sea itself.

He shifted into drive, then reached across the seat to clasp her hand. She felt him interlock fingers with her, strong and steady. The car cleared the summit, and they headed west, into the twilight, away from eternity and into reality. The encounter with Ian had brought them back into the real world very fast—and Susannah shut her mind against him. She held Grey's hand, closed her eyes as she felt his fingers holding hers, and pretended they were still in the sea's warm embrace.

FOURTEEN

*Susannah and Grey had kissed goodnight at her door, linger-*ing as long as they could, and she'd watched him drive away. She moved in a daze. Her mind kept drifting back over the day, to the way he'd held her in the water, traced her hand on the cave walls. She walked into the bathroom, splashed cool water on her face. She knew she should take a bath, but she didn't want to yet; she couldn't bear to wash the salt and Grey's touch from her body.

Parked at that overlook, gazing over the Mediterranean, she had known: everything would change the minute they started back. And it was true. With every kilometer, she'd felt them returning to their lives, back to reality, away from the place they'd somehow made in their brief time together.

Staring at her own reflection in the mirror now, she felt as if she were waking from the most incredible dream. She wanted to hold on to every feeling, every detail, and never forget any of it. She would have given anything to be able to trade her real life for the dream, but she knew that wasn't how it worked.

Things fade away. Today was already passing into memory. Maybe she could hold on to it a little longer, when what she really wanted to hold on to was Grey. She leaned on the sink, looking into her own eyes in the mirror. She barely recognized herself. She was a woman in love.

She felt thirsty, from the dive and the sun. She filled a tall glass with water and went out to sit by the pool. Somewhere down the street, a stray cat meowed. It sounded so yearning and so alone. Susannah walked over to the fence, peered into the darkness. She saw the yellow cat stalking along the alley behind her yard, crying and searching. She stared, watching it poke in and out of corners and doorways, until it stopped right in the middle of the cobblestone way.

The cat locked eyes with Susannah. It stared without fear, and Susannah reached out her hand. It held her gaze a moment longer, then darted away, continuing its search. Craning her neck, Susannah saw it disappear toward the waterfront. Even when it was out of sight, the plaintive meowing continued, reminding Susannah of her own deep longing.

Exhausted, she crawled into bed. She didn't want the day to end, but she also wanted Sunday to get here more quickly. It was a conundrum, and she was too tired to figure anything out. Lying still, images of the day filled her mind. She saw Ian, heard him telling her she ran out on people—ran out on her mother. The words were terrible, but they didn't have any power. Being here in Stes.-Maries had brought Margaret Connolly back to her. And being with Grey had made her realize she wanted love, wanted it down to her bones and into her soul.

The next day, she woke up early. Sunlight streamed through the window; she closed her eyes against it, holding on to sleep and her dreams as long as she could. Fragments filled her mind: kissing Grey, the feeling of his arms around her, the cave's shimmering blue light, the intensity of emotion between them. But she couldn't stay in bed forever. . . .

After her morning coffee, she did what she always did to get herself grounded: pulled out her work. Her briefcase was filled with file folders about the sites she'd been working on most recently, so she opened the one for Cosquer Cave, to add to her notes from previous dives there.

She always left a blank section, at the bottom of every page, for new observations. It was her experience that, no matter how many times she revisited a cave, there was always something new to see, brand new discoveries to be made. It might be an image obscured by dirt, filmed by time, it could be markings that hadn't been visible before—either because of lighting, or because Susannah had been distracted by larger, more apparently significant drawings.

This time, almost her whole attention had been on Grey. Seeing his excitement and reactions, gazing up at the prehistoric art all around them, had made her feel as if she'd just bestowed the best gift she could ever give someone. He was a world-class appreciator, and his joy in discovery had been a gift right back to her.

She'd stared at him as he examined the hand stencils, noticing everything. She'd seen his intellect—so apparent in the sharpness of his gaze, the intensity of his focus. She'd sensed him wanting to record his own observations, trying to commit it all to memory. It was exciting to work alongside a person like that, who could become completely engaged by something so esoteric and obscure.

He had seemed to know that her own fascination lay with the hand stencils instead of the more beautiful, dramatic, accessible animal paintings. He had immediately understood, even without her telling him, that the artists had needed to leave their mark, that human beings needed to know they mattered. She'd been immeasurably moved by the way he'd held her hand, pressed it to the rock wall, outlined it with his own fingers. He'd made them part of the history of the cave. . . .

So as she sat there at the desk in her rented house, surrounded by documents, by work papers, and by copies of her published work on the Cosquer Cave, all she could do was close her eyes and picture Grey. She wanted to hold on to every single moment; when she returned to Connecticut, she wanted the memory to be as distinct as it still was right now. She wanted to be able to feel the friction of his leg against hers, the way it had felt treading water together, the sublime luxury of kissing instead of studying the Paleolithic art in the undersea cave all around them.

By the end of the day, she needed a break from her papers. She walked into town, had dinner at a bistro along the harbor. Sipping a glass of rosé, she felt memories of the night before overtaking her. If she closed her eyes, Grey would be right across the table from her.

After dinner, she wandered through the town. She felt like the yellow cat, edgy with yearning. Every street made her wonder whether he'd walked along it; had he come here with Maria? Had they ever pushed Sari in her stroller along the quay? She realized she didn't like thinking of him with Maria any more than he'd liked seeing her with Ian.

Finally, she realized she was too restless to go on. If she went home, maybe he would call. What were he and Sari doing? She wished she could be with them, too; she had felt her own strong connection with the girl—when they had first met, and during their ride together.

Susannah wished things were different, so she could be more a part of their lives . . . and that made her think that maybe she could. Maybe the trail ride tomorrow would bring her and Sari closer together, let Sari begin to trust someone other than her father, and Laurent.

After half an hour back home, with the phone stubbornly

silent, the swimming pool called to her. That's what she'd do: take a swim, burn off some energy. She stretched, heading into the bedroom to change, when she heard a knock at the door. Thinking it must be Topaz, she pulled it open without even checking. Grey stood there on the top step, holding a book.

She stared at him, speechless.

"I know I should have called first," he said, giving her a wicked smile.

"Really?" she asked, stepping into his arms. "You think you should have called first?"

"It would have been the polite thing to do," he said, kissing the side of her neck, sending chills all through her body.

"Polite is overrated," she said, standing on tiptoes, lips against his collarbone, wanting to do the same to him.

"I'm glad you feel that way," he said. "Because here I am." He kissed her, long and hard, arms around her back. Something sharp pressed into her spine, and even though she wanted the kiss to go on forever, she pulled back.

"What's that?" she asked.

"My excuse for coming over."

"I thought we were past needing excuses." She smiled, and took the tattered red leather-bound volume he held out to her. "What is it?"

"It's an old book I found in Paris. At one of those stalls along the Seine . . ."

"I know them well," she said. On many of her past research trips to France, she'd based herself in Paris and spent hours browsing through the used books, maps, posters, and postcards of the *bookinistes*, the secondhand booksellers whose stalls ran along the river.

"You showed me something of your work," he said. "And I wanted to show you something of mine."

"You wrote this book?" she asked skeptically. "It looks a hundred years old."

"No," he said, laughing. "This is a biography of Django Reinhardt. There's a lot of material about Stes.-Maries, and the caravans. The writer spent time with Django himself, and really got into his early life. Lots of time spent here in the Camargue. I used the bio as background when I wrote these . . ." Tucked into the book was a sheaf of articles, published in *Harper's* and *The Atlantic;* she glanced at them, saw his byline, felt her heart turn over.

"Oh, Grey, thank you," she said, glancing through the pages. "I can't wait to read them."

"Being with you yesterday . . ." he said, trailing off. Then he looked her straight in the eye. "It really set me on fire."

"I know," she said.

"I want to research and write again. I think I told you—I wrote a series of articles about Gypsies and music. Now . . ."

"Now you're going to write a series about sea caves?"

He laughed, stepped closer, holding her again. "Yes," he said. "And other adventures. Riding through the marsh with a beautiful woman."

Susannah smiled, to hear him say that. "Helping her escape from wild bulls, you mean?"

He shook his head. "It's pretty clear that you can take care of yourself." He kissed her, his eyes open, then pulled gently away. "I saw the way you were with Ian. You took care of it really well."

"Actually, you did," Susannah said.

"Yeah," he said, holding her. "I got carried away. But he was asking for it. I couldn't let him speak to you that way."

"I don't want it to get to me, the way he sees me," Susannah said. "But it does . . . especially when he talks about my mother."

"Don't listen to him anymore," Grey said. "You've got to realize something . . ."

"What?"

Grey stared at her long and hard. "He knows he's lost you."

"He does?"

"Yeah."

"Because he saw us together . . ."

"Partly," Grey said. "But not only that. Guys know. They can feel when it starts to happen."

"When what does?"

"When love is over."

"If it was ever there," Susannah murmured, speaking of herself and Ian, wondering whether Grey was thinking of himself and Maria.

"You don't love him?" Grey asked, staring hard into her eyes. "You never did?"

"Not like this," she whispered. He pulled her toward him roughly, kissing her until she lost herself, until the ground tilted and she felt she was swimming in the sea.

After a few minutes, they stopped and stood there looking at each other, as if unsure what to do next. The air felt charged, and Susannah's skin tingled. "Would you like something to drink?" she asked slowly.

"Yeah," he said. "I would. But . . ."

She saw him glance at the clock.

"You have to get home?"

He nodded. "Sari was studying with Laurent, so I saw my chance to drive down here. I made an excuse . . ."

"The book?"

"Yes. She knows you went to the Cheval Blanc for work, and I let her think this was absolutely essential to your research. I lied to my daughter."

"You said you've done that before . . ." she said, thinking of what he'd told her about the woman he'd dated.

"I know. She's at Laurent's, working on a project. I didn't get the whole story, but it involved a field trip. I thought they were going to the library, but while you and I were in Marseille yesterday, Laurent took Sari to Avignon."

"That sounds wonderful for her; for both of them."

Grey nodded. "Laurent's a really good kid. He's very patient with her."

"Maybe that's because he loves her," Susannah said. She watched him, not sure how he'd take a statement like that about his daughter. He didn't reply, but just stood very still, staring at Susannah with deep thoughtfulness. After a minute, she said, "Young love, you know?"

"Young love is nothing," he said. "Compared with what can come once you know who you are."

"Do you think?"

He nodded slowly. It was dark outside. Susannah wanted him to stay on and on. She clasped his hand, led him toward the back door. The rising moon spilled white light into the small yard. She turned on the pool light, making the water glow like a blue jewel.

"Last time you turned on the lights, you lit up a whole cavern," Grey said.

"I have the power," she said, joking.

"Well, I'll try to light up the marsh for you tomorrow night," he said, gesturing toward the east, where the moon was rising. "It's almost full."

"I don't want tomorrow to come," she said, sliding her arms around his neck. "Because it's one day closer to the time I have to leave."

"Susannah," he said, pressing his forehead against hers, staring into her eyes.

"Grey," she said back.

He kissed her under the almost-full moon. The swimming pool's blue light reflected up, shimmering against the house's white plaster wall. It was no sea cave, but Susannah held Grey in her arms and made the most of it.

Sari sat across the kitchen table from Laurent as they worked on their homework together after dinner. For the first time in almost as long as she could remember, Sari was excited about something to do with school.

"Would you like a *tisane*?" Anne, Laurent's mother asked.

"Non, merci," Sari said. Anne smiled, poured hot water into the cups, making herbal tea for her and Claude.

"We're fine, Maman," Laurent said.

"You both seem very busy, writing so industriously . . ."

"Yes, working on our assignment," Laurent said.

"It must be quite ambitious, considering you didn't return from Avignon until so late last night."

"That was my fault," Sari said quickly, not wanting Laurent to get in trouble. "I was having so much fun, I made us miss the bus. We had to wait a whole hour to get the next one!"

"Sari, I'm just happy you both got home safely, and that you're so inspired by your project." Anne kissed the top of her head, then Laurent's, leaving them to their schoolwork. Sari had been writing nonstop, but she paused, gazing across the table at Laurent. She felt happy with her essay, and it was all because of him.

Usually she felt so left out. Not that she didn't have friends, or that the other kids weren't nice to her; it was more that she knew she was different. She didn't have a mother. She was half Gypsy, and sometimes that made her wonder which half of her was most real: the dark-skinned Romany half or the pale New England half. Her father loved her, no matter which she was, so she didn't worry too much about that part of things.

The real reason she felt left out was because the way she saw the world was poles apart from how others did. She was existing in a black-and-white movie while everyone else was living in bright color. It affected the way she learned; her teachers' lessons never really came alive to her. Descriptions of the court at Versailles, of the French Revolution, Madame de Sévigné in

the Midi, of the bloody doings at the Conciergerie, just felt flat
to Sari.

Until yesterday.

Their assignment was to write an essay about a place. It
could be anywhere in the world; the only requirement was
that the writer had actually visited it. Local, far away, it
didn't matter as long as it was real, and as long as the student
had been there. Laurent had said they were going to write at
the library, but Sari didn't want to go.

"What do I care about this?" Sari had asked. "All places
look alike to me. Gray, gray, gray."

"Pauvre p'tite," Laurent said, without a trace of sympathy
in his voice.

"You try being colorblind!" she said. "It's not fun, I promise
you."

Laurent had given her a long, even gaze. She instantly felt
remorseful; she knew that he, more than anyone, felt bad for
her, wanted her to be all right again. Sari was being difficult,
partly because she knew her father was going out of town.
He'd told her he had an errand to do in Marseille. And even
though that was just a hundred kilometers away, Sari felt nervous.

"You're in a bad mood," Laurent had said.

"No," she'd said. "I'm not."

"It's because your father has things to do, isn't it?"

"You make me feel like a baby when you say that," Sari had
said.

"He needs to have his life, too," Laurent had said gently.
"You should learn to let him."

Sari's eyes had filled with tears. She'd felt slapped. What a
terrible thing to say, that Sari didn't let her father have his
own life! She suddenly felt like a snail without its shell; everything hurt, and she felt as if Laurent, her best and oldest
friend, was prodding her with a stick.

"Sari," he'd said, just standing there, not backing away, not apologizing. "I have a plan for us."

"I don't want to go to the library, I don't want to do *anything*," she'd whispered. "I don't feel very good."

"It's for the assignment . . . for the essay."

"I've been plenty of places," she'd said stubbornly, wiping tears. "I'll write about one of them."

"No," he'd said firmly, matching her stubbornness. "We're going to go somewhere new—forget the library. And we'll be evenly matched. We'll see the place exactly the same way."

"Except you'll see it in color," she'd said, unable to stop herself.

"No," he'd said. "I won't."

And he'd meant it. After school, instead of going to the library, they'd taken the bus into Avignon. It was a very long ride, and Sari felt worried that her father would be upset with her for going. Laurent assured her that he'd cleared it with her father and his parents. That had reassured her somewhat, but it still seemed very out of the ordinary, and she'd wondered what he had in mind.

By the time they reached their destination, the sun was almost down. Avignon was a medieval city, surrounded by a crenellated wall. Getting off the bus, Sari thought it looked like a fairy-tale village, haunted and magical, with towers and castles, with Gothic slits for weapons in the walls, with the long, low fourteenth-century bridge, celebrated in the children's song, crossing the dark and mysterious Rhône River.

Laurent and she walked along the river. He teased her about the Tarasque hiding under the bridge, and she teased him back. The streets were paved with cobblestones, rounded and glinting in the twilight.

House windows glowed from within; iron grillwork looked glossy black, and the streetlamps threw long shadows onto the sidewalks and streets. Some of the busiest thoroughfares, still paved with cobblestones, had been paved over with asphalt. The ancient stones peered through, tarnished silver underneath worn blacktop.

They walked down some of the narrowest streets, lined with old wooden houses, tilting with age, paint peeling, reminiscent of etchings and woodcuts Sari had seen in museums, black-and-white or sepia-toned. Laurent walked her down a crooked cobblestone alleyway, and they emerged on a wide street, sparkling with shards of broken glass, overlooking the Rhône River.

The rising almost-full moon played on the water's smooth surface, illuminated the city's Gothic towers; they stood out in sharp silhouette against the moon's whiteness. Laurent steered Sari toward the Palais des Papes, built in 1335 by Pope Benedict XII; she stood there gazing up at the half fortress, half castle, listening to Laurent read passages from their schoolbook.

"Here's what Petrarch said about the Pope's Palace," he said. "*Écoute:* 'The houses of the apostles crumble as popes raise up their palaces of massy gold.'"

"Gold," she said. "Funny, because it looks silver in this light."

"Yes, it does," Laurent said. "Doesn't it?"

She nodded, gazing up at the castle; it was beautiful and mysterious. Darkness cloaked the city, and the moon had bleached every last spot of color away. Every brick, stone, tile, and window was edged with foil.

The whole night looked metallic, without any color at all. She glanced around. The light and dark contrasts were so vivid that she knew that even if, during daylight, this was the most brightly colored city in the world, right now anyone would see it as a cityscape of black, white, cream, charcoal, and silver. And then Sari got it. She drew in a sharp breath, turning to Laurent.

"You did this, didn't you?" she asked.

"Did what?" he asked.

"You brought me here because you knew Avignon would be black and white."

"Not always, but it is tonight," he said.

"How did you think of this?" she whispered.

"I wanted to see like you see," he said. "I can't stand thinking of you trapped in the dark, Sari. Missing all the beautiful colors that the rest of us don't even think about. When we got the assignment to write about a place, I didn't want to do it."

"Why not?"

"Because my places, anywhere I could think of, were all so bright. I thought about how it was for you, how different the world looks to you, and I knew—I had to make it the same for both of us."

"And you did," she said. "You made it beautiful for me."

"The moon helped," he said.

They walked under the plane trees of the Place de l'Horloge, around the massive clock tower, past all the brasseries and *bistrots*. They caught sight of their own reflection in a shop window; the light was dim here, and their faces looked back at them like two strangers. Sari reached out, touched the window's dusty surface with her fingertips, brushed the reflection of Laurent's face.

Past iron grates and steel fences, past shuttered shops and lonely alleys, they headed down to the river. Sari watched the moonlight glitter on the surface. She thought of the toy dragon Susannah had given her, wondered whether she would ever see it as bright green with red eyes, or whether it would always look gray.

"What are you thinking?" Laurent asked.

"About the toy dragon," Sari said.

"The one Susannah gave you?"

Sari nodded. She felt torn inside, liking Susannah, but feeling nervous about her. What did it mean that her father liked her so much? He did; Sari could tell. He'd told Sari he was going to Marseille on business, but she had the feeling it had something to do with Susannah.

"She's coming to the ranch tomorrow, isn't she?" Sari asked.

"I think so," Laurent said. "For the trail ride."

"I'm glad," Sari said, surprising herself.

"You really like her, don't you?" Laurent asked.

"I do," Sari said. She thought about it; she liked Susannah for being so kind, and for not pushing her, and for talking to her about dragons, and just because of the way she was. But that didn't automatically make everything easy. "She seems really nice, and I love the dragon she brought me. But she lives in America. We can't exactly see her very often, once she goes back there."

"You could visit," he said. "You and your father go to America in the summertime anyway."

"That's sort of what I've been thinking," she said slowly.

"Really?" he asked.

"It's not simple," she warned him. "It might seem that way to you, but . . ." It had been just Sari and her father for so long; that's how she'd stayed safe, how she'd healed from her fall, how she'd kept from going crazy when she thought of her mother. Her father had taken care of her.

"Believe me, I don't think it's simple. I've known you forever, remember?"

She nodded. "I want to be a good daughter; I want him to be happy. I'm thirteen, and I'm not an idiot. I know he likes her. And I . . . well, I like her, too."

"I know you do," he said, sounding proud of her for being so positive. "In fact . . ." Sari glanced over, to see what Laurent was going to say. But he fell silent, swallowing his words, as if he'd thought better of speaking them. They continued walking along the river.

When they got to the Pont St.-Bénezet, they turned onto the long, arched span, and walked out into the middle of it.

Traffic went past, but Sari hardly noticed it. She stared down at the river flowing below, and couldn't help thinking of the childhood song: *Sur le pont d'Avignon, l'on y danse . . .*

"Do you think people really danced on this bridge?" she asked. "In the old days?"

"I think so," he said, staring into her eyes.

The breeze blew off the water, making her shiver. Laurent was so close she could feel his warm breath on her forehead. She tilted her head back, looked up into his face. The moon made his skin look so soft; she wanted to touch it with her hand, but she held back.

"Thank you for this," she whispered.

"For what?"

"Bringing me to Avignon," she said. "For wanting to see it with me; for waiting for a night when it would look the same to both of us."

"I wanted to," he said. "But I wish . . ."

Sari stood still, trembling, waiting for him to tell her what he wished. She saw tears in his eyes. The moon made them shine so brightly. Staring up at him, she saw him wanting something so badly he could hardly stand it.

"I wish you could see colors," he said, his voice breaking. "I thought that day you rode with Susannah, it would happen. I thought that once you got back up on Mystère, you'd be all better."

"Laurent . . ."

"Susannah seems so kind, and she wanted to help you ride," he said. "And she understood that Mystère was all yours, that she was a one-girl horse. So I thought—"

"You thought that would cure me," Sari said. He nodded, and she had to look away. Now her own eyes blurred with tears. Staring down at the river current, she wished that anything were that simple. The idea that a woman, even one as nice as Susannah, could help Sari to see right again. "It's not going to happen," she whispered to Laurent.

"What do you mean?"

"I really like her, Laurent. And I'm trying to let it be okay that my father likes her, too. I'm glad she's coming to ride Sunday night, I honestly am. And maybe I'll even try to ride with her again." She stared at him, eyes filled with tears, wanting to please him, wanting every single thing in the world to turn out right. "But just because she's gotten me back up on my horse doesn't mean I'm magically going to be fixed again."

"How can you be so sure?" he asked.

"Because she's not my mother," Sari said, her voice cracking.

"Oh, Sari," Laurent said, grabbing her hard and holding her tight. She felt him sobbing; he didn't make a sound, but she felt his chest shaking.

They held each other, pressed together, feeling the bridge shake as traffic sped past, and Sari wished she could forget all about that night so long ago, the night the world fell apart, the night her mother pushed her away and disappeared, the night she took all the colors with her.

And she knew that, for Laurent, she would try to ride Sunday night.

FIFTEEN

*Sunday evening, Grey was finishing up the dinner dishes, star-*ing out the kitchen window at twilight settling over the marsh. The sky was clear, almost iridescent purple, and the wind had dropped. The first stars were just coming out, but they'd soon be erased by moonlight. He saw people arriving, car after car. None of them was Susannah. He felt spring-loaded tension in his shoulders, wanting her to get there.

Sari sat at the table behind him, intent on her homework, an essay about her excursion to Avignon with Laurent.

"When am I going to get to read it?" he asked now, standing at the sink.

"Read what?"

"Your paper."

"I don't know. Do you want to read it?"

He laughed. "When have I ever not wanted to read one of your school papers?"

"I don't know," she said, continuing to write. "I guess you always do." She glanced up, her eyes bright. "I think this one's pretty good."

"Tell me about it," he said.

And she did: it all spilled out, the trip to Avignon, Laurent planning everything so he could see the city through Sari's eyes, how he'd waited for the moon so they could see the cobblestones, city walls, bridges, castles, everything in black and white and pewter. Grey listened, moved that someone as young as Laurent could be so perceptive, that he was so obviously in love with his daughter.

"That sounds amazing," Grey said.

"Was your time in Marseille anything like that?"

"It was really good," Grey said, holding everything in, suspecting what she was hinting at. He'd been pleased that Sari was making strides, that with everything happening so fast, she'd been accepting of Susannah. The fact that she hadn't balked at the idea of Susannah showing up for the trail ride was a feat in itself. But now, with Susannah about to leave, Grey wanted to be careful. He wanted more than anything to start a real relationship with her, and for Sari to be okay with it, so they could make plans to see each other again.

"What time is Susannah getting here?" Sari asked.

"I thought she'd be here by now," he said.

Sari nodded. She glanced down at the table. One of the cats was lying on his side, his spine pressed up against her writing arm, right beside the toy dragon Susannah had given her. Sari moved Bruno a few inches away, and he rolled onto his back, to get closer to her again.

"You're happy she's coming?" he asked.

"Yes," she said. "I want her to be able to take the moonlight ride."

Grey gazed at her. She was concentrating, not even looking up. He couldn't quite figure this out—she never liked when he left the house after dark. Lately she hadn't objected at all; this would be two nights in a row.

"You know I'm leading the ride, right?"

"I figured that."

"You used to like it when Claude took riders out at night instead of me."

"I'm not such a kid anymore," she said. "I'm trying to get used to things that used to bother me."

Grey looked down at her pad of paper. She had a stack of neatly written sheets, along with a few pages she'd doodled on. He saw the letter "L," and knew it was for "Laurent." Right now people were congregating by the paddock, and he heard Laurent asking someone if he could help adjust the stirrup length. Sari heard his voice, too, and raised her head to listen.

"I guess I should get ready," she said.

"Ready?" he asked, not getting it.

His daughter stared at him, her eyes blank. But behind their gold-green prettiness, inside their lack of expression, he knew emotions were storming. It showed in the tightness of her face, the thin line of her lips. Riding horses at night was dangerous business in their family; to Sari, that was the greatest reminder of the night that had taken her mother away, and gotten herself badly injured.

"Ready for what?" he pressed.

"The trail ride. I'm going, too. I told Laurent I'm going to ride tonight."

Grey stared at her, feeling a million things at once. "What about your essay?" he asked.

She glared at him, then drifted back to the table. "That's not what you really mean, is it?" she asked, her lower lip wobbling.

He held back, not sure how to answer her. He was shocked that she'd even consider riding at night. While he felt elated by the progress she was making, he also felt hesitant. A night ride would be huge for her. Sari had had night phobia for as long as she'd been colorblind. What if something went wrong? He had thought she'd take it slow, go out on Mystère again in the afternoons, with him, with Laurent. But she'd ridden only that one time—with Susannah.

And he had to admit that he'd been thinking that he'd have Susannah to himself tonight. He couldn't believe his own selfishness.

Sari picked up the toy dragon lying on the rustic wood table, burying her face in its green fur and spiky felt spine, and his thoughts dissolved.

"What's wrong?" he asked, going to her.

Sari held the toy to her face, shoulders shaking in quaking sobs. Grey put his arm around her, trying to soothe her, aching for her.

"You know I can't go," she sobbed. "I want to so much. For Laurent—to make him proud of me. And to spend time with Susannah . . ."

Those words killed him, they really did. His heart was sliced open—to think of Sari wanting to spend time with Susannah. Nothing had ever made him happier, yet here she was sobbing into a toy animal.

"Sari . . ." he began.

Just then, a soft knock sounded at the back door. He glanced up, saw Susannah's smiling face in the glass. But as she caught sight of Sari crying, her happiness drained away. Sari glanced over, saw it was Susannah, and tore to the door. As Grey watched, Sari yanked the door open. She stood frozen for a few seconds, and Grey steeled himself for her to explode. Instead, still clutching the dragon, she moved forward to Susannah.

She stopped short, and then Susannah reached for her and hugged her. Grey thought he was already beyond shock, but he'd never seen Sari act like this with anyone outside the family before.

"I want to go riding with you and Papa," she wept into Susannah's shoulder. "But I can't . . ."

"Oh, Sari," Susannah said, holding her tight. "I'm so sorry."

"I want to so badly," Sari said.

"Yes," Susannah said into her hair. "It's so beautiful out, such a lovely night. You want to see the moon on the water . . ."

"I want to, but I can't!" Sari cried.

"Sari, there'll be other times. You know there will . . . you don't have to rush it," Grey said.

"No, Papa," Sari said, shuddering with a long sob. "I can't *ever* ride at night. It's not even possible. No matter how much I want to!"

"Do you want your father to stay home with you?" Susannah asked.

Sari looked up with tearstained eyes. Incredibly, she shook her head.

"You sure?" Grey asked.

"Yes. You have your cell phone if I need you," Sari said, trying to smile. She held up the toy dragon. "And I have Tarasque."

"One of these days, you'll feel ready to ride in the moonlight," Susannah said, smiling. "I know you will."

"I hope so," Sari said. "The moonlight was so beautiful last night; I'm sure it will be so pretty on the marsh. You'll have a wonderful ride. Susannah, will you come back and say goodnight to me? Promise?"

"I promise," she said.

And just then, Laurent ran over to bang on the door, letting Grey know that all the horses were saddled, that the riders were ready to go. He looked straight at Sari, and didn't even glance away.

"Only one thing," Laurent said. "Arabella has a stone in her shoe. She's a little lame tonight, not seriously, but it would be better for her to stay here—is it all right if Susannah rides a different horse?"

"Of course," Susannah said.

"Give her Mystère," Sari said instantly, the words spilling out as she stared at Laurent.

"Sari," Susannah said.

"Are you sure?" Grey asked, stunned and touched that Sari would offer, a little uneasy at the same time.

"Yes," Sari said. "Positive."

"I knew you'd say that," Laurent said, sounding proud of her.

"Thank you, Sari," Susannah said. She stepped forward to hug Sari again. Grey watched as they stood there, and as he did, he felt his heart settle down. Just one beat at a time, it went back to almost normal.

He stood still, knowing that no matter how the rest of the night went, nothing could ever be better than this, or erase the fact that it had happened. Standing in his own kitchen, seeing his daughter so happy, comforted by a woman he was pretty sure he'd fallen totally in love with.

Susannah had never seen anything as beautiful as the Parc Régional de Camargue at night. The moon rose in the east, just as Grey was leading the group through the paddock gates. It hovered, an enormous apricot-pink globe just on the horizon; then, mounting swiftly, grew smaller and whiter, until by the time they reached the first wooden bridge, it was a bright, gleaming disc.

The white horses looked luminous in the moonlight. The glow turned the reeds glittery dark blue, and made all the creeks and lagoons look like polished onyx. There were seven tourists in the group, and Claude had also come along. Susannah and Grey rode last in line, pulling back on the reins, letting everyone else move ahead, leaving them almost alone.

When the trail widened, Grey came up alongside Susannah. He took her hand for a minute, their fingers clasped as the horses stayed side by side. Susannah glanced over, smiled at him, felt him watching her.

"I can't believe we're back here in the marsh together," he said.

"Neither can I."

"I'm not sure you understand just how big a deal this is," he said. "On a whole lot of levels."

"Like what?"

"Like Sari letting you ride Mystère. And her being okay with my going out on a night trail ride."

"She doesn't like that?"

"Not at night," he said. Then he smiled, wonderful and incandescent, making his eyes shine. "That brings me to the biggest reason of all. That I'm out here with you right now."

"Me, too," Susannah said. "That's the biggest reason of all."

She'd been looking forward to this night every minute since he'd invited her; she still had the scallop shells in her pocket, and she'd looked at them a hundred times since Grey had left the house last night. They'd helped her get to this moment, and now that it was here, she wanted to make every moment last.

"Hold on," he said to her now, gesturing for her to stay back while he rode Django past the line of riders and spoke privately to Claude. When he came back, he gazed at her as Django and Mystère stood still and the rest of the riders followed Claude down the long trail around the lagoon.

"Where are they going?" she asked.

"Away," Grey said. Django took a step closer to Mystère, and Grey leaned over to kiss Susannah. His right arm slid around her waist, sending a charge through her body, making her grab onto him with all she had.

"What did you tell Claude?"

"To go the long way around," Grey said, and laughed.

Susannah laughed, too. They began to ride in the same direction they'd gone three days ago, toward the stony beach on the Gulf of Lions.

"Are you sure Sari is okay?" she asked.

"I'm in awe of how okay she is," he said. "This is a first."

"So I gather . . ."

"Nights are hard for Sari."

"With all the time I've spent with you these last days, you still haven't told me exactly what happened—the whole story."

"I've really appreciated what you've brought to us, not having to think about it so much these past days," he said. "You don't know how great that's been for me. Some of it you know, but there's more."

"Tell me," Susannah said as they walked along.

"Her mother left at night," he said. "You know that part. But it's not just when she left, but who she left with, and how they did it . . ."

"Who took Maria away?" Susannah asked.

"Her trainer," Grey said. He didn't sound angry, or on edge at all. It was just information now; it had lost its barb. "He came to pick her up. They'd waited until after Sari was supposed to be in bed, but she sensed something going on."

"Didn't Maria say goodbye to her?"

Grey stared ahead as Django walked along. "No. She was going to just leave. Bags packed, ready to go. But Sari heard her; she'd been asleep, and she woke up and ran downstairs." He paused, and Susannah heard the horses' hooves, and the sound of animals in the marsh. "She caught her mother just before she walked out the door."

"Did Maria explain to her?"

"I don't know; she might have tried. All I know is that Sari latched onto her, wasn't going to let her out the door."

Susannah could just see it, the child trying to keep her mother from leaving.

"I was in another part of the house," Grey went on levelly.

"All I heard was a big thud; I didn't realize until later that it was Maria shoving Sari away."

"Oh, no," Susannah said. She tried to imagine a scene like that between her and her mother and couldn't begin to.

"Sari chased her outside," Grey continued. "Maria was running by then, carrying her bags, out to the car waiting by the road. I guess Sari realized she wasn't going to catch up on foot, so she ran to the stable."

"Mystère . . ."

He nodded. "She opened that big barn door all by herself, climbed up on Mystère. I was downstairs by that time, and all I saw was Sari galloping by, full tilt, right past the window."

"Grey . . ."

He nodded. The horses walked on, so peacefully along the narrow sand trail, moonlight breaking apart bits of glass on the tidal creek.

"Sari rode off the ranch, onto the main road. I only know this from what I've pieced together over time, but what happened was that Adrien Ferret—'Matelo,' as he was known, Maria's trainer—had stopped the car. Maybe she was having second thoughts, maybe they were kissing, who knows? But Sari gained on them, was riding straight toward them—"

"The taillights," Susannah whispered, remembering that Sari had mentioned red lights.

"Yes," Grey said. "And the minute her mother saw her coming, she must have told Adrien to drive off. They did—speeding away, with Maria looking out the rear window. That's Sari's last memory of her mother. She was already sobbing, hurt from where Maria had pushed her away. She kicked Mystère harder, getting her to gallop faster—a car came around the bend from the other direction, and the lights spooked Mystère."

"She reared up?"

"Or skittered away—something. Sari was thrown."

"Oh God—I'm so sorry."

"So am I. It's been bad. She was in pieces—broken pelvis, broken arm, dislocated shoulder, fractured skull. She was in intensive care for weeks—I told Rosalie to get Maria the hell back here, but supposedly she couldn't be found. Sari was just lying there in a hospital bed, crying for her mother—"

"And Maria never came . . ." Susannah murmured.

"Never came, never called. Sari was in traction, and then in casts. She went through physical therapy—it hurt so much, she'd cry nonstop. She was colorblind. At first her vision was blurred, from the skull fracture. We thought it would all improve at once; her vision would clear up, and colors would come back."

"Her vision cleared?"

"Yes, it did."

"But the colors?"

"Didn't happen."

"At all?"

"No."

"You said she's seen a lot of specialists."

"Yes, and had every test known to all of them. They've all told us the same thing. Her eyes are fine; her brain is normal. It's all in her head."

"They say that?"

"Those aren't the words, but that's the message. Makes her feel she's crazy. That if only she tried harder, didn't take everything so seriously, relaxed a little, stopped trying to control the world, she'd be fine."

"That's a lot of pressure," Susannah said. "And why wouldn't she want to control her environment, considering what she's been through?"

Grey nodded, glancing over. "That's why her riding with you was such a big deal. That was the first she's been on a horse in all those years, since the accident."

"I really wouldn't have minded if she'd wanted to come tonight," Susannah said. "But she wasn't ready."

"No. Not for riding at night."

"Someday she will be."

"Yeah," Grey said. Then he looked over at Susannah, and the way he smiled did something to her heart. "But not tonight."

"Not tonight," Susannah said.

"You can't leave," he said.

"You're right," she said, laughing softly. "I can't, but I have to."

"If we didn't have tonight," he said, taking her hand again, "I'm not sure I'd be able to stand the thought of you getting on that plane. And even with it . . ."

"I know," she whispered.

"Susannah, I'm not going to let you go."

The moon lifted higher, and a light haze rose from the lagoon. It swirled around Susannah and Grey, hiding them from anyone who might be watching. They were almost to the beach; Susannah could smell its nearness in the salt air, the sharp breeze. An owl hunted silently overhead, its silhouette dark against the moon. In the distance they heard a loon, its cry long and joyful.

At least that's how it sounded to Susannah.

Sari finished her essay. She read it over, pleased with what she'd done. Her writing brought back the beauty of the night in Avignon, the mystery of walking along the cobblestones with Laurent, the black-and-white drama of moonlight spilling over the medieval stone city.

Her father used to be a journalist; had he felt this satisfied when he'd finished a particularly fine piece of reporting? She knew that he'd been writing about Marseille, and she drifted into his study. Her intention was to leave her own essay on top of his desk, but her attention was drawn to a pile of papers.

Glancing down, she saw his handwriting and read the top page. He had written about a secret cave, underwater, filled with prehistoric drawings and etchings. Sari read something about "hand stencils," then, in big bold letters, the words LEAVE YOUR MARK, DON'T FORGET TO LIVE.

What did that mean? She wasn't sure, but the phrase sent tingles down her spine. Don't forget to live . . . Was that what Sari had been doing? Friday night, walking with Laurent, she'd felt so amazingly, wonderfully, excitingly alive. She was so used to feeling guarded, as if everyone else was having all the fun, that she'd forgotten what it was like to just wander freely, feeling in touch with life.

Did her father feel the same way?

It disturbed and alarmed her to think that he did. Was that why he'd seemed so different ever since Susannah had come? Was she helping him to live in a different way? Sari knew she hadn't seen her father smile as often as he had recently—and if Susannah was the reason, what did that say about Sari?

She walked into the kitchen, picked up the small toy dragon, pacing back and forth by the window. The cats were sensing her excitement, weaving around her feet as if it were a game. She peered out the window, trying to see if the riders were back yet. Of course they weren't: they'd left no more than twenty minutes ago, and rides were an hour and a half long.

Bruno nearly tripped her, but she hardly noticed. She felt bad, and it was getting worse. Last night she'd stood on the bridge with Laurent, looking down at the Rhône River. She'd imagined dragons living in the shadows, but she'd felt so brave. Why was tonight different? Why did she feel her own private dragons rising up to attack her?

The dragon of fear, the dragon of horseback riding, the dragon of night, the dragon of her mother leaving, the dragon of no-colors, the dragon of her father riding in the marsh with

Susannah: they all lived together in one slimy lair, deep in Sari's body and mind.

Sari stared out the kitchen window. The moon was up, and so white. It reminded Sari of when she and Laurent had walked through Avignon, up and down every dark street. She hadn't been afraid at all.

Turning from the window, she hurried upstairs. Her pelvis still ached a little—or maybe she was just focusing on it because she wasn't sure she wanted to do this. Rummaging in her bedroom closet, she found the olive jar, hidden behind her rain boots, where she kept her allowance. Just looking at the jar made her shudder with emotion.

She'd been saving for such a long time, to be able to afford a round-trip ticket to America. She had always imagined landing in Providence, staying with her grandparents, and then putting her plan into effect.

She had saved all her money, so she could fly to Nevada to find her mother. So she could travel out West to the ranch in the desert where her mother lived, where the circus was located.

She pictured a dusty, dry yard. Deserts were filled with sand, not lovely reeds and lagoons like here. She imagined horses—not sweet, loving animals like Mystère, like the ones her father raised—but high-strung, performing circus horses that did what they were commanded for praise and applause, but never gave any love back.

Sari would knock. And when her mother answered—what would Sari do? Would she throw herself into her mother's arms? Would her mother push her away again, even harder this time, slam the door in her face? Sari crouched in the closet, thinking about her mother, starting to cry.

Everything was so wrong. She felt panic begin to bubble up, knowing her father was out in the marsh without her. The insecurity made her feel like a very little girl, and she hated that. Determined to get back the strength she'd felt last night, she dove into the closet for what she'd come up here for: her riding boots. Her old ones no longer fit, but her father had bought her this pair, for when she was ready.

Sitting on a pile of shoes, she pulled them on. She grabbed a sweater because the night was chilly. And she tore downstairs, into the kitchen, out the door. She was moving so fast, she almost let the cats out. They were circling by the kitchen door, and nearly squeaked out between her legs—but she stopped them just in time.

Running across the yard, she felt her pulse racing. She wished Laurent was here, but he had gone on the ride, she was sure. She still felt half afraid, but she was also half excited. She could do this. The moon was up, filling the Parc with white light. It illuminated the entire yard and paddock, almost as brightly as day. She told herself that this was nothing—nothing at all—like the last time she had ridden at night.

She walked over to Mystère's stall. Starting to open the door, she remembered: she had let Susannah ride Mystère. That nearly took all the wind out of her sails. No horses were left. But then, hearing a wild whinny, she turned her head and looked straight into the eyes of Tempest.

The new colt was small, stocky, very sprightly. He danced in place. She reached out her hand, and he buried his velvety nose in it. She tickled him under the chin, ran into the tack room.

Her mother's old black saddle was there, with its tarnished silver scallop shells hanging down, gathering dust—no one had used it since she'd left. The sight of the saddle made Sari shiver, but she just rushed past it to grab a bridle.

Sari hurried back to Tempest, tried to slip it over his head. He wouldn't take the bit, though. He tossed his head, pulling back with such force it nearly yanked her arm up, taking her with it.

Fine. She'd ride him with just his halter. The moonlight

reminded her of last night, of Laurent, and made her feel she could do anything. She led Tempest out of his stall, through the open door, into the paddock. The breeze was blowing, and he sniffed the air. She saw his ears twitch.

Leading him over to the fence, she planned to climb up to the top rung, grab his neck for balance, and then jump on. Tempest was frisky, sidestepping as she walked him over. His muscles rippled beneath his skin, and his white coat felt hot beneath her hand. She whispered his name, and told him they were going to go for a ride.

When they got to the fence, she looked into his eye. It was dark and mischievous. She swore to herself she was ready for this; she really thought she was. But Tempest must have thought otherwise. He reared back, pulling away.

Sari let him go. She really had no choice—he had a mind of his own. She watched with alarm as he ran in a wide circle around the ring. She remembered seeing Laurent trying to ride him, getting thrown. And suddenly she saw a ghost image of her mother on his back: standing proud, connected as if she and Tempest were the same.

And then her mother disappeared, and it was just the white colt. He ran in another circle, white mane and tail flowing behind him. Sari watched him rear up again, tearing wildly at the air.

"Sari, *ça va?*" called Laurent from his front door.

"What are you doing here? I thought you went on the ride!"

"No, I . . ."

Maybe it was Laurent's voice, or maybe it was the shock of running almost free in the ring, or maybe it was the moonlight: suddenly Tempest stopped dead-still, then got a running start, and suddenly charged like a bull, straight for the gate. She thought he was going to crash it, head down, but suddenly the young horse lifted off—powerful neck up, chest forward, legs thrusting—and jumped the fence.

"He's escaped!" Laurent said, running from his house, watching Tempest gallop into the marsh.

"And it's my fault," Sari said, panicked at the idea of losing the horse.

"No, he's wild," Laurent said. "He just saw his chance to go."

"I have to tell my father," Sari said, starting to shake. She ran to the house, into the kitchen, Laurent right behind her, and began to dial her father's cell phone.

"Papa," she said, when he answered, "Tempest got away! I wanted to find you and Susannah, and I led him into the paddock, and he ran into the marsh."

Her father said not to worry, he and Susannah would look for Tempest. And Sari felt slightly calmed by that, because she didn't want the half-tamed horse to go back to the wild, especially not wearing a halter, which could get caught on brush or wire or fences and trap Tempest so the bulls could gore him.

So she hung up feeling okay. Not quite happy, but all right. Still trembling, because she had let the horse get away, and she couldn't stand the idea of him being lost on the endless, lonely sea plain.

"Your father will find him," Laurent said.

"Do you think he will?" she asked, her eyes welling.

"Of course. And my father will help. They know more about the horses than anyone."

"I have to go look for Tempest."

"No," Laurent said, grabbing her hand. His touch made Sari tingle, and she looked into his eyes. Laurent had held her hand lots of times during their lives, but lately it had started making her feel so different. His eyes were steady, protective. "The marsh can be dangerous at night, Sari. It's not like walking through Avignon with me. Stay here. They'll be home soon."

Sari stood still, frozen by the fact Laurent hadn't let go of her hand. She felt something tumble inside. His piercing eyes held her still, even as her heart was tugging her to go after Tempest.

"If we go together, it will be safe," she whispered.

"You want me to come with you?"

She nodded, but even so, she couldn't move. All she could do was look into his eyes and hold his hand and worry about the young horse being lost and think about their night in the dark, silver city, wonder why being with Laurent had started making her feel this way inside.

The waves lapped the shore, the front edge white with sea foam and moonlight. The horses grazed in the salt meadow. Grey held Susannah in his arms. He kissed her, feeling his blood surge like the sea, when his cell phone rang. The sound was startling, so out of place, and he was so lost he nearly threw the thing into the water.

But of course it was Sari. And there was a problem: Tempest had run off. She sounded calm, pulled together, but there was an undertone of panic in her voice. And Susannah knew, the minute he hung up the phone.

"What's wrong?" she asked.

"A young horse ran off."

"Tempest?" she asked.

"That's right, you saw what he did to the stall . . ."

"He's a wild one," she said.

Grey pulled her close. They lay together on the cold sand, hearts beating together. She felt so warm in his arms, and he closed his eyes and wished the phone hadn't rung. But it had, and she was pushing back, standing up, giving him a hand to pull him to his feet. He felt wild himself, on the primitive edge of feelings he hadn't had in years.

Walking over to the horses, giving Susannah a leg up and then mounting Django himself, Grey felt almost out of control. His emotions were racing, and his blood was pounding.

He only wanted to go back to the beach with Susannah. But she was in charge right now, leading him back into the marsh, on their way to save a barn-crazed colt and give Sari hearts-ease. Watching her, he couldn't help spinning back in time, to the last time he'd been in love. With Maria everything had been wild—their horseback rides, their lovemaking, and their fights.

His passion for Susannah was no less intense; in fact he knew it was stronger. She hadn't hesitated for an instant—her concern for Sari immediately trumped whatever she'd been feeling back on the beach.

"Where should we look?" Susannah asked, pulling him back to reality, out of his fevered thoughts.

"Maybe over where Tempest's herd used to graze," Grey said. "There's a salt field behind the Pont d'Onorato." He rode up alongside her, gave her a long kiss—probably the last in a while—and urged Django into a gallop. Susannah followed closely behind. They charged along the narrow trail, through tall rushes painted sapphire blue by the still-rising moon.

Grey knew the horses were affected by the moon's phases; he had long noticed that mares went into heat during the full moon, that stallions became more fierce, that wild horses like Tempest were more likely to escape. He felt the moon's pull himself. Even as they galloped along, intent on their purpose, he was nearly overwhelmed with desire, wanting nothing more than to pull her off Mystère, make her want to stay in France with him forever.

They rounded a bend, and he slowed down. This was not far from where the bulls were concentrated. He swore the air felt different here—hotter, as if all that aggression poured off the bulls' hides and had nowhere to go. Mist from the creeks rose and swirled. Grey and Susannah rode through this ghostly world, straight to the Pont d'Onorato. After sand and the soft earth of the trails, the horses' hooves sounded loud on the wooden slats of the curved bridge. A creek rushed down below. Somewhere in the distance a nighthawk screeched. And very close by, something screamed.

"What was that?" Susannah asked.

"A horse," Grey said.

"It sounded human."

"Horses in distress do," he replied.

They listened carefully, trying to get the direction. The wind lifted and danced, blowing the mist. It was disorienting, all the more so because Susannah was so near. Grey had to block out everything except the sound of the horse. It took a moment, but he finally had it.

When Grey realized where it was coming from, he looked straight at Susannah. His stomach dropped, knowing she'd fight him on this.

"I want you to wait here," he said.

"Why?"

He hesitated. Maybe if he didn't tell her the truth, she would just listen to him and not try to follow. But there was something about her, and about the way they'd become over this very short time together, that made him know he never wanted to lie to her.

"Because there's quicksand."

"Is . . . the horse trapped?"

"It's possible," he said, hearing the sound of the horse's panic again. "I think so."

"Where is he?"

"Over there," he said, pointing into the mist, across the narrow creek. Climbing down off Django, he turned to see Susannah jumping down from Mystère.

"Susannah," he said.

She put her hand on his arm, her eyes wide. "First," she said, "I'm afraid of being alone with the bulls. And second, I'm not letting you go into quicksand alone."

"I know this area by heart. I'm not going into quicksand."

"Good," she said, trying to smile. "That means I'm not either. You swam into the sea cave with me, I'm heading down that path with you. Come on—let's go get Tempest."

He hesitated, then nodded. The pressure of her fingers on his arm was lighter than moonlight and a hundred times more intense. It made him grab her, kiss her hard. She tasted like the beach, and he swore he heard breaking waves until he realized it was just the sound of his own blood pounding in his ears.

Grey pulled the coiled rope off Django's saddle, took Susannah by the hand, and walked headlong into a place he'd been a hundred times, yet had never been before.

SIXTEEN

Susannah barely stopped to think. She trailed Grey, ready to help. The mist enclosed them, making straight-ahead visibility almost nonexistent. Up above was another story; the fog was pinned to the rivers and lagoons, barely higher than the reeds, and through a fine layer, thin as muslin, the sky overhead was a blue field for the moon and the brightest stars.

Her feet squished in damp earth, and she flashed back to her first day in the Camargue, when she'd stepped off the path onto terrain like this, gotten caught in a stampede of wild bulls. Would they come again? Her heart beat in her throat. Moray eels in the sea cave scared her less than those bulls. Her senses were on high alert as she paid attention to every sound, and followed Grey toward the frightened horse.

They edged along a creek. The tide looked to be ebbing, with the water rushing toward the sea. Moonlight revealed ghostly creatures clinging to the banks. Susannah crouched down, staring at them.

"Those are just *favouilles*—little green crabs," he said.

"I know them well," Susannah said. She'd grown up on the Connecticut shore, spent many happy childhood hours crabbing with her dad. She stared at the tiny eyes on stalks, their oval shells—dark on top, white underneath—their small pincers raised menacingly as she and Grey passed. The bank was also lined with broken shell; the moonlight glinted on them, and she saw the unmistakable ripple of scallop shells.

Mesmerized by the sight, Susannah barely noticed the ground shift. One step later, she stepped right into a black hole—her left leg went into the muck, right up to her knee. She gasped and scrambled, feeling the mud suck her down. But Grey reached back, she grabbed his hand, and she pulled herself out. Steadying herself against him, she looked up ahead, and saw.

The horse was no more than ten yards up the path. He was veiled by mist, but even so, his terror was unmistakable. He had sunk into a hole of black swamp gunk, was nearly up to his withers in it, and was thrashing so hard he seemed in imminent danger of drowning in mud. His back was a glossy hump under slick mire. His eyes flashed with black fire. At the sight of Grey and Susannah, he let out a guttural, screaming neigh.

"Tempest," Susannah said, shocked.

"Yes," Grey said. "He's really in there."

"Can we get him out?"

Grey hesitated; she saw him scouting around the area, staying on the path, but leaning into the tall grass, rippling silver in the moonlight.

"We have to," Susannah said, determined. Inching toward Tempest, wanting to reach out her hand and calm him, she felt the wet ground pulling her feet down, and she stopped dead. "We have to get him out."

"Here," Grey said, hauling a long, weather-beaten plank out of the reeds.

"What's that?"

"People go crabbing here, and stand on it so they won't fall in."

Susannah took one end, and Grey the other. They laid it down on the ground, pointing like an arrow toward the horse. Then Grey burrowed into the wet earth on the other side of the trail, emerging with another sea-silvered board, two inches thick and at least three feet long. Using the first plank as a bridge, he laid the second one even closer to Tempest. At the sight of him, Tempest tossed his head and struggled more.

"There, boy," Grey said. "Stay still if you can. That's it. Just wait a minute now. Just another little bit . . ."

"What are we going to do?" Susannah asked, inching out along the boards. They were six inches wide. She felt as if she was walking a tightrope. The planks distributed her and Grey's weight, making it possible for them to stand on the swampy mud.

"I don't know," Grey said. "I can get the rope around his neck, but how am I going to pull him out?"

"I'll help."

He glanced at her, gave a wry smile. "You're strong, but not that strong."

"Has this ever happened before?" she asked.

Grey nodded. And his frown and the line furrowing between his brows let her know it hadn't had a good outcome.

"He's really trapped," Grey said, tense and powerless as he watched the horse thrash again, sinking another few inches.

"This is quicksand?" she asked doubtfully, looking down at what looked much more like black, tarry mud.

"It's the swamp," he said. "More silt and mud than sand. But the same thing. Tempest can't get a foothold down there. There's no purchase. The more he fights, the deeper he'll go. He weighs a ton, so I can't haul him out myself. I need to keep his head above the mud." Grey started taking off his shirt and watch. He handed them to Susannah. She noticed his hard, tan chest and shoulders, the lines of his muscles, his strong arms, gleaming in moonlight. This was life and death, but she noticed anyway. This was going to turn out right, she was sure. She had confidence in them together. They were going to save this horse, no doubt about it.

"What do we do next?" she asked.

"We're going to pull him out," he said, holding her face between his hands. His fingers felt rough, but the way he held her was so tender, as if he knew how scared she felt. He touched his forehead to hers, then kissed her. In spite of the danger, of the fact they were balancing on boards, she leaned into his body and felt the heat pouring off him, and she felt another surge of certainty. They were not going to let this horse die.

"Hang onto my stuff, okay? Throw it on that patch of tall grass if you want—it won't sink there. Then, walk down the middle of the creek bed. The tide's out, so it won't be deep. The bottom will hold you—it's silted over with pebbles and hard sand. Go to the bridge, and get Django, okay?"

"Okay," she said.

Then she stood back and watched as Grey used the boards in a sort of hopscotch over the mud, walking across one and then the other, lifting up the first to move him closer to the horse, doing it again. When he was almost on top of Tempest, the front edge of the forward plank began to tilt down into the hole. Grey inched back, shifting his weight, to keep from tipping in.

He knelt on the board. She watched him move closer, nearly eye to eye with the terrified horse. He had the rope coiled around one arm, and talking to Tempest, his voice calm and authoritative, he slipped a noose around the powerful neck. As he leaned in, his arms went up to his shoulders in silt. Tempest neighed and started to throw his head around, buck backward, but Grey spoke to him sharply. And the horse stopped.

Susannah ran down the stream. Grey had been right; the creek bed held firm, all the way to the bridge. At the sight of her, Django and Mystère danced nervously. She climbed up the bank to them, untied Django. He tossed his head, nuzzled her shoulder. Petting his neck, she tried to lead him into the water. He balked.

"It's okay, boy," she said. "It's safe . . . hurry now, we have to go get Tempest."

Django was tall for a Camarguaise horse. He towered over Susannah, and when she looked up at him and saw moonlight spilling over his lush white mane and aristocratic head, she knew that he could pull away from her in an instant. She remembered her days at River Farms, how her teacher had taught her to be strong with the horses: kind but firm. *They sense fear, and it's all over,* he'd always told her.

So she kept her hands steady, her voice low, and she told Django what she wanted him to do, and led him into the shallow creek—it came no higher than his knees—just as if she knew what she was doing. The small crabs, *favouilles,* scuttled up the muddy banks, out of their way, their claws scrabbling in the tall grass. Susannah kept an eye on Django, worried the crabs might spook him, but the stallion just walked on, and she led him along the creek, back to Grey and Tempest.

They hadn't moved, but that last fight had taken Tempest down farther. Grey knelt upright; his jeans were soaked, and his upper body was black. Tempest's mane and forelock were coated with silt, and Grey leaned over to clean mud from around his nostrils. For the first time, Susannah felt panic in her chest, wondering how long they could keep the horse from sinking.

Grey had started digging out the area immediately around him. One scoop of black mud, then another, thrown into the reeds. As if Tempest knew he was saving his life—or perhaps just frozen with terror—he stopped moving. Grey leaned closer, kept digging.

Susannah felt the wind pick up. It blew in from the sea, bringing with it fresh scents of salt air. It rippled across her skin; she felt prickles on the back of her neck. The sea breeze cleared the mist, so she could see Grey and Tempest even more clearly. But at the same time, it seemed to have brought ghosts to the scene. She felt death hovering over her shoulder.

She thought of times she'd wedged herself into caves, narrow openings; times she'd gotten stuck in one place, having to wriggle free by inches. She knew that horrible feeling of claustrophobia, knew that Tempest and Grey had to be feeling it now.

Holding on to Django, she looked around for a place to tie him; an old post had been sunk on the creek's bank—some sort of marker, the lettering long worn off the weathered old sign. She knotted his reins to the splintered post then stepped from the creek onto the squishy ground. She felt her way along the still relatively solid ground about five yards toward the swamp where Grey was with Tempest and leapt onto the first plank. It clattered under her feet, tilted momentarily, but held firm.

The moon shined down, painting everything silver—the rough wood under her feet, the tips of the tall green grass, the ripples of black mud, the glint in Tempest's eyes, the shadows around Grey's muscles. He was stretched out, tense and hard as a board, physically holding the horse's head above the surface of the mud. She reached out, touched Grey's back.

"Don't get too close," he said quietly.

"He's sinking; we have to get him out."

"He's like a greased barrel. I can't even get my arms around him."

Silence. Susannah saw Grey's back muscles straining and bunching, and she heard him trying to breathe steadily, keeping Tempest's head up.

"Django's here, waiting," she said.

"I know," he said. "But what can I do?"

"Grey," she said, "put one of the boards under Tempest's front hooves, hold the line around his neck. He'll want to run up—and you'll be on Django pulling; he'll use that force to get himself out."

"Susannah, I can't let go of him right now. If I do, he'll drown before I get to Django."

"I'll hold his head up," she said. He glanced back over his shoulder. She moved closer, gestured that he should go, that she meant it.

"I can't let—"

"You have to," she said, strong and steady. "Do it for Sari. We have to save him, Grey. You know we can . . ."

He met her eyes; he saw her confidence, and she felt him taking it in. "Okay!" he said. "We'll try. Get in here, if you can . . ." He moved aside, so she could wedge herself under his body, wrapping her arms around Tempest's thick neck. Almost instantly she pitched forward, chest-first into the mud— but she caught herself, managing to hold tight, spitting out dirt.

"Got him?" Grey asked.

"Yes," she said. And she did. Nothing was going to make her let go; she reached forward, arms braced on the board. Grey reached around her, grabbed the first plank, wedged it down into the mire at a forward-tilting slant. She saw him soothing Tempest with one hand, while feeling his way beneath his legs with the other. Susannah and Grey were nearly chest-deep together, and he turned to give her one hard look.

"Keep his head up," Grey said. "But if you start to sink any more, let go. Got that?"

"Yes."

"I'll be just a minute. Shout to me if anything happens."

She nodded, to let him know she would. Then she handed him the rope he'd tied to Tempest, and heard him jump from the plank on which she was lying all the way to the solid ground yards away. His feet pounded across the damp marsh-land, then splashed into the creek. She heard Django whinny, and the slap of skin as Grey climbed up.

Tempest reacted; his ears twitched. His black eyes widened. Susannah did what she'd seen Grey do; she dug at the mud, brushed the worst of it from his nostrils so he could breathe. He sputtered; his lips sprayed her with a fine black mist.

"It's okay, darling," she said. "Don't be afraid. It'll be just a few minutes now. Stay still, Tempest. That's it . . . good boy."

"Get ready," Grey called.

She eased back, both arms around Tempest, line grasped in one hand, just in time for the rope to go taut and burn her fin-gers. The pain nearly made her cry out, but all her focus was on helping Tempest. She watched him start to panic—he thrashed again, legs spinning like a wheel. Only this time they found a step. He pawed at the weathered plank. Susannah threw her weight on the loose end; it was like a seesaw, with her on one side and the horse on the other.

"It's working," she called. "Pull harder!"

Tempest began to haul himself out. She heard one front leg pop free of the muck, then the other. She had just enough time to jump out of the way, watching him clear the stickiest part, moving into the creek, nearly swimming through the swamp, stepping here and there, his hooves getting caught in little mud holes.

"He's out!" she cried breathlessly.

Turning around, she saw Grey still on Django. In that in-stant, the rope went slack, and Grey jumped down and came running. He held the rope's end in one arm, and caught Su-sannah with the other. He pulled her into his arms, and they nearly fell into the mud. He held her face between his hands; they were slick all over, and his chest was slippery, covered with silt turning silver in the moonlight as it dried in the quickening breeze.

Tempest stood safely in the pebbly stream, tossing his head and dunking his face into the flowing water. Susannah glanced over at him, looked up at Grey with wide eyes, and was just about to say "We did it!" when he kissed her.

She'd been kissed before, but never like this, even by him. She felt the primal power of the wetland, and the fierce strength of the man she had fallen in love with, and his lips were hot and his chest hotter, and both of them were soaking wet and slick, and she had absolutely no idea of where she ended and he began. She thought of Sarah's latest miracle, wondered whether it was a direct result of her petition and the offering of one scallop shell . . .

A horse whinnied. It might have been Mystère or Django or even Tempest, but she was past knowing or even caring. Her hands slid across Grey's hard chest and up his muscular arms; her fingers caressed his face. The kiss went on and on, moonlight scoring shadows across their closed eyes, so that she barely noticed that they weren't alone.

Grey was the first to see. He stopped kissing her suddenly, looked over her shoulder. Laurent was walking along the trail, as if he knew the way by heart after years of horseback rides and crabbing expeditions. Right behind him, stopped dead in her tracks, one hand held over her mouth—Sari.

SEVENTEEN

Sari's eyes were bright with shock and moonlight, as if she'd just seen a ghost, as if she'd just been betrayed all over again. Grey watched the color drain out of her face, started toward her.

"Sari, Tempest's safe," Grey said. "Susannah and I saved him."

Sari didn't reply. She just stood still, staring straight into Susannah's eyes. "I didn't know it was like this," she said.

"Oh, Sari . . ."

"I thought you were my friend."

"I am your friend, Sari," Susannah said, walking toward her.

"No," Sari said, shaking her head, backing away.

"Getting Tempest out of the quicksand, I just kept thinking we had to do it for you . . ."

"No," Sari said again, shaking her head.

"Sari, don't . . ." Laurent urged.

"That's right," Grey said. "Come on now, Sari. Let's get the horses, and get everyone home."

"I don't want . . ." Sari began, her voice tiny. She closed her eyes, going inward, exactly the same way she had the first day Susannah had met her. Susannah's heart cracked, watching her retreat.

Laurent had begun rounding up Mystère and Django. Tempest stood to the side, mud dripping from his coat. Susannah and Grey flanked Sari, and Grey took a step forward, to touch her shoulder, but she seemed frozen.

"Sari?" he asked.

She just stared straight ahead, as if she had turned into a statue.

"Sari," Susannah said, moving closer, trembling with emotion at the girl's distress. She whispered that she was sorry.

Sari shut her eyes tight, retreating deep inside, blocking out the world. She swayed, as if about to fall, and Grey caught her in his arms. Her limbs seemed useless, as if they were made of wood.

Laurent walked over with Django and Mystère, and just then Claude came galloping over the bridge. Grey looked over at Susannah. His blue eyes glinted in the moonlight, but she felt as if she was staring at him from across the sea.

They all began to walk back toward the ranch. Grey lifted Sari, almost catatonic, onto Mystère, and he climbed up behind her. Laurent gave Susannah a leg up onto Django, while he rode behind his father, leading Tempest.

Susannah just sat there on Django, watching Sari. Grey glanced over at her, filled with longing and hopelessness. *This is what it is, my life,* he wanted to tell her. *This is what we're up against.* Sari was so pretty, and looked so normal, but her psyche was a Pandora's box of what had happened that night five years ago. In her frozen silence, he knew Susannah was finally starting to understand.

When they all got back to the ranch, they went to the stable to wipe the worst of the mud off themselves and the horses. Laurent got out the hose, and he and Claude set in on Tempest. Susannah watched them talking, heard Claude admonishing the young horse for his dramatic escape. Sari stood at Grey's side, glued to him.

Grey looked over at Susannah.

"Will you come into the house?" he asked.

Susannah looked at Sari, but she seemed locked into herself, completely shut down.

"I'd better not," she said.

"Sari," Grey said, looking his daughter in the eye. "Susannah saved Tempest . . . please listen to me, will you? You know how good she's been to you."

"I can't, Papa," Sari finally choked out, her voice breaking. And Grey knew that was true—she couldn't. He could see it in his daughter's posture of defeat, the way she hung her head and started to shudder with great, heaving sobs.

"That's okay, Sari," Susannah said. "I'm going to go now."

Grey shook his head; he couldn't believe this was happening. Their days together had been like nothing he'd ever known before, a revelation. He and Susannah had a life of their own, and he'd hoped it could last, hoped they could ease Sari along until she felt ready to accept things. But Susannah was leaving.

Grey watched as Susannah walked over, stood right in front of Sari.

"Sari?" she said, and even though Sari didn't look up, Susannah went on, through her own tears. "I want you to know how much I've loved meeting you. Spending time with you . . . I'm so glad to know you're riding Mystère again; I'm sure she's happy about that, too."

"Sari, please . . ." Grey said. But she didn't even register she'd heard.

"It's okay," Susannah said. "I just want you to know I'll be thinking of you. And if you ever get to the States, I hope you'll come see me. I'd really like that."

"She visits her grandparents in Rhode Island every summer," Laurent interjected. "Every single summer."

"It's true," Grey said.

Susannah nodded at him, obviously smiling the best she could; he saw the quick sparkle in her dark violet eyes. He wanted to touch her. His arm moved, aching to pull her close. But she stayed away.

"Don't forget the Tarasque," she said, looking from Grey to Sari. She directed her words at the girl, but she was speaking to both of them, and even to herself. "Don't forget that even when there's a dragon, you're safe. You can always sing it to sleep . . ."

"Susannah," Grey said, almost pleading.

She shook her head, stepped back.

"Good night," Susannah said. She blew a kiss to Sari, but his daughter didn't open her eyes to see it. Then, to Grey, "Thank you for everything . . . this has been the most amazing time . . ."

And then she got into her car and drove down the dusty moonlit road, and he watched her, thinking of how she'd brought such unexpected beauty, such tremendous life, into his dead world. He watched her drive away from the Manade du Dempsey, and felt the weight of the last five years come crashing back down.

Hours later, Grey couldn't sleep. The full moon was all the way up now, slanting through the windows, bathing the whole house in blue light. He showered off all the black mud, watched it swirling down the drain, felt the hot water all over his sore body, remembered what it had been like to hold Susannah in his arms on the beach and by the creek.

He relived the feeling of his skin against hers, the taste of her.

Sari, his traumatized child. If she hadn't come along; or if she'd seen him kissing Susannah during the day instead of at night, when all her fears and memories were fully alive . . .

Drying off, he walked through the house. Susannah was everywhere. He faced the fact that he'd started imagining her here. He'd pictured her in the salon—he'd find a beautiful desk for her, put it by the window, a place for her books, somewhere she could do her work and study. He'd seen her in the dining room, sitting between him and Sari at the table, eating together every night. Cooking with Sari, showing her all the things she wanted to know. The three of them riding together through the marsh . . . he'd find a horse for her, the perfect one. . . .

Dreams of a home life. He'd long stopped having them. Grey Dempsey, expatriate. His brothers still thought of him as Hemingway. Maybe he didn't have the bylines anymore, but he did have the bulls and white horses, and now he had the sea cave. Even a fight by the harbor. Perfect.

What would Oscar and Ben think if they knew his wildest dreams were to have Susannah Connolly move in with him, make a life together?

He walked through the silent house. Blue shadows fell everywhere. The tile floors felt cool under his bare feet. He'd fallen in love fast before. When it came to love, he had two speeds: fast and stop.

Look how it had turned out the last time. He remembered when he had bought this place. Nearly a year into his time with her, and already they were on the rocks. He'd become a rancher just to keep his wife.

The ranch had lasted; Maria was gone.

He kept pictures of her for Sari. They stood in frames in the family room, where he hardly ever went. Walking in there now, he looked at the family they'd once been. Maria holding the baby; Maria standing on the front step; Maria standing on the back of Django.

What was he doing, keeping alive the memory of a woman who didn't even want her daughter? Disgusted, he turned the photos facedown. He kept walking through the house, remembering how dangerous love with Maria had always felt, wondering why he had once found it so exciting. She was a circus rider now; she had adulation and cheering crowds and the adoration of the man she'd left with.

Sari was paying the price. An elusive wife was one thing; a disappearing mother was another. Grey didn't need all those doctors' diagnoses to tell him what was going on. His daughter was filled with rage—anger turned inward.

From the minute Maria had pushed her, Sari had needed to fight back. She'd watched her mother drive off, been completely powerless to stop her. She'd turned her frustration on herself.

Grey had often wondered exactly what Sari had seen, after riding Mystère up the main road, coming upon the car idling on the side, taillights glowing red in the darkness. Why had Maria and Adrien pulled over right there?

Had it really been so incredibly impossible for them to drive out of the region, away from the Parc, out of sight of Sari before making love, doing whatever they had to do?

Sari had always claimed she never saw anything. The trauma of her fall had—perhaps mercifully—blocked out any memory of her mother in Adrien's arms, whatever the two of them had been doing. But Grey had always had his suspicions, and after tonight, he thought he knew for sure.

Coming upon him and Susannah had brought it all back to her. A parent in the arms of someone else meant only one thing—they were leaving her forever. Why else would Sari have reacted the way she did? The way she shut down so violently, eyes squeezed tight, unable to let herself see . . .

Sari liked Susannah. But Grey had been deluded to think they could ever become a family. He had always thought the

Gypsy's curse was complete bullshit, but right now he found himself starting to believe.

As he walked upstairs, Grey's heart felt heavy. He loved his daughter more than his own life—but sometimes he felt that that's what he had traded, to love her the way she needed to be loved, to stay here and take care of her the way she needed taking care of.

He walked along the hall, wondered how Susannah was doing. She'd seen how upset Sari was, and she'd known. But did she know what all this was doing to Grey, how much it hurt to be without her now?

Pausing in the doorway to Sari's room, Grey checked on his daughter. She lay in bed, covered with a sheet and her duvet. The two black cats were curled up, guardians at her feet. She'd named them after his brothers, Ben and Oscar, with a French spin: Bruno and Oscar. They watched him with yellow eyes.

The moonlight, coming through Sari's window, caught something in her arms. He saw the red glints, took a step closer. There, clutched right under his daughter's chin, was the dragon toy Susannah had given her.

Don't forget the Tarasque, Susannah had said. *Don't forget that even when there's a dragon, you're safe. You can always sing it to sleep . . .*

The memory of her words was strong. It filled Grey, made him miss her so much he couldn't stand it. He pictured her lying in bed just a few miles away, her next-to-last night in the Camargue.

He wondered whether she was visited by dragons tonight, as he was. He wanted to grab Sari and shake her; he wanted to tell her she was ruining the best thing that had happened to them both in longer than he could remember.

He stood in the doorway, staring at his sleeping daughter. Then he whispered, "Good night, sweet dreams"—just as he always did—and continued down the hall to his own room.

EIGHTEEN

The next day was brilliant, full of springtime.
Susannah hadn't slept at all during the night. The full moon had poured through the window, straight into her eyes. Lying awake, she couldn't stop thinking of him, of Sari, of the evening's traumatic turn.

At first light, she went to the church to see Sarah one last time. She lit a votive candle, added it to the glow of a thousand others, letting the smoke drift up to the ceiling of Sarah's chapel, merging with the black soot of years gone by, just like the charcoal from ancient fires in the many caves she'd visited. She'd bowed her head, thinking of her mother. She'd wished she could have introduced her parents to Grey and Sari. . . . She left the second apricot scallop shell Grey had given her at Sarah's feet. For thanksgiving or for hope, she wasn't sure. Maybe it didn't matter; a prayer was a prayer.

Back at her house, Susannah felt the hours drag by so slowly.

She kept waiting for the phone to ring—for it to be Grey. She wanted to hear his voice, wanted to hear that Sari had come around, that the shock had worn off, that she'd felt well enough to go to school, that Susannah would have another chance to see them.

When Grey did call, mid-morning, he spoke in a low voice, as if worried that Sari might hear him.

"How are you?" he asked.

"Never mind me," she said. "How's Sari?"

"The same," he said.

"You kept her home from school?"

"I had to," he said. "It takes a while for her to come out of it . . ."

"I feel terrible," she said.

"Don't," he said. "You didn't do anything. You've come into something that was set in place long ago. She'll be okay."

"I just . . ." Susannah began. "I just hoped I could see you. I thought maybe you both could come for dinner tonight. I wanted . . . to be with you, my last night here, and talk to Sari about what happened."

"You have no idea how much I want that," he said.

"I understand, Grey. I know you have to take care of her . . ."

"Susannah . . ." he murmured. "You know I'd be there in a minute if I could."

"What about you?" Susannah forced herself to move on. "Will you be okay?"

"Yeah," he said after a moment, as if he had to think about it. "I will. Until tomorrow."

"Tomorrow . . ."

"Until you leave . . ."

They held on for another minute, then said goodbye. Susannah hated hanging up the phone, breaking the connection.

She couldn't bear giving up the idea she'd had of cooking for him and Sari, so she left the house and walked up the street to the market. She picked out the most delicious food she could find, brought it home. She'd gotten things that were meaningful, that would connect with this magical time she'd had in the Camargue.

Coquilles St. Jacques, glistening pink with the red roe still attached; small local crabs, just like the *favouilles* they'd seen last night; pencil-thin stalks of asparagus, as green as the fields all around the Manade; delicate squash blossoms, to be stuffed with a duxelles of mushrooms and herbs, the color bright saffron, reminiscent of the garland of flowers painted in the Dempseys' kitchen.

And then Susannah prepared the meal, just as if Grey and Sari were really coming. She filled the kitchen with the most beautiful aroma, grateful for every minute she'd spent in this enchanted place. The copper pans glinted, the olive oil poured in a cool green stream, the smells of sage and tarragon made her feel as if she were forever under Provence's romantic spell.

A knock on the door made her jump. Turning, she half expected to see them standing there. But it was Topaz instead. The setting sun shone on her burnished brown hair, dark tan arms, amber-colored silk dress. Topaz held a bag and a bouquet of dried lavender.

"I've come to say farewell," Topaz said. "And here you are, making a feast!"

"Please, come in," Susannah said.

"Who are you cooking for?"

Susannah smiled. "For my ghosts," she said. "The ones I brought with me when I came to the Camargue, and the ones I'll be leaving when I go. Since they can't very well eat all this lovely food, will you join me?"

"I'd be delighted," Topaz said. "Honestly, I smelled your cooking all the way down the street."

"I'm glad you followed it to *my* door," Susannah said. "You have the best market in the world, and I couldn't resist buy-ing all these good things . . ."

Of course Topaz knew where everything was, so she pitched in, helping to finish cooking the meal. Susannah poured them glasses of the lovely sweet-dry rosé of Provence; it would forever remind her of being at Cap Morgiou with Grey. They clinked glasses, drank to Susannah's stay in Topaz's house.

As Susannah set the table with Provençal cotton linens, the tablecloth pale pumpkin and the napkins printed with faded red and purple flowers, her throat caught. She had wanted to make this meal so special for Sari and Grey. She set out silver-ware, bright crockery, a Lucite peppermill and a blue container of Fleur-de-Sel de Camargue. She still had Grey's black scallop shells and she arranged them in the center of the table, around a vase of colorful wildflowers. When she lit the tall white ta-pers, she felt the tears start, gritted her teeth, and turned away for a moment while she swallowed them down.

Dinner was ready. The two women dined on *soupe de favouilles,* made with stock of onions, carrots, and celery that had been simmering for hours, enriched with crème fraîche, fla-vored with bright threads of fragrant saffron, and thick with fresh local crabmeat.

Next came coquilles St. Jacques, served in the shell after a quick sauté in olive oil, garlic, and finely chopped tomatoes; a green salad; *fleurs de courgettes* stuffed with a duxelles of wild mushrooms; a baguette and fresh farm butter. When dinner was over, Susannah put out the last of the cheese she'd been enjoying during her stay: Crottin, creamy St. Marcellin, and one small piece of Roquefort.

Susannah did her best to eat. She wanted to savor every bite, but she barely tasted anything. She made sure Topaz had enough, and she was aware of her friend watching how much she left on her plate.

"This was delicious," Topaz proclaimed. "But it's a good thing I came."

"Yes, it is, I loved having you."

"That's not what I meant," Topaz said. "I mean that this would have been much too much food for some ghosts and a woman who barely ate a single bite . . ."

"Oh," Susannah said.

"Indeed," Topaz said.

Susannah stared into the candlelight. It flickered, and a small breeze sent columns of smoke up to the ceiling. Topaz leaned forward, catching Susannah's eyes.

"I wanted them to come for dinner tonight," Susannah said.

"Sari and Grey?"

Susannah nodded. "I wanted it very badly."

"I'm sure he did, too," Topaz said. "In fact, I know. He called me and asked me to come check on you. He didn't go into detail, but I could tell he's concerned about you. He's in deep."

Susannah gave her a direct gaze. "Why do you say that?"

"Grey Dempsey hasn't looked seriously at a woman since Maria left," Topaz said. "He was burned by her, badly. But worse, he saw what it did to Sari."

"You should have seen her last night," Susannah said. The story started spilling out: the full-moon trail ride, the call from Sari, the lost horse, the ordeal of pulling Tempest from the quicksand. She got toward the end of the story, and Topaz guessed the rest.

"Sari saw you together?" she asked.

"Yes," Susannah said.

"That Rosalie . . ." Topaz said.

"What do you mean?"

"All the time she spent with Sari, drilling it into her head that her mother was both so special and so cursed. It's a terrible, heavy burden for Sari to carry. She thinks she drove her mother away." Topaz shook her head angrily.

"Sari thinks she drove her *away?*" Susannah asked. "Maria hit her."

"You weren't there, and neither was I," Topaz said. "But I know Maria, and she couldn't have hit her."

"Sari says she did," Susannah said. "Grey told me, and I believe them."

"You don't know Maria," Topaz said. "She didn't hit her child." She paused a moment, and then shook her head. "If something like that *did* happen, it was a terrible, terrible accident."

Susannah watched Topaz; she seemed so secure and calm, and her statement had the confidence of conviction.

"Will you tell me about Maria leaving?" Susannah asked.

"We all adore Maria," Topaz said. "If you knew her, you would, too." She spoke steadily, defying the doubt she saw in Susannah's eyes. "It's impossible not to—her *joie de vivre* is unparalleled. Her gifts in the realms of magic, horses, and balance are truly miraculous. Sari . . . the child must remember what it was like to have a magician as a mother."

"Maria is really a magician?"

"In a manner of speaking. She can charm a horse as no one else can. Our clan reveres horses. We grow up with them, almost like members of our family. But no one, not even the elders, could ride like Maria. To see her, you would swear she's floating on air, just above the back of the animal. It's beyond description . . . and it was too great a gift for her to let go."

"Let go?" Susannah asked, suddenly filled with fury, picturing Sari standing devastated in the moonlit marsh. "So she let go of her family instead?"

"I don't expect you to understand," Topaz said quietly. "You don't know her. I'm not saying that she did it well, or did it right . . . but she had to leave."

"What about the 'curse'? Did that have something to do with it?"

"Well, perhaps," Topaz said, sighing. "Zin-Zin was furious with Maria for marrying Grey."

Topaz reached out for the wine bottle, poured them each another glass. They sat there a few moments, calming down. After another sip of Bandol, Topaz raised her eyes toward Susannah.

"She left him for another man," she said quietly.

"The trainer."

Topaz nodded. "Adrien Ferret. His Gypsy name is Matelo."

"What happened?"

"He was the son of our greatest horse trainer, a genius in his own right; he'd frequently be hired by the best horse farms, from Normandy to Belgium. He was the only trainer some people would use. Even in Ireland, for the most magnificent Irish hunters, and even for Dutch hot-bloods. He was brilliant . . ."

"And he worked with Maria?"

Again, a nod. "Yes. Everyone thought they would be married—before she met Grey. Zin-Zin decreed it."

"That's why she was so unhappy when Maria decided to marry Grey instead?"

"That's putting it mildly. As I said, Maria was feisty and independent. No one was going to tell her what to do. She made her choice to marry outside our tradition. But she paid the price. She was so terribly unhappy—and so was Grey."

"And Adrien was waiting all that time?"

Topaz nodded. "We have a festival every May. Romanies from all across Europe make the pilgrimage to see Sarah. We have dances, and parties, and there are always a lot of horses. A tent is erected on the caravan grounds, and a small circus is held. It's not for the public—just for us. Tightropes, and trapezes, and the most exquisite white horses ridden by the best riders . . . it's a show that no one else has ever seen, one that most people would believe was sheer magic."

"And Maria . . ."

"She did some of the most spectacular riding of her life there, even after she married Grey. Adrien had her lead his group, in spite of everything. You have to imagine the tent—swooping material, parachute silk, in colors from midnight blue to glowing amber, printed with gold images of stars and the moon. And the tent was lit by lanterns, a hundred of them!"

Susannah pictured the tent, glowing with light, filled with Maria's clan, watching her perform her magic. She could almost see the white horses, the avid faces, the exquisite fabric of the circus tent, Adrien watching his prize rider. But all of those images were dimmed by the sight of Grey and Sari. Were they there in the crowd? Five years ago Sari would have been eight; how proud she must have been of her mother . . .

"It was the last week of May," Topaz said. "The month of miracles was almost over. Devotions to Sarah had been made, our circus had been held, the clan was dispersing for another year. Adrien was leaving for his latest posts—this time across the Atlantic. He had horses to train in British Columbia and Nevada."

Susannah nodded, listening.

"He went to the Manade du Dempsey; I'm not sure anyone but he and Maria, and perhaps Rosalie, know whether a plan had already been made. Rosalie has never told the truth of that. All I know is what happened next. Maria ran to his car, they drove away, and Maria never returned."

"Something else happened," Susannah said.

Topaz glanced over.

"Sari," Susannah said. The name hung in the air, reverberating. Susannah stared into the candle flame. She followed the smoke with her eyes, swirling up to the ceiling. She thought of Sarah's chapel, of the soot-blackened crypt. Her heart skipped, thinking of all Sari had gone through, from that terrible night forward. And in that instant, she felt anger at the saint.

"And now . . ." Susannah trailed off.

"Maria and Matelo run a horse facility in the desert," Topaz said. "In Nevada, just outside of Las Vegas. And they've started . . ."

"What?"

"A circus. Very similar to the magical little tented circus we have every May. It's not unlike Cirque du Soleil; they perform at one of the casinos."

"What's it called?" Susannah asked. When Topaz didn't reply, she leaned forward. "I can find out, easily enough."

"Clair de Lune," Topaz said.

"Light of the moon," Susannah whispered, thinking of the night before, picturing Grey swathed in luminous blue light. She could almost smell the sea air, feel the warmth of his arms around her.

"The show is brilliant, I've heard," Topaz said. "Friends have traveled to see it; some even work there. I'm told that one feels a spell has been cast, and—"

"What does her name mean?" Susannah asked suddenly, her head light as she thought again of the saint, and of a little girl left behind by her mother.

"Maria? She was named for the three Marys, of course," Topaz said.

"Not Maria. Sari."

"Well, it's a nickname."

"For what?"

"Sari's real name is Zinnia," Topaz said. "She's named for Zin-Zin, in honor of all her wisdom."

"In spite of her unhappiness with Maria's marriage to Grey?"

"Perhaps because of it," Topaz said. "It was Maria's attempt to mollify Zin-Zin, win back her love."

"It didn't work?"

Topaz shook her head. "Zin-Zin is very stubborn."

Susannah pictured the face of the very old woman sitting at

the Sarah Circle, her eyes kind and patient and full of love—how could someone supposedly so wise not have accepted Maria's choice? How could she think she knew better?

"What is her middle name? Sari's?" Susannah asked.

"You know already," Topaz said steadily.

"Tell me."

"It's Sarah."

Susannah stared at the candles, her eyes welling with tears. "Sarah . . . the saint hasn't taken very good care of this girl who has her name."

"Sarah takes care of everyone who asks her," Topaz said.

Susannah looked into the eyes of this woman who had so quickly become a friend. She felt Topaz's divided loyalties: between the women she cared about; and between Sara-la-Kali, to whom she devoted so much of her life, and the young girl who'd been left behind.

"She will take care of you," Topaz said. "She already has."

"I prayed for something yesterday," Susannah said. "I almost thought . . ."

Topaz laughed gently. "And you wanted instant results?"

Susannah stared at the candle.

"My dear friend. You, who know better than any of us the miracles Sarah can perform . . . even you took nine months to be born. Miracles don't happen overnight."

"But Sari . . . she's suffering."

"She has a good father," Topaz said. "And somewhere, a mother who loves her."

"'Somewhere' isn't good enough," Susannah said.

"So you say," Topaz said. "But do you know what would happen if Maria returned? Can you say that after all this time it would be the best thing?"

"For Sari it would."

"Are you so sure that it would be better for Sari to have a mother who longed to be somewhere else? I know how terrible that sounds to you, how much you want to judge Maria.

But not everyone is like your mother. Not everyone is like you . . ."

"I'm not a mother," Susannah said.

"Remember what Zin-Zin said," Topaz said gently.

"That I will be someday."

Topaz nodded and took her hand. Then, gently, "Just not today."

"Not today," Susannah agreed, the candlelight blurring as she stared at it through tears and thought of everything she'd be leaving when she flew home tomorrow, to her wonderful life full of friends, research, classes, and colleagues. And no Grey.

NINETEEN

Tuesday the weather changed again. The sky was dark, and the wind felt spooky and cold. Grey drove into Stes.-Maries-de-la-Mer, and headed for the white house just off the harbor. Whitecaps filled the bay, and flags snapped in the wind.

He parked in the driveway, and opened the car door just as Susannah was stepping out into the drizzle. Laden down with her suitcase and briefcase, she looked shocked to see him. He felt the thudding impact of her expression and realized—she didn't want to see him.

But then he stepped out of the car, and she dropped her bags, and she was in his arms, standing in the sharp, cold rain. He held her, rocking her, just standing there getting wet together and not caring. His mouth brushed hers, kissing her lightly and then deeply and wanting to give her everything he had. Her face was wet, only partly from the rain.

"I didn't think I'd see you again," she said.

"That could never happen," he said.

"But I'm on my way to the airport," she said. "My flight from Arles to Paris is this morning."

"I know," he said. "I'm going to drive you."

Her face fell; she pointed at the car in the driveway. "I have to return my rental car," she said.

Grey smiled. "Leave the keys; I made some calls last night, and we'll get it back to the airport for you."

"But who?" she asked.

"Topaz will drive it up, and Claude will meet her at the lot there and give her a ride back home."

She didn't need more than that. Grey lifted her bags, carried them to his car and stowed them in back. It was his battered old Citroën; their last ride in it had been to Cap Morgiou and back. Susannah climbed in, and gave him a smile, remembering.

He was hoping the weather would cause her flight to be canceled. "Did you check with the airline?" he asked.

"Yes," she said. "No delays so far."

"Well," he said, "maybe that will change."

He backed out of the space, pulled onto the road. As he drove through town, he felt eyes on him. Grey didn't care. Let them stare all they wanted. They passed Rosalie, coming out of the post office; she stopped dead and stared coldly at the car.

Susannah waved goodbye; Rosalie didn't wave back.

"Why is she that way toward you?" Susannah asked. "So much time has passed since Maria left . . ."

"It's the way life is here," Grey said. "Everyone's very raw when it comes to Maria."

"That's why Sari was so upset at me the other night . . ."

Grey took one hand off the wheel to reach across and hold hers. He wanted to hold her and reassure her, and also reassure himself.

"Sari walks a fine line," Grey said. "A razor edge, when it

comes to her mother. She got into trouble with Rosalie, for criticizing Maria to her. For saying she hates her. But she doesn't, not really. Sari has a hard time with women. If she gets too close to someone, she feels she's being disloyal to her mother. And if I do, she's afraid she's going to lose me."

"You'd told me that," Susannah said. "But seeing it was a whole other story. It was terrifying to see her that way."

Grey nodded. "I know. And she's such a wonderful girl, Susannah, she is. If only you could know her. But the line is so fine with her. She's made progress. She has. But I'm always afraid something will push her back to the way she was right after the accident. She's terrified I'll leave her, too."

"You'd never leave her."

"Of course not."

"I care about her so much," Susannah said. "I did from the moment we met. I'm not sure whether it was tied up with you or not. But I felt a bond. I wish she knew that . . ."

"Susannah, I think she does," Grey said. "And that confuses her more than anything."

When he glanced at Susannah, he saw her frowning, taking that in, as if trying to figure out what it meant, or what to do about it.

He pulled onto the road leading north, leaving Stes.-Maries behind. He watched Susannah gaze at the dark silhouette of the ancient church, the site of Sarah's chapel and so much history.

They drove through the Parc Régional de Camargue, washed with rain. The endless plain of sea grass was darkened by low clouds; white horses in the distance looked like ghosts or shadows. A herd of black bulls clustered by the road, on the other side of a fence, and Grey slowed down so she could see.

"They don't look so dangerous from in here," she said, squeezing his hand.

"If it weren't for the fence, they could do some damage to this little car," he said.

"I'll always be grateful to the bulls," she said. "When I see them in cave paintings, they'll always remind me of us. They brought us together."

He nodded. It was strange, how the most unexpected happenings could turn everything around, take life in a completely different direction. That day he'd been riding Mystère because she didn't get enough exercise. He'd crashed through the circle of bulls to rescue a stranger, who in turn had gotten Sari back up on Mystère again. Most of all, he had met Susannah . . .

"You've changed my life forever," he said.

"And you've changed mine," she said. "Let's not stop, okay? Let's keep changing our lives, until we come back together . . ."

He heard something in her tone, and when he glanced over, he felt a shiver shoot down his spine. She was on the edge of her seat.

He drove slowly away from the bulls, and checking his watch, sped toward Arles. He remembered how he had waited at the side of this road—on a rainy day just like today—and followed Susannah to the library. He'd lived here for over fifteen years, and suddenly the entire landscape was transformed. He would never again drive past these spots without thinking of Susannah, and how much he missed her.

"I want to do something," she said.

"Oh, Susannah," he said quietly, feeling another shiver. "You live in Connecticut, I live in the Camargue. But distance isn't the problem."

"I know," she said. "Talk to her, Grey."

"Do you think I haven't?" he asked.

"Maybe you haven't in a way she can hear."

"We visit the States every summer," Grey said. "My parents' house in Rhode Island isn't so far from Connecticut."

"You could visit," she said, and he felt her glance over.

"I want that more than anything," he said.

"But . . ." she began, trailing off, frowning.

He knew she meant Sari, too. Didn't she understand that wasn't going to happen? It was all over; she didn't know his daughter.

"She loves my parents," he said. "And they'd do anything for her. My brothers, too. The sun rises and sets on Sari for the whole Dempsey family. I'm thinking that maybe some day when she's out on my dad's boat, or fishing with my brothers, I can drive down to see you . . ."

"Grey," she said. And the sadness in her tone made him realize that she was backing away from him.

"I have to be with you again," he said, looking over. "It's why I had to drive you today, why I can't stand the idea of you going on that plane. Please say you'll see me when I get there this summer . . . we can meet somewhere, anywhere you say . . . I'll drive to your house, or we can go someplace else."

She glanced over, and he could see the longing in her face. He felt it, too. He wanted her now, and he'd be wanting her every minute until he saw her again.

"How long will we have?" she asked. "Will we have an hour, two?"

"Susannah, I don't know," he said, reaching for her, wanting to pull her all the way across the seat. "We'll be together as much as we can."

She stared out the window. He saw the worry lines between her brows, as if she was struggling with something.

"Of course, I want to be with you again, too," she said. "More than you can imagine. If that's all we have, then that's what it will be. But it seems so small and sad, compared to what I feel inside."

"Susannah," he said quietly. "You saw Sari in the marsh, and at the ranch afterwards. That's what I'm dealing with—

no matter how much I want you, want to be with you all the time."

Susannah nodded sadly, looking over at him, not trying to talk him into something he just couldn't do.

Grey got it. Susannah wanted what they had to add up to more than just a few stolen meetings—sneaking off to the library, to the sea cave, a moonlit trail ride, this trip to the airport. He wanted that, too, and he was driving himself insane trying to think of ways to speed the process.

"She slept with your Tarasque the last two nights," he said.

"She did?"

"Yes. I looked in on her, and she was holding it tight, right under her chin."

"Grey . . ." she began, then trailed off, as if she had already said what she had to say.

And suddenly, way too soon, they were at the Nîmes-Garon airport.

Susannah checked her ticket, and he took her to the terminal. She had a Ryanair flight to Paris, connecting with Air France to Boston. She sat very still, staring straight ahead, as if she didn't want to move.

Grey sat there, his heart pounding. He had so many things he wanted to say. For the first time in years, his heart and mind were connected. They were both unlocked, and words and feelings were flowing. Everything was directed to Susannah. He only wanted to talk to her; his thoughts were for her alone. Once she got onto that plane, how would he go back to the way things had been? Locked up, locked down.

"Susannah," he said, taking her hand. "Don't go."

She looked over at him, eyes welling with tears.

"But I have to," she said. "I have work, and my house, and my life to get home to. Besides—what would happen if I stayed here? Would I hide from Sari?"

He couldn't answer that.

"I'll tell you one thing," she said, taking his hand. "I know you say she's fragile. She's your child, and you know her better than anyone. But I'll bet you anything she's stronger than you think."

He gazed at her, listening.

"You said she slept with the Tarasque; you know why, don't you?"

"Why?"

"Because she's trying to *fight*. She's thirteen, and too old for stuffed animals, but she's up against something that's scaring her so much she can't stand it. But she wants to chase it away. She does."

"What is it?"

Susannah shook her head. "I don't know, exactly. But it came out the other night, when she saw us together."

"It's just like you told her," Grey said. "She's tormented by what happened with her mother, and she has to deal with it. And she gets that! She does. Susannah, you should see her hanging on to the toy you gave her, for all she's worth . . . I know she was upset to see me with you. But . . . she likes you, Susannah. She likes you so much."

Susannah smiled, but her eyes were so sad. "Her fears really don't have to do with me," she said. "They're five years old; they've been with her ever since the night her mother drove away."

"I know," Grey said.

She nodded, gazing into his eyes as if she understood him. They were in an impossible situation, and Maria had put them there.

"Can I write you? At least let you know when we're coming to the States?" Grey asked.

"Of course," she said. "And I'll write to you, too. In fact, I'll probably write you from the plane."

He laughed. Susannah fumbled in her bag, pulled out a business card from Connecticut College, wrote down her home number, address, and email. He scribbled his address, and email address, and phone number on a scrap of paper. She reached for the paper, and he caught her hand.

She gazed into his eyes. The car was idling, and an official was standing just outside his window trying to hurry him along, but Grey couldn't move. He sat there, holding her hand, roughened from scrambling over rocks, crawling into caves. He loved her hands.

"Thank you for everything," she said.

"I didn't do anything."

"Don't get me started. There's not one thing I regret," she said.

"There is for me," he said. "I have one huge regret."

"What's that?"

"That I can't throw Ian into the harbor all over again."

She laughed. So did he, and he felt how impossible it all was. How could he meet someone like this, and feel as if he were about to lose any chance with her forever? Suddenly the security official tapped on his window, gave him a stern look. Grey indicated that he'd move right along.

"I'll park the car and walk you in," he said.

"No," Susannah said. "Please, don't . . ."

"Susannah . . ."

"This is too hard," she said.

He stared at her. He knew what she meant, but he couldn't let her go; grabbing for her hand again, he pulled her close to kiss her. Her body felt so light, and already familiar. The way his arms went around her, the weight of her hand on his shoulder, the way her mouth felt on his. When she pulled back from him, Grey saw the official approaching again.

"I already miss you," he said. "More than I can believe."

She seemed about to speak, but instead she just turned away.

And then she was out of the car, a blast of wet air coming through. She grabbed her bags. He stared after her, and she didn't look back, not even once, before running through the airport doors. The official let him watch until the last moment, then tapped his window, moving him along.

Grey put the car in gear and drove away. He could still taste Susannah's kiss and feel her small, rough hands, but she was already gone.

The plane ride from Arles had been bumpy, never quite making it above the rough weather until they crossed through central France. Then they left the mistral behind, landing at Paris in nothing much more than light drizzle.

The flight from Paris to Boston was half empty, and the cabin crew upgraded Susannah to first class. She flew Air France a lot, and this had happened before, and she'd always enjoyed the wide leather seat, the soft wool blanket, and the complimentary glass of champagne. This time she was just glad to have a little extra privacy.

She had a window seat. As the plane took off, banking around Paris, she had views of the Arc de Triomphe, the Eiffel Tower, and the Seine. She stared down at the serpentine river, twisting north toward the coast and English Channel, but she was picturing a different body of water.

The Rhône River, making its passage through the Camargue, with its estuary of marshland, endless and green, filled with black bulls and white horses. Susannah closed her eyes, trying to hold on to everything she was feeling. She brought her left hand to her face, smelled Grey: horses, leather, salt air.

Her briefcase was filled with material she'd gathered for Helen. And her suitcase was filled with some of the souvenirs she'd bought, that would always remind her of this trip: a muslin peasant shirt embroidered with flowers, a book about Sarah with a beautiful picture of her statue on the cover, a small statue of Sarah, some candles, photos of the white horses, jars of delicious things from the *marché* at Stes.-Maries-de-la-Mer.

But most of what she was bringing home she could neither pack nor carry. She felt it deep inside: a change in her heart. It was a terrible heaviness—not of grief or regret, but of wild love. It was as if during this trip her heart had shed the pain of her mother's death, opened itself up for something new and completely unexpected.

Susannah had kept herself closed off for a long time. She'd focused on work to recover from grief. She'd grown up in a home feeling completely loved and cared for. Her parents had nurtured her talents and intellect; after her father's death, she'd grown closer to her mother. They'd had a special bond— her mother the teacher, and Susannah in the department of cultural anthropology at Connecticut College.

Susannah had wanted to fall in love, get married, have a family, but it had never happened. Perhaps she'd been too spoiled by so much early love from her parents. And then Ian had come along, and they had wasted years in their halfhearted limbo, trying to hold on even after she'd realized they were completely wrong together.

Suddenly it was strange flying in first class alone. She felt the funniest ache, wishing she could share it with Grey. All the nice things: the extra attention, the warm blanket, the flight attendant coming around to refill glasses. The flight felt so special, but what did it matter?

Now that she'd been with Grey, felt what it was like to love someone, it made being alone feel twice as hard. She'd never minded it before. She'd planned her trips solo; she'd had her books and writings for company. Right now, the seat beside her was empty, and it made her feel so hollow inside, she began to panic.

She looked out the window at the counterpane landscape of France. The coast appeared, a long jagged edge that fell into the Atlantic. She felt that once the plane flew over the water, she would lose everything: this trip had just been a vacation, a getaway, a little escape. Yes, she'd met people she liked, but what could they possibly mean to her, after all? And what could she mean to them?

Reaching into her carry-on bag, her hand was shaking. She pulled out a small silk pouch—bought only days ago, at the *marché*—just to reassure herself it had all been real. Unzipping it, she removed the black scallop shells Grey had given her on the beach. She placed them on the tray beside her seat.

And she tried to keep her heart calm, her mind from despairing, as she reminded herself it had all been real. So real, she began to cry. She hadn't asked for anything, hadn't expected to fall in love. She'd received so much more than she'd ever thought possible.

Staring down at the scallop shells, she thought of all she had left behind, on the ground in France—people she had just met and had never dreamed she could love so much—and tried to understand what it all meant, why she had fallen so deeply in love with someone she couldn't have. Why had such a thing happened?

But she couldn't answer her own question, so she just rested her head against the cold window and watched the ocean down below and remembered the peace and connection she'd felt with Grey under the sea.

TWENTY

School had never been so difficult. It was impossible to sit and think. Sari dragged herself into the building, made herself go to class, sat in her seat and pretended to listen. Her friends were all leaning forward, concentrating on what the teacher was saying.

They were all getting their *bac;* their baccalaureate certificate, necessary for continuing to college. Sari was in the A program, for arts and literature. Today's lecture had to do with themes of morality and rationality in Molière. Sari couldn't focus on a word.

Laurent met her in the hallway after classes were over. She bumped right into him, her books went flying, she was in such another world. He gathered them up without admonishing her, even as other kids were walking past, staring.

She cringed, embarrassed. What was wrong with her? Laurent followed her into an empty classroom. She sat down at one of the pale wood desks, and he stacked her books in front of her.

"What's wrong?" he asked. "You should be happy today."

"Why?" she asked.

"Your essay," he said. "Didn't you get it back from Mademoiselle Guillaume?"

"No," she said, staring at him. "You got yours back?"

He nodded. "With a good grade; I assumed your mark would be even higher, considering your essay was better."

Sari stared down at the desk. She had enjoyed everything about that essay—the magical trip to Avignon, the way she'd felt writing about the night, the way writing seemed to unlock something inside her. The words had spilled out, describing the night Laurent had planned for her, the joy she'd felt to wander the streets with her best friend, knowing they were seeing everything the same way.

"I wonder why Mademoiselle Guillaume didn't return your paper?" he asked.

"She probably hated it," Sari said.

"Why would you say that?"

"Because of how I am," Sari said. "I never should have written the truth . . . shouldn't have told about the city being black and silver that night, and how it made me feel as if I belonged. It was too much. I never know when to stop."

"That's what made your essay stand out," Laurent said. "You told the truth."

Sari sat there shaking. She was so tired of the truth. She wanted someone else's life. She wanted to be happy and pretty, with the same color skin as everyone else—either darker or paler than her in-between medium shade. She wanted a whole family, she wanted to put on a sweater and know what color it was.

"I bet Mademoiselle Guillaume is showing your paper to the other teachers. Just wait, Sari. You'll get it back with the best grade of anyone. You could be a journalist, just like your father used to be."

Sari glanced at Laurent. How did he read her mind the way he did? She'd had that same thought, writing the essay— maybe she could become a reporter when she finished school. But lately she'd felt too depressed to care.

"We could join the school paper," he said.

"It's almost the end of the term," she said.

"Well, there's one more issue to put out. We could write stories for it. Or help in some other way." At the look in her eyes, he stopped. He'd been sounding so enthusiastic, but she just couldn't join in.

"What's wrong?" he asked.

"Everything. I can't join the paper. Sometimes I feel as if I don't belong anywhere in the world. Here at school, on our ranch, nowhere. I'm completely different. I'm half Romany . . ."

"First of all, what does being half Romany have to do with joining the paper?"

"Nothing specifically; I just feel like an outcast," she said, struggling to explain what she felt inside.

"There are other Rom here at school," Laurent said.

"Yes, but they're all-Romany. Not mixed. My mother's people don't want me, and my father's live in America. Gypsy kids don't want anything to do with me—I can feel it, Laurent," she said when she caught the look of doubt in his eyes. "No one wants me."

"Sari, May twenty-fourth is coming—the Gypsies' Pilgrimage in Stes.-Maries. Every year you're invited to march in the parade, to carry the school banner or sing in the chorus, and every single year you refuse. *You're* the one who doesn't want anything to do with them!"

"Because of my mother! Everyone knows she just left me— it's shameful. People try to make up for it, like Susannah, but it doesn't work. I'm wrecked."

"Wrecked? You're getting better—you're so much stronger, Sari. You rode Mystère . . ."

"But I don't *want* to ride her again," Sari whispered, feeling despair. "It was just that one time. I thought I could do it. I thought I was going to be okay . . . Until that night with Susannah, when I ruined everything."

"No, you didn't," he said. "Susannah would understand, if you wanted to write to her, talk to her . . ."

"But I don't want that," Sari said, staring down at the desk. Everything was a gray blur. She'd gotten her hopes up last month; life had seemed to be changing. Her father had seemed happier, and as Laurent said, Sari had made strides. Now she felt trapped back inside the same old grainy black-and-white movie. Completely stuck, while everyone around was moving on.

"Okay, fine," he said. "Don't call her, then. Things will get better, Sari."

"I don't know . . ."

"You'll want to hold on to your paper when you get it back," he said. "Because someday you'll look back and want to remember how it was. What it's like to see through your eyes."

Laurent's words ignited something terrible in Sari. She suddenly felt her best friend didn't understand her, didn't get her at all. "What do you mean? Why would I want to remember 'what it's like to see through' my eyes? I already know!"

"I mean, once you start seeing colors again, you'll forget what it was like to see in silver."

"It's *not* silver," she said, her eyes filling with tears. "That was just how it was that night. It's gray, Laurent. Murky, muddy, colorless gray. I'm *colorblind*. I don't have to remember anything. Why can't you understand that it will never go away? It's how it's always going to be!"

"Sari, I didn't mean—"

She stood up to run away, but he grabbed her.

Laurent was tall and toughly built, like her father, and he held her away, and now she did start to cry; big shuddering sobs wracked her body. She had to hold the sound inside, stifled so hard it hurt, because her classmates were filling the halls now, getting ready to board the buses home. Laurent picked up her books, steered her outside, reached into his pocket for a folded handkerchief, handed it to her.

"I'm so sorry, Sari," he said.

"So am I," she said, wiping her eyes.

"You're very distressed, I know."

They began to walk toward the buses. Her eyes were red and swollen; she could feel them, puffy and stinging. That morning she had looked in the mirror, hating herself, and noticed dark circles beneath her eyes. Ugly! She hadn't slept well. Not since the night of the moonlit trail ride. The night of Tempest. The night she'd seen her father and Susannah . . .

As she got onto the bus, she paid close attention to all her classmates' faces—just to see if they were staring at her. They all seemed absorbed in their own conversations, except a couple of friends—Genevieve and Josephine—who smiled. Sari tried to smile back.

By the time she sat at the back of the bus, she was shaking all over again. Laurent slid in beside her. His shoulders were wide, and pressed against hers. She felt glad for his presence.

She glanced over, saw him staring down at her. He had medium-dark hair and bright eyes she remembered being hazel. He was handsome, and other girls liked him. Sometimes he rode the bus with Alice, other times with Jeanine. But for some reason, this entire year he almost always sat with Sari.

The way he was watching her felt protective. She looked up at him and wondered what he was thinking. He'd seen it all. He'd heard her screaming five years ago, the night her mother had left.

And the way she'd acted with Susannah.

"I'm tired," she said, stifling a yawn.

"You must be," he said.

"What do you mean?" she asked, feeling sensitive, girding up to be teased or criticized.

"Your light was on very late last night," he said. "What were you doing?"

"Work for school," she lied. "Molière . . ."

"Sari," he said, smiling indulgently. "Tell me the truth. Were you looking on Google Earth again?"

She shrugged. That very small twitch of her shoulders was like a toggle, sending blood into her face. Her blush gave it all away.

"For Las Vegas?"

She gazed out the bus window. Despite what she'd said, Laurent knew her so well. He spent enough time at her house to know her habits. More than once he'd caught her zooming in on Las Vegas—the strip, with all the stark lights and casinos, the dancing fountains of the Bellagio. So it seemed easier to nod now—lie again—than tell him the truth.

"Since you know your mother is there, why do you not write her?" he asked. "Care of the *cirque*? Or even of the horse farm. They both have the same name, *n'est-ce pas*? Clair de Lune."

"I don't want to write her," Sari said.

"Then why do you keep looking for her online? She's not there, on your computer screen. I wish I could find her myself. I'd tell her what she's done, who she's left behind."

"She knows," Sari said, holding herself tight.

Laurent was stirred up, and so was she. She partly wanted to tell him the truth, but she couldn't quite do it. It was easier to let him think she'd been searching for her mother. Instead, Sari had aimed Google Earth, the cyber eye-in-the-sky, at an address she'd found on a card in her father's bedside table: the same place he'd hidden that ribbon just two and a half weeks ago.

11 Blue Heron Drive, Black Hall, Connecticut.

The satellite image had shown a small house, surrounded by trees, very near the wide and rippling sea of marsh grass that was the Connecticut River estuary. So, Susannah lived near marshland, just like Sari and her dad.

Zooming back, Sari saw that Connecticut was very near Rhode Island. Her grandparents lived on the farm in Narragansett, and her uncles and cousins lived in Westerly. They were practically right next door to Susannah. At least, compared to Sari all the way in France.

"So," Laurent was saying. "What new things did you see in Las Vegas?"

"Un désert d'eau," she said without thinking. *"Étangs, sansouire, et les îles dans le marais."*

"Really?" he asked. "Lagoons, a plane of marsh grass, and salt-marsh islands? In Nevada?"

She looked up, caught by her friend.

"You were looking up Susannah, weren't you?"

"No," she said stubbornly.

"Are you to see her?" Laurent asked, ignoring her denial. "This summer, when you and your father go to Rhode Island to see your grandparents . . . will you drive to the marsh to see Susannah in Connecticut?"

Sari gazed out the window and shook her head. "No," she said. "It's better that she's out of our lives, and we're out of hers."

"Of course, you're right," Laurent said, amusement in his eyes.

"I mean it," Sari said again, just for emphasis.

"I know, Sari. I know."

Sari stared out the school bus window at the trees and houses and marsh. Laurent thought he knew her, but this wasn't like Avignon. It was daylight, so he was seeing blue sky, green grass, colorful houses. And just like every other day for the past five years, Sari wasn't, and never would.

*   *   *

Life on the ranch had always had its own rhythm. Springtime meant foals being born, horses being trained and penned, tourists returning to the Camargue. Grey had always spent the spring repairing the ravages of winter, looking forward to a busy summer both here and in Rhode Island.

The young horses always went a little crazy in spring. They kicked at their stalls, pulled at the bit, tried to escape any chance they got. This year, Grey felt that way, too. His brief time with Susannah had turned him into someone new. He went through the motions of being a good father, taking care of the ranch, but all he wanted to do was be with her.

That wasn't going to happen, so he thought about her all the time instead. He found himself taking long solitary trail rides, taking Django farther and farther into the Parc. When that wasn't far enough, he'd get into the car and drive. Sometimes, if he was in the right mood, he could almost believe she was in the car with him.

She'd been right there, in the seat beside him. They'd driven east, so that's what Grey started doing. The first time, he took the N568 as far as Fos-sur-Mer. The next day, he made it onto the A55. Caught in traffic, he remembered how he and Susannah had gotten stuck in Marseille's morning rush.

One afternoon he told Claude he was taking off. Sari's history teacher had pulled her aside, told her she wanted to submit Sari's essay on Avignon to the school paper. To Grey's surprise, Sari had agreed—not only that, she had reluctantly let Laurent convince her to get involved for the paper's last issue. It would mean working after school, and meant both kids would have a shot at becoming editors next fall. Grey was so proud of her, but almost more than that, he'd been relieved because it meant he'd have more time to himself.

Being alone was his way of being with Susannah. They

sent each other emails all the time. Grey checked his computer ten times a day, hoping there'd be something there from her. There usually was, and he'd write right back.

They called each other a few times when Sari was at school, but that was hard. The phone made things worse. To hear her voice and not be able to see her, to listen to the silence between words and wonder what she was thinking . . .

More than anything, Grey loved her letters. They came on fine blue stationery, embossed with a blue heron. She'd write about the marsh near her house, how it reminded her of being with him, how she'd walk through the reeds every morning just hoping he'd appear out of the mist on a white horse.

He'd hold her letters to his face, knowing the paper had been in those beautiful hands of hers, hoping for a breath of her scent. It wasn't enough, but it was all he had. He'd write back, trying to give her hope that someday everything would change, someday life would be different: Sari would grow up, get better. She wouldn't need him this much forever. And when that happened, he and Susannah could be together.

And Susannah would write back as if she believed him. She sounded so excited about Sari's essay, about the fact she and Laurent were working on the newspaper. "Following in her father's footsteps," Susannah had written. "I can't think of anything better!"

In spite of the closeness Grey felt, reading and writing those letters and emails, his heart felt heavy. He wondered how long Susannah would wait. Years would go by, and even if she didn't fall in love with someone else in the meantime, wouldn't she drift away? His thoughts raced, trying to think of ways to make it all work.

So the afternoon he'd lined up Claude to cover for him, he drove east again. This time he didn't turn around when he got to Marseille. He kept going, along the white limestone ridge, through the pine-scented olive orchard, over the crest of the Calanques, and down the switchback road along the jagged fjord that led to Cap Morgiou.

He parked the Citroën, grabbed his backpack, and scrambled down the steep steps cut into the white cliff. Bright flowers grew out of cracks in the rock; he wished Susannah could see them. The azure bay spread out between the steep headlands, and he stared out at it, reliving each moment of their day together.

Walking into the Caratini dive shop, he felt his heart turn over. He'd stood right here, handing Felix his certificates. Susannah had been with him, excited and happy. A group of young divers stood at the counter, speaking French to a woman Grey didn't recognize. Maybe Felix, Jeanine, and Jean were out on the water, leading a dive . . .

He stood by the wall covered with photos. There must have been fifty, maybe more, all overlapping. Scanning them, he felt his pulse racing. He'd come to town to connect with Susannah. To sit at the café and write her a letter, and tell her he was here. But standing in here, knowing that the picture of her and Ian was hanging somewhere among all the other photos of happy divers, disturbed him. He looked over and over the wall, but he couldn't see it.

"May I help you?" asked the woman behind the counter.

"Uh, no," he said. "Thank you."

"Are you sure?" she asked, smiling. "Would you like to dive?"

"Not this time," he said.

"You've been before?"

"Yes," he said, backing away. "With a friend. We dove on the Cosquer Cave."

"Ah," she said. "One of the most spectacular dives in the world."

Just then the telephone rang, and Grey took the opportunity to leave the shop. He walked along the quay, wondering why he'd come. Being here without Susannah felt so empty.

His chest hurt; his heart felt bruised. Taking a seat at the sidewalk café where he'd sat with her, he stared at the water.

The waiter brought him a glass of rosé. He pulled a paper and pen from his backpack, spread it out on the table, started to write.

Dear Susannah, he wrote, *I'm here in Cap Morgiou with you. You're with me everywhere, but this is our place. You showed it to me. It was brand new, just like so many things I experienced with you, and now I feel it's ours forever.*

A shadow fell across the paper, and he glanced up into a familiar face: Jeanine Caratini.

"It is you," she said. "When Amelie said a man had stopped in, speaking of the Cosquer Cave, I thought maybe it could be . . ."

"There must be many people who come here for the cave," he said, gesturing for her to take a seat. "Why would you think it was me?"

"Because Susannah said you would be back."

"Susannah?" he asked, startled and happy just to hear her name. "How would she know? I didn't tell her."

Jeanine was small and slender, with dark red hair and kind blue eyes. She stared at Grey, smiling gently. "When you love someone, you know them. You didn't have to tell her your schedule for her to know you'd be drawn back here."

The words rang in his ears. *Love someone.* He stared up at Jeanine, wanting to ask if Susannah had said she loved him.

Jeanine laughed, reading something in his eyes. "She didn't spell it out, if that's what you're wondering. Her reason for calling said it all."

"Why did she call you?"

"To ask me to take this picture down," she said, reaching into the pocket of her jacket, pulling out the photo of Susannah and Ian. She set it down on the brown paper, beside his glass of wine.

He stared into the picture. There she was, smiling into the

camera, her eyes so bright and clear. Ian stood close beside her, arm around her shoulder, looking as if she belonged to him.

"She called the day after she returned home to the States," Jeanine said. "She told me that you both loved it here in Cap Morgiou, that you were certain to return, and that she didn't want you to have to see this picture hanging on our wall. I should have thrown it away, but I'd just stuck it in a folder. Susannah is one of our favorite clients, and I don't have another picture of her."

"Thank you," Grey said, unable to take his eyes off Susannah.

"You sent Monsieur Stewart for quite a swim," Jeanine said, laughter in her voice.

"I got carried away," Grey said. "I probably shouldn't have done that."

"Oh, I'm certain you should have. Susannah wouldn't love you the way she does if she felt you had acted unfairly."

"Excuse me?" Grey asked, stuck on the word "love."

"She was adamant about my taking the picture down," Jeanine said, ignoring his meaning. "She wanted you to know he doesn't matter to her."

"You knew them together?" Grey asked, looking up.

"There was no 'together.' Both my husband and I knew that from the first time we met him. Surely you could tell, just from that one meeting. They are as different as two people can be. She is sweet and kind ... he ..." Jeanine shrugged. "Arrogant and very full of his own importance."

"But he thought they had something ..."

"That doesn't matter," Jeanine said. "It's what Susannah wants that we care about. Right?"

"Right," Grey said.

"Don't worry about Monsieur Stewart," she said. "I doubt very much that he will show his face in this town again."

"He managed to get out of the water okay?"

"Oh, yes. He climbed out at the boat launch ramp," she said.

Then she checked her watch, said she'd better be getting back to the shop; she'd been upstairs, doing paperwork. He thanked her very much, and she shook his hand, said that he hoped to come back and dive again.

"I'd like to," he said.

"That's what Susannah assumed, that you would," Jeanine said. "She told me that you'd had a very profound experience in the cave."

"We certainly did," Grey said. "And I'd like to do it again, but I couldn't without her."

"Then bring her back," Jeanine said, her gaze fiery.

Grey nodded. If only he could, if only it were that easy. He started to hand her back the photo.

"No," she said. "It's yours."

"But you said you don't have another of Susannah . . ."

Jeanine smiled. "As I said: bring her back here. Then we can take a picture of the two of you together." Without waiting for his response, she rose from her seat, and with a last pointed look at him, strode away.

He watched Jeanine walk along the seawall, back to the wharf. The harbor was full of boats, many more than had been here even two weeks ago. The warm weather was here, and so were the tourists. Grey looked down at the photo. He gazed at it for a long time. Susannah had wanted it destroyed, but he couldn't do that.

Instead, he ripped it down the middle. He crumpled up the half showing Ian, and he walked over to the bar to throw it in the garbage. Then he returned to his seat, lifted his glass. He remembered how he and Susannah had drunk to Henri Cosquer. But right now, feeling the warm breeze and looking at her picture, that didn't feel right.

"To you," he said to her picture.

TWENTY-ONE

Susannah tried to return to life in Connecticut, but the best part of her was back in France. She couldn't really do anything about that either, except write letters as often as she could, check email constantly, and think about Grey all the time. She felt more like a college student—young and in love—than one of their professors.

Helen was away, delivering a series of lectures at UCLA; Susannah took the opportunity to write up all the notes she'd taken on the trip: about Sarah, the *Livre du Grand Voyage*, the Cosquer Cave. In a separate journal, she poured her heart out about everything else, the things that would never be found in a scholarly paper: everything about Grey. She went out, saw friends, kept busy, but felt herself far away.

One early evening she went for a walk behind the Renwick Inn, to see the light reflected in the river. By this time of May, the air was warming up, and new leaves were on the trees.

The river glistened, golden in the last rays of the setting sun. She stared out at the river, seeing the butterscotch light play on the water's surface. She thought of the Parc, of all the creeks and reeds, of how the landscapes were so similar. They were both fed by the same ocean, but they were so far apart.

She sat on a rustic bench, lost in thoughts of Grey until the waning moon lifted into the sky, through the trees. It glowed, as white as ever, but it looked as if it had been torn in half, tipped on its side.

The breeze picked up . . . a salt wind, blowing inland from Long Island Sound. Susannah felt it ripple through her hair as if it were coming straight from France. She remembered getting Tempest free of the quicksand, the way the moon had looked that night. Moonlight just pouring down . . . She'd felt it on her skin, just as she felt the breeze now.

The moon that night had seemed to belong to her and Grey. And when she looked up now, seeing it rising higher in the sky, she realized that he had seen the same thing just hours earlier in France. And she knew that it was waning; the moon had been full, and soon it would disappear.

Sitting alone on the bench, she felt the same thing happening to her, Grey, and Sari. They'd had their moment, but it was over . . . disappearing. All she wanted was to hold on to the feelings she'd had in France. But staring up at the moon through the new leaves, she felt everything ebbing away.

In her office the next day, Susannah was surrounded by papers, transcribing notes onto her computer. Lost in work and thought, she barely heard the door open behind her.

"Hello, Susannah," came the low, elegant voice.

Susannah glanced over her shoulder and smiled, so happy to see her mentor, just back from Los Angeles, tall and thin, with her white hair pinned up in a French twist.

"Hello, Helen," she said. "It's good to see you . . ."

"The same to you, Susannah. Why don't you bring every-thing into my office, so we can catch up?"

Susannah gathered the material she'd brought back from France, and walked down the hall of the anthropology de-partment. It was long and dark, with sunlight slanting in through several open office doors. Susannah entered Helen's office, and took her customary chair opposite the wide oak desk; she'd been sitting there for years, ever since their first interview, when Susannah was just out of grad school.

Helen stood in a corner of the room, waiting for the kettle to finish boiling. Their meetings always included tea and short-bread, and Helen always arranged them herself. Susannah no-ticed her leaning on the table, favoring her weak leg; she got up and walked over.

"Please let me get the tea today, Helen," she said.

"You know, I think I'll take you up on that," Helen said gratefully. "My trip was rather arduous, and I'm a bit tired."

Susannah nodded, noticing her pallor, feeling a ripple of worry. She heard the professor limping back to her desk, and finished making tea. She arranged it just as Helen always did: on a linen-cloth-covered silver tray. The cups and teapot were porcelain; the tea was loose Darjeeling, held in a silver strainer.

"So," Helen said after they were settled. "Tell me about your visit to the Bibliothèque in Arles."

"Yes, of course," Susannah said, removing from the sheaf of papers the sketch she'd made of the cover: the title, the dragon with burning red eyes, and the gold cross blessing it all.

"And page 321? Did you read it?"

"Yes, I did," Susannah said. "I was so struck by the love Saint Martha had for the dragon. It reminded me so much of 'Beauty and the Beast.' "

"It's archetypal," Helen agreed. "I've always believed the legend of Saint Martha was the genesis of that fairy tale."

"I was very moved by the idea of her singing hymns to the dragon," Susannah said, thinking of Sari, of the toy she'd given her. Lost in the thought, she looked away.

"What is it?" Helen asked.

"Oh, nothing," Susannah said, shaking her head. "I just . . . well, I met a family over there. A man and his daughter. I gave Sari a Tarasque toy . . . anyway, never mind. Back to Saint Martha . . ."

"Ah, yes," Helen said after giving Susannah a long look. "Well, as Saint Martha taught us, love is the most effective way of taming our 'enemies.' I learn it repeatedly, yet forget each time I go to war for more funding, slugging it out with boards and directors for foundation grants. Perhaps only a saint is truly capable of such gentleness . . ."

"Perhaps," Susannah said.

"Years ago, while in Tarascon, I focused my research on a work written by Vincent Phillipon in 1521: 'The Legend of the Saintes-Maries.' It was all about Sarah and her miracles. Vincent was abbot of the Franciscan monastery at San Vigilio at Bolzano . . ."

"Italy?" Susannah asked, amazed that Sarah's legend had spread so far by that time, and that it had been taken up by a member of the Catholic Church. "But Sarah isn't a real saint . . ."

"Oh, my dear," Helen said, laughing. "She absolutely is. Just ask her devotees! What you mean is, she hasn't been canonized by the Church. She was a poor girl of such humble beginnings, overshadowed by everyone else in that boat . . . Anyway, Vincent must have been a true visionary. Some archaeologist friends of mine worked on a dig at his monastery; they unearthed gardens and a greenhouse, along with notes by the master gardener—Vincent himself. So of course I had to see for myself, and spent some lovely times there, getting to know the monks. Vincent, one of them told me, was cultivat-

ing a variety of lily called 'Sara.' It was black, and named
for . . ."

"Sara-la-Kali."

"Yes. Now . . . tell me more about the women you met.
From what you say, many of them have actually settled in
Stes.-Maries, just to be near her?"

"Yes," Susannah said. "Topaz Avila told me about several,
and she took me to her caravan, so I could meet the Sarah
Circle."

"How fascinating. I knew that your trip to the Camargue
would bear riches! Just to think—getting such an inside look
at so secret a society. Do you know, after studying women of
Tarascon—which isn't so far away—most of my professional
life, I've never once even heard of the Sarah Circle." She gazed
across her teacup at Susannah, her eyes bright with admiration.

"Well, your focus has always been on Saint Martha and the
dragon," Susannah said, feeling a pang as she thought of Sari.

"You're far too modest, my dear. You've breeched some
closely guarded gates. Topaz Avila must have really trusted
you, to invite you in."

"We became friendly . . ."

"Avila," Helen said. "That's a Spanish name. As in Saint
Teresa of Avila?"

"Possibly. Topaz told me that some of her ancestors were
Spanish. She told me about loyalty and allegiance within the
group, and how her family was stigmatized by intermarriage.
And . . . that seems to be an issue even now, with modern
women."

"Examples please, dear. You know I live for the specific."

"Well, the story involves Grey—the father of that young
girl I mentioned . . ."

"Sari?"

Susannah nodded, beginning to tell the story of Grey and
Maria. She started with academic detachment, telling about

his career as a journalist, the gypsiologist, his trip to the Camargue.

But once she got to his marriage to Maria, and the birth of Sari, and Maria's abandonment, the details began spilling out, and her emotions began rising. She told Helen about Grey rescuing her from the bulls in the marsh, and her first meeting with Sari, and the child's long aversion to riding, and how the night Maria left had devastated Sari so completely.

"Such pain for a young girl," Helen murmured.

As Susannah continued talking, she realized how terribly she'd been missing her mother; she'd wanted to tell her all about meeting Grey, and responding so deeply to him and Sari, and wondering what she could do to help them. Helen listened, her eyes grave as she heard about Sari's anguish.

"Sari hasn't seen her mother for five years?" Helen asked.

"No. Not since she was eight."

"Important years," the professor said. "Where is Maria now?"

"In Nevada," Susannah said. "She and Adrien, her trainer, have a stable there. They run a small circus, Clair de Lune."

"Maria remains devoted to horses," Helen said, still holding the cross medallion.

"Instead of her daughter."

Helen shook her head. "You must guard against making such assumptions," she said.

"What do you mean?" Susannah asked, shocked by Helen's statement.

"Society can be cruel to women," she said. "Many cultures force a woman to choose between motherhood and her own dreams. Even here and now, Susannah. Surely you of all people know that. It's a myth, that one can 'have it all.' "

"Plenty of people do," Susannah said stubbornly. "My mother was a teacher—work that she adored, and felt challenged by—and she also had me."

"Your mother was lucky. And you're right—many women

choose to do both. Others don't, or can't." She paused. "I, for instance. With all the travel my work entails, the long periods of time I've spent in the field . . ."

Susannah sat still, listening. In spite of their closeness, she and Helen rarely talked about her personal choices.

"I'm not letting Maria off the hook," the professor said. "Sari is not an abstraction. She's a real person, and Maria left her. I'm only suggesting that there may have been powerful forces at work here."

"Internal forces?"

Helen nodded. "And perhaps the influence of a man. Adrien Ferret."

"Matelo," Susannah said. "That's his Gypsy name."

"Well, you'll have to learn the truth," Helen said.

"Excuse me?"

"When you visit the Clair de Lune, you'll have to observe their interactions."

"Visit—what do you mean?"

"I think you should go there . . ."

"Helen, I can't meet Maria!"

The panic in her tone made Helen glance over. She poured the last of the tea into their cups. Susannah's heart was pounding as she waited for her to speak.

"It will be necessary," Helen said, gazing at Susannah. "For our further study. Now that we've learned about the Sarah Circle, and the extraordinary pull Sara-la-Kali has over her modern-day devotees, we must learn what would cause one of them to run away. Especially from a daughter named for Sarah. What an insult, what dishonor to the saint! You said Sari's middle name . . ."

"Yes, it's Sarah," Susannah said. "But Helen . . ."

"Don't you want to know?" Helen asked, leaning forward. The look in her eyes shocked Susannah with its vehemence. "Don't you want to meet this woman, who walked away from her family, and caused her daughter to live in such agony?"

"I can't be objective," Susannah said, breaking down. "I love . . . Helen, I've come to love them both—Grey and Sari."

She bowed her head, crying quietly. Helen reached over, took her hand. With her eyes closed, in the quiet of the office, Susannah could almost believe her mother was with her, sitting right here, understanding the way her heart was breaking. Silence filled the room.

"You just said you love them, Susannah," Helen said finally. "So you must ask yourself: what are you willing to do for them?"

Late the next night, the road was flooded. There'd been an unusually high tide, and as Grey drove south through the marsh, his tires splashed through puddles of salt water. Sitting at the café in Cap Morgiou, trying to figure out a way to Susannah, he'd come up with an idea. He felt driven, as if he had a rocket in his chest.

The diminishing moon spread sallow light across the wet pavement—it was nothing at all like the sharp, bright, ferocious white moonlight he and Susannah had had on their ride. He drove into Stes.-Maries-de-la-Mer, passing through town with barely a glance from people walking along the glassy black harbor. He turned up the winding road that led behind the old church, and followed it a few miles.

When he reached the caravan park, he hesitated for a moment, staring at the sign: *Mas SLK*. Sara-la-Kali. He had a violent reaction to the sight of it; it reminded him of the closed world Maria had come from, and suddenly he thought about turning back. What made him think he'd get anything from this? But he called up a picture of Susannah, and then one of Sari, and he drove the Citroën in through the gates, over the rutted field toward the circle of caravans.

The *roulottes* were parked in a wide circle. Even in the shadowy dark, he could see their colors: brick, amber, purple, rose. He had been here just once before—again, uninvited. Maria had never once brought him here. Five years ago he'd had to find his way himself—and for the exact same reason.

He wondered whether tonight was a Sarah Circle meeting night. Before he married Maria, she used to attend the group nearly every week. Afterwards, once she'd broken out of the clan by marrying him, she'd stopped going. Sometimes he'd see her standing by the window, looking longingly into the middle distance, and he'd always wonder whether she was seeing the Circle, seeing the faces of her family and friends, seeing a place she was no longer welcome and wishing she'd made a different choice.

Now, pulling into the grassy area where other cars were parked, he noticed someone tall coming toward him. He heard the creaking of doors, saw light pouring out of several being opened around the circle as people looked out. Music drifted across the field—guitars, violins, bells. But after a few moments, they stopped.

"Well, well," said the man's voice. "Are you back to follow up on your research?"

"Hello, Baro," he said. *Baro* meant "big," for the firstborn son. Maria's older cousin . . .

"A man comes to write an article about Romanies, but interviews weren't enough, were they? You had to marry one. Just to see, right? Just to get inside our circle, and have a bird's-eye view."

Baro got in his face. Grey stood his ground. He felt Maria's cousin spoiling for a fight, and he almost wanted to get into it himself. Baro was darkly tanned, his moustache a thick, sharp line above his mouth, his eyes narrow, bright, glowering, as if he'd been nursing hatred these last five years.

"I'm not here to see you," Grey said.

"You're not welcome here at all—no matter who you came to see."

"I'll let *her* tell me that."

"Leave now, and there'll be no trouble."

"There already is trouble, Baro. Now, let me past."

Baro shoved his face into Grey's, and Grey felt the heat pouring off him. Grey had plenty of heat of his own. This guy had never sought Sari out—not once. None of them had. She was their blood, and they'd forgotten her.

"Stop that! Both of you!" Zin-Zin stood in the doorway, on the top step of her caravan, thumping her cane.

"She's right," Topaz said, hurrying over. "Don't be idiots, acting like little boys. Baro, enough."

"I'm not turning my back on this one," he said. "Don't ask me to, Topaz."

"Why are you here?" Topaz asked, eyes nearly as fierce as Baro's, but with a tone of beseeching in her voice.

"I want to talk to Zin-Zin," Grey said.

"She won't see you," Baro snapped.

Topaz gave him a look. Then, taking Grey's arm, she turned him around, walking him away from Baro. Grey felt his heart beating overtime, pumped for a fight. Just because Topaz was leading him out of Baro's range didn't mean the clash was over. Grey knew it was just beginning.

"Wait here," Topaz said, hands on both of Grey's shoulders. She looked him long and hard in the eyes, exacting a silent promise that he wouldn't get into anything with Baro.

He nodded, and she ran up the steps to Zin-Zin. Others had started to gather—either in the windows of their *roulottes* or in the open area in the center of the circle. He glanced up, saw Rosalie hurrying over from her caravan.

She gave him a quick, harsh glance, ran up the steps to join in the talk. Grey watched the three women consulting, Rosalie obviously disagreeing, shaking her head the hardest. Zin-Zin disappeared inside her caravan, Rosalie following her. Grey's heart fell, but he knew he wasn't going home until he'd talked to the old woman. He'd force his way in if he had to.

But just then Topaz returned.

"She'll see you now," she said.

"Alone?"

"That's not possible," Topaz said.

Grey nodded. He didn't care if he had an audience or not. He climbed the steps after Topaz, walked into Zin-Zin's dusky blue caravan. Nearly every wall bore a painted swag, just like the one in his own kitchen. Draped and swooping lengths of flowers woven into silver-green laurel leaves. His stomach churned, seeing the artwork, reminded of the symbol that united the women of Maria's clan.

"Come," Zin-Zin said. "Sit." She was stationed in a deep armchair, and she gestured at a straight-backed kitchen chair that Rosalie had drawn up alongside. The lights were dim, each lampshade covered by a rose silk scarf. Several candles burned around a makeshift shrine, a carved statue of Sarah in the center. He turned his back on the shrine.

Pulse racing out of control, he sat in the chair.

Zin-Zin sat back, regarding him with wide brown eyes. She wore her gray hair in a bun. Her face was deeply lined, reflecting a lifetime's worth of joy and pain. Grey had been so charged up outside, but right now he relaxed under her steady gaze.

"Hello, Grey," she said.

"Zin-Zin," he said, bowing his head.

"Why have you come?"

"It's about Maria."

She shrugged. "You know that I have no power over my niece. She makes her own decisions. It's been five years now since she left. Can you not make peace with her choice?"

"She has a daughter," Grey said. "Who is suffering."

"Zinnia Sarah," she said.

"Yes, Sari," Grey said.

"She misses her mother," Zin-Zin said.

"Every day."

Zin-Zin took in the words, closed her eyes. His stomach tensed, anticipating any number of reactions that might cause him to blow up. If the old woman defended Maria—or if Rosalie or Topaz did—he'd lose it.

"What would you have me do?" Zin-Zin asked.

"What do you want from Zin-Zin? You already know where Maria is," Rosalie interjected.

"I know. Nevada. I know all about Clair de Lune. I've written her letters, even tried to call. She's never responded."

"Because she's—" Rosalie started to say hotly, but Zin-Zin held up one hand.

"I know you don't understand her," Zin-Zin said. "In some ways, none of us do. She defied all of us when she married you. Made her choice, told us we had no say in it. It angered me so terribly . . . She lived on your ranch, but it might as well have been India—she was lost to us. All of us except Rosalie . . . and Matelo."

"I could never hold anything against Maria," Rosalie said.

Grey looked at Maria's old friend, her eyes tearing up. He'd been very angry at Rosalie over the years, for many things, but he knew that her loyalty to Maria had kept her close to Sari. She'd helped out at the house and ranch, stayed even after Sari's rage at Maria had first boiled over. He saw the tension in her face, and knew that Maria's leaving had been devastating to her, too. His gaze swept back to Zin-Zin.

"Do you ever think that you're the reason she can't come back? Your 'curse'?"

"That was anger; she knows I'd never truly curse her."

"You raised her—don't you think she'd believe it was real?"

Zin-Zin just stared at him, silent.

Grey stared back at her, felt the pity in the other women's gazes. He reddened, knowing they thought he was trying to justify Maria's staying away for any reason other than the fact she couldn't stand him, and didn't want to see Sari.

"We make allowances for Maria," Topaz said gently, "because of how talented she is. Her riding is almost like flight, so we don't bind her with the same earthly rules as everyone else. Please, Grey—for your own sake, let it go. Move on with your life."

Move on with his life: that's all he wanted to do. He wanted to be with Susannah; that's what coming here was about. He knew Topaz knew that: he'd never forget that she'd called to let him know when Susannah would be at the library. But right now she was missing the point.

"Even if I could go along with that," Grey said, "her daughter can't."

"What do you mean?" Zin-Zin asked.

"Sari is hurting. She's angry. Her injuries have healed, but emotionally she's damaged. You know about her colorblindness; it hasn't gone away. Her feelings about Maria are coming out all over the place . . ."

"This is about that woman, isn't it?" Rosalie retorted. "You're upset because Sari won't accept your seeing someone."

"Rosalie, stop!" Topaz said.

"I just—" Rosalie began.

"Yes!" Grey exploded. "It's about Susannah. She's an incredible person. She was so good to Sari, and Sari responded to her. Do you know how important that is to me?"

"What would you have me do?" Zin-Zin interrupted.

"I'd like you to intervene somehow. I know that Maria respects you. Even during the years when she was separated from all of you, and even after you cut her off for marrying me, she never stopped hoping for your love, Zin-Zin. She named our daughter for you."

"I was honored by that," Zin-Zin said, voice shaking. "Maria's own mother died when she was just a baby. I raised her as if she were my own."

"That's why I'm begging you now," Grey said. "Please contact her and tell her that Sari needs to connect with her."

"And what do you think that will do?" Zin-Zin asked softly.

Grey stared into her eyes. Rosalie hadn't been all wrong; his motives very much concerned Susannah. He had the feeling that Sari needed a mother so badly, and Susannah could be that for her. The two of them had connected just as he and Susannah had—he had seen it. Every night Sari slept with that toy dragon. And although she hadn't ridden again, she'd started grooming Mystère, and walking her on a lead line. Grey knew such things were a connection to Susannah. But there was no way Sari could let herself completely trust another woman until she found a way to let go of Maria, and what she'd done to her.

"She needs to say goodbye," he said. "Sari wasn't given that chance five years ago. She's trapped in that moment when Maria drove away . . ."

"Time heals," Rosalie said.

But Grey didn't look at Rosalie. He held Zin-Zin's gaze, and saw that she understood what he was saying. Perhaps she was old enough to know that there were some things that didn't heal on their own, not without outside help.

"Not for a thirteen-year-old," he said, staring at Zin-Zin, "who still remembers that night when her mother left her lying in the road."

"Maria didn't see the accident!" Rosalie exclaimed. "That's what I keep telling Sari! Maria wouldn't have left her there if she'd known . . ."

"Sari can't hear it from you," Zin-Zin said, looking over her shoulder, patting Rosalie's hand on the back of her chair. "There's only one person who can get through . . ."

"So, will you help?"

Very slowly, resolutely, Zin-Zin nodded. "I'll do the best I can. Know that I can't promise anything."

"Are you in touch with her regularly?" Grey asked. "Do you speak to Maria? Does she ever come back here?"

But those questions were beyond what was permitted. Zin-Zin just shook her head to all in a way that let Grey know he'd crossed the line. He'd always been an outsider here. The Manouche stuck with their own; Baro and many others still vilified him for stealing Maria away in the first place.

Standing, he bowed his head in thanks and respect. "Thank you for seeing me," he said.

"Grey," Zin-Zin said. "It's an unusual name to give a little boy," she said.

"It was my mother's maiden name," he said.

"In our culture, it means 'wisdom.' For someone to be gray, to have lived life and experienced many things. I shall pray for your daughter. And also for your continued wisdom."

"Thank you," he said. "I appreciate that. Goodbye, Zin-Zin."

Then Rosalie opened the door, indicating that it was time to leave. He said goodbye to her and Topaz, walked past Baro and a group of other men standing at the foot of the stairs.

As he crossed the dark field, he looked up. There was a yellow smudge in the western sky, the last remnants of the once-full moon.

TWENTY-TWO

Laurent had been right; Sari couldn't stay off Google Earth.
While her father worked in the barn—later and later each
night, it seemed, as if he didn't want to spend time with her at
all—Sari sat at her computer, soaring across the Atlantic.

She had three favorite locations to visit online: addresses in
Narragansett, Rhode Island, where her grandparents resided,
and Black Hall, Connecticut, where Susannah lived. She enjoyed getting the satellite image as clear as possible, so that
she could see the roof of Susannah's small house, the trees in
her yard, the car in her driveway.

The third address was just outside Las Vegas, Nevada. The
satellite picture showed garish structures, a grid of streets and
highway, and then nothing but desert spreading out as far as
she could see. Sari knew how hot and parched the desert
sands were, and that's how she felt whenever she looked at
Las Vegas.

Dry, hot, as furious as the sirocco that blew through there. How could her mother raise horses in such a place? After riding here, in the beautiful green marshlands of the Camargue, how could she have flown to such a terrible, arid land? Sari's eyes sometimes filled with tears, thinking of her mother in such a place.

Every time Sari looked at Las Vegas, she'd find herself shaking so hard, she could barely see the screen. To be able to see her mother's house, right there on the computer, and not be able to reach her. So she'd click back to New England, the two southernmost states, Rhode Island and Connecticut, where her grandparents and Susannah lived almost side by side.

She wondered what Susannah was doing. Did she have any idea that Sari was spying from the sky? Possibly she would be upset to know. After the terrible way Sari had treated her at the end, Susannah probably wanted to forget she even existed. Sari wouldn't blame her. She'd thought about sending Susannah her essay about Avignon: it had been printed in the school paper.

Sari looked up, over her computer screen, out the window. The horse barn and ring were between her house and Laurent's. Summer was coming quickly. Soon she'd be traveling to the States with her father. She thought of how much Laurent did for her; if he hadn't encouraged her, she wouldn't have allowed her essay to be published.

Maybe her father would let her invite Laurent to take the trip with them. Her grandparents had such a big old farmhouse; her father and his brothers had grown up there, so there were plenty of bedrooms. They could have so much fun, surfing at the beach, riding the family's horses, maybe even visiting Susannah.

Thinking about everything, Sari just stared out the window . . . Laurent and her father were in the paddock, her father holding Tempest at the end of a longe line. She heard him talking to the feisty horse in a low voice.

Her stomach clenched, remembering that night when Tempest had gotten caught in the mud. If only Sari could do that night over again; if only she could make everything right with Susannah. But that only made her upset; she had messed it all up.

Turning away from the window, she saw her computer screen glowing. Down in the lower left corner was the icon for Las Vegas. She had minimized it. Just seeing the name gave her a start. It was like the code for a dragon, or a demon: the bad things that haunted her dreams, and, she was sure, haunted her father's.

Only her father probably dreamed in vivid color, while for Sari even the world of dreams was black and white.

Grey stood in the ring, letting the young horse run around him in circles. Tempest was stocky and muscular, and he seemed full of primal power. That night in the swamp had both broken and energized the colt, and these last few training sessions he'd seemed eager to please Grey.

Laurent helped out. Grey noticed how the boy kept looking up at Sari's window. The kids were nearly inseparable, and Grey was happy his daughter had such a good friend.

Grey forced himself to concentrate on training Tempest, because otherwise he'd go crazy missing Susannah. The colt cantered around the ring at a good, steady pace. Grey tried to stay focused on discipline, on keeping the longe line taut but not tight. The horse's hooves pounded the soft earth in gentle rhythm; Grey listened, and observed, still alert for any sign he'd been injured in the marsh. But just then, Laurent waved up at Sari's window, and Grey looked up. She waved, and his heart caught.

When she was little, and would see him exercising one of the horses, she'd come running out to watch. She'd been irrepressible, his Sari. Maria had already started fading away. She'd finish dinner, and say she had to go to town, meet Rosalie—the only one of her old friends who still welcomed her.

Looking back, Grey had realized that Maria had been meeting Adrien in the horse ring out by the caravans. He'd probably even known at the time—but he'd blocked the knowledge out, thrown himself into working with their horses, and entertaining Sari, trying to deny their family's reality.

"Papa," Sari would say, running out of the house in her nightgown, "let me help!"

"You should be in bed, asleep," he'd chide, but not very convincingly.

"I'm not tired," she'd say.

So he'd let her sit on the top rail of the fence, one arm clinging to his neck as he stood beside her, and they'd watch whichever young horse he was working with at that time. His own mind would be racing—thinking of Maria, wondering what he could do to make her happier, trying to figure out a way to help her.

"Where's Mama?" Sari would inevitably ask.

"With Rosalie," Grey would reply.

"But it's late," Sari would say.

"Yes, honey," he'd say. "But they have important things to discuss."

"Like what?"

"Secrets," he said. "They tell each other secrets."

"About what?"

"White horses," he'd always say.

"Secrets about white horses?" she'd ask.

"Oh, yes."

Sari would clutch his neck, staring at the white horse in their ring. She'd grown up here in the Camargue, knew the horses' mystical origins, running wild through the marsh and along the beach.

"She should stay here," Sari would whisper. "We have white horses here . . ."

"But Rosalie is in Stes.-Maries," Grey would say, making excuses for her. Even after he'd started to realize Maria wasn't sitting in a café with Rosalie—after he'd started noticing the smell of horse, and the bits of hay stuck in her dark hair, and the fact she always left the house wearing makeup and her brightest silk shirts—he'd cover for her with Sari.

Maria had brought home a saddle made of black leather, decorated with silver scallop shells, purposely tarnished to resemble the black coquilles St. Jacques found along the rocky strand on the Gulf of Lions. She had had it made for herself, she'd told Grey. But he'd known that was a lie, and that it had been a gift from Matelo.

And she'd been in such a hurry to leave with her lover, she'd left the saddle behind; it still hung on a peg in the tack room, gathering dust.

Back before she left, on nights after she'd been meeting Matelo, Maria would drive in, park the car, sit in the dark with her cigarette glowing for a few moments. That time was the worst for Grey, he'd feel how much she didn't want to see him. He told himself that's all it was—she was tired of him, their marriage; he'd never let himself think she was also burdened by Sari.

"Mama!" Sari would call. Even then Maria wouldn't hurry. She'd take her time, getting herself together. And then she'd walk over to the ring.

"What are you doing up so late?" she'd scold as Sari threw herself into her arms. "What can your father possibly be thinking?"

"She wanted to see her mother," Grey invariably replied.

"It's time for bed," Maria would say.

"She's waited for you all this time."

"Yes, Mama," Sari would say, arms around Maria's neck. "Tell me secrets about white horses! Tell me!"

"Secrets about white horses?"

"Yes, I want to know!"

Maria had laughed. "Those aren't half as interesting as the horses' own secrets. You have to learn to let the horses tell you their secrets themselves."

"Horses don't talk!"

"They do, Zinnia Sarah. To people who listen to them."

"How do they do that?"

Maria's laugh held hidden sadness. Her wide almond eyes showed secret sorrow and longing. Her long dark hair flowed down her back; it sparkled with bits of bright straw. She'd been lying with Matelo, and couldn't even be bothered to clean herself up. Even before he'd let himself realize the truth, Grey would be seething inside. His body had known what his mind couldn't yet recognize.

"They do it all the time," Maria had said to Sari. "You just have to train yourself to tune in, and think like a horse."

"Train myself?" Sari had laughed, her voice spilling like water. "That's funny! Papa, you train horses, not people, right?"

"To be truly connected to the horse," Maria had said, still holding Sari, "the only training necessary is of yourself. You must listen, Sari. Let your instincts come out, and you'll hear all the secrets in the world."

"I want to," Sari had said.

And then, Grey remembered—he could see it as if it were happening right now: Maria had walked into the stable, come out leading Mystère. She had jumped up without a mounting block, without any help from Grey. And she'd pulled Sari up in front of her—Sari flying onto the horse as if she had just sprouted wings.

Grey had stood aside, watching the two dark-haired beauties, mother and daughter, ride Mystère bareback in the night.

Sari had clung to the flowing white mane, her head bent as if to listen to the horse's secrets, seemingly oblivious to her mother behind her—Maria no longer sitting, but rising up on both feet, reaching up toward the night sky, graceful arms outstretched, slowly raising one leg, balancing on the toes of one pointed foot.

Tempest cantered around and around now; Grey closed his eyes and went back in time. Listening to the horse encircle him, seeing his daughter listen for horse secrets, seeing his wife stand tall on horseback, reaching for the stars, for anything that might take her away, help her escape.

From both of them: Grey and Sari.

That was the part that killed him most. Literally killed him. He loved Susannah, but he wondered what she saw in someone like him. Until she'd come, he'd felt dead inside. One legend of the Tarasque, the dragon who lived in the Rhône, was that it devoured its victims from the inside out. Grey had felt that that had happened to him. But not by some evil dragon: by the woman he'd loved. Maria had taken his guts and spirit. If she'd just left him, maybe he could have survived. But she'd left Sari, too, left her broken and blocked to the beauty all around them.

He found himself thinking back to when he'd first met Maria. He had come down here to the Camargue a brash, cocky journalist, out to file the definitive story on Gypsy women. Guys at the brasserie in Paris had teased him, told him he'd have to sleep with a Gypsy to really write the whole thing.

He'd had that in the back of his mind. He wasn't averse to the idea. He was a young jerk, a guy who'd moved to Europe to become a hotshot. He hadn't had any sisters—and certainly not yet a daughter—so he'd traveled south with certain ideas about hot sex with a beautiful Gypsy.

He'd met Maria right away, ironically at Adrien Ferret's family's horse stable; even then, Maria had been a star. While many of the other local women worked at the market, making and selling crafts, or tending to Sarah's chapel, Maria Loisy had been born to ride. Grey's first sight of her had been on the back of a white horse. She'd been wearing a short silver dress—setting off her gorgeous, strong brown legs, and just about finishing Grey off then and there.

Grey had asked permission to interview her. While Monsieur Ferret—Adrien's father—had said absolutely not, Maria had defied him and said yes. She'd climbed into Grey's car—the red Alfa Romeo he'd driven back then—and decided Stes.-Maries would be too filled with prying eyes.

They'd gone to Arles. He'd taken her to a café by the Arènes, he'd put his tape recorder on the table, and she'd started talking. Her voice was so sexy and raspy, but also, somehow, so vulnerable: she was the best rider in all the Manouche, but she'd led a completely sheltered life.

As they talked, and the hours passed, she'd flowered with confidence and trust under his rapt gaze. She told him that her parents had died in a fire when she was just a little girl; she'd had to depend on the kindness of others. But the deaths had left her feeling alone—as if she'd always be alone, no matter who else was around. She knew she had to make everyone proud of her—there were circuses in Paris, Brussels, Vienna, and she had ridden in them all, from the time she was twelve years old. And at night she would crawl into her bed and know she was all alone. It was the emptiest feeling in the world, as if she were flying through space, past the stars, with no one to hold or catch her.

At the time Grey met her, he was thirty-one and she was twenty-two. She hadn't ever fallen in love before; she knew it was expected that she marry Matelo—Adrien Ferret, son of her trainer. His nickname meant "Sailor," and that was because he rode a horse as if he were sailing the sea . . . with great beauty, grace, and majesty . . . as mystical as the boat

that had carried the three Marys across the Gulf of Lions—
surely Grey knew that story?

"But do you love him?" Grey had asked, focusing only on
the fact she was promised to someone else.

She had shrugged, beautiful bare brown shoulders rippling
under the fine silver straps of her tight dress. "How do I
know?" she asked. "I have no time for love . . . only riding."

"But you're a beautiful young woman," he'd said.

"Beautiful?" she'd asked, blushing.

Hadn't anyone ever told her she was beautiful before? Was
everyone in her clan too focused on her skill as a horsewoman,
her potential to make money as a circus rider, to let her just be
herself, figure out her feelings?

"Yes, Maria," he'd said. "So beautiful."

"I don't think of myself that way," she'd said, eyes darkly
luminous, staring into his, locking in.

"How can you not?" he'd asked. "From the moment I saw
you on that horse, you were the most . . ."

"You're mistaking me and the horse—*that's* beauty," she'd
said. "My wonderful wild white horse . . ."

"Oh, Maria," he'd said. "You just have no idea, do you?"

"Everything I do is by the grace of Sara-la-Kali. My saint;
she has blessed me with many gifts. I am nothing on my
own."

"But you are, Maria. You're like no one else in the world."

She'd laughed shyly. Her eyes gleaming, hungry for his
praise.

He'd known then—he wanted to take her away. He'd forgotten all about his friends at the brasserie—what did they
know, anyway? He'd looked into her ebony eyes, and wanted
only to be with her. He wanted to love her, so she'd know she
was incredible on her own, without a horse under her, and
without the hopes and dreams of her whole clan on her shoulders.

The rest was history. They'd gone to Paris; she'd cried with homesickness for horses and the marsh, so Grey had sold his Alfa, cashed in the bonds he'd inherited from his grand-mother on Block Island, and bought Maria a ranch in the Camargue.

The fact that it was ramshackle, run-down, and disreputable didn't really matter. It came with five horses—including Django. Grey hired a couple to run the place: his friend Claude—whom he'd met years back, bellied up to the bar near the bullfight arena in Nîmes, when Grey was there on assignment—and his wife, Anne.

Maria got pregnant with Sari. Grey worried, because she seemed quiet, distant. It soon became obvious she was withering without her clan. As the months passed, her depression turned to anger. "I've gone against nature!" she'd screamed at Grey one terrible night just before Sari was born. "I've sinned against my family. Zin-Zin was right, I swear. I've brought shame on myself and my baby. Sarah will punish me."

"What kind of saint would punish you for who you love?" he'd asked.

"I don't love you," she'd said. "You took me away from everything I knew, everyone who knew me. Now it's all gone! And all because of you and this!" she'd tapped her big belly.

"This? You mean our *child*?"

"You've taken everything from me!" she'd screamed at him, pounding herself with closed fists.

Grey had grabbed her hands, afraid she'd hurt the baby with her violence. Those days had been nightmarish in the extreme—the way Maria would weep all the time, the way she'd go riding even late in her pregnancy. Sometimes Grey thought she purposely wanted to fall off.

The baby was born at home; she'd refused to go to the clinic in Stes.-Maries for medical care, so with Anne's help, Grey had arranged for a midwife from Arles. Maria had threatened to not feed the baby, but the minute she saw Sari, that changed: she looked into her daughter's eyes, and for the first time in months, Grey saw love in his wife's face.

Even now, holding the longe line as Tempest cooled down, he had to admit that she'd loved their child. He swore she did, even to the end. Her reasons for leaving had been about herself—not Sari. She'd named their daughter for the oldest, wisest woman in the Manouche, and for Sara-la-Kali herself. Even so, no one but Rosalie had come to see the baby. That rejection had nearly destroyed what was left of Maria's self-esteem, and turned her even more bitter.

When she and Matelo—Adrien—ran away, Grey knew that it was because she'd felt she had no real choices left to her. She couldn't live with Grey, and she couldn't return to Stes.-Maries; and Adrien didn't want anything to do with her child by another man.

Grey held the line while Tempest slowed to a walk; he thought about Susannah, wondered where she was tonight. He missed her with everything he had, but he imagined her in a peaceful place, among friends and people who loved her, far from him and the terrible, unsolvable turmoil of his life.

"Papa!" Sari called now, out the open window of her room.

"What, Sari?"

"It's late! Aren't you coming in?"

"In a few minutes. As soon as I get Tempest into his stall."

"You need sleep," she scolded. "Make him stop for the night, Laurent."

"I will," Laurent called back.

Grey chuckled despite his dark mood. The kids were ganging up on him. Walking Tempest into the barn, he stopped by Mystère's stall. He stared at her, remembering how he'd bought her for Maria and Sari. Then, a more recent memory arose: of grabbing Susannah's hand, hauling her up onto Mystère's back, feeling her arms around him. That first meeting had been as sudden and passionate, or more so, as his and

Maria's. But he and Susannah had connected at a deeper level—the core place that made them who they were.

And everything that followed had felt completely real—and right. He stood in the cool, dark barn, missing this quiet, steady woman who seemed to love him and his troubled daughter without conditions or reservations. He wanted her back, he wanted her here with him right now. The feeling nearly knocked him over.

Several nights after their last meeting, Helen Oakes gazed across the table at Susannah. She had sensed a slight distance between them, ever since she had proposed that the younger woman travel to Nevada. But she cared deeply about Susannah, and she had a secret promise to keep, and she was determined to forge ahead. She had insisted on this dinner.

"Isn't this lovely, that you were able to join me tonight?" she asked, her tone formal, although inside she felt anything but. Her heart was racing. The respect and admiration she felt for her protégée was mutual—she knew Susannah returned it tenfold. But like Helen herself, Susannah was also extremely circumspect—guarded even—about her private life, and Helen knew she had to be careful to not drive her away by pushing too hard, and with what she had decided to reveal.

"I'm always glad to have dinner with you," Susannah said.

"This house has been my home base forever," Helen said, looking around. Her gaze took in the dark mahogany furniture that had been her parents', the oil paintings she'd bought in Provence over the years, the French country sideboard she'd acquired on a study trip to Tarascon, the richly woven rugs she'd purchased on meditation and research trips to northern India. "If you're going to make a life in cultural anthropology, and plan to travel a great deal, it's important that you have a home you love—and that loves you back."

Susannah nodded, sipping mineral water. Perhaps she was wondering when Helen would get to the point; she'd certainly been a guest here several times over the years. This was hardly the first time. Helen's heart thumped, but she held back. It wasn't yet time . . .

They dined on Provençal specialties: *soupe aux legumes,* duck with olives, and for dessert, warm apricot soufflé. They moved from the dining room into the salon, a long room with a lovely view of the mouth of the Thames River. With the days getting longer, the sun was just getting ready to set, and the two women sat by the window overlooking Ledge Light, drinking an after-dinner marc.

"Have you given any more thought to going to Nevada?" Helen asked.

"I've thought of pretty much nothing else," Susannah said.

"And have you made plans?" Helen said.

Susannah shook her head.

"Think of what you might learn from Maria," Helen said. "And how it could further our understanding of the Sarah Circle."

Susannah gave her a long look. "I think you know me well enough," she said, "to know that if I went, it wouldn't be about research."

"Even research isn't always, only, about research . . ."

"What do you mean?"

"Sometimes it's more about life . . . you already know that. It's about the way we relate very personally to our material," Helen said slowly.

"We study what matters to us," Susannah said.

"Yes," Helen said. "We're drawn to subject matter because it speaks to us, touches us . . ."

"Like you and Saint Martha . . ."

"Yes. Hers is a great love story."

Helen saw Susannah's eyes flicker at the word "love." Margaret had been her daughter's greatest supporter; Helen wished she could be here now, to see Susannah's strength and intelligence. She wished she could see how deeply Susannah had fallen in love.

"You know I was married," Helen said.

"Yes," Susannah said.

"Twice, as a matter of fact. One marriage to a man I loved deeply, but who left me for someone else. The second to a man I'd met at a symposium: handsome, brilliant, and cruel. Not unlike your Ian. Neither marriage lasted longer than five years."

"I'm sorry . . ."

"Please don't be."

"Did you ever find love again?" Susannah asked.

Helen shook her head. "I threw myself ever more deeply into my studies," she said. "But I began to focus on love as a subject. Particularly, as you know, Saint Martha and the Tarasque."

"You really think they loved each other?"

"Very much so," Helen answered.

"Metaphorically?" Susannah asked.

"Why not literally?" Helen asked, smiling. "At least on an emotional level . . . just like . . ." She paused. "I may have mentioned to you that when I traveled to that monastery in Italy, to visit the garden of black lilies—devoted to Sarah—I met a monk. We became close friends. I still remember his kindness, feel his spirit."

"Is he . . ."

"He died," Helen said, feeling her heart skip just to say the words.

"I'm sorry," Susannah said.

"We didn't even speak the same language. But our hearts spoke. We were good friends—I often think back to the first trip I took to San Vigilio—his monastery. I'd been very tied up with work, and almost hadn't gone. There were so many good reasons not to. Work deadlines, and classes to teach, and papers to grade. But something pulled me there—I had to see those black lilies . . ."

"And you went . . ."

"I had to—I can't even tell you why. A desire deeper than words. And my journey took me to a place where I met the best friend I've ever had."

Helen leaned forward, took Susannah's hand. She stared into her eyes, wanting to make this point more than she'd ever wanted to tell anything to anyone else in this world, living or dead. "Choose wisely, my dear friend," she said. "Right now."

"What do you mean?"

"I mean that you can either stay and do nothing—work in your cubicle, rise in the anthropology department at Connecticut College, watch your wonderful adventure in the Camargue fade into memory. Or . . ."

Susannah stared, nodded, as if she already knew.

"You can fight for what you love."

"Grey and Sari?"

"Yes. Grey and Sari. Go to Clair de Lune, and help Maria understand what needs to be done, so that all of you can move forward in your lives. Not just you and Grey and Sari—Maria, too. You will be doing her a great kindness."

Susannah took another sip of her drink. The sun had finally gone down, and Long Island Sound and the mouth of the Thames River were a sheet of black glass. Ferries shone their yellow lights on the water, and the beam of Ledge Light swept across the rocks. Helen Oakes savored a long, hot sip of liquor, waiting for Susannah to ask the last question.

And of course she did: Susannah was as bright a protégée as any college professor could ever hope to have.

"There's something I've been wondering," Susannah said.

"Go ahead."

"We both have such old connections to Sarah. You through your research about Martha and the monastery with the black lilies . . . and your monk. Me through my mother and her prayer at the church in Stes.-Maries. Don't you ever think about what a coincidence it is, that I wound up working with you?"

"Do you really think it's a coincidence, Susannah?"

"How else . . . ?"

"Think back," Helen said. "You'd just finished grad school at Yale, a star in your class. You could have worked at any anthropology department in the country. Stanford, Harvard, Chicago, Michigan, Yale itself—any of the top programs. Ian Stewart was pressuring you to move to California. Yet you chose my department. Why?"

"My mother suggested I apply at Connecticut College," Susannah said. Suddenly her eyes grew wide, and filled with tears. "I miss her."

"I know you do. Tell me . . . why do you think she wanted you to come to work with me?"

Susannah spoke, her voice cracking. "I've always thought it was because she hoped I'd stay close to home. But Yale was close to Black Hall as well . . . and she was so positive about my sending my application to you."

"Your mother came to me right after you were born," Helen said, holding Susannah's hand. "She'd seen a story about me in the *New London Day*—a review of my book, and an account of my research on Martha. She thought I'd like to know about the miracle in your family."

"My birth . . ." Susannah whispered.

"I held you when you were a baby," Helen said, remembering the radiance in Margaret Connolly's eyes, the glow around the infant herself. "And I knew your mother was right—she had been blessed by Sara-la-Kali. As I've been blessed all these years to work with you."

"Oh, Helen," Susannah said, breaking down and burying her face in her hands.

"I was with her when she died, you see," Helen said softly.

Susannah raised her head, gazing through tears.

"She called you?"

Helen nodded.

"So you were there," Susannah whispered. "She didn't die alone . . ."

"She didn't die alone," Helen said, taking her hand, her throat catching as she remembered those last hours.

"Why didn't you tell me?" Susannah asked.

"Because she asked me not to. She was afraid you would be hurt, that she didn't want you to be there. She loved you so much; she knew she couldn't bear to leave if you were right there with her. Do you understand?"

"Yes," Susannah said. "It's how she always was toward me . . ."

"She made me promise that you would visit Sarah. To thank her for the life you had together . . ."

"Is this why you encouraged me to go to the Camargue after her death? The reason why you asked me to visit the library in Arles?"

"Of course, my dear," Helen said, welling up as she saw the truth dawning in Susannah's eyes. "I promised your mother I'd look after you when she was gone. I swore to her that I'd make sure you made that visit . . . and that I'd do my best to make sure your life was full of love."

TWENTY-THREE

Susannah knew she had to go. By the time she booked her flight, she realized she didn't really have a choice. Talking to Helen about her own mother made her more determined them ever to do what she could for Sari. After all she had learned in France, she wasn't at all sure or even very hopeful about what the visit to Maria would accomplish, but she had to try, for Grey and Sari.

The flight to Las Vegas was smooth, blue sky all the way. Susannah started a letter to Grey, replying to the one he'd written from Cap Morgiou. At the end, he'd mentioned Sarah's feast day coming up at the end of May.

Come back for it, he'd written. *The procession is really something to see. Laurent has been trying to get Sari to go this year. They're on the school paper now, and he thinks it would make good material for them to cover. The truth is, I think he hopes Sari will connect with her heritage a little more. He thinks it will help to heal her. As for me, I just want to see you. Please come back.*

Susannah wrote that she wanted to be there more than anything. She started to tell him about her plan to see Maria—if all went well, maybe she could get Maria to reach out to Sari, maybe that would speed the healing along. But everything was too uncertain, so she just folded the paper, stuffed it into a book she'd bought in Stes.-Maries, with Sarah on the cover.

The sight of Sarah calmed Susannah's nerves, gave her strength, and she slid the book and letter into her briefcase. When she got to the airport, she went through the motions of renting a car, getting printed directions, and driving onto the highway toward the Clair de Lune Ranch.

The landscape was so different from the salty blues and greens of home. As she drove off I-15 and into the Clark Mountains, she climbed into high desert. Jagged sandstone ridges threw shadows, turning the rocks red, brown, umber, and black. As unfamiliar as the terrain was for her, from coastal Connecticut, she figured it had to be the same for Maria, from the watery marshlands of the Camargue.

She passed Joshua trees, saw eagles circling overhead, jackrabbits in the scrub. The landscape was rugged and foreign; she felt farther from home than she had in the Camargue. The road ran straight for a long stretch, and she saw cattle and horses grazing in rough fields under endless blue sky.

Helen had shocked her with some of the revelations she'd offered three nights ago. Susannah held on to the part about her mother. She could imagine what it must have been like for her, driving onto the Connecticut College campus with a new baby, searching the halls for Professor Oakes's office.

Susannah's mother had always revered education. She'd been a teacher herself. But Susannah knew, from the pride and awe with which she'd tell people about her daughter working at the college, that she had held it in special regard.

Susannah pictured her mother holding her, knocking on Helen Oakes's door, asking if she could tell the professor their story.

And Helen had known, the minute she saw Susannah's application, that she was that baby, all grown up. She'd always remembered Margaret Connolly and her daughter Susannah, the way Margaret had been drawn to tell her story. And later, when Margaret was dying and Susannah was so far away, Helen had sat with her until the end.

Now, just fifty minutes away from Las Vegas, Susannah turned onto White Horse Road and into another world. Eerie cactus and mesquite trees clawed the sky. The pavement ended after a mile or so, and the road became gravel, climbing higher; Susannah shivered, knowing she was near.

When she'd checked the website, she'd looked at the ranch calendar. The circus performed only one day each week—tomorrow night, in Las Vegas. All other times, the circus personnel were on location at the ranch, training for performances and offering trail rides. Accommodations were also available, and Susannah had booked a room.

The ranch came into sight. There were several rings, including one covered by a deep blue tent and set up with trapezes, tightropes, and safety nets. The rustic buildings around the property's perimeter were long and low. In the distance, purple peaks were silhouetted against the sky. Closer up, sandstone ridges, sculpted by wind and blowing grit, rose out of the hard, dry ground.

She parked in the lot, carried her bag to the door marked Reception. She walked in, expecting to be greeted by an employee, by someone hired to run the front desk, so the circus star could train or rest. But standing at the counter, going over papers, was Maria Loisy Dempsey herself.

That it was Maria, Susannah had no doubt. This was Sari's mother: cascading dark hair, wide, intelligent forehead, exquisite brown eyes, and the same shy smile. Her legs were hidden behind the counter, but Susannah saw she wore a white shirt printed with the circus's logo: a galloping silver horse leaping toward a crescent moon. Her bare arms looked tan and strong.

"Allo," she said, her French accent thick. "Welcome to Clair de Lune."

"Thank you," Susannah said. "I'm glad to be here."

"We have lovely weather today. Yesterday there was a sandstorm, not so good. The horses did not enjoy it." She dropped the "h" in "horses," and finished with a bright smile. "But today—all is fine. Your name, please?"

"Susannah Connolly," she said.

"Ah, yes. For two nights. I have you here. You are staying in the Soleil d'Or building. Golden Sun," she translated.

"There are so many French names," Susannah said. "Clair de Lune, Soleil d'Or . . ."

"Yes, my husband and I are French," she said, and smiled again. "You can tell by my accent."

Susannah nodded. So, Maria and Adrien were married.

"Are you the owners?" Susannah asked.

"Yes," she said. "I'm Maria Ferret."

Smiling, Susannah hesitated. She hadn't planned exactly how she would handle her reasons for coming. She wasn't sure whether to speak openly, jump right into the story, be honest up front about her purpose here.

"You're well known," she said. "You're the star rider in Clair de Lune."

"You know our circus?" Maria asked, pleased.

"I've read about it," Susannah said. "I hope to see tomorrow's performance. Will you be riding?"

"It's possible, although I may not be," Maria said. "I have to see."

"Honestly . . . I'm surprised to find you here, working at the desk."

"Oh, I do some of everything," she said. "We are a small operation. Mom-and-pop." She laughed at the American phrase. "Have you also come to ride?"

"Yes," Susannah said. She filled out the registration form, gave Maria her credit card to swipe, and glanced through the brochure.

"We have lovely trails," Maria said. "Our hundred acres runs right into one hundred thousand acres belonging to the Bureau of Land Management. It's almost endless, and so beautiful . . ."

Almost like the Manade du Dempsey and its location by the Parc Régionale de Camargue, Susannah wanted to say, studying her face. Maria looked happy, bright, almost glowing. Her cheeks were pink, the rest of her face burnished and tan. She seemed utterly comfortable with who she was, and quite kind. Could this possibly be the woman who had abandoned her eight-year-old daughter?

"You must be tired from traveling," Maria said. "I will show you your room. Would you like some iced tea? I'll have it brought over . . ."

"Iced tea would be great."

Maria made a call to the kitchen, spoke not in French, but in the language Susannah had heard in Topaz's *roulotte,* the language of the Manouche. The sound sent prickles up Susannah's neck, and she felt the blood rising in her face. She picked up her bags, waiting for Maria to come from behind the desk, and when she did, Susannah's jaw nearly dropped.

Maria Ferret was pregnant.

The path from the main building to Soleil d'Or went directly past the stables. Several brown and white horses stood in the ring, all saddled up and ready to ride. Maria had tried to take Susannah's bags, but Susannah refused.

"I can't let you carry them," she said, glancing down at Maria's belly. Maria tapped it with her hand, and laughed.

"There's no need to coddle me," she said. "I don't believe in being an invalid during this time . . ."

"When are you due?"

"Not for another four months. At the end of September . . ."

"And you still ride?" Susannah asked, thinking of what she had said about the circus.

"Honestly, not so much. I just . . . well, I don't want people to stop going to the circus just because I'm not performing. Many people associate me so completely with the Clair de Lune. When, in fact, there are performers every bit as gifted . . ."

"Gifted," Susannah said, catching her use of the word.

"Yes. It is a great blessing to be able to ride."

"Especially the way you ride," Susannah said.

"You have heard such things?"

"Yes," Susannah said, her blood pounding. This would be the time to speak out. She could tell Maria everything. Surely, if she were expecting another child, she would be tuned in to the needs of her firstborn, the daughter she'd left in France.

But just then she heard a horse's whinny, and the sound of hoofbeats, and turned to see a parade of white horses trooping out of one of the barns, toward the tented ring. Susannah's heart caught, seeing such gorgeous animals, knowing they were just like the ones in the Camargue.

"Beautiful white horses," she said.

"Yes," Maria said. "They are magnificent—we use them in our circus. When we bought this ranch, we renamed the access road White Horse Road. It is a way of honoring our beautiful horses . . . and our homeland."

"Your homeland?"

Maria nodded. "My husband and I are from the South of France. An obscure area—not well known, like Cannes and Marseille. But it is Eden, truly. A paradise filled with white horses."

"Do you miss it?" Susannah said.

Again Maria nodded, but nothing more was forthcoming. She hesitated on the path for a moment, shielding her eyes against the desert sun, watching the horses file into the tent.

One horse held back, prancing in place, allowing the others to go ahead. The rider was a dark-haired man wearing a black hat. Even from so far away he looked striking and handsome, with strong features and a wide moustache, and to Susannah it was clear that he and Maria were staring at each other.

"That's my husband," Maria said.

"He's in the circus, too?"

"Adrien trains all the horses and riders," she said. "He's brilliant with horses."

Susannah nodded. *And at taking women away from their daughters,* she thought. As Maria unlocked the door to Soleil d'Or, Susannah realized that she wanted a villain. She had expected to detest Maria on sight; to her surprise, she felt the opposite. So she glanced back over her shoulder, at the man in the black hat, and felt all the anger she'd been holding inside come pouring out—at him.

The building seemed to be all one story. Maria led Susannah down the long hallway, and unlocked the door to the last room on the left. It opened into a soaring space: rustic barnboard walls rising to a cathedral ceiling.

Picture windows overlooked a landscape of cactus and sage, dry desert, and purple mountains in the distance. As Susannah stood by the window, she saw what appeared to be a trail ride returning home, four brown horses winding their way down a path from the nearest foothill.

"What a beautiful view," Susannah said.

"It's very majestic," Maria agreed. "There is something so vast about the desert."

"I agree," Susannah said. She knew they called the Camargue *un desert d'eau:* a desert of water. But she held it inside. Her heart was racing too fast, and her nerves were too much on edge to tell Maria the things she'd come to say.

"I'm sure the iced tea will arrive any moment," Maria said. "After you've refreshed yourself, if you would like to ride, just call the barn. It's marked on your phone. Someone there will assist you."

"*Merci bien,*" Susannah said.

"You speak French!" Maria said, her smile gleaming.

"Yes," Susannah said, then, in French, that she traveled to France as often as she could.

"It is so welcome to hear the language."

Susannah nodded, suddenly feeling exhausted, wanting to be alone. Nothing so far had gone as she'd thought it would. She had expected to arrive at the Clair de Lune and have to seek Maria out. She'd thought she would hate her on sight. Certainly, she'd never expected to find her so gentle and sympathetic—and so pregnant.

"Please call if you need anything," Maria said.

"I will," Susannah said.

Then, just as Maria was about to close the door behind her, Susannah called out. "Maria!" she said. "Just one question . . ."

"Of course," Maria said, halfway out the door, standing sideways so the silhouette of her belly was apparent.

"Why did you name your ranch and circus Clair de Lune?"

"It means 'light of the moon,' " Maria said. "Moonlight . . ."

"But what is its significance?"

Maria hesitated. For a moment Susannah thought she saw pain flicker across her eyes. Had the moon been out the night Maria had run away with Adrien? When Susannah pictured the moment, she saw Sari riding after her mother under a moon, the car pulling ahead along the moon-white marsh road. Maria blinked, holding whatever she was thinking deep inside. Then, the smile again. "Moonlight is romantic, *non*? And it looks so beautiful on the white horses."

"Yes," Susannah said, remembering that last ride with Grey, him on Django while Susannah rode Mystère, the full moon pouring its light on the swamp while they rescued Tempest. "It does."

And then Maria left.

Susannah had started unpacking—placing her jeans and boots in the closet, setting her books and the letter she'd started to Grey on the desk by the window. She called over to the barn, told the woman who answered that she would like to ride, made an appointment to go out in an hour.

Just then a knock sounded at the door. She went to answer it, found a young woman standing there, holding a glass of iced tea on a tray. Susannah opened the door wide so she could come inside.

"Hello, madame. Shall I put your tea on the desk?" the woman asked, and Susannah was struck by her accent—it was exactly the same as Maria's, Topaz's, Rosalie's: French mixed with something else, which Susannah knew to be Manouche.

"Yes, please," Susannah said.

"Did you have a good trip here?" she asked, pausing to give Susannah a smile. She had very curly dark hair, tumbling to her shoulders. Deep brown eyes peeked out from behind thick bangs, filled with friendly curiosity.

"Very good, thank you."

"I hope that you will enjoy the ranch," the young woman said, continuing over to the desk. Susannah had placed her books and notes there, but the woman gently moved some of them aside and lowered the tray.

"I'm sure I'll enjoy it very much," Susannah said. She went to her purse, to get some money for a tip. When she turned, to hand it to the woman, she saw her frozen in place—staring down at the desk, as if she had seen a ghost, or a rattlesnake, or something else that scared her. But when she looked over at Susannah, her eyes were suddenly wide and filled with joy.

"You know Sarah?" the woman asked.

"Excuse me?" Susannah asked.

"She is my family saint," the woman said. "We love her very much, are grateful for all she has given us, but do not hear of her here in the United States. She is very personal to my relatives, and our people."

When Susannah still looked puzzled, the woman pointed at the desk. Susannah had taken the book from her briefcase—the one in which she'd placed her letter to Grey, with the picture of the statue of Sarah on the cover.

"Sara-la-Kali," the woman said, pointing. Her voice trembled with emotion.

"Oh, yes," Susannah said. "Yes, Sarah . . ."

TWENTY-FOUR

Maria returned to the reception desk, sat down in the swivel chair. Being on her feet was getting harder. Summer was coming, the heat rising; yesterday her ankles were so swollen, Adrien had made her lie down and put her legs up. The baby had been kicking a lot. Adrien said that meant it was a boy. Maria wasn't so sure. She wasn't sure at all.

Sitting at her desk, she looked at the pile of calls she had to return. One of their top horses had had a bad hematoma and needed surgery last week, and she needed to check with the vet on how long he'd be out of commission. Several travel agents had called, wanting to arrange for special riding packages. And Rosalie had phoned twice; both times Maria had been tied up with customers, unable to settle in for a good, long talk.

Now, wanting to ensure she'd have that opportunity, she buzzed the kitchen and asked Chata to come and cover the front desk. Then she went into the inner office, just off the lobby, and closed the door behind her.

The windows gave onto the riding rings and barns. As she watched, Susannah Connolly—the new guest—walked out of Soleil d'Or, across the yard toward the barn. She wore jeans and boots, ready to ride. Her hair glinted reddish-gold in the sun. She had pale and striking purple eyes. Maria thought she was very beautiful; she also seemed very powerful, in the way that meant she had inner strength.

Checking the time, Maria realized that it was nearly nine at night in Stes.-Maries. Her blood quickened, just dialing the number of her friend's cell phone. It brought her home, hearing the foreign ring tones, and she imagined the smell of the marsh wafting through town, mingling with fog off the sea.

"Hello," Rosalie said.

"It's me."

"Finally you call back!"

"What a crazy day it's been," Maria said. "All week, as a matter of fact. I'm so tired, and it's not even summer yet. The heat . . ."

"Never mind the heat. So much time since I left those messages for you! I started to think you really have forgotten us. Life in the States is so glamorous . . ."

"Yes," Maria teased. "I'm as big as an ox, the lovely young Zuna has taken my place as star performer, and I'm soaking my feet to keep them from swelling. Okay then; surely that's not why you've called so often. What is it? Have you finally decided to come over here and see me?"

"That's not it."

"No, of course not," Maria said. "It's May, nearly time for Sarah's feast. You must be so busy. Is the town filling up?" She stopped, caught for a moment in a wave of homesickness.

On May 24 each year, all the Gypsies made a pilgrimage to Stes.-Maries. They would travel from all over to see their saint; the town would be decorated, and the statue of Sarah paraded through the streets, down to the sea in a wooden boat. It was such a beautiful ceremony, and the memory of it pierced Maria with homesick longing.

"Zin-Zin wants to talk to you," Rosalie said.

Maria thought she had misheard, lost in dreams of home. Her chest felt hot, and quickly the blood rushed up into her neck and face. "What did you say?"

"She asked me to call you for her."

"Why? After all this time?"

"Maria, you know she still loves you . . ."

"How could I know that?" Maria asked. "She sent me away . . . she spat at me. Cursed me."

"She was angry. You married him, you let him take you away from us."

"The ranch was just ten kilometers from Stes.-Maries. Now I am ten thousand kilometers away, and she wants to talk to me?"

"Yes, I told you! She had me call you," Rosalie said, sounding eager.

"Does she know about the baby?"

"I haven't told a soul—just as you asked me."

"What does she want?"

Rosalie was silent; Maria heard her tapping her fingernail on the telephone. The women had a long friendship, stretching back to when they were little girls. Maria knew all Rosalie's nervous habits.

"Come on now," Maria said. "Tell me. What does she want, Rosa?"

"Grey came to see her," Rosalie said, lowering her voice—with shame or sadness or a combination of both, Maria wasn't sure.

The sound of his name jolted Maria. It wasn't that she never thought it—she did, more often than she wished. But she had arranged her life to protect herself from unexpected mentions. She had traveled across an ocean and three-quarters of another continent to escape the dishonor of her past. Her hand was trembling; it strayed to her belly.

"What did he want?" she asked.

"You must let Zin-Zin tell you," Rosalie said.

"Rosa, no," Maria said. She cringed, thinking of Grey and Sari, shame and pain washing through her. "The past is over. Tell Zin-Zin I will not talk to her about him."

"It's not," Rosalie said, "really about him . . ."

The baby kicked. Maria bent her head down, toward her belly. She had shortness of breath—it was part of pregnancy, she'd had it the first time, too. Other similarities existed: the quality of movement, the way the baby seemed to swim inside, the quick staccato bursts of kicking.

All reminded Maria of her first pregnancy, of Sari . . . So much so that, although Adrien said this was a boy, Maria secretly called the baby Tchaj—for girl, or daughter—just as she had called her first baby when she was born.

"I do not want to hear," Maria said.

"Then you won't hear," Rosalie said. "Not from me. Zin-Zin will tell you . . ."

"No. I won't call her."

"Surely you won't ignore a request from the woman who loved you as a mother, who raised you as her own. Maria!"

"She disowned me after I married Grey," Maria said. "You're the only one who stayed loyal to me, who still loves me." Maria paused, catching her breath. "Besides, I cannot bear to hear anything she might say."

Just then Maria heard the sound of scuffling, and of muffled words, as if Rosalie had covered the receiver with her hand. Definitely—the sound of a door being closed.

"Rosa, are you walking somewhere?"

"No," Rosalie said. "I'm already here."

"What are you talking about?"

"I've just walked into Zin-Zin's *roulotte*. She is here now. I love you, my Maria . . ." and with that, before Maria could open her mouth and object, Rosalie was off the line.

"Maria." The voice was deep yet frail. It brought back worlds of memories to Maria, filled her with love, and with anger. She'd loved Zin-Zin so much, and felt so hurt when the old woman had cut her off.

"Zin-Zin," Maria said.

"I've kept track of you through Rosalie, and through Matelo's brothers. How is he?"

"He is fine."

"And you, my Tchaj?" My girl. . . . The old nickname brought tears to Maria's eyes.

"I am well, Zin-Zin. And you?"

"Old, my darling. Very old. When one reaches this age, one has crazy thoughts. Memories become weapons . . . clubs, daggers, that one uses on oneself. That is how I spend my days, Tchaj. Living with memories I wish I could undo."

Maria squeezed her eyes tight. She could hang up the phone. She could stop this conversation right now instead of going on with it. Memories she wished she could undo. Oh, Maria's heart had broken over and over again because of memories she wished she could erase. She didn't need to hear about Zin-Zin's.

"It's impossible," Maria said. "To undo memories."

"Do you think so?"

"Of course . . ."

"You, the one who can fly? Who can tiptoe across a horse's back so lightly he doesn't even know you're there? You can swing from the stars, hand-over-hand, all the way to the moon, and you can turn white horses into white doves, wings and all . . . you can do anything. Those are magical things, Maria. Supernatural."

"They are illusions," Maria said. "No more than that."

"Maria, you don't believe that."

"Of course I do. It is how I make my living; it is the premise of Clair de Lune—and of all circuses."

"I shall prove to you you're wrong," Zin-Zin said. "Prove that you are capable of performing supernatural acts."

"Such as what?"

"Taking away my regret. Erasing the terrible thing between us . . . Undoing my memory."

"How could I possibly?" Maria asked. She held the phone tightly; her tone of voice was angry. But inside her heart was racing, because she thought: what if she could do those things?

"You start with the bad night; the worst night: when you came to me, here in my *roulotte*. It was filled with pictures of you back then. On nearly every surface, photos of my darling Maria, on white horses, in costume, on the church steps. Many pictures, remember?"

"Yes," Maria said, picturing the caravan where she had once felt so loved, the wall painted with garlands of sunflowers and lavender, painted by Maria as a gift for Zin-Zin.

"Fine. You are back in time, the night when I shouted at you. When you came here to tell me about Grey Dempsey. When I told you that you were making a terrible mistake, worse than death—that I was glad, in fact, that your mother was dead, rather than see you marry such a man . . ."

Maria remembered those words. She had felt them like a knife in her heart, and the pain came back now—but Zin-Zin was wrong; that wasn't Maria's worst night.

"That night when I disowned you," Zin-Zin said. "When I cursed your marriage, and any children that might be born of your love for him. And when I told you that you would never escape your destiny, that you would leave him and destroy him and marry Matelo instead. Do you remember?"

"How could I forget?" Maria whispered, hot tears flowing from her eyes.

"Maria, that is my worst night. That is the memory I would like you to undo."

"How can I?" Maria asked, voice breaking. "It happened!"

"You can forgive me," Zin-Zin said, begging. "That is all you have to do. I pray, Maria . . . please, find the understanding to do this for me. Go deep inside your own heart, look in there and find the forgiveness. Please, oh, please . . ."

"I forgive you," Maria said. Was that it? Is that all Zin-Zin needed? "I forgave you long ago . . ."

The phone line was filled with soft weeping. She heard Zin-Zin's lips brush the receiver, and the word *"merci"* being repeated over and over. Maria shut her eyes tight, unable to take it in, afraid of what it would dislodge. If only she could undo her own terrible memories.

"Maria," Zin-Zin said after a few moments, "was that your worst night?"

"No," she whispered. "No, it was not . . ."

"What was that?"

Maria rested her hand on the curve of her belly, almost as if she could protect the child inside the way she had failed to protect Sari. She had blocked these thoughts for so long, done whatever she could, at whatever cost, to keep them away. But Zin-Zin's question broke the dam, and they flooded in.

Packing her bags, stealing out of her house, being confronted by Sari. Sari clutching her, begging and sobbing, Maria crazed, pushing Sari away, pushing her hard. Not just a shove—she admitted that now. A slap—hard. Wanting her baby to go away, so this would be over, so Maria wouldn't have to hear her crying, so this could be over.

Those cries, her child weeping.

Climbing into the car. Telling Adrien to drive away fast—*faster!* Faster, oh, hurry. The night so dark, the road so slick. There'd been a rainstorm one hour earlier, after a season of wet weather. The road buckled; the pavement gave way; Adrien's tires stuck in the mud.

By that time, Maria weeping so hard, the sight of Sari's face seared into her eyes and brain, the terror in her daughter's eyes as Maria had shoved her, slapped her—she'd never hit her ever—the sound of Sari's helpless, confused weeping.

Maria had thrown herself into Adrien's arms, crying that she couldn't stand what they were doing, sobbing that she wanted to die. And that was the moment they'd heard hoofbeats: looking out the rearview mirror, they'd seen Sari on Mystère, bearing down on them at a gallop. Sari's last view of her mother had been in the arms of another man.

And Adrien had hit the gas just right to pull out of the rut, and they'd gone speeding up the road. Thinking of that moment, hearing her daughter's voice ringing in her ears, Maria held tight to the phone and couldn't speak. Maria hadn't stayed around to see what happened next. She'd heard about it, and that was even worse.

"It's a memory of Sari, isn't it?" Zin-Zin asked.

"Yes," Maria whispered.

"The night you left her?"

"Yes, God help me."

"Would you like to heal that memory, my darling Maria?"

"More than anything," Maria said. "But it's not possible. The hurt is too deep. When you and I fought, I was a grown woman. I left Sari when she was only eight years old. I hit her. I pushed her so violently, Zin-Zin, just to get her away from me."

"You left her because you love her," Zin-Zin said.

"How do you know that?"

"Rosalie told me. We talk of you often, Maria. Over the years, Rosa has helped me understand what you were thinking. You felt my curse was real. When I swore against your husband and any children . . . Oh, Maria."

"No, Zin-Zin," she said, shaking her head. "It wasn't you who cursed them. I did that. By being selfish—always taking what I wanted, starting with Grey, ignoring the truths I knew. Sari . . . needed a chance without me."

"What do you mean?"

But Maria couldn't explain. She felt her heart shut down, turn into a stone. She heard the old woman speaking gently in her beloved language, but she barely registered a word. She caressed her belly, silently whispering, "Tchaj, tchaj." Girl, girl . . .

If only she could be given a second chance. A way to make up to one daughter for the pain she'd caused another. She'd named her daughter for the wisest woman in the clan, and for Sarah.

She'd always trusted Grey to care for Sari, to give her everything she needed, to shower her with more love than most children received from two parents. She'd trusted him. But even all that love and care had been unable to heal what Maria had done. Maria knew everything; she had made Rosalie tell her every last detail.

"Maria," Zin-Zin said, "Sari needs something from you now."

"What do you mean?"

"Grey came to me. The child is very troubled. The color-blindness . . "

"Hasn't gone away," Maria said. "I know. I ask Rosalie every time we speak."

"There's something else. There is a woman; someone Grey cares for very deeply."

Maria heard the words, felt her heart turn over. She was in love with Adrien, she had left Grey long ago. But still, it was hard to hear. Another woman in Sari's life?

"Even more, Sari seemed to take to her at first. But then . . ."

"Then what?"

"Sari can't let herself be happy, Maria. She feels too hopeless. Can you understand? To be thrown away by her mother . . ."

"Stop," Maria said through clenched teeth. How could Zin-Zin tell her such things?

"Think of my rejection of you—and, as you said, imagine how such a thing would feel to a child. Then you will know what you must do."

"Must do?"

"To undo the memories of that night."

"I can't!" Maria yelled. "They're in too deep—those memories will never leave me, Zin-Zin. Never!"

"I'm speaking of Sari," Zin-Zin said quietly, with almost unimaginable tenderness. "I'm speaking of what you must do to undo those memories for her. Think this over, Tchaj. You will discover the answer . . . turn to Sarah. Pray to her for help and guidance."

"Sarah . . ."

"Even now, I hear the violins and guitars, the musicians preparing for her feast on the twenty-fourth. May, the loveliest month, Maria. Surely you remember . . . Blessings are great in May, if you open your heart to them."

Maria heard Zin-Zin say goodbye; the phone was hung up. Rosalie didn't come back on the line.

She sat in the office rocking back and forth, clutching herself, staring out the window. Matelo was in the circus ring; she could see through the panel that had been rolled up. He looked her way, grinned, blew her a kiss. She wanted to blow a kiss back, but she couldn't move.

A tap sounded at the door.

If she ignored it, the person would go away.

Two seconds later it came again, a little harder: knock, knock, knock . . .

"What is it?" she called.

"Maria!" Fayola stepped through the door. She was only twenty, already a great talent on horseback. It was a shame to use her in the kitchen, even part-time. She should be training to become a star rider, like her sister Zuna, and like Maria herself.

"Yes?" Maria asked. She felt too exhausted to even try to smile.

"That woman in Soleil d'Or? You had me bring her a glass of iced tea?"

"Yes, what about her?"

Fayola smiled wider, and her eyes gleamed. "She has a book of Sarah," she said.

"What are you talking about?"

"Sara-la-Kali. Right here, at our ranch! She has it on her desk, right now."

TWENTY-FIVE

Because she had arrived midday and the other riders were already out, Susannah found herself alone on the trail ride with a young instructor named Christiane. Christiane saddled up two horses, a pinto named Bero for Susannah, and they started into the desert. The day was spectacular, with rock formations stark against dazzling blue sky, and Susannah felt as if they were riding into a postcard.

"What does *Bero* mean?" Susannah asked.

"It means 'bear' in my language, miss," Christiane said in the same accent—French mixed with something else—as Maria and the woman who'd brought Susannah her tea.

"What language is that?" Susannah asked.

"Romany, miss."

"Oh," Susannah said. Maria and Adrien must have brought many people over with them; so far everyone Susannah had encountered had been Romany. But Christiane must have misinterpreted Susannah's tone of surprise for alarm.

"Bero is a fine horse," she said. "He is gentle, nothing like a real bear. We named him that because when he was very young one of the circus bears escaped, and this one helped find him."

"Brave horse," Susannah said, patting his neck.

"Yes," Christiane said, pleased by Susannah's compliment. "He is. . . ."

They headed along a dusty trail into the brush, flushing jackrabbits who went tearing over the dirt. Following a ridge bleached white by the sun, they wound up the foothill to a higher elevation, emerging on the side of one of those purple mountains Susannah had seen from her room.

The view gave onto a long valley running beside a dry riverbed, deeply scored into the hard and rocky desert soil. The mountain terrain made her think of caves; she wondered about tribal art hiding in crevasses above. Susannah gazed down as Bero walked along, feeling his gentle rhythm, grateful for this chance to just ride and think. Her love of riding had flooded back to her in the Camargue, and now it brought her back to that time, and to Grey.

She stared down the mountainside at the dry creek, wondering what it must be like for Maria—coming from such a lush, verdant estuary—to be transplanted into this rough, stony land. Certainly all the people Susannah had met seemed kind, nurturing; and obviously Maria was flourishing. That in itself disturbed Susannah; how could Maria so easily make this new life for herself, have another child, while she'd left Sari in such a terrible way?

The trail widened, and Christiane fell back to ride alongside Susannah. She glanced over, making sure Susannah was fine. "You ride very well," she said.

"Thank you," Susannah said. "I rode a lot when I was young, and just took it up again recently."

Christiane nodded. "You should continue. You have a good seat, and a good rapport with your horse."

"Have you been riding long?" Susannah asked.

"All my life," Christiane said. "Like many of my people, I could ride before I could walk. My father operated a small circus outside Paris. It was very popular; many people from the fashion world would come. Our tents were very beautiful, and the models wanted to be photographed on the white horses."

"The white horses," Susannah said. "I saw some down below, at the ranch here . . ."

"Yes," Christiane said. "They are the same breed as at my father's circus."

"What breed is that?"

"Camarguaise," she said, and the word alone sent a delicate tremor down Susannah's back. "They are an ancient breed, dating back to the Paleolithic period—seventeen thousand years old! They're found only in one place in this entire world—the salt plains of southeastern France. Very beautiful place . . . There are only thirty herds of white horses in existence; they run wild through the salt water."

Susannah listened silently, holding her thoughts inside. She pictured the herds she'd seen with Grey and Sari. She could see Tempest still young and wild, trying to escape into the marsh. She thought of what Grey had said, that horses always felt hunted. Now, hiding her true reasons for being here, Susannah felt like a hunter. She was after something from Maria, that was certain.

Susannah felt that there was something so primal about riding through the mountains, with the blue sky enveloping them, that made dishonesty impossible. Susannah's gaze flicked over to Christiane.

"I've been to the Camargue," she said.

"You have? Then you know! Isn't it magnificent?"

"Yes, it truly is. You said you're from outside Paris," Susannah said. "How did you wind up here in Nevada?"

"Oh, for the chance to ride in Clair de Lune," she said, almost breathlessly. "My father reveres Matelo—that's Adrien Ferret; he and his wife are owners of this ranch, and of the circus. He is the best trainer in the world. All Gypsies want to ride with him. And Maria is famous everywhere."

"But you're so far from home," Susannah said.

Christiane smiled, a little sadly. "That is our way," she said. "Gypsies are wanderers, did you not know? We began in India, and followed the Romany Trail all the way to Byzantium, and from there to Europe. *Romany* means 'human.' We are at home in the world, wherever we go."

"That's beautiful, Christiane," Susannah said softly.

"Clair de Lune is my family now," she said. "I work in the stable, hoping for the chance to move to the circus. For now I am needed on the ranch; but I work out and practice. Matelo trains me when there is time. I am very good."

"I'm sure you are," Susannah said.

"With Maria no longer performing, others have moved up to become stars themselves. Zuna, Chata—they are both brilliant. I'm hoping to take their places in the ranks, when the time is right."

"That will happen, I bet," Susannah said. Then, "Maria no longer performs? She's expecting a baby . . ."

"Yes," Christiane said. "She stopped riding just before her pregnancy. Some women continue for at least the first few weeks, but not Maria."

"No?"

Looking uncomfortable, as if she'd said something wrong, Christiane shook her head and looked away. Susannah followed her gaze, down the long slope toward the ranch. The sun had moved behind the peak, and long shadows had begun to fall. From here, the dry riverbed looked like a hard black line through the high desert.

"She and Matelo wanted a child." Christiane paused, glancing over with excitement in her eyes. Susannah had the feeling that she didn't ordinarily gossip with guests, but that she was overflowing with the story and needed to pour it out. "They hoped for a long time, but they were under a curse."

"Really?" Susannah asked. "A real curse?"

"A spiritual sickness," Christiane said. "I don't know why, or what caused it, but Maria's soul was ailing."

"And this 'curse' was lifted?"

Again, Christiane nodded.

"How did that happen?"

"Through grace and the intercession," Christiane said. "And by Maria giving up what she loves most: riding and horses. Offering it up to God."

"Did she tell you that?"

"It is known among us," Christiane said confidently. "And now we know that she is expecting, and we are so happy for her, that soon she will have a child."

Susannah didn't reply to that. The trail took a wide, looping turn, and then began its way down the mountain—a series of switchbacks that took them back toward the ranch. The path seemed very close to the edge; Susannah's heart raced when she saw what a sheer drop there was to the bottom.

But even when they'd leveled out, walking slowly along flat even ground, her pulse refused to steady. Christiane's words stuck in her head: Maria was pregnant through grace and intercession. And in France, four thousand miles away, there was still a little girl without her mother.

Maria watched her come back. The two horses meandered down the trail, seeming to take forever to get from the last plateau of the mountainside to the barn. She stood in the hallway of Soleil d'Or, holding the book of Sarah, eyes glittering, gripped by such powerful emotion she didn't even know what to call it. Was it rage? Or sorrow? Or a word that hadn't been invented yet?

Once she was sure the horses had returned, she used her key to let herself back into the room. She was tired, and her lower back hurt. Pulling out the desk chair, she sat down—as she had two hours ago, after Fayola had run to tell her about the book.

Maria held the book now, hands shaking as she touched the single sheet of paper, folded within its pages. Her eyes had felt scalded, burning right out of her head, when she'd opened it, read the words *Dear Grey* . . .

What had inspired Maria to ransack a guest's room? She had never done such a thing before. But then, she'd never gotten a call from Zin-Zin before, followed so quickly by an employee nearly hysterical over the discovery in one of the guest rooms of a book on Sarah.

Maria had instructed Fayola to stay at the front desk, and she'd hurried here to Soleil d'Or. What had she expected to find? Looking back, it was impossible to remember or know.

Her emotions since then had been like an earthquake: rumbling, tearing, apocalyptic, destroying the familiar landscape, leaving something brand new and terrible in its place. Maria had let herself into the room, gone straight for the desk. The book was there in plain sight. The price tag—tiny white rectangle, stuck to the back cover, marked in euros—showed that the book had been sold at the gift shop in Stes.-Maries-de-la-Mer.

That's when she'd known: this wasn't an accident, wasn't a coincidence. Gypsies didn't believe in such things anyway. Maria had been taught by Zin-Zin long ago to look past the simple explanation for the deeper, darker truth. Simplicity was a myth. Gypsies knew that truth was layered, and life was complicated. Persecution had been their lot. They had been hunted and hated, and Maria knew that was why they all loved horses so much: they shared a sense of having suf-fered predation.

Now, here was this woman with a book on Sara-la-Kali, and a letter to Maria's ex-husband—filled with love, and aches, and promises. And Maria had a new baby kicking inside, and she hadn't been on a horse in months, almost a year, and her soul felt as if it were withering, and right now she thought she might die before Susannah Connolly returned to her room.

A buzz sounded—her walkie-talkie. Someone looking for her. She reached for it, to shut it off, heard Adrien's voice: *"Ou est tu, cherie? Ma p'tite? Viens, Maria . . ."* Her hands were shaking so hard, and she couldn't bear to speak to her beloved, so she just clicked the damn thing off.

Maria stared out the window at the Spring Mountains. She used to look at them, feel they were mocking her. *Spring* meant fresh, flowing, growing; but Maria had been as barren as the twisting, cruel, dried-up river running across their ranch.

She had gazed at those mountains, thinking of how ridicu-lous their name was, considering they'd spawned such a use-less, dry river. Adrien had had to pipe in water for the horses. The river had gone dry the same year they'd bought the ranch; it was as if Zin-Zin's curse had spread and grown, af-fecting not only Maria's body, but even the land on which she and Adrien lived.

Having walked away from one child—in pursuit of riding, her miraculous "gift"—she had found the meaning of a true curse. Losing Sari, she ached for a child. She wanted a baby to love, to make up for what she'd done to Sari.

Maria had tried everything. She'd undergone in vitro fertil-ity treatments. Adrien had brought in a Manouche healer from Bruges, and Maria had consented to many sessions that involved candles, chants, and holy water. Still, every month, she'd see those hated drops of blood, and she'd fall deeper into despair.

She would dream every night: Sari's face. That was all. Those precious eyes gazing into Maria's with such questions, such wondering. *Why?* Sari seemed to be asking. *Why did you leave me?*

I can never explain it to you, my love, Maria would try to reply. But every time she opened her mouth to let the words out, Sari would close her eyes.

That's what Sari used to do when she was little: whenever something she didn't like would happen, her big green eyes would shut tight. When Maria had tried to feed her home-made vegetable soup—eyes shut. When Grey had tried to give her medication for a bad cold—eyes shut.

Maria had felt shut down herself. She had felt her own body turning against her; she felt such shame from what she'd done to her daughter. Why should she be given a second chance to be a mother, when she'd thrown away the first one so cruelly? She'd prayed for guidance.

The dreams of Sari, the dry river, the uselessness of her body. She knew she needed to do penance, so she decided to stop riding—the greatest sacrifice she could make. Maybe if she did that, deprived herself of the thing she most loved to do, Sarah would take pity on her and let her have a baby.

Adrien had been furious. Not only because she was the greatest draw their circus had—people came from all over to see the "Gypsy princess" and her white horses—but because he knew what it would cost her spirit to stay away from horses. He had held her while she'd cried, and she had finally been able to convince him that this was something she had to do, a sacrifice she had to make.

Her last night on horseback: she and Matelo riding together in the moonlight, standing tall on the backs of their most exquisite steeds, flying through the night under a crescent moon. She had felt the horse's power moving into her bare feet, up her legs, into her body. She'd reached up, fingers stretching toward the thin moon.

Tears had fallen from her eyes, blinding her, absorbed by her horse's white coat. Even without vision, it didn't matter: she rode as if she and the horse were the same animal. Matelo—she always called her husband by his Romany nickname when they were riding—had galloped beside her, and they'd switched in midair—she jumped onto his horse, and he onto hers.

They had crisscrossed through the desert, riding blindly, switching off, back again, until finally she felt him leap up behind her. His horse whirled and fell behind while he stayed with her, holding her. She'd leaned back into his strong body, eyes wide open, taking in the field of stars and the romantic curve of moon.

His body had pressed into hers—two crescent moons becoming one. She'd been wearing her silver dress, covered with glitter like tiny stars. He'd slid his hand underneath, guided himself inside. Maria had felt him explode, and she'd known right then, that was the moment.

And she'd been right: the miracle had happened.

Adrien was careful to keep her pregnancy out of the press; he didn't want people to stop coming to Clair de Lune, and he wasn't quite ready to promote Zuna and Chata as the new stars. Maria didn't care. She just wanted to make it to full term, for the baby to be born healthy and happy.

Zin-Zin's call . . .

Forgiveness and a challenge: to "undo" the memories of that night. That night, that terrible night, Sari with her eyes open coming fast. Zin-Zin had spoken of Grey and a woman, said that Sari had taken to her—at first. Maria sat very still, holding the book and letter, thinking of her daughter taking to another woman. In spite of her own selfish grab for happiness, it hurt to think of such a thing.

The baby kicked, as she always did. Tap, tap, tap . . . memories of Sari at this stage. *Tchaj,* Maria thought. *Tchaj . . . my girl . . . my daughter*. Maria's arms encircled her growing belly, as if she could keep the child inside safe. She, more than anyone, knew how illusory safety could be.

Footsteps sounded in the hallway. The click of heels meant it was someone in riding boots, but the tread was light, so she knew it was a woman. Maria pushed herself out of the chair and rose to face the door.

The key turned in the lock; the rustic oak door swung open. Susannah Connolly stood there with a look of shock on her face. Maria felt her own mouth twitching—with nervousness and fury and words of rage. But she watched Susannah's gaze fall upon the book Maria held in her hand—watched her look at the image of Sarah—and saw Susannah's expression soften.

"Maria," Susannah said, walking toward her with an outstretched hand. "I've come here about your daughter. About Sari . . ."

TWENTY-SIX

Susannah walked forward, propelled by a force deep inside, hands outstretched to Sari's mother. Maria stood by the desk shaking, eyes red-rimmed, tears pooling, book clutched to her breast, the picture of Sarah peeking out above her hand. Susannah watched Maria flinch, withdraw, and then finally reach out her hand.

"I've come about your daughter," Susannah repeated.

"Does she know you are here?"

"No. They have no idea."

"They—Sari and Grey?"

"Yes," Susannah said. Still holding Maria's hand, she led her to the sitting area at one end of the room. A sofa and two chairs had been grouped here, cozy and intimate, around a fireplace for chilly nights. Maria sat on the sofa, and Susannah perched on the edge of one of the armchairs. She stared down at the small book, saw the corner of the letter she'd written to Grey sticking out. Following her gaze, Maria looked her hard in the eye.

"I don't usually read guests' letters."

"But you read that one."

"Are you the woman Grey 'cares about deeply'?" Maria asked, emphasizing the phrase.

"Who told you that?" Susannah asked.

"Zin-Zin," Maria said. "The matriarch of my clan."

"I've met her," Susannah said.

"But that's not possible," Maria said. "Zin-Zin doesn't associate with outsiders."

"Maybe I'm not as much an outsider as you think. What did she say about me?"

"Nothing about you. Just that Grey went to see her. And that my daughter . . ." Maria trailed off, as if the next part was impossible to say; or maybe she just found it too difficult to discuss Sari with Susannah.

"That your daughter is in pain," Susannah said quietly.

"How dare you!" Maria said, jumping up. Her eyes were wild and fierce. She clutched her pregnant belly as if protecting the child inside from this stranger's influence and judgment.

"I spent time with her," Susannah said. "I saw . . ."

"Saw what? What can you understand of my daughter? She is mine—no one knows Sari as I do, and don't you dare judge me for what I did, for what I know to be right!"

"Right?" Susannah asked. "You pushed her away—shoved her so hard, she hit the wall. You ran out the door to be with Matelo, and you never looked back long enough to see Sari lying in the road."

Maria yanked her hand back as if to slap Susannah, but she didn't follow through. She crumbled inside, felt the world end.

"Stop," she gasped.

"It's true, isn't it?" Susannah asked. "That's why you didn't slap me just now; you know I'm just telling you what you already feel."

"You don't understand; you can't begin to imagine."

"Maria . . ."

She closed her eyes, as if she could block out Susannah's voice. But Susannah saw the torment on her face and knew that Maria was still seeing the shock and betrayal in her daughter's eyes.

"I had to get away," Maria whispered.

"Your family," Susannah said. "You defied them by marrying Grey and they cut you off. That's why you're here now, isn't it? So far from the Camargue, from the place you'd always known as home . . . it's why you and Adrien had to travel so far away. Because you were shut out of your own clan."

"You don't understand us," Maria said.

"I'm not part of you," Susannah said. "But I'm doing my best to understand. Because I care about . . ."

"About Grey? About taking over as the woman in his life, mother to my daughter?"

"About you, too, Maria," Susannah said. She felt emotion welling up, thinking of Helen Oakes and all she had said about Romany tradition, women's choices, the difficulties of being true to oneself.

"Don't waste your energy thinking of me," Maria said. "I am fine."

"I don't see how you could be, honestly," Susannah said. "You're pregnant again, and that is wonderful. But what did you have to give up, to get to this place? Your gift—riding the horses you love so much . . . just so you can feel you deserve to have another baby? What about the daughter you already gave up?"

"Leave me alone," Maria wept, collapsing into the desk chair. "Please, leave my ranch and let us be . . . go away and stop this talk . . ."

"Maria," Susannah said, crouching beside her, "stopping the talk won't help you. And it won't help Sari."

"Is she still suffering?" Maria made herself whisper.

"Of course. She misses her mother."

"She's still colorblind." It wasn't a question.

Susannah steeled herself. "Yes," she said.

"Zin-Zin cursed us," Maria said. "I told myself, and her, that it wasn't possible, that it's just old-world, superstitious foolishness. But maybe it's true."

"Maria, the only way a curse can work is if you let it. If your psyche is fragile, if you already feel bad about yourself, a curse can find its way in. It becomes a self-fulfilling prophecy. You believe it will work, so it does. I think you've been punishing yourself ever since you left."

"I brought it on myself, marrying an outsider."

"What happened to you was so unfair," Susannah said, thinking of Topaz and all she had said about her own family, the ancestor who had defied their culture and married a Spaniard. "You loved someone, and deserved happiness. You didn't bring *anything* on yourself. They did it to you."

"I was young," Maria said. "Zin-Zin was like a mother to me. I hated myself for hurting her. There are traditions, and she taught them to me. Her wisdom always meant so much to me—I named my daughter for her, even though I knew Zin-Zin would never approve. She was so wise . . . she even predicted my love for Adrien."

"But you had to find out for yourself," Susannah said.

Maria paused, then went on. "I left Sari to save myself, and *her*. I thought she would do better without me. Our lives, our home—they were terrible. I could never live between two worlds. . . ."

"The world with Grey and the world of Stes.-Maries?"

"Yes. I wasn't Gypsy anymore. I tried to fit into Grey's life, but it never worked. I was dying there . . . He loves Sari so much. I tell myself I wanted to do the best for her—leave her with her father, so she wouldn't have to be so divided. Matelo and I . . . we didn't know what we were going to do . . . where we'd end up . . . I knew Grey would take care of her."

"He does."

"I told myself she would be better without me. I was so unhappy. I'd ride all day, tears flowing the entire time. Sari started thinking mothers were people who cried. She looked at Anne—Laurent's mother—and wondered why she smiled so often. In my selfishness, to do what I wanted, I told myself she'd be so much better off without me."

"But she wasn't," Susannah said, touching Maria's hand.

"How do you know?"

"Because you're her only mother," Susannah said.

"How do you know so much? Do you have children?"

"No," Susannah said. "But I had a mother. She died last winter, and I miss her every day. I miss her right now . . . I wish I could tell her about you, ask her what I could do to help you."

"Why do you want to help me?" Maria asked harshly. "When it's Grey you love? Grey and Sari?"

"Because they can't move on."

"What do you mean?"

"Sari is trapped, Maria. Trapped in the world of that night."

"She can't be," Maria whispered.

"But she is."

The words made Maria start to cry again. She bowed her head, her shoulders shook. Susannah felt tears come to her own eyes. She'd thought maybe she would try to convince Maria to return to France, just to give Sari the chance to say what she needed to say, including a proper goodbye; what she realized now was that they needed to say hello. Sari needed a life that included her mother.

Just then Susannah saw that Maria was still holding the Sarah book. Reaching over, she gently pried it from her hand. She looked down at the book, felt flooded by realizations about her own life—the time she'd spent in Stes.-Maries, the history her mother had had with Sarah.

"I told you before," Susannah said, "that I'm not as much an outsider as you think."

"Because you have that book?" Maria asked, her voice hollow.

"No. Because I've been to the Sarah Circle."

At that Maria raised her head, looked at Susannah with wet eyes. She blinked with disbelief. "No one is invited there who is not Rom."

"I was invited," Maria said. "By Topaz Avila."

"The others would never accept you."

"But they did, Maria," Susannah said. "When they heard my story."

"Which is—" She left the question in the air.

"My mother was unable to conceive," Susannah said. "My parents had tried to have children for years; they were giving up hope. My mother was in despair, and to help her, my father planned a trip. He knew she loved horses, and there was a place he'd heard about, where white horses run free . . ."

"The Camargue," Maria said.

Susannah nodded. "Yes. They explored their way down through the park, and wound up almost by accident in Stes.-Maries. My parents were so taken by the story of the boat . . . without rudder or sails, that left Palestine . . ."

"Carrying the three Marys, and Martha, and Lazarus, and . . ."

"And Sara-la-Kali."

"You call her by her Gypsy name?"

Susannah nodded. "She's my saint, too."

"How could she be?" Maria asked.

"My mother went into the church that day. She described the statue—Sarah, so beautiful, made of ebony, dressed so lovingly by women of the village. Surrounded by candles."

"Thousands of candles, all glowing," Maria said, as if she could see it.

"My mother knelt at her side, and looked into her eyes. She prayed to Sarah, that she be blessed with a child."

"The child is you?"

Susannah nodded. She stared into Maria's face and saw something change: a shift in her gaze, in the focus of her brown eyes, in the way tension seemed to spiral right out of her.

"Sarah blessed your mother?"

"Yes," Susannah said. "And after my mother died, I kept a promise I'd made to her—to visit Sarah. I rented a house that turned out to be owned by Topaz. She was so friendly and welcoming, and when I told her the story, she insisted . . ."

"That you visit the Sarah Circle."

"Now do you understand why I was allowed to enter?" Susannah said.

"It's because Sarah caused a miracle in your family," Maria said. "And you are that miracle. They would want to meet you. You would be very holy to them . . ."

"I felt honored to meet them all. They were very kind to me. All except Rosalie."

"My best friend," Maria whispered. "The only one who stayed loyal to me after I married Grey."

"She's still loyal," Susannah said.

"She never liked to tell me about Sari; I would ask, and she would hold back. She couldn't bear to tell me my daughter was suffering. But I knew. I made her tell me everything."

Susannah paused. A group of riders was returning from the tent to the barn; she heard thundering hooves, looked up in time to see a blur of white horses going by. Maria's shoulders tightened, and she refused to look out the window.

"I think Rosalie wanted to protect you," Susannah said.

"From what?"

"She knows you have a great gift," Susannah said. "Everyone talks about the way you ride, your love of horses. Not everyone can communicate with them the way you do. Rosalie, and in fact everyone I talked to, spoke of your leaving as a necessity for your spirit. They said you had to ride with Adrien, that to stay home would have stunted you, broken you down. Maybe that was part of the 'curse.' You didn't believe you deserved to ride, to have everything."

"Everything? What do you mean?"

Susannah thought of Helen, of their last talk, of all she believed she'd had to give up in order to rise so high in her field. Had she really had to sacrifice so much? Did any woman? Maybe that was just one version of a modern-day curse: being told you couldn't follow all your heart's desires, limiting yourself to just one.

"I mean stay in Stes.-Maries. Be with Adrien, and perform and ride, but also see Sari. Also be her mother . . ."

Maria listened. Susannah looked at her, believed that all the fight had gone out of her. She listened, really thinking about it. Her hands rested gently on her round belly. Her gaze swept from the book of Sarah to Susannah's face, the expression in her eyes thoughtful and without defiance.

"I could undo the memory . . ." Maria said.

"The memory?" Susannah asked, but Maria didn't reply.

Just then footsteps sounded in the hallway outside. Strong, powerful, running fast. Someone pounded on the door. Maria's eyes brightened; even before she answered the knock, Susannah knew who it was.

She pulled the door open, saw a man standing there. Not very tall, slightly built, he was nonetheless very strong-seeming. His eyes were black and wide-set, his cheekbones high and sharp, his mouth open to speak beneath a thick moustache.

"I'm looking for my wife," he said, looking over her shoulder.

"Mr. Ferret?" she asked, putting out her hand. "I'm Susannah Connolly. Please come in. Maria's here . . ."

He nodded, brushed past to go to Maria. Knelt down beside her on one knee, took her right hand, brushed the dark hair back from his wife's face in a gesture so tender that Susannah felt tears spring to her own eyes. She stared at the couple, saw them whispering, heard Maria say the name "Sari" just before dissolving in another flood of weeping.

Adrien just caressed her. He listened to her speak, his ear close to her mouth. Susannah watched as Maria reached for the book on the desk, pulled it to her lap, pointed at Sarah's picture and whispered some more.

Susannah had to turn away. The moment was too intense and intimate for her to watch. And she was filled with thoughts of her own. She was picturing Grey and Sari, knew that it was the middle of the night there, hoped that they were sleeping. She remembered her last sight of Sari, being led away in the moonlight by her father; she thought of all the nights Sari had spent without her mother, knew what a toll they had taken.

Even with her back turned, she could hear Maria and Adrien talking, whispering. Their voices rasped with emotion, and she knew, even without understanding the Manouche language that they were speaking, that Maria was telling him what she needed. She had a heart's desire that needed to be fulfilled, and Susannah knew—with everything she had—that Maria was going to make sure it was.

"Tchaj," she heard Maria say in a voice full of tears. And then, in response, Adrien whispering back, "Tchaj, Maria . . ."

And Susannah stood there with her back turned, feeling someone beside her. Fingers brushed her hand. She felt the warmth, as if she were standing in a chapel filled with the light of a thousand candles. Outside the window, the rest of the white horses galloped out of the circus tent, but Susannah barely noticed. She was standing with Sarah, and they were both waiting for Maria to decide what she was going to do.

TWENTY-SEVEN

The month of May passed so slowly, Sari sometimes thought the calendar was going backward instead of forward. In nature, things happened in their own time. The marsh turned a little greener every day. The birds built nests, and eggs were hatched, and suddenly the air was filled with song. Dragonflies hovered over the ponds, iridescent wings gleaming. And the lunar cycle came around again so that soon the moon was growing full once more.

Sari looked up in the sky from her room at night, wishing time *would* go backward. She wished she could return to that last night Susannah was on the ranch, when Sari had turned into a baby beast. She had taken the Tarasque story to heart—how could she not, sleeping with the soft dragon toy every night—and decided that *she* was the creature who needed taming.

If Sari could go back in time, she would tell Susannah she

was sorry. She would ask her to go riding with her again. As time went by, she realized that her worst memory was the night her mother had driven away; now, staring up at the growing moon, Sari realized that that had happened again, with Susannah. Sari had chased her away from here. . . .

The next day at school was very busy. May 24 was coming up fast, and all the Gypsy kids were getting ready for the celebration. To honor the feast days of Stes.-Maries-de-la-Mer, the school was preparing a banner to be carried in the procession. The band would play, and the equestrian team would ride in formation.

Sari watched the team practicing from the window of her literature class, and felt an ache. She wished that she would someday be able to ride as well as those kids, and represent her school at important occasions—just not the Gypsy procession. She wished with all her heart that these festivities would end soon. That would mean summer was here. . . . Staring into the field, she saw—or remembered—a shimmer of silver-green.

"Why are you so quiet?" Laurent asked, sitting beside her on the bus on the way home.

"I'm just thinking of summer," she said, shocked by the sight-memory of color.

"That's not for a few more weeks," he said, frowning. "Why are you hurrying through May, when there are so many exciting things we're going to do?"

" 'We're'?" she asked.

"Well, we have to go to the procession, to write an article for the paper."

"Laurent, the last issue has already come out."

"I told you. It would be for next September," he said. "The fall issue of the school paper should have some really good, strong reporting in it. All about the Pilgrimage of the Gypsies."

She just gave him a look, as if he was crazy.

"Not only that, someone has to carry the banner for the school, in the parade," he said. "I figured we could do it, and then we'd have firsthand experience. It would make the story even more powerful."

"I don't go to the procession," she said, staring at him, wondering why he was blushing. "You know that, and I keep telling you."

"You're related to so many people in town," he said. "They'd be proud of you, marching in the parade."

"Don't say that," she said, shaking her head. "You know they don't want any part of me." When she looked up, she saw Laurent staring down at her.

"You can go to the procession whether they want you or not," he said, his voice low and gravelly, "when you're with people who do want you."

"What do you mean?"

"You'll be with me," he said.

Sari felt the blood rush to her face. She had always known and loved Laurent; they had learned to walk and ride together. When the bad times started, he'd heard her crying late at night; she'd look out her window and see him standing in the yard. One night when they were nine, just a year after her mother had left, he'd climbed up the vines to lean into her window, give her a kiss. But it had been a brotherly kiss. The way he was looking at her now didn't feel like a brother.

"We'll march with the school," he said. "And our fathers will be there, and my mother."

"My father doesn't go to the procession," she said quietly.

"I think he's going this year," Laurent said. "My father told me."

Sari looked up, surprised again. Why would her father be going to the Pèlerinage des Gitans—the Pilgrimage of the Gypsies—the largest gathering of Romanies held anywhere, at any time of year? And why wouldn't he have told her? She'd noticed him being very odd and quiet lately. He'd gotten a letter in the mail two days ago. She'd seen the envelope, seen the postmark.

Then she'd seen him reading the letter. He had taken it outside, to stand by the ring where Tempest was, to lean against the tall fence and read the pages. Watching from the kitchen window, Sari had seen there were several pages. Her father read them slowly; and when he'd finished reading the letter once, he read it through again. Of course it was from Susannah; Sari knew they wrote to each other all the time.

Her father had seemed different since that letter. Sari had stared at him just this morning, sitting at the breakfast table. He'd been so quiet, staring at the morning paper, seeming not to see the words. Sari had thought how thoughtful he seemed, just gazing into space. She had watched him, thinking he looked as black and white as the newspaper he held, and wishing she could see the color of her father's eyes.

"Will you go with me, Sari?" Laurent asked her now.

"I don't want to see those people," she said.

"Rosalie will be there," he said. "You know she loves you."

"I remind her of my mother," Sari said, shrinking. "She quit because of me."

"She still loves you."

"Everyone quits because of me," Sari whispered. "They leave."

Laurent gazed down at her. She had slunk low in the bus seat, knees drawn up almost to her chin. She wanted to disappear, but she didn't want to stop looking into Laurent's face. His eyes were filled with fire, but they had the effect of calming her down.

"I won't quit because of you," he said.

The bus drove through the Parc, crossing a bridge that rattled beneath the wheels. Out the windows, a herd of white horses grazed on the salt plain. Sari gazed out, saw a shimmer of silver-green. *Was* it? Had she just seen color? Or was she just remembering it? She thought about it now—ever since the night in Avignon with Laurent, things had looked different to her somehow, more vivid, even in black and white. Maybe that's all it was.

Laurent watched her, and Sari knew he could see every emotion she was feeling inside. Her skin was as thin as wet paper; everything showed. Laurent could see all the worry, pain, shame, fear she'd been feeling all this time, passing just under her skin. And now this shocking feeling, seeing a burst of green. She couldn't hide it from him.

"What is it?" he asked.

"I don't know," she said. "Something strange . . ."

"Tell me."

She shook her head hard. "Maybe it's just thinking about that parade. It's crazy, my father wanting to go. What could that be about?"

"I don't know," he said. "What do you think?"

"Susannah, maybe," she said. "She and my father write to each other."

"I wonder if she's coming back to France," Laurent said after a long pause.

Sari stared out the window, wishing for another flash of green. She thought of Susannah coming back to France; it surprised her, how much she hoped that could happen.

"I'll be with you," Laurent said. "If you go to the procession."

"I'd be too afraid," Sari whispered, shutting her eyes.

She felt Laurent take her hand. His fingers slipped around hers, and he pulled her hand up to his chest. Her eyes were squeezed shut, but she felt his lips brush her knuckles. Her heart beat as if there were a dragonfly trapped inside. "I'll be with you, Sari," she heard him whisper. "The whole time."

The morning of May 24 dawned foggy and cool. Mist hovered over the marsh as the sun began to rise. Grey stood in the barn, brushing Mystère again, making sure her tail and mane were brilliant, flowing white.

Grey could hardly keep his feelings in. He felt as if he were trying to hold back the Atlantic Ocean—as if all the waves that had traveled across the sea were gathering force, ready to wash over him—and he had to slow them down. It was his job to stay calm, act "normal," when every cell in his body was raging to go see her.

Susannah; he felt her presence as if she were standing right here beside him. He felt her in the air, on the breeze, in the sounds of the marsh all around him. He swore Mystère sensed her, too; she pranced in place, letting out a long whinny.

"There, girl," Grey said, petting her. "Just a little longer now."

"She looks good," Claude said, poking his head into the stall. "Beautiful."

"This is her big moment," Grey said.

Claude chuckled. *"Hers?"* he asked. "Maybe you mean yours?"

"You know what I mean," Grey said.

"Indeed I do," Claude said, giving Grey a long look before he nodded, heading into the tack room to make sure the saddle and bridle were polished and ready. He'd been careful to leave some tarnish in the grooves of the silver scallop shells, giving them the blackness of coquilles St. Jacques.

Grey saw Laurent out in the yard, pacing, waiting for Sari to wake up. Grey hurried, wanting to get Mystère ready before she did. He had asked her to lay out her best clothes before bed, to dress in the morning as if they were going to church. When she'd asked him why, he'd told her he wanted her to look pretty for the procession. She'd turned over, hidden her face so she wouldn't have to reply.

He'd stayed calm, kissed her goodnight, told her he'd see her in the morning. Now, looking back, maybe he should have told her what was going on. He felt as if he was balancing between wanting to tell her everything, so she would be prepared, and wanting to hold it all back—letting the day unfold, not getting her hopes up about something that might not turn out the way he prayed it would.

As Claude came out of the tack room, holding the gleaming bridle ready to slip over Mystère's head, Grey saw his old friend smiling. Claude knew Grey very well.

"Today will be a great day," Claude said.

"I hope so," Grey said.

"You have nothing to worry about. Anne and I will make sure Mystère gets to the parade grounds . . ."

"That's not what I'm worried about," Grey said.

"Sari? Laurent knows everything, and he'll see to it that everything goes smoothly. You can count on my son. And on me . . ."

"I know that, Claude," Grey said. "I've always been able to. You're a great friend."

"All will be well, understand?" Claude asked, hand on Grey's shoulder. "Laurent will be right there with Sari. We'll all be there together."

Grey nodded, shaking Claude's hand. Then, taking Mystère's bridle, Claude led her toward the trailer parked in the yard outside. He loaded her in, and Anne came out dressed in a light blue dress and beautiful straw hat. Waving, they drove away.

Steadying himself, Grey walked into the house. He went upstairs and shook Sari awake. She ignored him for a while, but then she climbed out of bed and turned on the shower. He went into the kitchen for another cup of coffee, listening to her move slowly, watching the fog burn off over the marsh.

"Is she ready?" Laurent asked, standing in the kitchen door.

"Not yet," Grey said. "But at least she's moving."

"She will love the parade," Laurent said, smiling. Oddly, the boy's words gave Grey real hope. "I'll call up to her and see how she's doing," Laurent continued.

Grey nodded. He watched Laurent go to the foot of the stairs, heard him call up to Sari and her brief reply. Then Grey walked out into the yard. He was filled with pent-up energy—all of it had felt almost impossible. He stood in the dusty ranch yard, staring across the fresh green marsh and in the direction of the road where he'd first met Susannah the day he'd rescued her from the bulls, thinking of all that had happened since then. . . .

A half hour later, he pulled the Citroën to the kitchen door just as Laurent came walking out with Sari. She looked beautiful, with her brown hair loose and flowing and wearing the black dress she reserved for special occasions and the pearls his mother had given her for her last birthday.

"Come on, kids," Grey said, leaning over to open the door. "Hurry up, we don't want to be late."

"I don't even want to go," Sari said quietly, climbing into the back seat.

"Sit up front," Laurent said.

Sari just shook her head, arms clasped across her chest, gesturing that Laurent should sit beside Grey instead. Grey knew her so well—she was making her point: she might be complying, but she wasn't going to enjoy it. Laurent shrugged and got into the front seat. Like Grey, he knew Sari.

Grey pulled out onto the main road, into a heavy stream of traffic. Every car held a Gypsy family, coming from all over Europe. Every hotel in Stes.-Maries and the surrounding area had been booked for months.

It was the same every May—the Pilgrimage of Gypsies took place each year, and Romanies traveled from wherever they were to venerate their saint. As Grey concentrated on driving, his heart was racing. He hadn't been to this procession in so long. But all those memories faded: he could think only of what was about to happen.

Now, pulling into town, he drove to the field where the horse trailers were parked, and where the locals were staging for the procession. He knew exactly where to go, where they had arranged to meet. Passing a cluster of kids from Sari's school, he saw them wave and heard Laurent exclaim. Glancing in the rearview mirror, he caught Sari's eye. She was inching down in the seat, and her gaze seemed desperate.

"Drive me home," she said.

"Sweetheart," he said to her, "trust me."

"I can't," she said, and he watched as she did the familiar thing of closing her eyes. "I thought I could do this, but I can't."

"Sari," Laurent said. He reached into the back seat, grabbed her hand. Grey glanced over and knew with certainty—he saw something in Laurent's eyes, in the way he was being toward Sari—this wasn't just a boy comforting his childhood friend. Laurent was a young man in love, just as Susannah had said.

"Tell my father," Sari whispered, eyes shut tight now. "Tell him to take me home."

"We're carrying the banner for our school," Laurent said. "You'll be with me, and all our friends. We'll remember everything, so we can put it in the paper. You'll be fine."

"You will, Sari," Grey said. "Look—some people have come to see you."

His heart was in his throat. He parked in the appointed area in the field, saw Topaz and Rosalie coming toward the car, big smiles on their faces. Turning around, to tap Sari's hand, get her to open her eyes, he pointed out the window. "Look," he said.

And Sari did look.

The field was thronged with people. Men and women dressed in traditional Gypsy garb, prancing white horses in ornamental saddles, schoolchildren holding bright flags and banners. Grey climbed out of the car, pulled the front seat forward so Sari could climb out. Laurent came around from the other side. He and Grey flanked Sari, standing still as Topaz and Rosalie came through the crowd toward the car.

When they got closer, they stepped aside, and Grey could see who was walking behind them. His face broke into a smile; he felt he'd been holding it inside this whole month, ever since she'd left. The wave he felt was the dam breaking, the ocean flooding in, the wave knocking him over.

And then Grey didn't have to hold back anymore. He left Sari standing with Laurent and the others, and he ran through the people milling between them, his gaze locked with Susannah's. They were bumped and jostled, people kept getting in the way, car horns were blaring, horses cantered by, but Grey didn't see or hear anything.

Except her: except Susannah. She beamed to see him, her eyes were so bright, and her arms opened wide, and then he was there in front of her and he held her against his chest. They stood in the middle of the crowd; he felt his heart pounding against hers, and he heard her say his name over and over, until he leaned over, kissed her so gently, as if they were all alone, as if the rest of the world had disappeared and they were just floating together, holding on tight, never letting go.

TWENTY-EIGHT

Susannah felt Grey in her arms, and she closed her eyes and held him as long as she could. They'd been apart for so long, nearly a month, and every night she'd dreamed of this—of kissing him, her body against his, his arms around her. He felt so wonderful and familiar, as if he'd somehow become part of her those weeks last month, as if without him, she had lost part of herself.

Then, suddenly, they were surrounded by other people, reminded that they were not alone, that they had things to do. Reluctantly they broke apart. Susannah glanced over, worried that Sari might have been watching; but the crowd was so thick now, it was impossible to even see her.

"Where are they?" Susannah asked.

"There's a staging area over there," Grey said, gesturing toward the top of the street. "Laurent knows where they all have to be. We'll meet them in a minute. First, let me look at you again. Stay with me."

Susannah held his hands, and they gazed into each other's eyes. She couldn't stop smiling, just because she felt so happy to be with him.

"I've been thinking about seeing you again every day since I left," she said.

"Same with me," he said. "It's been the longest month of my life."

"So much has happened . . ."

"Thanks to you," he said.

"Don't say that yet," she said, smiling. "We still have a long way to go. There are probably a hundred things that can go wrong."

She and Grey headed for the staging area. Seeing Sari with Laurent, Susannah slowed down. Sari spotted her. Her eyes widened with happiness; she started over, then hesitated. Susannah held back, too, unsure of what Sari was feeling. But then, to her great joy, Sari rushed forward and threw her arms around her.

"I think about you a lot," Sari said shyly, stepping back a bit. "I'm so sorry about what happened."

"Oh, Sari," Susannah said, reaching for her again. "That's okay. You didn't do anything wrong. Not one thing."

"I didn't mean to drive you away."

"You didn't," Susannah said, hugging her, looking over the top of her head at Grey. "You couldn't."

"Thank you," Sari said. "I'm so glad you came back . . . did you know about the parade?"

"I absolutely did," Susannah said. "And I've even heard that you're going to be representing your school in it."

"We are," Laurent said, stepping over. "We're marching, and then we're going to write about it."

"Congratulations on your piece in the paper. . . . I was so proud of you; I told everyone at the college about it." Susannah glanced around, saw Helen right in the midst of everything, taking pictures with her digital camera. "In fact, let me introduce you to someone . . . Helen!"

Helen turned and saw them. She waved, walking over.

"Hello, everyone," Helen said, stepping forward. "Susannah has told me so much about all of you. . . ."

Susannah beamed. "Grey, Sari, Laurent . . . this is my mentor and dear friend, Professor Helen Oakes."

"It's wonderful to meet you," Helen said, shaking hands all around. She told them about how she'd first come here to study Saint Martha and the Tarasque, Sarah and the Marys, how fascinating she found the region, and how excited she was to see the procession.

Susannah looked at Grey; they'd had almost no time at all to talk. She knew that he'd set the ball rolling, and she only hoped it all worked out the way they planned. His gaze was powerful and constant, as if he couldn't look away from her. Even with people jostling, the crowd crushing in, the suspicious glances of people who knew his story, he didn't take his eyes off her.

After a few minutes, Laurent turned to Sari, reminding her their school was getting ready to line up. Sari reluctantly pulled herself away. Helen asked if the kids would mind if she accompanied them, so she could see their school organizing for the procession. They seemed excited to have her, and they all went off together.

Susannah was alone with Grey in a crowd of thousands. Now he took her hands, pulled her close again, and held her hands between them. Lowered his head to her, kissed her. She wanted to disappear into him, just feel his lips against hers and forget where they were. But there was still so much to do.

"I can't believe we're all here," she said when they pulled apart. "That it's actually happening."

"I've done the best I could," he said. "But where is—"

"Rosalie's been wonderful," Susannah said. "She and Topaz

have arranged everything." The two women had already left to join the procession, and looking at her watch, Susannah realized that time was flying by.

"We'd better get to the church, I know," he said.

But he just held her hands, pulling back just slightly so he could look at her, swaying a little as the crowds rushed by. "I don't want to let you go again."

"I don't want you to, either."

"I feel as if I've been living through your letters," he said. "I can't believe you went to Nevada."

"We have Helen to thank for that. She convinced me . . ."

"You took that all on yourself . . ." he said. "I never would have asked you to."

"You didn't have to ask," she said quietly. He leaned down, kissed her again, and it lasted a long time, until the bells began to ring, letting everyone know Mass was ending and the procession was about to start.

He held her close against him as they made their way through the throngs of people. Women were dressed in embroidered blouses, full skirts, kerchiefs, adorned with gold and jewels. The men wore dark suits or dress shirts, some embroidered with colorful yarn.

Horses trotted toward the staging area, riders sitting tall and proud, on fancy tooled-leather saddles. There were all kinds of breeds and colors, but Susannah was struck most of all by the large numbers of Camarguaise, the beautiful white horses that had drawn her here in the first place.

As she and Grey made their way into the center of town, Susannah became aware of people staring at them, whispering.

"It's not you," he said, and she felt him tensing up. "They're talking about me."

"Don't let it bother you," she urged. "Just keep walking."

A group of men jeered, and Susannah heard someone spit on the sidewalk as they passed. Her heart was racing, and she felt the crowd crushing in. She swore she heard the name "Maria" being said over and over, and she imagined people recounting the story, telling each other how Grey had stolen the beautiful Gypsy circus rider for himself. He held her tighter as they walked, as if trying to protect her from what they were saying, and she gave him a look to reassure him that she didn't care.

When they got to the main street, they joined an already excited and anticipatory crowd. She and Grey edged toward the front, wanting to have a good spot from which to watch Sari march past with her school.

The doors to the church opened, and the faithful came pouring out. Susannah craned her neck, knowing that soon the statue of Sarah would emerge from the church—the only time of the year she was taken from her crypt, paraded down the street to the harbor, washed in the sea.

This was what everyone had come to see; Susannah looked for Helen, hoping she was taking everything in. There were bowers of black lilies, and Susannah had no doubt that the seeds had come from the monastery of Sarah's biographer, Vincent Phillipon, deep in the Italian countryside, the holy sanctuary where Helen's beloved monk had lived and prayed.

Susannah thought of her mother and father, of how they had come here to pray for a child, and she knew how lucky she had been to have had her mother as long as she did, and that when the statue of Sarah passed, she would be thanking her on behalf of her parents, too.

"Where is Maria now?" Grey asked as quietly as he could, considering the pitch of voices around them.

"She's with Zin-Zin," Susannah said. "She and Adrien spent the night in her caravan."

"This is her homecoming," Grey said. "Look at all these people. All of them . . . it seems they're waiting for her."

"Only one person really matters," Susannah said. "There's only one person here that Maria is coming home for."

"I know," Grey said, looking into her eyes. "Thank you, Susannah. This is because of you."

"Because of Sari," she said. "I just hope it all works the way we planned."

And just then, it seemed as if it wouldn't. Helen was making her way through the crowd, just ahead of Laurent, with one arm around a sobbing Sari. Head bent, long hair falling in her face, Sari was weeping into her hands.

"What happened?" Grey asked as Sari flew into his arms.

"They were lining up with their class," Helen explained, "when two old men started pointing at Sari, speaking in Manouche."

"They were making fun of me," she wept. "Saying that my mother left me, that she ran away in disgrace, that our family should be ashamed."

"Sari," he said, "don't listen to what people say."

"You didn't see them pointing and laughing!" she cried. "We shouldn't have come, Papa. I want to go home!"

"Sweetheart," he said, "we can't yet."

"I can't stay," she said, shuddering. "Please, please don't make me."

"No one will make you," Grey said. "Of course we won't."

Susannah stepped forward, toward the curb, to look up the street. She heard music playing: flamenco guitars and hauntingly beautiful violins. The procession was just starting. The priest in his black robe came down the church steps, followed by a throng of people carrying Sarah. The statue gleamed in the sunlight, and everyone stopped to watch.

Sarah was in a beautiful carved boat. Her faithful surrounded her, reaching out to touch her as she passed. Behind her came the children of local schools, including Sari and Laurent's. Susannah watched as they passed by with their homemade banner, smiling and waving at their friends. Laurent waved back, but Sari just buried her head in her father's shoulder.

Next came groups of Gypsy women—Susannah recognized so many of them from the Sarah Circle. Her heart sped up, anticipating what was next. Zin-Zin, Topaz, Rosalie, Florine, Ana, Naguine, all dressed in their finery, grinning with pride and overwhelming happiness. Susannah's eyes met Zin-Zin's, and she smiled as the old woman blew her a kiss. The sound of hoofbeats grew louder; the horses were coming now.

"Grey," she said, catching his eye.

"Sari," Grey said softly. "Open your eyes."

"I just want to go home," she cried.

Susannah stood beside the young girl. She thought back to their first, beautiful ride. Sari had been so brave, climbing back on Mystère, the animal she'd loved so much but had been unable to ride for so long.

"Look who's coming, Sari," Susannah said, taking her hand. "It's Mystère . . ."

"Sari, look . . ." Laurent said.

And with that, at the urging of her best friend, Sari opened her eyes.

The horses were all in a line; it seemed to stretch on forever. There were black horses and gray horses, pintos and palaminos, and, especially, stunning white horses from the Camargue. Their riders were adorned in embroidered cloaks, flowing capes, studded leather chaps.

Circus riders were performing: standing on their horses' backs, swaying to the music, playing guitars and mandolins and tiny silver cymbals. Susannah watched as Adrien led the entire troupe of Clair de Lune—all of them adorned in the circus colors of blue and silver, their costumes imprinted with the signature crescent moon.

The crowd gasped with delight and shock, and cried out as he passed: *Matelo, Matelo!* He obliged by waving and beaming, by standing on the back of his white stallion, doing pirouettes in the air.

If Sari recognized him, she gave no sign. Susannah watched

her face. She had eyes only for Mystère, and the woman who was riding her.

The greatest rider of all, and she wasn't doing anything but sitting still in the saddle. The crowd fell silent as she passed, except to whisper her name: *Maria!*

"Mama!" Sari cried.

Maria beamed. She balanced in the gleaming black saddle, reaching her arms out. Grey stepped forward, lifted Sari off the ground. Maria held out one strong hand, swung her daughter out of Grey's arms, onto the saddle in front of her.

Susannah saw Grey and Maria lock eyes for a moment. Then she watched as Sari leaned into her mother's body, her eyes wide open, gazing straight up at the sky, with Maria's arms wrapped around her.

Maria clutched Sari, riding past. Her right hand dropped down, just long enough to brush Grey's fingers, then Susannah's. She met Susannah's eyes with a glance of gratitude. And she held Sari tight again and rode on.

Susannah turned to Grey. For once, she was the one who couldn't quite look. She pressed her face into his chest, eyes squeezed tight, feeling tears and love well up inside.

She heard Helen ask Laurent if he wanted to walk alongside Maria and Sari, heard him say yes. She heard them walk off together, heard the uneven pace as Helen walked slowly and Laurent supported her.

"Thank you," Grey whispered into her ear, holding her as tightly as he could. "Thank you, Susannah."

"Oh, Grey," she whispered back, mouth against his shirt. "I'm not the one to thank."

Susannah heard Mystère's hoofbeats clacking on the pavement, heard the jingle of silver scallops on her saddle, glistening black in the sun. She smelled the sweetness as wagons of black lilies clattered by. And then she heard Sari cry out. Grey heard it, too, and they started running down the street, behind Laurent, who was tearing as fast as he could toward Sari and her mother.

And when they got closer, they saw Sari turning, tears streaming from her eyes. Her mother's arms were around her.

"The day is so bright," Sari cried. "And I think . . . oh, I know, the sky is so blue . . . Laurent . . ."

"Sari," Laurent said, walking alongside, reaching up to touch her hand. "You mean—?"

"You have hazel eyes," Sari said, gazing at him. She'd seen that shimmer of silvery green in the marsh, and now she saw a burst of blue overhead, and looking into Laurent's eyes, they were the hazel she remembered. Her mother held her, and Laurent was by her side, and her father had always been right here. . . . She looked over at him with Susannah, and she felt such radiant joy mingling with the colors, she couldn't tell where one let off and the other began.

Susannah rocked in Grey's arms, holding on to him as the parade went on. Mystère walked proudly along, Maria holding tight to Sari. The most famous circus rider in the world wasn't standing, wasn't doing any tricks at all: was simply riding through the crowd of the people who had never stopped loving her, embracing her daughter as they moved along, past brightly colored flowers that seemed to have been set out this day just so Sari could see them, down to the sparkling blue harbor, where Sarah was being washed in the sea.

EPILOGUE

They sat on the seawall across the street from Dempsey Stables in Narragansett, Rhode Island, gazing out over the still, black water. Grey's arm was around Susannah's shoulders, and she leaned into him. The sky was perfectly clear, and midnight blue. Stars blazed overhead. Susannah wanted to ask him if the constellations looked the same as at home, in France. But she was too mesmerized, watching the horizon.

"Is that it?" Grey asked.

Susannah squinted, staring at the thin dark line where the sea met the sky. She looked for a glow, but saw only darkness.

"Not yet," she said.

As if he knew that meant they had a reprieve, he kissed her. She could have gotten completely lost in his kiss, pressed against his body, sea mist on both their faces, but she forced herself to stay present. She caressed his cheek with her hand, pulled back enough to look into his blue eyes.

"You know it's already risen in France," she said.

"But not yet here," he said. "And not yet in the desert."

"Do you think Sari will watch later?"

He laughed. "I think she wants to see everything. It's all new to her. Especially with Laurent there, and the fact they're staying at a ranch called Clair de Lune . . . and she's with her mother."

"She sounded so happy on the phone," Susannah said. She thought of the conversation, of how excited Sari had sounded, describing all the colors in the desert, and the circus, and her mother's eyes.

"I know," he said. "She's been looking forward to this visit with Maria ever since the parade."

"How is it for you?" Susannah asked.

"Me?"

"Yes," she said, stroking his face, staring into his eyes. "You've raised her alone for so long."

"Seeing her mother is good for Sari," he said. "So it's good for me, too."

Susannah nodded. She'd been with Grey when he'd driven Sari and Laurent to the airport. They'd been staying with his parents in Rhode Island, and now the kids were out in Nevada for a week, spending time with Maria. Susannah had watched Sari hug her father in the departures building, so hard it seemed she'd never let go.

But when it was time for her to go through security, she and Laurent on their way to the plane, she'd given both her father and Susannah exuberant waves, excitement in her dark green eyes.

"It's because of you," Grey said to Susannah now. "You brought them together."

"No, it wasn't me," she said, knowing she couldn't take credit for something so powerful and right. From the minute Sari had jumped up on the horse with Maria, the bond between them had started to heal. What they'd both wanted for so long, a way back to each other, had started to happen. And it was happening in full, glorious color. . . .

Now, gazing out at the water, Susannah saw a golden line where the horizon had been. It shimmered, growing wider. The full moon began to crest, and then to rise. It had been two months since that magical trail ride, the night they'd rescued Tempest, and one month since the Gypsies' Pilgrimage, the festival of Sarah.

Susannah watched the moon rise out of the sea, wide and bright as a basket of gold. It overflowed onto the water's surface, painting a gleaming path that seemed to stretch straight to her and Grey. She felt the moonlight on her skin, stared at its trail across the sea. It looked almost solid enough to walk across.

She thought of Sari and her mother, getting to know each other all over again, and of her own mother—how much she missed her, and wished she could introduce her to these people she loved. She thought about how grateful she was to Helen, and to Zin-Zin—for helping her forgive herself for leaving her mother alone. She gazed at the moon's bright path and imagined herself walking it with Grey, taking him to meet her parents.

"If only," she said out loud.

"What?" he asked.

"If only we could all be together."

"Who do you mean?"

"Us," she said. "And all the people we love."

"I'm with you," he said, holding her.

She nodded. And she had met his parents and brothers, and Helen had given her her blessing to move to France, live on the ranch, and work on her own book, a study of Sarah's miracles in the lives of women who loved her. Sari was so happy about it, had asked Susannah to promise that they could go riding together, that they could all take a moonlight ride as soon as Sari was ready. Susannah had promised.

Right now, staring out at the moon, she felt the kind of piercing sadness that comes from so much love. She felt it so fully and completely for Grey and Sari, but she wished that she could have just one more thing, one more miracle.

"They know," Grey said.

"What do you mean?" she asked.

"Your parents," he said, holding her hand. "They know about us."

"How can they?" she asked, tears filling her eyes. "You know my mother died six months before I met you."

"Yes," he said. "But don't forget, she sent you."

Susannah stared at the sea, feeling the salt breeze in her hair, a long tingle shivering down her back.

"Sent me," she whispered.

"To thank Sarah," he said. "Do you really imagine she didn't know what would happen?"

"That I'd travel to France and meet you?"

"Exactly that," Grey said, holding her. Then, looking straight into the sky, where the moon glowed, he said in a voice almost too quiet for Susannah to hear, "Thank you—for sending Susannah to me."

Whether he was speaking to Susannah's mother, or the moon, or Sarah, Susannah didn't know. She just held Grey's hand and watched the soft white light fall on the dark and lovely sea, and they sat there together, in the light of the rising moon.

About the Author

LUANNE RICE is the author of twenty-four novels, most recently *What Matters Most, The Edge of Winter, Sandcastles, Summer of Roses, Summer's Child, Silver Bells,* and *Beach Girls.* She lives in New York City and Old Lyme, Connecticut.